Gul
Guler, Kathleen
In the shadow of dragons
$ 25.00
1st ed.

# Author's Notes

## The Macsen's Treasure Series

Often, when a society struggles to right itself in the face of devastating outside pressures, it will also struggle within itself for a long period until it finds its voice, its courage, and its strength in a leader who will guide it safely to peace and freedom. There will be those few selfless souls who mold events in the direction needed to attain that peace, not just for themselves but for the people and the nation as a whole. They suffer dearly, but even so, they refuse to stray from their course until the right leader takes command.

Dark Age Britain of the fifth century was embroiled in just such a dual struggle; the indigenous Celtic tribes fought amongst themselves as much as they did invaders from the continent and other places. In conjunction, it is generally believed that the Arthurian legend's historical side belongs to that same era. This is the backdrop for the Macsen's Treasure series.

Though historical in concept and loosely based on Geoffrey of Monmouth's 1136 narrative, *The History of the Kings of Britain,* as well as other sources, the Macsen's Treasure series should be regarded solely as fiction. Upon completion, the series will be comprised of four novels, their scope extending over the twenty-five year period leading to King Arthur's rise to power in the fifth century. Each book can be read alone, but their prominent characters, chronology, themes, and historical background will tie all four to each other.

The goal of an historical fiction writer is to meld fact and imaginative storytelling into a seamless tale, at once fresh and exciting as well as timeless and realistic. My intention in writing this series is not to merely retell a portion of the Arthurian legend. That has been done many times. Rather, I wish to bring alive a period of history through the eyes of Celtic people who could have lived then, blending the events leading to Arthur's rise to power as a reciprocating influence upon their lives.

While Geoffrey's *History* provides framework for the legend aspect of the series, it is only a small part of the sources used to create this work. Extensive research of related documents and literature, travel in Britain to experience first hand the pertinent archaeological sites, and examining clues found in cultural traditions and ancient beliefs have enhanced my twenty years of studying Celtic history. I have also (and continue to do so) listened to and participated in an on-going group discussion conducted by prominent scholars, historians, and enthusiasts of the Arthurian legend. They often broadly disagree; however, they have willingly and freely shared their vast knowledge.

## The Historical Background

In brief, it is known that Britain was originally populated by unknown Neolithic peoples and then by Celtic tribes. In AD 43, the Romans conquered the island, occupying it as far north as Hadrian's Wall. Although the Romans imposed political, military, and economic rule, the natives kept their languages, cultures and basic way of life. The conquest spilled much Celtic blood, but the legions posted across the island deterred invasions from outsiders; and after four hundred years of relative peace, many native Britons found an incentive to keep their Roman governors.

As the empire faltered in the late fourth and early fifth centuries, the legions gradually evacuated, many leaving with the emperor Magnus Maximus, (the hero called Macsen Wledig by the Welsh) who died in AD 388. Roman influence upon Britain's economy and organization lingered for many years after in spite of a Celtic revival of sorts. The last of the legions left around AD 408-410, laying Britain open to invasions, first from Picts from north of Hadrian's Wall, Irish from the west, then Germanic tribes (Angles, Saxons, Jutes, among others) from the continent.

## The Legend

In working with eras such as the Dark Age Britain of King Arthur, accuracy can be notoriously difficult, given that very little documentation to work from remains. That which does remain is unreliable. From the fall of the Roman Empire in the fifth century until the Renaissance in the sixteenth, events were written down with little or no scholarship.

One extensive document which tries to place Arthur historically is Geoffrey of Monmouth's *The History of the Kings of Britain (Historia Regum Britanniae)*. Geoffrey was a cleric who attempted to write a history encompassing nineteen hundred years of British kings, from the first, Brutus, to the last before the Saxon conquest. However, Geoffrey was *not* a good historian. While some of his figures and events probably were historical, his work includes many blatant inaccuracies as well as outright patriotic and ecclesiastical posturing. His narrative served to popularize the legend more than provide an accurate account. Numerous variations and related tales followed in the Middle Ages, including the well known *Le Morte d'Arthur* by Sir Thomas Malory. The legend grew more literary than historical as it became infused with each author's current beliefs and cultural standards.

The story continues after the Roman withdrawal — according to Geoffrey — when in time, a British leader called Vortigern came to power. Needing help to fight the Picts, he imported Saxon mercenaries from the continent. With his campaign successful at first, he rewarded the Saxons with land along the southeast shore of what is now England, the area becoming known as the Saxon Shore. Eventually too many mercenaries came, took too much land, grew out of control and began to displace the native people. In reaction, civil violence spread. The economy disintegrated along with trade with the continent, and the Celtic tribes fought amongst themselves as well, warring for land and cattle. Others, especially Irish along the western coast from Dun Breatann (now Dumbarton in Strathclyde) to Dyfed in South Wales and Cornwall, invaded, displaced and settled.

Vortigern lost control of his mercenaries. He was dubbed "the Traitor" for having brought them into Britain, and the drive to depose him began. Two brothers, Ambrosius and Uther, sons of the previous king Constantine, had been exiled in Armorica (Brittany) and were attempting to raise an army.

Ambrosius and Uther returned to Britain and defeated Vortigern, landing the kingship in Ambrosius' hands. Vortigern's youngest son Pascentius made various alliances and attacks against Ambrosius, trying to regain his father's crown, but was continuously defeated. Within a couple of years, Ambrosius was assassinated by poison, and his brother Uther then became high king. Pascentius continued his bid for the crown, but was finally killed at the battle of Menevia (Mynyw).

### Notes for *In the Shadow of Dragons*

*In the Shadow of Dragons* continues the saga of Marcus ap Iorwerth and his beloved wife Claerwen, begun in the first book of the series, *Into the Path of Gods.*

Many figures in the book are probably historical: Ambrosius, Uther, Pascentius, Vortigern, Octa, Ceredig, Cunedda. The battles at Caer Ebrauc and Mynyw most likely were real. The principal characters of Marcus ap Iorwerth, his family and clan, Daracha, Banawr and Girvyn are fictional.

The character of Myrddin is of course the legendary Merlin the Magician. Within the legend he is probably fictional, though it is believed he may be a composite figure of several historical bards. For the purpose of the series, I have fictionalized him as the last "high druid." Druidry virtually vanished after the Roman conquest; their enclaves and priests were annihilated out of the Romans' ignorance, prejudice and need to remove the druids' influence over the people. It is now believed that these holy men and women had advanced knowledge of the sciences — astronomy, engineering, medicine, mathematics — and all of this was lost in the extermination. To the average relatively uneducated person of those times, demonstrations of that knowledge could have appeared to be magic.

Welsh names for places and people have been used as much as possible in trying to evoke the sense of language for the era, although the tongue actually was a precursor of Old Welsh. Of course the Roman influence is there as well and is necessary. For example, Marcus ap Iorwerth's name is as paradoxical as he is himself; while his given name is Roman, the structure of his full name is purely Welsh. The word "ap" means "son of", hence, Marcus, son of Iorwerth. In contrast, Winchester is an Anglicized place-name, and was probably not used until after the Saxon conquest that led to the eventual creation of England, after Arthur's demise in the sixth century. It is used in this form solely because of its familiarity to the reader. A pronunciation guide/glossary is included to help with the more obscure.

To retain a sense of Celtic beliefs before Christianity's conversion was completed in Britain, I have chosen to instill a bit of mysticism through the visionary element of Celtic spirituality called "fire in the head," as well as Druidry and references to the Celtic pantheon. To some, the visions may represent an element of fantasy; however, I believe it belongs within the historical belief system still in use among the more remotely located native Celtic people of Britain.

And lastly, within the context of this series, Macsen's Treasure is a five-piece set of ceremonial symbols sacred to the high kings of Britain, consisting of a crown, a torque, a spearhead, a sword and a grail. It is purely fictional and does not exist in the Arthurian legend or in history. However, trappings of kingship such as special crowns, scepters, and swords have been held dear by monarchies throughout the centuries. Couldn't it be possible that the famed sword Excalibur and the Holy Grail have descended from symbols such as these?

Kathleen Cunningham Guler
March 2001

# Pronunciation Guide/Glossary

The following list should help with the more frequently used names and places that are difficult to pronounce. These pronunciations are approximate. Where useful a translation or notation is provided.

Brynaich: BRUN-eick
Caer Ebrauc: Car EB-rock
Caernarfon:  Car-NAR-von
Ceredig:  Ker-EH-dig (King of Strathclyde)
Daracha: Dar-AHK-ah
Diolch yn fawr: DEE-olk Un Vawr (many thanks)
Drysi:  DRUH-shi
Dun Breatann: Dun BRET-on (Ceredig's stronghold)
Dyfed:  DUH-ved
Eryri: Eh-RUR-ee
Faolan: FAIL-an
Gwyddbwyll: GWITH-booihl (a precursor of chess)
Gwynedd:  GWIN-eth
Hafod: HAH-vod  (summer dwelling)
Iorwerth: YOR-werth
Iwerddon: ee-WER-thon (Ireland)
Mynyw: Mun-EE-oo
Myrddin: MUR-then (aka Merlin)
Pascentius: Pas-KENT-shus
Sinnoch:  SHIN-ock
Uther: YOU-ther
Y Gwalch Haearn: Uh Gwalk Hahern (the Iron Hawk)

The most noteworthy differences between Welsh and English are as follows:

The Welsh "dd" is like English "th," as in *them*. A "w" is either a consonant or a vowel; as a vowel it has an *oo* sound. A "ch" is hard as in the Scottish *loch*. The "ll" is not found in English but can be approximated as a very rough combination of *hl*.

And "Celtic" is correctly pronounced with a hard C: *Keltic*.

Britain in the
5th Century

ALBA

Northern fort

Dun Breatann

Antonine Wall

GODODDIN

STRATHCLYDE

BRYNAICH

Hadrian's Wall

Octa's
farm

RHEGED

Saxon landing

Marcus escapes

EBRAUC

Caer
Ebrauc

Ynys Môn

Caernarfon

Dinas
Beris

GWYNEDD

POWYS

Afon Hafren

Irish landing

Mynyw

DYFED

Hillfort

Winchester

SAXON SHORE

Tintagel

CORNWALL

# Chapter 1

**The lands of Dinas Beris, in the mountains of Eryri,
Kingdom of Gwynedd
Autumn, AD 470**

*The goddess of the pond waited, prepared to listen to all those who came.*

*Well hidden within the thick, cloud-shrouded woodlands of Dinas Beris' mountain pass, her unreadable waters rippled in the rain. On the muddy brink, nearly invisible within tangled and dripping bracken, stood a wooden carving, some long ago human's idealistic vision of how the goddess should have looked. She often laughed to herself, not in ridicule of the carver's ignorance, for no human understood she was the ensoulment of the waters. In truth, she was proud someone had cared enough to remember her, and because of that she had given herself as a place of comfort and contemplation.*

*The goddess waited. Patient for those who needed to unburden themselves, she accepted their tears of anguish, joyous memories and endless beseechings without question. And just as easily as she received those confessions, her waters adamantly refused to give them up. Never had a secret been betrayed.*

*So many flaws had been revealed in those secrets. One upon the next. So many that they blended together, hiding each other, layer upon layer until they created a perfect camouflage. In time, the goddess thought, the suffering and sacrifices would be forgotten. Only the illusion of an idyllic life would be left behind. And of this idyllic life, the court bards would sing, praising grand heroes and their courageous deeds, calling for cups held high in cheer.*

*The rain passed. The waters calmed, lying utterly still, deep, eternal, waiting patiently for the next mortal to approach. Would there be a happy prayer this time, she wondered, or another shattered soul come to reveal its flaws?*

*The goddess waited...*

The face that stared back must have belonged to another woman. Floating on the water's still surface, it was pale, ragged and smudged, the clear green-blue eyes iridescent with tears that had been swiped aside and replaced with more. Nearly knee-length, tawny brown hair clung uncomfortably, soaked from a cold rain shower that had passed earlier. Thin and worn clothing only added to the aching in the woman's eyes. She blinked at the face, disbelieving.

The tiny pool had often been a place of peace and privacy, and she hoped to once more find comfort in its gracious ambience. Fingering a smooth and greenish speckled pebble, chosen on her way there, the woman began to sense the presence of the pond's spirit. She looked up at its wooden icon presiding from the surrounding underbrush. It gazed at her with wistful eyes. Then she reverently placed the pebble among many others that had been left as offerings to the carving by passing travelers and thirsty local people.

The woman dipped her fingers into the pool, dispelling the reflection. Too warm in spite of the chilling dampness, she pulled out a handful of water, poured a few drops in reverence to the goddess then drank the rest. Closing her eyes, she savored the fresh, cool feeling as it flooded her dry mouth and slid down inside her throat.

Images of her husband's face crept into her mind, becoming so substantial that she traced every detail of his treasured features from memory, as if she could just reach them with her fingertips. "How can I tell you..." she breathed, and the hope of finding solace disintegrated. Bowing her head, she spread her hands over her belly. Then her thoughts scattered like leaves, refusing to assemble coherently, and the tears began to spill again.

The surface of the water rippled languidly. It was the color of burnished steel, dark from its depths and the murky light of dusk. Suddenly distracted, the woman shivered and was irresistibly drawn to lean forward and watch again. But instead of her reflection, she found a drifting, fluid image of the mountain pass road that crossed below the pond.

In the water she saw two horsemen stopped on the road, facing each other, a stone's throw apart, not far below the pass' summit. The first was heavily cloaked against the foul weather, and she was unable to see his face. The second horseman, a husky, rough-looking stranger the woman did not recognize, confronted the first man with a drawn broadsword. No voices sounded, but she understood they shouted at each other by their angry gestures and the stamping of their horses' hooves in the deeply churned mud of the road.

The first rider drew his own sword, but his grip on the hilt was unsure, even unfamiliar, belying his fear and lack of ability with weapons. He intently concentrated on the challenger; then, as if realizing it was in the way, threw back his hood, revealing a pale, thin face framed by wavy brown hair.

"Myrddin Emrys!" the woman cried out his name. Leaping to her feet, she abandoned the vision and started running down through the forest towards the road, dragging along her sodden skirts. Halfway there, she caught a glimpse through the trees of the two horsemen set to charge one another.

"No!" she screamed and raced onward.

Myrddin's head whipped around at the cry, and he saw her descend the path.

"Go back!" he yelled, recognizing her. "Don't come this way! Go back, Claerwen!"

The stranger saw his advantage in Myrddin's distraction and

spurred his horse savagely. Lurching forward, he narrowed the distance between them in seconds, his sword raised high. But before he reached his quarry, Claerwen skidded into the road, halting before Myrddin, her bare feet nearly sliding out from under her in ankle-deep mud. Too late to haul on the reins, the attacker was too determined and too close to his objective to give it up. He kicked the horse again.

Myrddin froze in horror as Claerwen struggled to keep her balance. His skin crept coldly as he realized she was utterly doomed in the path of the charging horse. A cry rose from deep within his lungs, but his throat constricted, choking it off. He held his breath, waiting for the horrible impact.

Claerwen whipped around. With her feet now planted solidly in the ground, she flung her hands up in the air and shrieked an eerie, haunting cry that seemed to stir from the earth itself. The horse shied, disobeying its master, and reared, its eyes rolling with fear. It stood on its hind legs and backed, turning, neighing loudly in discomfort. Crashing down again, it wheeled violently and bucked twice, throwing the man into the roadside bracken, then bolted down the road.

Claerwen turned, eager to speak to Myrddin, but she stopped, astonishment on her face. Behind him, a husky grey stallion suddenly crested the summit, pounding hard at a full-tilt run. Relief flooded her as she saw her husband Marcus astride the grey, crouched forward, his shoulder-length black hair and long, drooping moustache both flying out wildly from his intense face. She moved back onto the grassy edge of the road, but as she watched him approach, his eyes lifted and locked above. Following his line of sight, her panic jolted alive again when she realized another man straddled the tree limbs above Myrddin, leaning to pounce.

"Move away!" Marcus roared, pulling a dagger from the back of his belt.

"Ride!" Claerwen screamed.

Confused, Myrddin could not react in time.

Reaching him, Marcus kicked him off his horse. Myrddin dropped like a rock, his sword bouncing out of his grip. The assailant plunged from the tree, grappling Marcus instead, wrenching him off the grey. They fell and rolled together, grunting, hurtling into the brush. Moments later, his dagger bloodied, Marcus emerged alone.

Claerwen rushed towards him, calling his name, but he held up a hand, signaling for her to halt. Silence drew in, and he scanned the roadside for the first assailant. Nothing moved, but the hair on his neck prickled and he hefted the knife, assuring his grip. He held out his other hand to Claerwen, now wanting her to come forward. His eyes continued moving, shifting, watching intently. Cautiously, she started for him.

Behind her, the first attacker reappeared, springing from the side of the road, his own dagger ready.

"Run, Claerwen!" Marcus shouted abruptly, but it was too late.

The man broadsided her, locking a thick arm around her waist. Pressing his blade to her neck, he commanded, "Lose the knife, or she dies right now!"

Stopping short, Marcus let the weapon slip out of his fingers. He flipped his hands up to show they were empty.

The next order came: "Now the sword."

Marcus slowly unbuckled the baldric that held a huge two-handed sword at an angle across his back. He eased it onto the ground next to the dagger.

"And you, come forward."

Myrddin pulled himself up, rubbing his side where he had been kicked, and moved next to Marcus.

"Now isn't this fine indeed?" the stranger drawled scathingly. "The High King Ambrosius' son Prince Myrddin Emrys, and Marcus ap Iorwerth, Prince of Dinas Beris, along with his wife, all at the same time." He half-dragged Claerwen, forcing her to lean awkwardly and hindering her attempts to find solid footing in the slick mud. Pushing her up against a birch tree, he pinned her there with one cold hand around her neck, the knife flat under her chin. He paused, savoring his moment of power, then pressed the blade in slightly, scratching her.

She winced. Glancing aside, she saw Marcus flinch.

The stranger saw him flinch as well. He sneered, "If you move again, I will slit her throat like a pig's." Then he whispered to Claerwen, "Of course, you know I'm going to do that anyway, sooner or later, whether or not he moves. But before I do, luscious lady, you and I are going to have a bit of fun, quite a bit of fun. And, of course, I will need to be certain that your husband and Prince Myrddin don't interfere."

His lips pulled back into an ugly smile, showing stained and rotting teeth as his eyes roamed down, anticipating what lay beneath her well-worn and threadbare dress. He liked how it clung to her, showing the fullness of her breasts, rising and falling with the distress of her breathing. "Not what a princess is reputed to wear, but it can be useful for tying you up," he muttered and slipped the dagger under her belt. He sliced through it.

Outraged, Claerwen sprang like a coiled cat.

The man had not expected her to react. Dumbfounded, shocked and in sudden pain when her knee rammed into his groin, he staggered back, involuntarily releasing her throat. She grabbed for the dagger, pulling it from his grip.

"Stay here!" Marcus ordered Myrddin, sprinting forward.

Claerwen's kick had been off-center. The assailant quickly recovered and he dove for the weapon, his hands raking over her. She tried to escape his reach, backing, twisting, ultimately stumbling, and she fell into a patch of ferns. Jarred loose, the dagger soared out of her fingers and disappeared. The man fell on her, his weight forcing the air from her lungs. But as she gasped, the weight suddenly lifted again. Through dazed eyes, she saw Marcus above, taking hold of the man's tunic and yanking him off her.

"*Twll dy dîn!*" Marcus cursed furiously. He heaved the attacker away, flinging him like a sack of dead rats. Charging, he intended to pull the man off-balance and take him captive, but the stranger kept his footing and countered the advance, blocking with a solid shoulder to the chest. Stunned, Marcus hit the ground facedown with a heavy grunt.

Claerwen crawled through the ferns. Reaching the road again, she watched the assailant clamber to the sword Myrddin had lost and turn back towards Marcus.

Horrified, she screamed.

Marcus' head jerked up at the shriek. Pulling his feet under himself, he sprang as the man lunged. The weapon came around hard but missed, slicing deeply into the mud. Before the assailant could pull back for another try, Marcus closed in on him, catching him around the knee and lifting, tumbling him backward across the road. Undeterred, the attacker came up once more, slashing, but missed again as Marcus rolled away, reaching his own sword and freeing it from its scabbard. In one ringing blow, he blocked the next assault and sent the man down hard on his backside, ripping the weapon out of his hands.

"On your feet!" Marcus ordered. The blade's tip hovered over his adversary's chest, and he watched the man's eyes move slowly upward to the hilt. Fear suddenly filled the stranger's face as if an unearthly chill had claimed his bones. Bolting, he scrambled desperately in Myrddin's direction.

The dagger Marcus had given up lay between them. The assailant grabbed it, racing straight for Myrddin. Marcus bellowed another curse and tossed aside the sword, dashing after him. He leapt, crashing into the man, somersaulting over. The dagger flew free and dropped into a deep puddle. Marcus came up again onto his feet, whipping his hair back from his face, and he caught the assailant's tunic in his left hand, pulled him upright, then smashed his right fist into his face. He felt the nose break with the impact. The attacker stumbled back several feet, turned and fell.

"Get up!" Marcus ordered, gasping for air. The man did not move. Marcus ordered him again, booted him, and still received no response. When he rolled him over, the lost dagger was imbedded squarely in the body's chest.

"By the gods," Myrddin mumbled, coming forward. "That weapon must have been stuck by its hilt, straight up in the mud."

"Marcus?" Claerwen called, interrupting.

He turned, his cold expression fading as she ran towards him. He caught her in his arms.

She hugged him tightly. "Are you hurt?" she whispered, not caring if mud from his clothes came off all over her or if Myrddin watched.

Marcus clutched her, needing to touch her as well. "Fine enough, fine enough," he answered. Then releasing her, he lightly traced her throat with his fingers where the dagger had pressed. They came away smudged with blood.

She assured him, "'Tis, nothing, I'm only shaken."

He frowned, his heavy brows shadowing his deep-set black eyes.

"'Tis nothing," she repeated, trying to smile away his concern.

It began to rain again, heavily this time. Myrddin removed his cloak and slipped it around Claerwen's shoulders. "I owe you both my life," he said.

Marcus grunted an acknowledgment as he collected the weapons and cleaned them, then asked, "Who were they?"

"They followed me from Caernarfon."

"Caernarfon?" Marcus reacted, handing Myrddin's sword to him. "Why would assassins ambush you here? There are far more secluded places in between."

"I don't know."

Marcus' eyes narrowed slightly, studying Myrddin's thin face. It was haggard, accentuated by the bedraggled appearance of his travel-weary clothing and wet hair. His brown eyes were glassy and unreadable, as if to avoid telling the true answer. Raising one eyebrow, Marcus offered, "I didn't mean to hit you so hard."

Myrddin cast a wry grimace and replied, "If you hadn't come when you did, and if Claerwen hadn't spooked that horse, I'd be dead for certain. How did you know to come?"

"I was looking for her. Then I heard this strange..." Marcus swung around and met his wife's solemn eyes. "That was you, wasn't it?"

She slipped a hand to his arm. "There was a vision in the pond above the road. I saw Myrddin in trouble, so I did the only thing I could think of. Had you been looking long?"

"The house guards said you went out this morning with no food or anything else; they thought you would return shortly. I became worried when you didn't come home." Studying her eyes intently, he was disturbed by the fact that she had not informed the house guards of her intended whereabouts, a rule strictly adhered to by all within their clan, a rule she never broke herself.

Claerwen held his gaze without wavering, her fingers squeezing his arm. She rationalized, "The gods must have kept me away for the reason of drawing you out. It was to help Myrddin, more than to look for me."

Myrddin stepped forward, a grim but knowing regard in his eyes. "'Fire in the head.' The power of visions grows in you, Claerwen, very much since the last time we met. Strong and powerful."

They looked from one to the other. Marcus sensed Claerwen's calm face hid more than visions and misinformed guards, but he decided to leave his questions for the privacy of their house. Unsatisfied and uncomfortable in the silence that followed Myrddin's comment, he broke away. Moving to the second assailant's body, he declared, "I wanted to take this one alive, to question him."

Myrddin winced at the shattered face then glanced at Marcus' large hands, scarred and calloused from hard work, including blacksmithing and laying stone. "No matter now," he muttered.

Marcus gripped the dead man's ankles and dragged him into the heavy brush near the other body. Scavengers would take the remains. "Aye, no matter," he echoed, returning to the road and whistling for the grey horse to come.

For several moments he leaned his head back, letting the rain rinse the mud from his face and hair. When he straightened again, he found Myrddin regarding him with somber curiosity, as if struck by some compelling thought.

Claerwen moved forward, touching Myrddin's wrist lightly. "You will come to the fort with us and stay the night." It was more a command than an invitation.

His thoughts interrupted, Myrddin nodded in agreement. Too tired to protest, he climbed onto his mount.

Marcus lifted Claerwen onto the grey, then dragged himself up behind her. Riding in silence, Myrddin behind them, they followed the road to the summit and turned into the path leading to the fort of Dinas Beris.

# Chapter 2

## Dinas Beris

"So this is Dinas Beris," Myrddin remarked as he entered the hillfort's courtyard with Marcus and Claerwen. With an educated eye he scanned the small complex, citing his approval of how the well-fortified structure was perched on a rocky hill spur high in the pass, overlooking the lands Marcus and his ancestors had held for generations. Well-blended into the surrounding mountains known as Eryri, the fort's location had not been apparent until they were nearly at the gates. Myrddin recognized this as a defensive tactic devised by its original builders, allowing patrollers to easily warn of approaching strangers.

They were interrupted when Marcus' seneschal suddenly appeared before them. Crusty but good-natured and full of wisdom, Padrig was past sixty winters and more like a grandfather to most of the clan of Dinas Beris. Before Marcus could request it, the seneschal assessed that a hot bath, plenty of food and large drinking horns of good, strong mead should be delivered to the guesthouse for Myrddin, as well as Marcus and Claerwen's house. He then took Claerwen by the elbow, escorting her home.

Marcus pointed out the arrangement of the various structures to Myrddin. In the center of the fort stood the great hall; rows of houses and storage buildings fanned out behind it. The courtyard, broad and earthen, now a rain soaked mire, spread from the gates to the hall. Stables and a smithy were built to the right of the gates. The outer wall, topped by ramparts, was of spiked, upright timbers set into a stone foundation. All of the buildings except the hall were round in the traditional Celtic style and made of dry stone, recently rebuilt after sustaining severe damage through war and a prolonged occupation. The fort was simple and spare, but highly functional.

Marcus watched Myrddin warily and was reminded of a haughty, prowling cat. "It's not the fancy court to which you're accustomed," he barbed, attempting to put the high prince at ease.

"I don't care much for court life," Myrddin responded blandly, "but I think it is rather appropriate, Lord Marcus."

"It's comfortable enough for us."

"Claerwen likes it, then?"

Marcus' left brow moved up slightly at the question. "Aye, she does," he answered, feeling the hair on his neck bristle again. Then curiosity prickled him, and his eyes narrowed. He asked, "Why are you here?"

With unreadable eyes, Myrddin held the stare a little too long, as if to reinforce the effect of his remoteness. Finally, just as a guardsman signaled the guesthouse was ready, he said, "We will talk after we've been refreshed." He slowly moved away, following the guard.

Irritated, Marcus retreated, striding swiftly for his house. Once inside he paused in the anteroom entrance, temporarily isolated between the thick door shut against the outside world and the leather drape that hid the inner space. He gathered his thoughts. Though puzzled by Myrddin's sudden appearance in his lands, he was more concerned with Claerwen. He had known her too long and too well to believe her strange disappearance was an aspect of a vision or the gods' higher intentions. Her eyes had been too careful to hide something more, and she had never been given to deception. Then he realized no noise came from inside. Frowning, he pushed aside the drape.

The tiny oak vat they used for bathing was pushed close to the hearth. Claerwen sat in it, perfectly still, facing away from him, her hair swirling around in the water. Steam rose upward, mingling with the fire pit's smoke, drifting into the rafters, seeking escape through the roof's smoke hole. Her head was bowed, her shoulders drooped.

"Claeri?" he called softly.

Her hands came up, quickly swiping at her face, and she twisted, looking up at him as he took the first step into the room.

As he approached he noted her eyes were not red enough to show she had been crying, but she was very good at hiding tears from him. She watched him slowly cross the room and lay his sword on a table, then come to kneel next to the vat.

"You're shaking," he said, picking up her hand from the vat's rim and lightly stroking it. Tenderly he kissed her palm. In spite of the bath's heat, her fingers were tense and cold. She sat folded up like a crumpled piece of cloth, trembling enough to make the water's surface ripple.

Claerwen gazed into his black eyes. They were so dark in color that the iris and pupil were indistinguishable from each other except in very bright sunlight and then only by the merest shade. Though he still frowned, with his heavy brows jagged down and making him almost look angry, she knew from his expression that he was offering an apology for not preventing the attack.

She smoothed her palms over the craggy surface of his face, her touch flowing from the network of fine lines that fanned out around his eyes, down over his high, proud cheekbones, to the rough beginning of stubble that shadowed his cheeks. "I'm so glad you were not hurt," she murmured as her hands came to rest on his shoulders, her fingers tangled in the ends of his hair.

His eyes dropped as if burdened by the questions that filled his mind. They rose again, leveling with hers, and he cupped her chin in his palm, his thumb brushing her cheek. Then he kissed her, tilting his head and pressing his mouth to hers, intense, deliberate, enduring, warming her far more than the bath ever could.

Pulling back, he studied her green-blue eyes, their clear beauty fascinating him as always. He asked, "Do you want to tell me why you were out all day in the rain? With no cloak, or even shoes?

And without telling the house guard?" His words were a little harsher than intended. Her eyes clouded, greying visibly, the sadness he had sensed before filling them. His tone softened, "Claeri, something is wrong. I can see it."

Knocking interrupted. Marcus grunted and pulled away, strode for the door. There Padrig offered a wooden platter of food, a horn of mead and a great amount of concern. The seneschal asked about the attack, having not learned much from Claerwen earlier, and Marcus spent several minutes recounting the ambush. After being reassured that both were fine enough and they would speak more the next day, Padrig expressed his relief, bid a good night and left.

When Marcus re-entered the room, he found Claerwen already out of the vat, dried and wearing a thick woolen shift. She stood before the fire pit, trying to comb the tangles from her hair.

"Padrig brought a sleeping potion for you," Marcus reported, setting the platter on the hearthstones.

Claerwen grimaced, returning, "I'd rather not take it."

He crossed to her and lifted her chin, waiting for her to raise her lashes and meet his eyes. When she did, she blinked several times and sniffled. He smiled, deciding to leave his questions for another time and said, "Look at you, you're nearly in tears, and you're trembling so hard you can barely hold that comb. You won't be able to sleep. It would do you good, I think." He took the comb and tossed it onto the table.

She said, "I will never become accustomed to watching you fight."

He grinned and stepped back, held out his arms and turned around once. "See, I am perfectly fine. Not a scratch. Rather dirty, but I'm ready for the next challenge. You have one for me?"

She could not keep from smiling back, momentarily catching his good humor.

"Go on and eat," he encouraged, starting to pull off his muddy clothing. He tossed each piece unceremoniously into a pile with Myrddin's borrowed cloak and her bedraggled gown and shift. Sinking into the vat, he relished its warmth and the chance to rest. But as he settled back, giving in to tiredness, he watched

Claerwen's mood rapidly deteriorate again. Her face reflected the brooding, lonely secret she protected as she picked at her supper. Marcus hoped the night and Padrig's sleeping potion would bring her peace, and on the morrow she would find the courage to confide in him. With his concern deepening, he poured another cauldron of hot water into the bath.

———————

"You want to tell me what this is about, Lord Myrddin?" Marcus demanded as he entered the guesthouse an hour later. Dressed in a fresh tunic and breeches of dark homespun, he carried a full drinking horn of mead as he crossed to the fire pit.

Myrddin had just finished his meal and he stood, joining Marcus at the hearth. "Then you do understand that I have specifically come to see you," he stated, looking for confirmation.

"I suppose so," Marcus replied impatiently. His hair was still damp, and he raked his fingers through it, trying to keep it in place. He rested his left foot on the hearthstones, rubbing the knee.

"Still bothers you?" Myrddin asked, dipping his head towards the knee.

"Aye, but not much. It's only if I wrench it hard, like today. Claerwen and Padrig take fine care of it."

"I'm sure they do. She told me how you took an arrow there and what she had to do to heal it."

Marcus sniffed absently, then sat on a nearby table, his feet on its bench. He picked up the drinking horn that had been part of Myrddin's supper and found it untouched. Handing it to him, he pulled the stopper from the one he had brought. Drawing a long swallow, he indicated for Myrddin to do likewise. The high prince sipped his mead slowly.

Watching him, Marcus realized that Myrddin's face had aged significantly since the one other time they had met, only a year earlier. He wondered if it was merely the course of years — he guessed Myrddin was close to thirty — or if the stress of supporting his father's kingship had worn so heavily on him. A dusting of grey beginning in the prince's dark brown hair emphasized the age in his face. Marcus took another long swallow of mead, wiped his mouth with his hand, then queried, "You have work for me, don't you?"

Myrddin stared into the fire pit a full minute, then finally answered, "Aye. I do."

"Those two on the road have something to do with it, I presume?"

"Aye," Myrddin muttered, his jaw working as he stalled again.

Marcus guessed, "It's regarding your father Ambrosius, isn't it? They've tried to have him assassinated? But you don't know who?"

When Myrddin hesitated to speak further, Marcus moved off the table and returned to the fire pit, thinking it ironic that he was almost reading Myrddin's mind, Myrddin who was well known and hailed for the same gift of visions as Claerwen had. He prompted, "Well, talk, man. 'Tis safe enough here. I can't decide if I'm going to help you, if I don't know what you want me to do."

The weariness in Myrddin's face gave slowly away to disappointment. Marcus even thought he could see fear. Finally Myrddin spoke, "'Tis true, what you guess. There is evidence of a more elaborate plot that will be implemented soon. I believe Octa is the source of it."

"Octa? The son of the old Saxon leader Hengist? So the peace he made with Ambrosius didn't last. I suspected as much would happen."

"But I can't prove it. And without proof, I cannot act. If I am wrong..."

"If you are wrong, the true assassin will strike while everyone is hunting for Octa."

"Aye. When my father defeated Vortigern, the old high king, the Saxons he controlled under Hengist lost most of their power. A few like Octa were pacified with exile on a small piece of land in the distant north. But Octa enjoyed the power he lost; he wants it back, and he wants revenge for his father's death. Of course, my father has him watched constantly, but his men learn nothing. I need to know what Octa is about, who his connections are within the nobility's hierarchy, then eliminate his power."

Marcus rolled a mouthful of mead across his tongue a few times then swallowed. For several moments he considered the precarious state of Britain's political and social structure. For sixty years, since the end of the four hundred year Roman occupation, their lands had been left foundering, first in anarchy, then under the poor leadership of Vortigern. More than fifty small kingdoms filled the lands of Britain, creating multiple factions. Always in a state of volatile flux, some clung stubbornly to Roman ideals; others strove to revive the ways of their Celtic ancestors from pre-Roman days. They fought constantly, both internally and between each other. As violence escalated across the lands and raiders harried the island's borders, Vortigern had sought to control all sides by using fierce Germanic mercenaries from the continent. Collectively called Saxons by the Britons, the mercenaries were given land on the southeast coast in return for their services, displacing the native people. In outrage, the Britons dubbed Vortigern "the traitor," and began to fight back, worsening an already perilous way of life.

Finishing his thoughts, Marcus muttered, "Damn. Why me?"

Myrddin's eyes took on a blank, inscrutable glint. He glanced into the flames jigging in the fire pit, then swept his gaze back to Marcus. He paused, an almost dreamy look coming into his eyes, and he said, "For you are content to walk in the shadow of dragons, rather than to become the dragon itself."

Marcus felt his hair tingle as if in the moment before a lightning strike. Unnerved, he held his mouth in a flat line, his brows jagged down.

Myrddin almost smiled, having expected Marcus' reaction, then continued, "You know very well why I have come to you. My father is desperately trying to unite this island's factions and control the Saxons, and he has begun to have some success. But he needs help, he needs someone truly loyal who can annihilate an assassin as you have today. And you are a son of Gwynedd, a *Cymro*, a Celt of the ancient clans. You believe in the old ways. I don't need to explain further. In Ambrosius' name, I am prepared to offer you anything you want, land, cattle, gold —"

"We don't need any such things, Lord Myrddin," Marcus cut

him off. "*If* I offer you my services, then I will ask for payment only in goods my clan needs as I have always done. All Claerwen and I have ever wanted was freedom and peace for our family, our home, our people. Nothing more, nothing less."

"If Ambrosius is killed there will be no peace. The Saxons will spread their hordes across Britain far and wide. Including these mountains of yours."

"You would be high king, no? You are saying you cannot hold them?"

"I am a druid, not a warrior, and my birthright is clouded by illegitimacy — it would be endlessly disputed. No, my father's brother Uther, would become king. He has his flaws, but he is capable of holding the Saxons at bay. And he is the rightful heir. But regardless, we must continue to draw together our many kingdoms and not let the factions tear apart the fragile unity we have begun to achieve. We have all worked too hard to let it die now."

Marcus moved to one of the windows and opened the shutters. He stared across at his own house and swore again. Claerwen would not take this news well, he thought, grinding his teeth, then said to Myrddin, "I will need time to consider it."

"I am going on to Powys and will be back within a few days. You can give me your answer then. But I cannot wait long." Myrddin rose, then paused, watching Marcus. He asked, "Is she well?"

Marcus looked up sharply, his eyes tensely narrowed. He remained silent, stretching to his full height, and crossed his arms over his chest. Myrddin was still a full hand taller, but Marcus' proud stance and presence gave him a commanding aura that filled the room. He answered, hedging, "Not a word of this to her yet, Lord Myrddin. She is more distraught over the ambush than she will admit. She finally took a sleeping potion just as I left the house and should sleep for quite some hours."

"Will she be all right?"

Marcus nodded, saying, "Aye, you know how tough she is. It's the shock...suddenly there are two men dead on our lands after the peace we've had — relatively — for about a year now. You must realize that this was a trap for me as well as for you. And I am sure she has understood that."

"Lord Marcus, I do apologize that Claerwen was caught in my problems. I never intended for her to be hurt."

With his face sternly unmoving, Marcus silently regarded the strife he and Claerwen had surmounted, spanning the previous seven years, sometimes catapulted by her visions. He said, "I know you didn't. It's that bloody 'fire in the head' of hers. It's what always brings her trouble." Suddenly he smiled with warmth and humor, declaring, "And she's as bloody stubborn as I am."

Myrddin caught the wryness in Marcus' words and agreed, "Aye, that she is." He smiled tiredly for a moment, then as his thoughts reverted to Ambrosius, he said, "I knew of no one else I could trust with this."

All of his mirth now gone, Marcus returned, "I will consider it and have an answer when you return. For now, I suggest you leave by first light, before Claerwen wakens and has a chance to drill you with questions. If you want an escort, I can provide you with one. I don't understand why you came alone. You're the high king's son, by the gods."

Myrddin deflected the criticism, saying, "You prefer to work alone, don't you? Then you understand about moving swiftly and without the encumbrance of guards."

Slyness showed in Marcus' expression. Hinting at the irony he had sensed earlier, he said, "Aye, and, as 'Merlin the Enchanter,' you should be able to disappear in a puff of mist, so it is said…"

"By the light, I hope you don't believe the drivel that's been said about me," Myrddin objected.

Marcus almost laughed, "Ah, but you use that drivel to your advantage, I have noticed. Such as when, years ago, you 'persuaded' Vortigern not to use you as a sacrifice at Dinas Brenin. You have promoted well your prophecy in which the red dragons of the Britons defeated the white dragons of the Saxons. Ah…I know…that truly was a prophecy. But I believe much of your cleverness comes from the many years of learning alchemy and healing arts and other mysterious wisdoms, all necessary to become not just a druid, but a high druid. The best education the wealthiest nobleman can buy is far less broad. And to the average person who cannot even read, you *are* magic."

Uncertain if Marcus was complimenting or accusing, Myrddin countered, "I know that you value learning and are well-educated yourself, having fostered in the court of Lord Ceredig of Strathclyde in the northern kingdoms. Your work has made you wise of the world as well, possibly even leading you to places where you could have learned the use of secrets belonging to those such as myself. Perhaps you have...your own kind of magic?" Myrddin lifted one eyebrow questioningly, testing for an acknowledgement.

Marcus only returned a look full of irony

Annoyed and too tired for further wordplay, Myrddin abruptly said, "Give my regards to Claerwen. I will leave early as you suggest. Tell her we will speak when I return. And now, if you don't object, I'm going to bed."

---

Claerwen slept until well after sunrise. With the sleeping potion still strong in her blood, she struggled to waken, trying to focus on the ceiling above. Built into an alcove along the wall, the bed was draped off from the central room by heavy calfskin curtains meant to keep out draughts. In the dim light she realized Marcus was still abed as well, sprawled on his belly, one arm draped over her. Wriggling, she rolled over to face him. He stirred sluggishly but did not waken.

Waiting for her mind to clear more fully, Claerwen concentrated on the pattern of scars etched in his skin. Most were from sword and knife cuts now dimmed with time. She pressed her fingers to one in particular, newer than the rest, running in a deep line from his shoulder to his elbow. It came from a wound she had seen him take the year before. Underneath, trim, sinewy muscles showed, hardened from countless hours of fitting stones into place while rebuilding the fort. Glancing up at his two-handed sword, hanging in its scabbard on wall pegs just above them, she recalled his occasional mention that hard work helped his swordsmanship by strengthening his arms and shoulders. She was grateful for his strength, both in his arms and in his soul.

Marcus stirred again. This time his eyes slit open. Finding her watching him, he sighed into the bedding, smiling at the questions he saw in her face. He said, "Myrddin is fine. A little sore from where I kicked him, but no more than a bruise. He will have left early this morning."

"So soon?" Claerwen's disappointment showed.

"Aye, he was in a rush to reach Powys. He has business there but should return in a few days."

She frowned, thinking to herself, then asked, "Is it safe? That he went on? Alone?"

"I can't say," Marcus answered, then half-sat up to face her. Hoping to distract her, he ran his hand along her arm. "And you? How are you feeling this morning?"

Claerwen rubbed at the sleep in her eyes. "I'm so groggy from that sleeping potion."

"Padrig said you should stay in bed today; he's afraid you'll take fever from being out in the rain so long." He leaned to kiss her. "He also said it will take most of the day before you regain full alertness. I'm going to work in the smithy while you rest."

Claerwen watched him move off the bed and pull on a loincloth, then walk across the room, limping slightly from his bad knee. He picked up a small iron cauldron left on the smoldering coals of the fire pit. Testing that the water in it was still warm, he took it into another draped alcove used as a lavatory. She listened to him splash water onto his face.

"I don't understand why Myrddin came this way. It makes no sense," Claerwen said.

Marcus hummed in response.

"Did he say anything else?" she asked.

She heard him begin to shave the stubble from his face and after several scrapes, he answered, "Not about much."

"Did he suspect an ambush?"

"He always suspects trouble because of who he is. Just like I do."

Claerwen grimaced; he was evading her questions. She sat up and pulled on her shift, then moved to sit on the edge of the bed.

Dizziness swept over her as the sleeping potion clung stubbornly to her senses. It cleared gradually, and she pushed off onto her feet. Slowly she made her way across the room, moving from one piece of furniture to the next for support. She pushed the lavatory's drape aside and leaned on a beam.

"Something bothers you," she said, her eyes drilling into his face. He grunted then adjusted a small bronze mirror and continued to shave around his moustache.

"Marcus, what is it? Is Myrddin truly all right?"

He glanced at her between strokes and said, "Myrddin is fine." His eyes were full of unyielding silence.

"There's more than what you say. You would talk, not brood, not like your cousin Owein. What are you not telling me?"

He ignored her question again, prompting her temper loose.

"Marcus!" She leaned forward and caught his wrist, suspending the shaving knife in mid-air. "If Myrddin is not the problem, then something else is wrong. He came here to see you. For a purpose. The high king's son does not come to see Britain's best spy for purely social reasons. Especially with two assassins trailing him. Now talk to me!"

Marcus lowered the knife, ejecting his breath sharply, his eyes squinting with dread. "So be it, then. He believes Octa the Saxon is planning an assassination against Ambrosius. He wants me to find proof, then sabotage it." There was an aching in his dark eyes, coupled with a combination of stubborn determination and no apology.

The angle of light made Claerwen look harshly ragged as she looked up into his face. Then she abruptly turned away, speaking low, "You're going to do it, aren't you? And you weren't going to tell me until you were nearly ready to leave."

"I wanted to wait a few days to talk about it, until you weren't so shaken by the ambush." He wiped his face dry.

Staring across the room, her eyes hardened. She said, "You're going back to your spying and the danger and I'm going to lose you again."

"Claerwen, I haven't committed to anything — "

"But you will. I can feel it in you."

"Claeri, no — "

"Aye! What happened yesterday rekindled it in you. You hunger for that adventure. And you'll put on all those mad disguises and worm your way into the deepest and worst places, until one day you're killed, and I won't even be able to find your bones to bury on *Yr Wyddfa.* "

"Hush, Claerwen," he soothed, catching her arm and turning her around.

But she could not stop. She hated the sound of her own voice, shrewish, nagging, but the words refused to end, and they were the truth. "You will! Admit it, Marcus! Don't make me force it out of you, like the night the Iron Hawk — "

"Don't ever speak of that, even here." He jerked her arm, not hard enough to hurt, but to make her understand he was going to lose his temper. They glared at each other, his fingers pressing into her skin.

Slowly her anger retreated. She opened her lips to speak, closed them again, then finally whispered, "I'm sorry. I do not wish to argue with you. I...I just don't want to lose you, Marcus. I knew one day you would go again, and I'm not being fair, it's not my decision to make. You warned me." Again turning away, she finished, "And I will lose everything..."

The poignancy in her voice wrenched inside him. He came up behind her, placing his hands on her shoulders. Leaning slightly, with his lips next to her ear, he spoke gently, "Claeri...I'll admit it. I want to go. I need to go. I have said, 'a spy is a spy until the day he is dead.' If I don't continue, I will lose control of changes in the politics, the alliances, the feuds, the information I must know to keep myself alive. I'm already too long separated from it now. If I don't go, eventually someone, somewhere, *will* kill me, because I won't recognize who that man, or woman, is. It could have happened yesterday. That was a trap for me as much as for Myrddin, and I think you know that."

He paused, hoping his calculated reasoning would calm her. She remained quiet, still facing away from him, and he used those several moments to finish dressing. Then he pulled her around again. The heartache in her eyes confirmed what he had sensed the day before, that the ambush, and now Myrddin's proposal, had little to do with her distress. "Claerwen?" he began tenderly, "I am not the only one of late who has been hiding a secret. Talk to me, please. What causes you such pain? What do you mean, you're going to 'lose everything?'"

Claerwen bowed her head. The tears were coming again, unstoppable, and she did not want him to see her cry. She did want his comfort, needfully, craving the warmth of his strong arms around her and his breath in her ear speaking words only he could say, but neither could she bear to let him know how weak and lonely she felt at that moment. She pleaded, "Go, Marcus...please, just go to work."

He sighed, frustrated. Raking his fingers through his hair, he complied with her request and started for the curtained anteroom, stopped, turned to see that she had not moved. The expression on her face filled him with guilt, but he was lost as to how to comfort her when she would not accept his compassion. Torn, he hoped she would find the courage to give up her secret to him before Myrddin returned. He sighed again and pushed through the curtain, then the outer door, leaving the house.

# Chapter 3

## Dinas Beris

Several days passed.

Long after midnight, Marcus lay half-awake, listening to Claerwen's steady breathing as she slept next to him. He had tried to talk with her again, several times, but she always turned away, ending the attempts in frustration, tears, lonely time spent alone. And the time left until Myrddin's return was running short.

"Will you come with me to the standing stone?" Her voice slipped through the darkness without warning, startling him. He turned on his side and touched her face, needing to see if she was awake and had truly spoken, or if he had only been dreaming. Her hand came up and held his palm to her cheek.

"When?" he asked.

"At sunrise. Please?"

"Of course, Claeri."

Her tension released, like water draining out of a broken crock. Marcus could not see her in the dark, but he gazed steadily at the dim outline of her face, thinking of the last few days. Now she snuggled down closer to him, hugging his arm, gently tucking his hand between her breasts. As she drifted into sleep once more, he wondered what had changed.

———

At first light, Marcus stood in the center of the courtyard, looking up past the ramparts. Beyond, through heavy drizzle, loomed the mountain his people called *Glyder Fawr*. Its mostly rock-strewn slopes swooped down into the pass. Among its lower levels was a crag ringed by an ancient oak grove, the trees both out of place yet perfectly appropriate within the wildness of the mountains. In the center of the grove, not visible from the fort, stood a single standing stone, marking a place of spiritual power used by local druids before Roman prejudice had driven them into hiding. It had also been the site of his wedding nearly three years before, during a Midwinter celebration.

Claerwen quietly approached, bringing Marcus' sheathed sword. Heavily cloaked against the cold and dampness, she said, "I am ready."

Signaling for the gates to open, Marcus hung the sword across his back and walked with her out of the fort. They moved slowly up the rocky hillside, following a terraced path that ended at the outer edge of the grove. Penetrating the barrier of trees, they emerged into a small, grassy clearing. Claerwen paused a few moments, eyeing the upright slab of granite, then strode forward. She knelt before it and pressed her hands to the rough surface as if in search of something within.

Marcus came around the other side, facing her, his arms folded. He guessed she sought power from the stone, the same power that fueled her visions, but the pale light of the fire's presence was not in her eyes. Instead, a stunning sadness grew in her face. She did not speak for a long while.

In time, he knelt next to her, laying a hand on her shoulder. She looked up into his dark eyes, her own flicking back and forth, seeking his thoughts. "You have reached your decision, I believe," she whispered.

He nodded.

Her eyes closed, and the sorrow in her face grew even more intense.

"Claerwen," Marcus murmured and took her hands. "I've decided that I will not be separated from you again. My life belongs to you now, to our family, to the clan, to the children we will raise. There are others who can help Myrddin. He will have to find them."

Claerwen stared blankly at his hands as they held hers. Her fingers looked tiny as they rested in his thick, rough palms. She said, "I wanted you to make your decision before…before I could tell you…" Her voice caught in her throat.

The daylight grew stronger, and her face showed as pale as it was on the day of the ambush, her eyes tinged grey again. Marcus smiled, stroking her cheek with his thumb. "I think I know."

Her eyes came up, so utterly appalled that it startled him. "You can't possibly know," she breathed roughly.

"Owein told me you had been to see Bronwen the midwife. You had forgotten your shoes at her house, and she was bringing them when he met her on the road. He brought them to me last night."

"Oh, no…" Claerwen exhaled, her eyes dropping.

"It's true, then? You carry a child?" He lifted her chin, an uncontrollable grin stretching across his features. "And you didn't want to influence my decision by telling me? That's why you've been so distraught and sad, thinking I would leave you alone with a child?"

Claerwen's eyes closed again and she shook her head slowly. "No, Marcus. By the gods, would that it were true."

"I don't understand," he said.

Still holding his hands, Claerwen rose, drawing him with her. "Come," she said, "It is time to talk now." She led him to a low, rocky ledge among the trees where they settled.

Pulling in a great, wavering breath to compose herself, Claerwen began, speaking low and clear, "'Tis true, I went to see Bronwen. But it was because I have not conceived. Now that there's been a period of some peace, I had hoped to start the family you wanted so much. But the months went by and nothing happened, and my hopes dwindled. Finally, I decided to see Bronwen. I didn't tell you because I wanted to know first…"

"What did she say?" he prompted when she did not go on.

She whispered, "The miscarriage I had two years ago…she believes there was too much damage from it, that I will never conceive again." She forced herself to meet Marcus' eyes.

His mouth opened in astonishment, then his face softened in empathy. Pulling her into his arms, he breathed into her hair, "You were right, I didn't know. Now I understand the anguish in your eyes...and why all the tears." Disappointment was in his voice.

She leaned against him, her hands tightly gripping his tunic. Marcus fully expected her to begin weeping; but her hands began to gently stroke his chest, giving him the sense she was trying to comfort him instead.

The depth of her compassion had always struck him; she gave it freely even when she should be the one taking comfort. As he held her now, Marcus thought back on the first year of their marriage, when he had been betrayed to Vortigern, imprisoned, then left to die. At the same time, unknown to him, Dinas Beris had been sacked, forcing her to flee shortly after learning of her pregnancy. She had suffered a nearly fatal miscarriage, leaving her ill for a long time afterward. Then, guided by fire in the head and a profound inner strength, she had trekked alone, for hundreds of miles, in the sole purpose of finding him. And when she did find him, on the verge of death, she spent every bit of her energy bringing him back to life, and never with a word of complaint.

Marcus felt that strength in her now, trying to ease his disappointment. He had known of men who had gone to great trouble to swell their clans with children; craving sons who would bring in dowries upon marrying a wealthy woman, and daughters whose marriages were purely strategic political alliances. Celtic law allowed divorce from a barren wife and recognized the rights of illegitimate children as equal to those born in wedlock; however, households were often torn apart when wives were set aside or fertile concubines taken. Marcus thought of such men as full of greed and false pride. He refused to forswear Claerwen's loyalty, love, and strength.

His lips pressed tightly together for a few moments then he licked away their dryness. He took Claerwen's shoulders, holding her gently and so he could look directly into her eyes. He asked, "When you said you would lose everything, did you think I would set you aside? Is that what you meant?"

Her expression told him he was right.

"Ah, Claeri," he said affectionately. "When we pledged marriage, I told you I would never marry for greed or political reasons. All I wanted was you and that's not changed. Children would be a fine thing, but I will not destroy all of our lives just for the sake of having them. Rather, I would give up everything else, without question, without remorse, because wherever you are, is the heart of our home."

His eyes were soft and wistful, and she could see his soul showing nakedly in their depths. He meant what he said. There was no hesitation in his words, no lie just for comfort, only his honesty, only the trust between them.

She smoothed his shaggy hair back from his temples and pressed her cheek to his. She whispered, "You are a fine man, Marcus ap Iorwerth."

After a long silence, Claerwen rose and paced slowly towards the stone. Watching her move, Marcus realized a change had come, that cool, clear serenity had pushed away the turmoil of grief. He followed, compelled by curiosity.

Claerwen confided, "The day I was gone, before I went to the pond and before the ambush, I was here most of the time. I needed to be certain that Bronwen's suspicions were true. I asked the god if I would ever bear you a child."

"And the god said there would be none?" Marcus asked.

She nodded. "The stone remained absolutely cold."

"And you stayed here, all alone? In the cold rain? Why didn't you come to me?"

"I didn't know how to tell you something so…so dreadful. So disappointing." She turned to him then, her fingertips hooking into his belt. Looking up into his face, she said, "These past days…I wanted to come to you so much for your comfort. But after Myrddin came, your decision was more important, so I held my tongue. And I needed time to understand it myself. I did not want to use this misfortune to influence you. But I'm afraid that you were influenced anyway, if incorrectly. Now you will reconsider."

He smiled, and the lines around his eyes deepened. "No. My

decision is done. I don't want to be alone anymore, child or no. If I am called selfish, so be it."

Claerwen studied his eyes a few moments longer then pulled away, returning to the ledge. She remarked, "You have a saying, 'Turn the disadvantage to the advantage.'"

Marcus expected her to react with warmth, with joy, but she remained pensive. Puzzled, he confirmed, "Aye."

"It is the crux of how you work..." She turned towards him, her face still somber, but a path of earnest thoughtfulness had emerged. "...your work as a spy."

Apprehensive, he joined her at the ledge, resting his left foot upon the stone and rubbing his bad knee. He gazed through the trees towards the fort and asked, "Why do you mention this?"

"Is it right for us to deny Myrddin?"

His head turned sharply, his brows knotted in a stern, wordless frown.

She went on, "I believe that you and I are bound to do as he asks." Her eyes locked onto the incredulous expression Marcus made at her, and she braced for his reaction.

He rubbed a hand over his mouth, pulling on his moustache, then stood straight to pace a few steps, one way, then the other. He silently bounced from anger to amusement to confusion, but with his calm good sense, decided to ask a question instead of speaking without thought.

"Why have you come to the stone today? To ask the question about the child again?"

"No, Marcus. I have had time to think now. I did want so much for you to say you would stay home. In truth, I wished that you would end that kind of work altogether. But we both know the truth of the situation Ambrosius faces every day of his life. We both know what can happen." She glanced at the stone, and her sadness returned for a moment. "I asked if we would find peace if we do not act."

Marcus felt a chill trace his skin as her eyes lifted to meet his. "You saw the future?"

"It was more...a foreboding. The stone radiates the feeling of empty, cold unforgiveness." Her words felt heavy, ominous, flowing like molten lead.

"You have said 'we' several times." He raised his eyebrows in question.

"We are bound to this, both of us, as much as we are bound to each other."

This time sadness clouded Marcus' eyes. "I cannot take you into such danger, Claerwen."

"You know I am capable."

She watched his face reflect how torn he was, his eyes squinting, then alternately growing sad, worried, calculating. Finally, he said, "Aye, you are capable, but I will not risk your life. No, Claerwen."

"You know I will follow, if you go."

His jaw was tensely set and he gnawed at his lower lip. He returned to pacing, his mind running through the years of conflict they had endured, picking out the times she had followed him — in defiance of all good reason — and more than once had saved his life. And to leave her at home could never guarantee her safekeeping. Dinas Beris had been sacked while he was gone before, placing her in terrible danger. And it was true as well that she was as stubborn as he. Running his fingers through his hair, he swore to himself, paced further, came back to her, then conceded, "Aye, you would follow me, that you would. Myrddin will be here in a day or two. We have time to think more on this."

"It is too late for thinking, Marcus. 'Tis not a choice."

He stared at her. "What else do you know?"

The vision light came into her green-blue eyes then, and she stiffened when it took hold of her, as if someone had put cold fingers on her neck. Marcus nearly stepped back, disturbed, but held his stance to disguise how unnerved he felt. He watched Claerwen go to the stone again and lay her hands on it, stroking the surface almost sensuously. He wondered if she saw it glow now, in the way she had once described to him, like the aftermath of a lightning strike. He could see the light in her eyes, but not in the stone. After a few moments she turned back to him, swaying slightly as her eyes cleared.

"Soon, things will be set in motion," she spoke, then paused for breath, gripping his arms. "When you and I are old, there will finally be peace across Britain. There will be a warrior to lead us like no other before and no other to come after. He will unite us all against the Saxons, the Northmen, the Irish, the Picts. And he will hold it in trust and strength for many years, until another traitor destroys that trust and strength and the cycle returns to darkness and the wasteland..." Her voice trailed off and she panted slightly, but her expression was one of wondrous hope.

Marcus stared into her face. He asked, "What does this mean, that things will be set in motion? You are saying that we must accept Myrddin's proposal? Or this warrior will not be part of the future?"

She dredged her mind, looking for a deeper understanding of what she had sensed, but no details grew any more distinct. She answered, "I don't know how it will all happen, not yet. Or when. Each time brings a few more clues, just enough to haunt me. But I believe we must do this because it will in some way affect what will happen to this man."

"You once said a name, a long time ago. A man who would be called Arthur — "

She pressed her fingers to his mouth, stifling his words. She whispered, "Aye, but we must not say it again. It must remain secret until the time is right or we could endanger his life."

For a moment, Marcus frowned, but with the rise of his curiosity and the power of his belief in her words, his confusion dissolved. He accepted both her admonition and her proposal. With a smile beginning in his eyes, he declared, "Then so be it."

---

Myrddin did not arrive on the day he had designated. Claerwen fretted, afraid another attack had been staged. A few days later, however, he did arrive, late in the evening, safe but tired from the grinding ride across the mountains. She greeted him warmly at the gates, then led him to the great hall.

"You don't need to fuss over me," he told Claerwen after she brought him food and mead.

"But I want to," she returned. "Marcus is with his cousin, I will go find him." She turned and strode out the door before he could protest. He had wanted to ask how she was faring since the ambush, and he guessed from her exuberance that she was doing very well indeed. Then he surmised that Marcus must have decided to decline the work, if she was in such high spirits.

Myrddin ate quickly, his mood darkening as he anticipated Marcus' negative answer. He was swallowing the last of his supper when he heard Claerwen's laughter from the rear doors of the hall. They were open, and he could see her coming from between two of the houses beyond, bantering with Padrig. She said goodnight to the seneschal, then Marcus appeared directly behind her, looming out of the dim torchlight.

Marcus caught Claerwen's hand and pulled her around, holding her closely. She tilted her face up and met his dark eyes, wondering why he was so deeply serious.

Speaking softly to keep Myrddin from hearing, he asked, "Are you sure you want to do this, Claeri? Are you absolutely certain?"

She nodded, her fingers smoothing his tunic. "I'm not changing my mind, and I will not sit at home to keen uselessly over something that won't happen. My weeping is done. In truth, I am surprised that I feel so comfortable with this decision."

"Making the decision itself will do that, but now is the last chance to reconsider. I must be sure that you are absolutely committed or we stay home. Both of us."

She held his eyes for several moments, thinking of how his enthusiasm had grown over the days as Myrddin's arrival neared. In past years she had thought that his work was a game for him, one he played with great ease and confidence. But with time, she had learned that his clever ruses and unwavering courage were inspired by a steadfast conviction to freedom, earning him much respect from many Celtic clan chieftains and kings for whom he had worked. She appreciated his dislike for leading men into endless and useless bloodshed as a military leader, and that he had chosen instead to create a successful style of espionage. Having come to share his vision of freedom, she had caught his sense of hope as well.

Claerwen answered, "Eventually you will go, with or without

me. No, don't deny it. I cannot sit at home waiting for you. I can't go through that again, not knowing where you are, if you are even alive. That's the selfish side of it. Beyond that, I do understand the danger because I've seen it, experienced it many times. We could fail and be killed. But this is something we both believe in, something we cannot leave be. And at least we'll have tried, and for that I will have no regrets. I will go with you."

Marcus smiled then, nodding his approval. "Then we go in and tell him."

They came through the doorway, pausing to find Myrddin scowling at the fire pit. The hall was silent except for the hissing of the burning peat, mirroring the prince's uncomfortable exhaustion. Myrddin turned his face to them, and his eyes traced from one to the other. He would have liked to wait until morning to talk, but in deference to his friendship with Claerwen, he greeted Marcus politely enough and waited for them to begin.

They circled around the fire pit and stopped on the opposite side from Myrddin. Gathering his thoughts, Marcus folded his arms, then spoke formally, "We have thought long on what you have asked me and discussed it at great length. We agree that Ambrosius' hold over Britain must be preserved."

Myrddin rose slowly from the table. The flames from the fire gave just enough light to make his face look stark and brooding against the dim and smoky air of the hall. He waited for more.

"We will prepare and leave within the next few days for Brynaich, for the homestead of Octa the Saxon." Marcus stated.

Myrddin held his face in unreadableness again. He asked, "Who is going with you? Your cousin?"

"No, Owein remains here whenever I am gone. Claerwen is coming with me."

Myrddin's eyes sank and he turned, seeking the comfort of the dark space behind him. He muttered, "I was afraid of this."

Marcus frowned, but Claerwen stepped forward before he could speak further. She moved around the hearth, taking Myrddin by the elbow, and asked, "You have seen the same portent, haven't you?"

His brown eyes filled with regret, telling her it was true.

"Would that I had asked the Iron Hawk instead," he said with some bitterness. "Would that he were not so elusive a warrior, but such is what legends are made from..."

Alarmed, Claerwen's eyes snapped up, seeking Marcus. He squinted back, waiting for Myrddin to go on, but when the prince did not continue, he tilted his head slightly, indicating for her to ignore the comment. She blinked her understanding.

Drawing a long breath, Myrddin came back into the light. He faced Marcus. "What do you require as payment?"

"Five years of tithes in fine quality cattle, paid to the king of Gwynedd," Marcus answered.

Myrddin frowned at the odd request.

Marcus explained, "I do not charge tithes of my clan. In return for the use the land, their payment to me is purely in loyalty and the defense of our borders. This has been our way since my grandfather's time. Because I do not take tithes, I likewise do not pay Cunedda of Gwynedd, and he has been long displeased with me for that. However, I have provided him with enough of my services to more than make up for the lack of cattle or other payment. It is the same form of remuneration I require from others."

"Five years of good, fat cattle should keep him, or his sons or grandsons if he should die within that time, quite happy. Very clever," Myrddin conceded, then asked, "Why not for yourself, then pay the king?"

"I don't need to be a livestock broker in lands where cattle don't do well."

Myrddin half-smiled wryly, then asked, "What else do you require?"

"A year's good wool and flax. And salt. That should be enough."

"All useful," Myrddin observed.

"Survival is better than waste."

"Done."

"You're not going to condition it? What if we fail?"

Myrddin studied Marcus' face, then Claerwen's. For a fleeting instant, sadness flashed in Myrddin's eyes. "You won't," he said, then turned abruptly and stalked out of the hall.

Marcus squinted through the open doorway after him, his lips pressed together in consternation.

Claerwen crossed to him. She whispered urgently, "Does he know who the Iron Hawk is?"

Their eyes locked. For a full minute, they wordlessly sought each other's thoughts, then Marcus finally said, "No, I don't think so. I think he is only fishing, that perhaps I might know." His lips flinched nearly into a smile and he finished, "Let him keep guessing."

The ties of his tunic were loose and Claerwen slipped a hand inside. Seeking to ease his tension, her fingers lightly stroked his chest. She told him, "I was afraid before, that I would be a hindrance, not a help, just what Myrddin meant to say, but didn't."

Folding his arms around her, Marcus pulled her closely, rocking her, enjoying the feel of her pressing against him, but he remained tense, remarking, "He is worried well beyond that. There's something he's not saying. Is there another piece of this vision that hasn't been told?"

Looking up, she found he was still staring out through the doors. She started to speak then stopped, realizing she could not answer his question. "I don't know. It's possible he has seen something different than I have, perhaps a more complete vision. Should I try to learn what it is?"

"No. Let him rest. Perhaps his mood will improve by the morrow."

"You don't like Myrddin much, do you?"

Marcus gave a rough laugh. "He has an aloofness that makes my teeth ache, and he likes to speak in riddles instead of just saying what he needs to say. I suppose that's part of being a high druid."

She offered, "I think that's just the way he is. He's always spoken like that. Sometimes it sounds like arrogance, but he doesn't truly mean it that way. I've seen other people react so when they meet him."

"And I seem to bring out the worst in him as well," Marcus said with wryness.

She leaned back to watch his face, catching the tease. "And why is that?"

One eyebrow lifted and he answered, "I'd wager he thinks I'm an overbearing tyrant."

Claerwen frowned, not understanding.

"He's only seen one small side of me."

"Because you were very careful to only show your 'overbearing tyrant' side? On purpose?"

Marcus nodded, "Aye, on purpose."

"You don't trust him?"

He replied, "I know you do, you've been friends a long time. And through fire in the head, you have a connection to him that most would never have. Oh, I trust him as a prince, but as a man, I don't. I can't, not yet."

"Why?"

He shook his head. "Oddly, I'm not sure. Instinct, perhaps?"

Claerwen considered his remarks, then said, "I will not defend Myrddin to you."

"And I will not naysay him to you, either."

"As a Celtic prince, you need his alliance."

Marcus grunted, "Aye, you are right. And he has helped you considerably in the past when I wasn't able, and for that I owe him greatly. He certainly didn't do it for me."

"He didn't even know how you were involved with me at those times..." she countered, then tilted her head slightly and added with just a hint of coyness, "...until I told him I had married you."

The lines around his eyes deepened into a smile and his tension drained away. He leaned, whispering, "It's late. Let's go to bed."

Claerwen's hand moved upward from his chest, sliding along his throat and into his hair. She caught his lips in a long, fully indulgent kiss.

"Ah, it is definitely time to go to bed," he reiterated afterward. Arms snuggly around each other, they walked through the open doorway and crossed to their house.

---

Myrddin's grim mood had not improved by morning. In the

guesthouse he sat idly before a board game called *gwyddbwyll*. He picked up one piece, noticing it was different from the rest. It was the piece representing the high king and had been carved by a more skillful artist than that of the original set. He studied it for a few moments then closed his fingers around it as he heard knocking at the door.

"Come," he called, already knowing Marcus was the owner of the knock and would be seeking answers to a long list of questions.

Unfortunately, Myrddin did not have much more to tell. He explained, "Octa has remained in seclusion on the small northern homestead that was given as a peace offering. His brother Ebissa and their kinsman Eosa are allegedly there with him. No one has seen any untoward activity occurring there, but I strongly suspect Octa is league with someone at court. Two serious attempts on Ambrosius' life have already been made — mysterious accidents with few or no clues left behind. We guard my father constantly, but disloyalty is too easily bought."

Marcus sat across from Myrddin, poking his fingertips together as he thought. "You are absolutely certain Octa is still in Brynaich?"

"He and the others haven't moved off the land for the last month. They're as quiet as a nest of snakes."

"Describe them."

Myrddin characterized Octa as a large man, taller than himself, blond haired, with dark blue eyes that bulged out slightly from a long thin face, usually bearded with hair quite darker than the rest of his hair. He had a jagged scar from a sword cut across the back of his left hand. "He is known to be a berserker. He is extremely dangerous in a fight when he has the killing madness in him. But, I suppose your swordsmanship speaks well of itself, as I have seen."

"He is one to approach by stealth when possible, rather than force," Marcus countered. "He sounds similar to his father, whom I have seen. What else can you tell me?"

"Ebissa is similar to his older brother; Eosa is not as big and he's uglier than an old dog."

Marcus nodded his acknowledgment. "I want a written proclamation or some symbol that will authorize Claerwen and myself to dismiss the men you have watching the homestead now. She and I will need to have complete control.

"Consider it done. My father will be holding a temporary court in Caer Ebrauc, beginning within the next few days; I will be heading directly there. How will we stay in contact with you, once you begin?" Myrddin asked.

"We will contact you when we are able. It will be too dangerous to arrange meetings, and messengers are not viable for the situation. We will find ways to get information to you, but I cannot say how just yet."

"You're not going to plan ahead? You will walk into this as if blindfolded?"

"There is no telling what we'll find until we're actually there. Instinct is more useful than all the planning I could do. So far, it has served me well."

Myrddin exhaled slowly, the same look of dread in his face as the night before.

Marcus leaned forward, his black eyes tightly studying the prince. As he opened his mouth to speak, the wall of aloofness rose up around Myrddin like a shield covered with spikes. Marcus squinted, irritated, but spoke anyway. "If you have seen something more than Claerwen has, Lord Myrddin, speak it now, at least to her. I'd wager you won't tell it to me."

He waited for Myrddin's response but received none, as expected. He went on, "If you doubt her involvement in this, understand that I have no regrets in this decision, and this is why: Three summers ago, I was forced into a war against one of Vortigern's traitors, the man called Drakar. You'll remember Claerwen had been contracted to marry him four years before that. I discredited him because he was importing Saxon mercenaries for Vortigern. The contract was broken, but he never gave up hunting her down after that. His force outnumbered mine three to one in the final battle, and she insisted to come with me. I refused her, of course, but because of fire in the head, she still followed me. I was ambushed, and she killed Drakar, saving my life. That was when I fully accepted what the fire does to her, and I learned to trust it with no question. When she says something must be so, I do not doubt her."

Myrddin murmured, "You cannot understand it the same way."

Marcus returned, "I know that. I never will, but it will not prevent me from following the chosen path that the gods have lain out before me." He suspected Myrddin was frustrated, as Claerwen was at times when the fire only showed her hints and clues of events to come. She had explained that there was no prodding the gods into revealing more through the fire, regardless of how important, and that Myrddin had no more control over it than she.

Myrddin remained silent with his head bowed for a moment, eyeing Marcus' big hands and remembering the smashed face of one assassin.

Marcus guessed his thoughts and said, "No, Claerwen is not a warrior woman, and she doesn't have the same physical strength I do, but she has something more valuable than what a lifetime of experience, or even what the fire can give her. Whether it's inner strength or an iron will or just plain courage, I have no name for it. She is not a foolish woman, Lord Myrddin. Not at all. I don't like the idea of taking her into such danger any more than you do. But if I had to pick one person to help me, anyone at all, I would choose her first, because I know I can trust her with my life. Completely."

Myrddin rose abruptly, saying with brutal finality, "And Claerwen trusts the path of her life to you as much as the gods." With his eyes watching on some other plane of time and distance, he placed the game piece he had been holding into Marcus' hand, then strode out the door on long, regal steps, as if already on his way to Caer Ebrauc.

Marcus frowned at the tiny figure of a king, pondering Myrddin's words and why the prince had been so cryptically ceremonious about the game piece. Holding it up, he realized it was the one he had carved himself to replace a broken king. The wood from which it was made had a slight flaw in it, but he had carved it in such a way that it scarcely showed.

"*Gwyddbwyll*, 'Wooden Wisdom,' a game of strategy between powers," he muttered to himself, and he wondered if Myrddin's gesture held symbolic significance or was merely more frustrating aloofness. Pressing his lips together, he returned the king piece to its place on the wooden board and left the guesthouse.

# Chapter 4

**Near Hadrian's Wall, Kingdom of Brynaich**

Squinting into the last of the evening's glaring sunlight, Marcus peered down across a vast stretch of rolling moorland scattered with farmsteads. He knelt within the edge of a thick grove, tucked in a fold between two low hilltops. Claerwen waited beside him.

The sun's appearance was brief, dropping out of a heavy layer of cloud above the western horizon. Brilliant light beamed outward like an immense golden fan, scattering sparkles onto a dozen carefree streams jigging through rocky cracks in the moors. Mesmerizing, it made the eyes ache, even water, yet enticed with irresistible beauty. Minutes later, the sun took refuge, gathering up its light like a woman's skirts, ready to flee, and leaving the entire expanse murky and sullen.

Marcus swung his arm from one side to the other, stopping periodically to point out each camp of Ambrosius' watchmen. "They want to call themselves spies," he commented. His voice reflected the quiet melancholy of the darkening landscape. "Their camps are so bloody obvious, it's not a wonder Octa has made no move. Or, I suspect, he may have left long ago. That's why I want them out of here, they're not helping anyone but Octa."

Mist rolled from behind the hilltops, wisping down over them. Marcus stood, watching its flow with approval. He adjusted his baldric, the thick leather strap that held a broad-bladed, hand-and-a-half sword diagonally across his back. He had left his favored two-handed sword at home, opting for the shorter weapon's lighter weight and quickness over the other's heavier power and longer reach. In addition to the sword, he checked the multiple daggers he carried, hidden in boot tops, the back of his belt and under his left sleeve in a wristband sheath.

Dressed identically to Marcus, Claerwen wore dark walnut-dyed deerskin breeches, boots, leggings, a tunic, a heavy hooded overtunic, and a thick grey sheepskin cap. While she tucked a few stray strands of hair into the cap, Marcus surveyed the weapons she concealed as well, a similar array of daggers to his. An accomplished archer, she carried a small bow and arrows instead of a sword, intended for hunting as much as defense. Their horses, a pair of sturdy mountain greys, were tethered and well hidden, each packed with only absolute necessities for travel.

Confirming they were ready, Marcus converted to silent hand signals. They moved down the hillside, fast and light, quickly reaching the lead observer's camp.

In a tiny clearing, centered in a thick stand of trees, two men squatted beside a small cooking fire. Each held a chunk of dried meat on a stick. As the cold drizzle descended, causing the fire to smoke and sputter, the men grumbled to each other that the food was bad enough already, and now they would be unable to heat it.

Observing them unseen, Marcus had an almost amused look in his eyes. He touched Claerwen's hand, indicating she should follow, then silently moved forward.

"Greetings, from Prince Myrddin Emrys," Marcus declared, layering authority into his voice. He stopped just where the fire's heat struggled to dissipate the mist.

The two men started, reached for their weapons.

"Hold!" Marcus ordered, lifting his hands to show they were empty.

The leader, a wiry man with curly dark hair and wary grey eyes, slowly put down his supper and rose. He stared long at

Marcus, particularly noting the sword, but found no hostility.

From behind Marcus, Claerwen appeared, walking out of the mist and startling the men again. She held out a rolled parchment imprinted with Myrddin's symbolic seal. Though surprised to see a woman, the leader held his thoughts to himself and took the parchment.

Marcus said, "The prince told us you could read."

The man nodded, broke the seal, pulled off the thin leather thong knotted around the roll, and read aloud:

*The bearers of this document are granted the authority to dismiss all concerned observers of the farmstead known to be the home of Octa the Saxon. All observers shall depart immediately upon the reading of this document and return to the military station at Caer Ebrauc. Authority is given in the name of the Lord High King Ambrosius, evidenced by the unbroken seal of his son Prince Myrddin upon its delivery.*

*Signed, Prince Myrddin Emrys*

The man read the document twice more. When his eyes rose to meet Marcus' solemn face, he plainly showed his discomfort at the dismissal.

"Why? And who are you?" he asked.

"We are merely couriers," Marcus replied.

The leader grimaced at the parchment a few moments, then rolled it up and slipped the thong around it again. "I suppose we have no choice. We will leave at sunrise."

"According to the orders, you are to leave immediately," Marcus pointed out.

"In the dark? In this mist?"

"You've been here long enough to know your way around without benefit of light or clear skies. The orders are for immediate withdrawal."

The man glared at Marcus, then again at the hilt behind his shoulder. He realized that this man was not just a messenger, but an enforcer as well. With no further word, he signaled his partner to pack and alert the other camps.

Within minutes Marcus and Claerwen were alone in the clearing. By sunrise, hours later, they had completely circled the area and confirmed that all observers were heading south towards Caer Ebrauc. Then, after carefully approaching the homestead, they settled in an overlooking willow copse to observe.

"It's too quiet," Marcus commented.

"You were expecting a military buildup that the king's men missed?"

Turning to her, he realized from the mischief in her face that she was teasing. Grinning, he said, "I meant there's not even enough activity to say this is a working farm. There's no livestock, no herdsmen, no crops."

"Aye," she agreed, gazing below again. "Do you think it's abandoned?"

"No, not completely. Someone is keeping it ready for when Octa comes home — if he comes home. See how the grass is trampled along the path leading to the door? There's probably a caretaker who uses the fire pit in the evenings, making just enough smoke so the house looks like it's occupied."

"Why wouldn't Ambrosius' men have suspected the same and reported it?"

"You can wager payment was given for their silence. That's why they were angry at being dismissed so abruptly. We will need to be very careful and very quick. They will have alerted those who paid them by now."

"Quick?" she queried.

"We will search it tonight."

Claerwen's eyes widened. "Won't the caretaker be there?"

"Aye, but he won't know *we're* there," he grinned at her wariness. "You will see. For now, we will eat, rest, until it is time."

They used the depth of night to their advantage, leaving the willow copse and descending down into a long, narrow stand of trees. The wood divided Octa's lands from his neighbor's, curving around behind the rear of the house, and Marcus followed along the inner lengthwise edge, leading Claerwen by the hand. They stopped a short distance from a rough barn, the closest outbuilding.

Rain began to fall heavily, making the night difficult to penetrate. Undaunted, Marcus pulled his overtunic's hood tighter around his face and peered through the wet shield, reconnoitering. Satisfied no one watched, he crossed the final spread of open space and came up against the barn, Claerwen close behind him. Moving along the exterior in search of an opening, he found it was a small, round, loosely built structure of rough branches tied together with leather hitches.

Finding a door, Marcus unlatched the tie that held it shut, tugged it open and slipped inside, pulling Claerwen in after him. He left the door slightly ajar and waited, watching for movement.

Rain thudded on the thatched roof, leaking through in a few places. The interior stank of rancid straw. Claerwen circled, groping slowly through the dark and over the spongy ground. Midway around, she stumbled, her foot finding a slight depression with a hard surface inside it. Dropping onto her knees, she cautiously dug with her fingers. Several straw-laced clods fell apart when she picked them up, and from the smell, she realized it was dung, so old it powdered when disturbed. She dropped them, disgusted, but continued to explore, knowing the solid object she had tripped over was out of place. Finally, she felt cold metal, half-buried in the ground, and pried it out. Its surface was uneven, one end tapered into a sharp point.

Marcus closed the door. As he came towards Claerwen, she rose and gripped his hand, turning his palm upward. She laid the metal object in it and kept her hands on his, preventing him from closing his fingers, communicating he should be careful, it was sharp.

Marcus traced the metal and discovered the shape of a spearhead. He squeezed Claerwen's arm in approval, wishing for light to examine it, but knew it would have to wait. He tucked it into a small leather pouch hung on his belt for the purpose of collecting anything useful.

Outside, the rain continued in a steady drenching. Returning to the door, they gazed across to the house, but only saw it as a vague shape. Not willing to wait longer, Marcus clamped his hand around Claerwen's and pulled her outside. Dashing across, they rounded the backside of the house, sliding on the slippery turf with each step. The shutters on the first window Marcus tried were not bolted. Without hesitation, he pushed them in and boosted himself through, Claerwen following.

The house was long and narrow, the interior one large open space broken only by a few support beams. A fire pit glowed softly in the center, giving dingy light. They had entered at one end, and Marcus crept forward, moving slowly through a common living space and into an area used as a sleeping room. A lone man lay in an uncurtained bed, snoring loudly.

Pulling off his right glove, Marcus pressed his thumb and forefinger into the caretaker's neck. The man struggled slightly, his snoring interrupted, then fell limp.

"He'll sleep a good while," Marcus said, breaking his silence as he straightened.

"He didn't see you?" Claerwen asked.

"No. He lost consciousness without waking."

"A rushlight," Claerwen blurted, her hands exploring an iron wall sconce. She pulled the rushes out and took them to the hearth, lighting them.

"That will help," Marcus said, wiping his dripping moustache. He directed, "Quickly now, while I bind and gag him. Look for anything that can tell us where they've gone or that would incriminate them."

"What kind of things?"

"Anything. Like this spearhead you found." He pulled it from the pouch and held it to the light. Where it was clean, simple chasing showed. "This is excellent. The Saxons use decorative patterns like this on their spearheads; each war band has its own pattern. We can identify them, using this. But we must know where they've gone. Most of those small buildings were probably filled with weapons, and I suspect Octa has taken them somewhere to arm a war band."

They found no other evidence in the house. Methodically, they searched every outbuilding and found a few more spearheads identical to the first one, and some old, nearly useless tools that were left behind. None of it was worthwhile to take.

The rain had nearly ended by the time Marcus declared the search done. As moonlight attempted to break through the clouds, he returned to the barn and stood inside its doorway, surveying the turf towards the wood. Beyond the house, a wide, churned up ditch had been dug just in front of the first trees.

"That must be their latrine pit," he observed, then strode out towards it.

Claerwen trailed him, slowing in astonishment when she saw him pick up a stout stick and begin prodding at the ditch's edge.

"You're not going to dig...in that...are you?" she asked, revolted.

"I learned a long time ago, people drop things into their latrine pits. Most goes unnoticed. Of course, being Saxons, perhaps they don't mind to retrieve..." He spread his fingers out as if to plunge them into the muck.

Claerwen's face curled up in disgust, thinking the dried dung she had accidentally picked up was bad enough. Then as he illuminated his face with the rushlight, she saw he was grinning broadly. She muttered, "Padrig is right, there is no remedy for you."

Rustling came from the trees. Abruptly sober, Marcus held up a hand for silence and watched Claerwen listen and sniff the air.

She said, "An owl. It missed its prey and went back up to roost." They waited. Moments later, the owl hooted its discontent.

He grinned again, this time in appreciation of her knowledge of the wild.

Claerwen smiled back wryly, and said, "Now, teach me more of this...work."

Marcus found little to collect. He hurried, hoping to finish before the rushlight burnt out. He also sensed Claerwen had become uncomfortably chilled from the dampness. The only items he found were a pair of small, well-rusted bosses that had been lost from someone's leather armor.

As they neared the end of the ditch, Marcus tossed his branch far back into the brush and doused the rushlight. "There's nothing more to do here —" He stopped when Claerwen suddenly moved away from him.

She ran into the trees where the owl had flown earlier and crouched, pushing aside thick fern fronds. Underneath, a large rock sat perched on top of several smaller ones set in a rough circle like a cairn. Marcus approached and knelt, studying the arrangement, then carefully removed the top stone. Inside, a space had been dug into the earth and was filled with an oilskin-wrapped object.

Marcus looked up at the sky, waiting for the clouds to part momentarily. He wished he had kept the rushlight, needing more than sporadic moonglow to see clearly. Unless he re-entered the house, he would not find dry tinder without a long search. Gradually, however, luck drove apart the clouds.

He wiped his moustache again, preventing it from dripping into the tiny cairn, and flung the rainwater off his hand. Reaching in, he cautiously pulled the bundle out, then opened the edges of the oilskin. His hands suddenly stopped moving, the object lying across them. Slowly, stunned, his eyes lifted to Claerwen's face.

"If this is what it looks like..." he whispered. His eyes dropped, staring at an oversized spearhead elaborately chased with intertwining lines and a bold, raised dragon symbol studded with jewels. The shaft it had been attached to was chopped away.

"By the light," Claerwen ejected, tentatively touching the silken surface. "Do you remember the vision I told you of, the one I had when Dinas Beris was sacked? I saw all five pieces of Macsen's Treasure, the crown, the torque, the sword, the grail, and the spearhead. The shape and pattern of this perfectly match the ceremonial spearhead."

Once more they stared at each other. Both thrill and horror swept them. In Marcus' hands lay a piece of Britain's ancient soul, one of the five symbols forged by the smith of the first high king Brutus and passed down over fifteen centuries into the hands of Macsen Wledig, the ruler near the end of the Roman occupation. It was utterly priceless. And as they pondered the significance of this discovery, they also wondered how in the gods' names had Octa become possessed of it.

A shout wailed from the moors, distantly.

Marcus' head jerked around. He peered into the darkness but found it useless to speculate if the shout was merely that of a farmer chasing predators from his livestock or from someone deliberately approaching. Not willing to wait for confirmation of either, he chose the latter as more likely.

"We must hide this and go north," he whispered tautly, wrapping the spearhead again and stuffing it inside his tunic. "If we can reach Hadrian's Wall before daylight, it's our only chance for escape."

The gravity of his tone scared Claerwen, but she appreciated his directness. She held the questions gathering in her mind, trusting that his judgement was wise in taking the spearhead. Glancing at the house, she saw nothing stir. But she also understood that others would be coming, and soon, especially if Ambrosius' observers had been paid to be disloyal. Carrying Macsen's stolen spearhead was not going to win them a grain of reprieve if they were caught by Saxons, whether only a few or as many as a full war band.

Reverting to silent hand signals, Marcus directed her to find a fallen branch. He replaced the stone and settled the ferns over it. With the branch, he swept across their tracks, obscuring them, then tossed it far back into the trees.

Another shout, closer.

"To the horses," Marcus signaled. They began running through the woods.

Claerwen could not guess yet what he had meant by escape, whether they would dig into a secure hiding place, go to the coast in hopes of boarding a ship bound for some distant port, or seek some other form of flight. She knew he would not speak his plans aloud where they could likely be overheard, and it was possible he had not even decided; but however he did, she trusted him and his experience, knowing how many times in the past he had wriggled out of trouble.

The clouds closed in again by the time they reached the horses. While the darkness blessed them with invisibility, it also cursed them with slowness. Marcus was familiar enough with Brynaich to weave a path in spite of the lack of light, following no road or track throughout the night. They emerged on an escarpment overlooking Hadrian's Wall, just as the eastward sky began to glow with first light. A river followed the wall, its water broad and fast moving, swollen with the recent rains.

Marcus halted several yards from the escarpment's edge and dismounted. For several minutes he carefully surveyed the river and its banks as well as the marshy land beyond that led to the Roman wall, listening, sensing every detail with his warrior's wariness.

"Rest here for a bit, but stay within the trees," he finally said, breaking hours of silence.

Claerwen dropped off her horse and explored the immediate area for food. Finding comfrey among the overgrowth, she pulled a dagger and began digging for the roots. Marcus joined her.

"You are tense," she remarked, noting his narrowed eyes were constantly scanning in all directions. "They are out there, aren't they? We haven't lost them."

"I have heard and seen nothing," he replied, turning his head to listen again, then shook it in frustration.

Her voice lowered, "But you feel someone is there?"

He nodded, rubbing soil off one of the roots she handed him. He took a bite, chewing slowly, thinking, still listening. Swallowing, he said, "By now they will know this has been stolen." He laid his hand over his tunic where the spearhead was hidden.

"They certainly won't let it go easily," Claerwen agreed.

"Neither will I," Marcus said, watching the concern in her face deepen. He explained, "I know this kingdom well but it's become nearly as hostile as the Saxon Shore in the south, because there are so many Saxons and Angles who have settled since Octa was exiled here. They are starting to call it by their name of Bernicia now, instead of Brynaich. I have an ally, directly to the east, on the coast. He will hide us for a while. But we will need to scout his lands first, and if it's safe, be careful not to lead anyone there."

"How far is it?"

"If we could ride out in the open, one long day. But we need to stay hidden — I think we should travel only at night. It could take two or three days, depending on moon and starlight."

"Why not go directly to Ambrosius?"

"We don't want to carry this any longer than we must. Caer Ebrauc is too far away and too much in the open. If we are delayed, Ambrosius might have already moved his camps and court again by the time we reach it. Because of the spearhead, we know Octa is guilty of its theft. I'm certain he planned to use it as a symbol of authority in the attempt to take Ambrosius' throne, but it is still not enough evidence. If he plans an assassination, we must find proof of the actual plot while preventing its occurrence."

Claerwen considered his prudence, his concise logic, and nodded her acceptance.

Marcus smiled then, approving of her agreement. "Then we shall camp for the day, but not here. I know a better place."

He led her to a depression in the escarpment hidden by thick evergreen trees. There was room enough to hide the horses and make a comfortable shelter protected from weather and predators, both animal and human. They took turns throughout the day, watching and sleeping, then ate again at dusk.

That night they began the trek eastward. Marcus continued to sense someone followed, but he never heard or saw anyone. He speculated that perhaps Octa had hired a Pict, from the wild northern tribes of Alba, known for their instinctive, relentless tracking. He and Claerwen redoubled their efforts to remain hidden, making no fires for cooking or heat, camping only in well-camouflaged places, not speaking aloud for hours.

Closer to the coast, the patches of woodland grew scarce except along the riverbanks. Marcus and Claerwen closely followed the winding course of the water, trying to stay hidden. By the end of the third night, they came within a mile of the shore. Marcus had hoped to reach his ally's holdings that night, but they were obliged to stop with daylight quickly approaching.

From their position, they could see the mouth of the river broaden into a marshy estuary that emptied into the sea. Directly below, exposed sandbars and sea-smoothed boulders indicated the tide was out. The shores to each side were narrow, rumpled with coarse gravel.

Dismounting, Marcus tramped along the thicket-lined south bank, looking for a safe place to camp. Not finding a satisfactory site, he turned back to where he had left the horses. Claerwen had gone the other direction on a similar quest, and he waited for her to join him.

Time passed. Marcus grew impatient, then worried. He breathed a low, soughing whistle they used as a signal between them. No reply came.

Then he saw the tracks. Cursing to himself, he pulled his sword and trailed them. Claerwen's footprints were not visible, but he knew she was capable of leaving no trace of her presence. There were two sets of male tracks, immediately fresh, running several yards along the bank. They paused between two willow thickets, turned, then headed away from the river.

Marcus stopped between the two willows, scanning in all directions, whistling once more. Still no answer came. He swore again and turned, intending to follow the prints away from the river. Then he halted, his eye catching a displaced patch of leaves. Turning back, he knelt and pressed aside the reedy branches of the thicket to his right. The earth had been disturbed, scrape marks running downward from the top of the embankment. Unable to see through the dense overgrowth, he lifted his sword and sliced away a chunk of the thicket.

The narrow shore below became visible, and Marcus felt his stomach shudder. In the moment he saw her, lying at the water's edge, he knew Claerwen must have been pushed, or startled into falling. She lay flat on her back, her right arm in the river, the water dragging at her hand.

A sound came from behind him, a lush and silky slither.

Marcus whirled, his sword moving so fast that it sounded like rushing wind. Within the same instant, an unforgiving thud pounded under his left ear. Pain grabbed him in the neck and along the side of his head. He never saw the man he struck with his sword, but the recoil jarred all the way up his arms, into his shoulders. Yellow and red colors flooded his eyes, drenching his sight like an excruciating, bursting waterfall. Screaming, he felt his voice scrape in his throat, roaring Claerwen's name from the depths of his lungs, but he could no longer hear anything, not even himself. The sword slipped from his hands, no strength left in them to grip the hilt. He was going down, on his knees, falling forward, hurtling into the muddy darkness of unbearable pain and helpless grief, utterly powerless to stop it.

# Chapter 5

### The northern moors, Kingdom of Brynaich

Rasping grated, a distant, hollow sound that faded, grew stronger, faded again. Marcus gradually became aware of it, listening, curious, confused. Then pain slowly awakened in his head and body, and he drew a deeper breath, trying to forestall it against an annoying, steady, icy draught that coaxed the dull ache towards torment. Cold drizzle soaked him and an uncomfortable, foul taste clung inside his mouth. As the drizzle thickened, droplets formed on his moustache and he licked at their refreshing taste. He realized the rasping was his own rough breathing.

His eyes slit open, revealing only a disorienting darkness, but rocks carving their shapes into his back told him he was lying on the ground. The sounds of working people drifted around him amid the smell of peat smoke and pungent, damp earth. A voice grumbled somewhere, suddenly a little louder, using words of a Saxon dialect. Alarmed upon recognition of the language, though he did not understand or speak it, Marcus forced himself to remain limp, steady his breathing and struggle to bring his mind to full awareness.

Two men approached, muttering back and forth, their words curt and on the verge of arguing. One grunted a final answer; the other walked away. The grunting one leaned down, sniffed roughly, then dropped a coil of thin rope from his shoulder. He bound Marcus' wrists to iron pegs that had been pounded into the ground to each side of where he lay. Lingering a moment longer, the man mumbled a few more contemptuous thoughts aloud, the last punctuated with the Saxon word every Celt understood, the word for foreigner, *wallia*.

The man paced away. Noise and movement gradually diminished. Lying quietly and listening, Marcus guessed he had been brought to a military camp, noting the authoritative tone one set of voices had over the subjective ones that answered. He also speculated the men were bedding down for the night and they had bound him to prevent his escape should he regain consciousness when no one was watching.

*Claerwen!* Marcus' mind suddenly wrenched fully awake. His abrupt recollection of her lying on the rivershore nearly compelled him to sit up. Nausea roiled in his stomach. He raked his mind for more memories but nothing came to him. Her fall from the embankment had not been far, he reasoned, but he could not guess if she had slid down by accident or dove off as a result of a strong-armed push. Either way, surviving the fall meant little if she had remained unconscious for very long. The coming tide would drag her out to sea.

The nausea grew worse as the dreadful sense of failure engulfed him. His stomach recoiled, then heaved. Unable to hold the bile down, he turned his head aside and retched.

Expectedly, it brought attention. Emitting grunts of disgust, two guards stalked forward and untied Marcus. They dragged him to a nearby latrine pit, forcing him onto his knees, pushing him down until his face hovered just above fresh, raw sewage. The stench made his stomach rumple and grip itself in pain, but he was through vomiting and spit the remnants in the attempt to clear his mouth.

One guard snapped a command in Saxon, but only received a look of honest incomprehension. Growling impatience, the man gripped the back of Marcus' tunic and wrenched him onto his feet, then grumbled a string of orders to the second guard. Other men gathered, curious and scornful, most apparently of the warrior class, the rest foot soldiers, all of them well armed.

Marcus eyed them one by one, deliberately showing only a defiant mask of cold regard. Feeling the extra space in his boots, belt and wristbands, he knew they had found his weapons, but even if armed, fighting his way out would be useless against so many. And, he speculated, Macsen's spearhead must now be in the hands of the camp's commanding officer. Presumably that officer was Octa.

The second guard acknowledged the orders with an indifferent mumble, then marched, shoved and dragged Marcus across the camp to a section crowded with filthy, unkempt men. Lying on the wet ground and already trying to sleep after an endless day of grueling work, each was shackled to a long common chain, one after the next in a long row. The guard tripped Marcus, dropping him flat next to the last man, then locked a pair of shackles around his wrists, the common chain threaded through both of them. Another pair of shackles went around his ankles, a short chain running between them. Like the other men, Marcus was given no blanket. Food and water would wait for the morrow; it was already too late for that day. His status had changed from prisoner to slave.

Exhausted, in pain and frustrated, Marcus guessed they would break camp and move a long distance the next day, given that the warriors would otherwise be drinking and gambling late into the night. He levered himself up onto one elbow, needing to learn the camp's layout before the evening firelight died. One string of patrollers paced around the perimeter. Another, smaller group watched the slaves. The guards were not many, he observed, counting them and memorizing their routines. Beyond the slave quarters, he saw a small portable smithy, two large tents just past it. Soldiers were clumped around a haphazard collection of fires, trying to keep warm as they sought enough comfort to fall asleep.

Then, on the farthest side, he saw dozens of carts, piled high with supplies and loosely covered with leather tarpaulins. Metal shined from under the edges of many of the covers. The field in which the camp lay sloped upward from the slave quarters to the carts, affording Marcus a slight advantage in his surveillance, but at that distance he was unsure if he was looking at stockpiled weapons or something else. It was very possible, he knew, and hoped, that this was the camp Octa had supplied.

A low, sharp call hissed beside him. Turning his head, Marcus saw the next slave was awake and looking appalled. "Get down," the man whispered.

"You are Cornish?" Marcus queried, relieved he could understand him.

"Aye, but get down before they see you. And be still, unless you want a beating."

A guard swung around then and peered across the row of slaves. The Cornishman closed his eyes, pretending to sleep. Falling back, Marcus turned his face away from the Saxon. The soldier frowned, unable to see the men well in the darkening camp. Hearing no more voices, he decided nothing was important enough to investigate. He continued his patrol.

Marcus waited several minutes then prodded the Cornishman with his elbow. Whispering low, he asked, "Have they brought a woman to the camp?"

The slave stared at him, wishing this stranger would go to sleep.

"Please, tell me," Marcus prompted.

"Who is this woman and why would you want to know?"

"It's important to me." Marcus' eyes bored fiercely, as if they could tear open the slave's mind in search of the answer.

The Cornishman grimaced. There would be no avoiding this newcomer. Glancing at the guards, he said, "No. Only you. There is no woman here. Now, be quiet." He tightened his arms over his chest, against both the cold and any more questions. He shut his eyes again, determined not to invite the Saxons' annoyance.

Marcus stared into the black, drizzling sky long afterward. Though relieved to learn Claerwen was not in the camp, he could not lose the harrowing memory of her lying on the rivershore, her hand in the water; nor was he able to stop his mind from conjuring one additional image, that of Claerwen being swept to the sea. With his lips pressed together in consternation, he lifted his wrists and scowled at the shackles, trying to determine if they had a weakness, a loose link in the chain, a lock he could open without a tool. He had to escape before the camp moved; he had to find Claerwen, and it would need to be that night.

"You!" a guard shouted, startling him. "Get down!"

Marcus transferred his smoldering glare to the Saxon, a grey-haired man with a face as hard and cracked as the granite cliffs of Eryri.

"Now, *wallia!*" the guard ordered again, then, without waiting for Marcus to comply, signaled to another patroller, a younger man in his charge. They spoke briefly and the second man ran across to one of the supply carts, returning with four metal stakes.

Marcus' head throbbed with each loud ping and vibration of a hammer on the iron pegs as they were driven into the ground. Sitting up, he watched his future punishment unfold. His face remained coldly unreadable, but in his mind, he calculated that his only chance to escape would come when they transferred him from the slave line to the stakes. He knew he could rip the chain out of the guards' grip, but even if he could avoid their weapons and overpower them with his bare hands while still encumbered by the heavy irons, he could never elude the camp's other hundred warriors. He would have to find another way.

The older guard approached, speaking again, his menacing tone and gestures indicating the gravity of the coming punishment, and upon finishing, he signaled to the younger guard. They detached the chain from Marcus' shackles and forced him at knifepoint to the center of the stakes. Each wrist and ankle band was linked to an iron ring on the top of each stake, stretching him uncomfortably. To add a final insult, they forced a large stone under his back, intending to cause enough discomfort to keep him awake the rest of the night. They stood over him, smirking, then returned to their rounds.

Marcus laid his head back, closed his eyes, and let his breath out slowly in a long, bitter curse.

The camp broke at first light. For two days, the men marched across bleak and rain-swept moorland heading south, from dawn to dusk. As they followed the warriors, the slaves were forced to endlessly load and unload supplies, cook the meals, dig the latrine trenches, set up and break down the camp. Except to relieve themselves, and even then they were still tethered to a guard, they remained chained, all together in a line or in small work groups. They were allowed one meager meal of gruel in the morning, another in the evening. By night, they dropped in exhaustion, still all in a row.

Although he was not staked down again, sleep did not come easily to Marcus. The farther from the river he was forced to travel, the more miserable he grew about Claerwen's fate. The discomfort from the blow to his head and neck annoyed him far less. Always chained and always watched, he had not yet discovered the opportunity to attempt an escape.

Nearly fretting him as much was the idea that no one had interrogated him regarding Macsen's spearhead. He was certain the Saxons knew he had stolen it from Octa's farmstead, and surely the only reason he was still alive was to provide them with further information. He puzzled long into the night on this odd lack of interest in him, contrasting it to the horrors of his last imprisonment, when Vortigern's brutish men had beaten him beyond most men's endurance in the hopes of learning what he had known then of Ambrosius' activities. The toll of that time had left gaps in his memory, but he well remembered the Saxons' penchant for torture.

By the third night they reached heavy forest and camped in a small clearing. As he lay in his usual place in the slave row, Marcus folded his arms over his chest as much as the chain allowed. He watched the guards' routines, noting that their patterns and positions had changed, leaving longer spaces between rounds, and he wondered why the security was looser. The camp settled into a low rumble of snoring.

The evening fires died down. High, thin clouds scudded above the treetops, causing the moonlight to flicker. Lying on his side, Marcus kept still, but his eyes moved warily. He reached his thumb and forefinger under his left wristband and pinched, slipping out a small piece of scrap iron, long and very thin. Angling it back, he pressed its tip into the lock of one shackle, wiggled it, turned it, wiggled it again. The lock clicked quietly, opening.

He picked the lock on the other wrist shackle, then drew his legs up to open the ankle bands. To keep the chains from clinking, he remained on his side and drew his arms and legs out of the irons with painstaking slowness, freeing himself. Calculating, waiting, he watched the next guard approach, pass, move on.

In the space of a few seconds he was up and darting into the trees. Pausing, he glanced for an instant from behind a heavy trunk. The last guard had not turned, and the next one had not yet shown. Satisfied, he slipped farther away, disappearing into the forest.

The thick trees and the near-complete darkness beyond the circle of the camp's firelight made movement difficult, but as his eyes adjusted, he gained speed. The persistent dampness of the past days kept the ground's leafy covering soft and pliable and prevented his footsteps from crunching.

Within a few hundred yards, he heard the whip of tree branches slap somewhere behind him. He halted, backing to a tree trunk, listening, waiting, peering across the area he had just covered. Nothing more disturbed the silence. The trees were less dense where he had stopped, their lowest limbs higher than his head. As the clouds struggled to clear again, moonlight offered more definition to the murky landscape. A short distance away, a bulky, out of place form was piled at the base of one tree. He listened a few moments longer, still heard nothing, then decided to investigate.

Before he was halfway there, he knew by its gear that the form belonged to one of the Saxons. Marcus stalked all the way around him, scanning the area and watching the soldier for movement. He stopped behind the man's shoulders and with his boot, gave a quick, hard shove. No reaction. Kneeling, he found the man was breathing and only unconscious. Though knowing well this could be a trap, he decided both the risk and opportunity to re-arm himself were worthwhile, and he reached for the soldier's belt dagger.

He stopped, aware of a presence standing behind him.

A figure was silhouetted, backlit by dim light from the partial moon straining to penetrate the clouds. Marcus stared, dumbstruck by the eerie image. The figure was slight, wearing male clothing and holding a heavy piece of deadwood as if to strike. A sword hilt showed high over its right shoulder

His hand darted for the dagger.

"Marcus..." the figure called softly.

He froze, his fingers pressed around the hilt, and he stared again. It was a woman's voice. *His* woman's voice.

But Claerwen could not possibly be there. She was three days to the north, lying on the cold rocks, alone.

Disappointment flooded Marcus. The image that had haunted his mind was real after all, put there only for the purpose of warning him. She was gone, gone along with the tide, swept to the sea, and this was her spirit standing before him, come to say farewell before she passed through the gates of *Annwn, y dan fyd,* the Otherworld. He had wanted to believe so much that she would still be there when he went back.

The figure slowly lowered the wood, dropping it to the ground, then came forward and pulled a glove from one hand, reached to him.

"It's me...Marcus? Are you all right?" Claerwen touched his arm.

Her hand was warm and comforting on his flesh, and he felt her life flow alive like breath in his lungs. Slowly he rose, realizing she was no spirit to flit away with the capricious moonlight. His mouth dropped open, and his dark eyes moved from despair to utter astonishment to unabashed joy.

"Come, I have a shelter we can hide in," she said, tucking her hand in the curve of his big fingers, eager to put more space between them and the camp.

"Claerwen," he finally whispered, his face bursting into a broad smile. He gripped her hand, holding her back. Too overjoyed to speak more, he laid his palm to her cheek, closed his eyes a moment.

"*Diolch yn fawr...*" he thanked the gods.

She flung herself into his arms, relieved that his rich voice was still steady, his hands still strong as they ran down her back.

"Ah, I am so very fine now," he answered, hushing the question he knew she would ask.

"Come, before they start looking," she coaxed, taking his hand again.

"How did..." He needed to ask so many questions of his own, but she was right that they needed to be farther away. He sheathed the dagger in the back of his belt, then regarded the hilt behind her shoulder. "Where did you get...this is mine. You found my sword..."

"Aye, if it was your other one, it would be too long for me to carry," she teased, unbuckling the baldric and awkwardly slipping it off her back.

He took the weapon, countering, "I'm glad to have this, no matter the size. Aye, show me this shelter."

"It's only made of branches and leaves, but it will keep out the wind and hopefully keep us hidden for the night," she said as she led him straight up a hill, arriving at a low structure wedged between a pair of boulders. It looked like a pile of debris blown into the rock crevice. "When the mist is gone, you can see straight down through that gap in the trees and observe most of the camp. In the late afternoon, the sun is behind the hill. If they would look up here, all they would see is shadow and a lot of glare."

"You chose well," Marcus commented, exhaustion coming into his voice. "It's far enough to be safe, yet watch them easily. From how it looks, no one would guess it's not a natural fall of leaves.

"I have food and water here. Are you hungry?"

When he did not answer at first, she moved to retrieve the food, but his hand darted out, catching her arm. "No...no, Claerwen. Not now. Sit here with me, and tell me what happened. I was so sure you were...gone."

They sank down in front of the shelter, and as he settled back against one of the boulders, the dim light illuminated his tired and battered face. Several days' growth of beard had begun to cover it, but the bruises and swelling were still obvious, running along his jawline and neck. "By the gods..." she sputtered and gripped his arm, pulling him back when he tried to turn and prevent her from seeing it.

"It probably looks worse than it feels," he shrugged off her concern, then teased, "You know my head's harder than an anvil."

"In many ways," she shot back.

"Claeri, what happened?" he prompted, returning to his earlier question.

Her eyes dropped as she fingered the familiar texture of his tunic's leather. She started to speak, caught her words, tried again. Finally she looked up, her face full of frustration, and said, "I don't know."

"Do you remember the river?" he asked.

She answered slowly, trying to find words to fill in the blank spaces in her mind. "I was lying on rocks, half in the water. I don't know how I got there, but I crawled up the embankment when I realized the tide was coming in. At first I thought I'd gotten sick because my head hurt and I was dizzy, and I couldn't understand why I was alone. When I found your sword and the pouch with the Saxon spearhead in it, it became clear...there had been an attack. I never saw or heard anyone."

Marcus frowned. "They left the pouch behind?"

She showed it hanging from her belt.

He grunted in puzzlement, then explained how he had last seen her and what he remembered of fending off the attack.

"Then that's what happened...I found..." she half-choked on her words, then began again, "...a beheaded man in the trees."

Marcus groaned, realizing why he had seen so much red before blacking out.

Claerwen continued, "He looked Pictish; I think you were right about the tracker. Your sword, your cap and the pouch were underneath the body. Everything else, you, the horses, my bow, everything except one small waterskin I was still carrying, was gone." She took his sheepskin cap from the pouch and gave it to him. "They have Macsen's spearhead, don't they?"

"I believe so, though they never questioned me about it."

"Will they still be coming after you, even now that they have it back?"

"Aye. They won't forgive me for stealing it, for escaping, or for killing their tracker." He felt her hands come up onto his shoulders, resting heavily there, her fingers curling into his hair.

She said, "When I realized there had been an attack and you were gone, I guessed they had taken you. So I tracked them and found the camp yesterday in the evening. I tried to find a way to help you, but there were too many scouts patrolling, I couldn't get close enough. It wasn't until tonight, because of the forest, that I was able to get near enough to see you, and that you were already trying to escape. I wish I could have done more."

He reminded her of the unconscious soldier, saying, "You cleared the path of my escape tonight. If you hadn't been there, I might not have been so lucky."

"Will we be safe here?"

Marcus looked up and saw the clouds thickening. With the tiredness in his voice growing deeper, he answered, "Aye, it's too dark for them to search now. They'll wait for daylight. Until then we should rest and eat, keep watch."

He wanted to ask her more, but his head ached badly and he did not want to think anymore that night. For the moment it was enough to know she was alive and unhurt and they had found each other. Pausing before entering the shelter, he leaned to gently touch his lips to her mouth and wrap his arms around her.

She smiled at last, savoring the warmth of his embrace. She asked, "Did you think I was a spirit?"

He nodded and laughed at himself. "Aye, and this is one time I'm very glad I was wrong. Let us go in."

# Chapter 6

**The northern moors, Kingdom of Brynaich**

"You know that I must go back," Marcus said softly, lying on his belly, propped up on his elbows in the shelter's entrance. He winced, waiting for Claerwen's reaction.

She lay next to him, looking up and wishing morning had not come. "I know," she answered. Her lips curled halfway into a smile as she reached to touch his face.

One of his thick black brows lifted slightly, and his eyes slid down to meet hers. When she nodded, he realized she had never expected him to walk away from the camp without further investigation. With a spare squint, he communicated his appreciation, then returned to watching. "It's odd," he stated. "There has been no fuss whatsoever about my escape. No alarm was given in the night, none now. You've heard nothing unusual, have you, when you took the watch?"

She shook her head.

He continued, "There are two leaders. I'm almost certain one is Octa and this is the camp he is supplying with weapons. The other man wears Roman-style clothing. I was never close enough to absolutely identify either of them."

"I probably saw less than you did," Claerwen added. "It was after nightfall when I finally drew close to the camp. They had already gone to their tents. Do you think they will move on today?"

Marcus shook his head. "They're not stirring enough to indicate they will do so."

"Perhaps they wait for more weapons? Or warriors?" she asked.

"Possibly."

She studied his face a moment, puzzled by his tone. "You don't think so?"

He squinted into the distance, then smiled slightly, a sardonic, sly twist to his lips. "I believe they wait for me."

"You jest!" she blurted, rolling towards him and pushing up onto one elbow.

He lowered his face, almost touching her cheek with his lips, and spoke low and intense, "I believe Octa knows who I am. Likely, the Roman does as well."

"But, how?"

"I don't know. After thinking on this half the night, I can't lose the uncanny sense that this has all been planned to draw me into an elaborate scheme. It all leads back to the assassination attempt at Dinas Beris. When I spoiled that for them, they decided to use me for a while instead. They let me escape because they expected me to do it. Likewise, they expect me to come back, to try to steal Macsen's spearhead again. Why, I can't guess yet."

"And you're going to walk into the trap for them by attempting just that?"

He turned his face fully to her then and suddenly grinned. "No. I am going down there tonight, but *not* for what they are waiting."

---

During the daylight hours, they surveyed the camp from all sides, circling it twice, studying the surrounding landscape for resources and escape routes. As suspected, the Saxons remained settled in the small forest clearing, sending out no scouts or search parties, and using only limited patrols to guard the camp's perimeter.

"They must feel safe in their isolation, so deep in the forest,"

Marcus concluded to Claerwen after they returned to the shelter at mid-afternoon.

She added, "Most people are afraid of forests, believing they are full of faeries, spooks and evil spirits. It's an excellent defense against the average person."

"Aye, and to me, it's almost like an open gate of invitation. Octa has to know I won't come before nightfall."

They ate another cold meal and rested, patiently waiting for the dark. Marcus sat as still as stone. He had shaved the stubble of beard, revealing that the bruises and swelling were now beginning to retreat.

Claerwen leaned against one of the boulders, watching him meditate on the camp. She knew he must still have pain by the way he stiffly held his jaw, but as the wind blew his hair back from his face, she saw his eyes were full of intense anticipation.

The moonless night darkened completely, and the soldiers bedded down. Marcus slipped the Saxon's confiscated dagger into the sheath along the back of his belt, then strapped on the sword. The rest of their sparse gear — the waterskin, and the lone pouch now containing both the Saxon spearhead from Octa's barn and a small amount of food — was slung onto Claerwen's shoulders. Moving down the slope, they approached the camp on the side where the tents had been pitched.

Lack of light kept their progress slow, but they easily remained undetected. Reaching the edge of the trees, they crouched, waiting, listening for the sound of restless men settling into the rumble and buzz of snoring. Only a handful of guards patrolled, and those watching the stockpiles were more dozing than awake.

Lamplight flickered in one tent, casting silhouettes against the cloth walls. Voices mumbled softly, mingling with the sounds of a meal. Using his hands, Marcus signaled a request to Claerwen, asking if she could climb up a particular tree, onto a specific branch. Examining it, she nodded, understanding that from there she was to look directly into the tent's smoke hole. He further instructed her to lie along the heavy limb, letting it hide her from the light below. She nodded again, then questioned where he would be.

When he pointed at the lighted tent, her eyes widened. He took her hand, and though she kept her objections silent, her fingers dug into his palm, belying her fear for him. For a moment, he held her by the shoulders, smiling with his face full of confidence, conveying that he knew what he was doing. Then he cupped his hands, boosting her a step up to the lowest tree branch, and waited until she was perched solidly in the correct place.

Marcus pulled his sword and hid its scabbard and baldric below the tree. Lying on his belly, the sword in one hand, he wriggled through the brush from the trees to the clearing's edge. Only a brief, grass-filled distance sloped down to the rear of the tent.

Motionless, Marcus watched a sentinel approach slowly. Humming nonsense, the patroller carried his spear without conviction and made unpolished steps as if slightly drunk. He passed, never looking other than a few strides' length in the direction he was going.

Scanning from one side to the other, Marcus confirmed the next patroller's location and that the gap between him and the last one was wide enough to penetrate unseen. He turned and swiftly rolled sideways. The tent had been placed on a dug out, flattened surface of earth, and he dropped off the grass into a border of this space, coming up against the tent's hem. He held his sword underneath himself to prevent it from reflecting light, and once he lay still, his black hair and dark clothing made him completely invisible.

Marcus lifted the lower edge of the tent. Not daring to risk shaking the cloth, he could gain only a narrow wedge of sight, partially blocked by an ornate chair and a raised pallet. Octa's legs descended from the chair, stretched out to a brazier towards the tent's front. His feet were out of his boots, and he wiggled his toes. Two servants stood by, waiting for permission to remove the remains of the meal. Octa spoke in Saxon, giving them the orders.

The second leader stood before the Saxon, but Marcus could only see him downward from the hips. His Roman-style clothing, including a short Roman sword in a belt scabbard, was long out-of-date. Once of good quality, the apparel was now very worn.

The two men were silent until the servants departed. Then they spoke again, very low and muffled. And they used Latin.

Surprised by the language, Marcus concentrated intensely, but most of the conversation was unintelligible. The Roman's voice seemed familiar, and as Marcus considered his accent, it occurred to him that this man was probably a Briton, Latin being the only likely common language between a Briton and a Saxon.

The talk continued for some time. The Roman names for Britain and some of her larger regions were mentioned often, and Marcus gained the impression that the men were holding some sort of strategy session for another invasion. But, he wondered, was it just another raid like all the rest, scattered along the coastlines, or was this to be pointed directly at taking Ambrosius' life as Myrddin feared? Marcus gritted his teeth in frustration and hoped Claerwen could see the Roman's face clearly.

The next guard marched along the camp's rim, steadier and faster than the last. Marcus lay absolutely still again, his face down in the ditch, and watched boots stride by from the corner of one eye. He waited until the soldier was well past before turning his head again.

Octa said goodnight to the Briton. Seconds later, the tent flaps opened, closed, and were secured shut, the lamps snuffed. Footsteps crunched across to the other tent. The Briton did not even light a candle; he went straight to bed, probably without undressing.

Marcus twisted around, looking for Claerwen in the tree, but he only saw leaves lit dimly from the campfires. After glancing for the patrollers, he rolled back across the grass, turned and crawled into the woods, pulling his hidden baldric and scabbard with him. As he rose, a low, soughing whistle breathed, and Claerwen's face appeared before him. Clasping hands, they wove far into the forest, halting only when they had covered nearly half a mile. There they broke silence in a swiftly whispered trade of information.

"I forgot you speak Latin. You never use it at home," Claerwen commented when Marcus had finished his account.

"Aye, and I'm not in practice. I only use it when I must be at a noble's court, for some formality."

"Did you learn it because your half-Roman grandmother insisted? Like she insisted that you carry a Roman name, instead of one from our language?"

"She was very pleased that I learned Latin, but I would have been required to anyway during my fosterage, because it is considered part of a good education, and because it is still considered the language of the nobility." Then, shifting his attention back to the quest, he asked, "Could you see their faces?"

"I couldn't see Octa at all. The other man was tall, dark haired with light eyes, grey, I think. He has a large, hawklike nose. It looks like it was broken once. He wore a long plain cloak, faded red, no badge. His hair is very short and curled. They were looking at a map of Britain on a table between them."

Marcus was silent a few moments. Claerwen could tell he was thinking, remembering the voices he had heard, going over the indistinguishable words in the seldom-used language. She could only see the outline of his face, then heard him say very softly, "Of course." He gripped her arm and repeated, "Of course. The other man is Pascentius. I knew I heard that voice before."

"Pascentius? Vortigern's youngest son? I thought he'd been killed with his father."

"That was only speculation. I have seen and heard him before, several times. It was the Latin that made me miss it..."

Marcus paused, his mind piecing together the few words he had understood. His eyes gazed into the darkness, moving back and forth as if reading. Then abruptly, they came up, ardently fierce. "*Lleu da!* Most of these soldiers belong to Octa, but it is Pascentius who has shaped this. He's planning to fight for the crown, using Octa and his Saxons as mercenaries and Macsen's spearhead as part of a claim. They've been marching straight in the direction of Caer Ebrauc...and Ambrosius."

Claerwen held her breath, realizing the gravity of his statement, then blurted, "And I'd wager he's hoping to use you against Ambrosius, like Vortigern tried, perhaps even making you a bargaining tool, if they catch you again."

"I'm not that important."

"But you are. For what you know, Marcus, you're a mine of information that's invaluable to anyone's side. No one knows as much as you do about this land's politics. Not even Ambrosius. Or Myrddin."

Marcus felt the blood drain out of his face. Her logic was sound, and the prospect of another imprisonment wrenched inside him. His eyes hardened, and he forced the dread back, plunging it down into an iron section of his mind where he would clamp the door shut on it once more. He said, "Regardless of me, Ambrosius has Macsen's crown and torque. If Pascentius should defeat him, with the spearhead he will have three out of five pieces of Macsen's Treasure, enough to secure a strong claim, especially with support from the factions that backed his father."

He had spoken with a raspiness, and though his tone was calm, Claerwen felt the hoarse quality of his voice reflected just how his sense of honor strained at the thought of such a misguided claim. After all the years of struggle to bring Ambrosius to power and to see their land begin the long journey to stability at last, a fall backward into the habits that perpetuated civil violence would be devastating. Pascentius had been known in the past to follow his father's style of rule, and to Ambrosius' supporters, any claim for the high kingship by Vortigern's spawn would be utter sacrilege.

Claerwen suggested, "Surely there's not enough of them here to take on Ambrosius' army."

"No, but I'd venture a good guess there's a bloody lot more of them coming in from the coast, and they'll join these within days."

"What do we do now?" Claerwen asked. "Go to Caer Ebrauc and warn Ambrosius?"

"Aye, but not yet. First, and right now, we are going to disarm this group."

"What?"

"Come with me. We must do this quickly." He grabbed her hand and pulled her with him, circling around and approaching the camp near the tarpaulin-covered carts. Crawling to the border between forest and clearing as before, they halted only a few feet away. Watching carefully, Marcus found only one guard on duty, and at that, not attentively. He guessed most of the patrols were deliberately concentrated in places it was thought he would be more likely to infiltrate. Thanking this good luck, he pressed Claerwen's shoulder in reassurance and made the hand signal for her to stay where she was.

Creeping up behind the lone guard, Marcus slipped a hand around to the man's throat, just under his jaw, and pinched hard with his fingers. The guard faded into unconsciousness, dropping his spear and falling to the ground.

With his eyes continuously watching for other patrollers, Marcus lifted the edge of the nearest tarpaulin. A variety of weapons were stacked underneath, even more than he had suspected, straw in between to protect their edges. Finding the straw dry and unspoiled, he stuffed several handfuls inside his tunic. He turned back, dragging the guard and the spear to Claerwen.

"Take off his helmet and get out the iron and flint," Marcus whispered, searching for weapons and valuables. Aside from the spear, he only found a small dagger and slipped it into one of his boots. He instructed Claerwen to hold the spear horizontally, and he pressed the helmet's crown to the tip. Pushing, he impaled it onto the spearhead.

Turning the helmet over, he placed straw inside, then carefully sparked the iron and flint together, setting the material to smoldering. He fanned it gently until a tiny flame ignited. Then before it could burst up, he extended the speared helmet, like a bucket on a long arm, across the narrow space to the cart. With great discretion of movement, he pushed it under the cover's edge and turned it over. A small puff of smoke escaped as the straw dropped, spilling fire down into the packing.

He pulled the helmet back, refilled it and repeated the act, until all the tarpaulins smoldered underneath. At the last stockpile, he left the helmet to burn with the weapons, then ran back into the trees with the spear where he broke the head off its shaft. The head matched the one Claerwen had found, and he gave it to her for safekeeping.

Marcus dragged the unconscious soldier up, lifting him onto

his shoulders. "Clear our tracks," he ordered Claerwen and began to carry the Saxon away. She followed him, wiping out their footprints with a leafy branch, and they circled around to the eastern side of the camp, locating a wide track bound for the coast.

"Help me strip him," Marcus said, dropping the heavy man. Within minutes the Saxon was absolutely naked, sprawled in the middle of the road.

The smell of burning wood and leather filled the air, and the trees around the clearing were suddenly lit. Seconds later, the entire camp erupted with shouts of alarm.

"Come," Marcus said, taking Claerwen's hand, the guard's clothing under his other arm. He sensed her confusion but smiled to himself, holding back his explanation. They ran, disappearing into a ditch off the side of the road

Men poured out of the camp, filling the trackway as they raced for the closest source of water, Octa and Pascentius among them. Within moments, the naked guard was found. Halting, Octa stared, anger rising in his face, the shouting of his warriors diminishing with their surprise. He whipped around, spitting orders at his second-in-command to assemble and account for their men. Without pausing, he marched to Pascentius and roared indignantly at him, his language ricocheting between Latin and Saxon. Pascentius shouted back in imperious Latin, criticizing Octa's failure to prevent the sabotage. The argument grew vehement, and Octa's warriors edged into a circle, surrounding Pascentius and his small group of loyal followers.

Tension rose like boiling grease, threatening to burst and spew. For a few moments, the arguing actually halted, the two leaders glaring at each other in the circle's center. Then the second returned, speaking quietly to Octa. The Saxon leader's face evolved into a combination of hatred and disappointment. With the report finished, he spoke again to Pascentius in a tersely worded statement, then turned to his men, gave the order to break camp, begin a northward march, and take the incompetent, naked guard with them.

Likewise, Pascentius ordered his men to abandon everything

except their personal weapons and what food and water they could carry. They took the eastbound route. Once abandoned, the road and the clearing took on the silence of a burned out battlefield, except the only dead bodies left behind were the destroyed weapons.

Marcus released his breath as the last man disappeared to the east.

"I thought they would all slay each other for certain," Claerwen whispered. "How convenient it would have been, if Octa had killed Pascentius."

"Aye, that would be true, ugly as it may sound," Marcus agreed, then speculated, "He certainly had the opportunity, well out-numbering Pascentius' men. Perhaps Octa is thinking that they will eventually make amends, and that's why he held back. I doubt it will happen. Both want the power to take the crown from Ambrosius, and neither has that kind of strength. In the alliance just broken, each was attempting to use the other to gain that power. Of course, they most assuredly would have crossed each other in the end. Sounds familiar, doesn't it?"

Claerwen agreed, having seen the vicious results of such dangerous posturing. It split every social entity, from the highest-ranking political rivals to the poorest of clans and was the basis for endless bitter civil battles and feuds. No one was exempt.

"Come. We're going to follow Pascentius," Marcus said, easing up from the ditch, Claerwen following.

They dashed across the road, moving in a southeasterly direction, straight through the forest. For the first two miles, they traveled without speaking, concentrating on keeping their direction well plotted and their strength conserved. Finally pausing for rest, Claerwen's curiosity broke through the silence. She asked, "Are you sure he's going to the coast?"

"Aye, and we're going to get there first."

"Is this a shorter way? What if he doesn't go there?"

"He will. He wasn't even born until more than a generation after the end of the Roman occupation, but he's one of those Britons who refuses to let go of their influence and acknowledge his own heritage. Romans always trained in strict discipline. That makes them not only tough, but exceedingly predictable."

"Marcus, I don't…" When he started grinning, she realized he was bursting to explain.

He said, "I needed the soldiers out of the camp long enough for the fire to burn the weapons beyond use. They had very little water in the camp, so I knew they'd need to run for it. The nearest source was to the east and hard to find, especially in the dark. The naked guard on the eastbound road created two diversions. The first was meant to stall them on the road outside the clearing. Secondly, he was stripped for the purpose of making them think that *I* had taken his clothes for a disguise, and that I was still in the camp. It forced them to assemble and take count."

"Because finding you was more important than saving the weapons?"

He nodded.

"Did you know they would break their alliance?"

"I couldn't guess that in advance, but humiliation can be the catalyst for many events," he winked, then went on. "I couldn't understand all of what they were screaming about, because Octa spoke the most and mostly in Saxon, but the trap for me was his idea. They had expected me to get inside the tents. After the lamps went out, both he and Pascentius were exchanged with elite warriors. Of course I didn't appear, and Octa broke the alliance because Pascentius blamed him for the mistake. He's going home to brood, and he is one I will need to watch because he will not forgive me. Or forget. What will make it worse is that Pascentius now has control of Macsen's spearhead."

"Pascentius? Not Octa?"

Marcus shook his head.

"How could Octa walk away without it, especially when he out-numbered Pascentius?"

"Pascentius stole it. He told Octa it was for its safekeeping — obviously from both Octa and me. I think he must have sent it far out of the camp with a well-trusted man. For now, there's little we can do about that, but we need to go to the coast. There we should be able to learn what he plans to do next. Perhaps the spearhead will turn up there."

Claerwen's brow rumpled in confusion. "But...how can we follow Pascentius, if we're ahead of him?"

Marcus grinned again, saying, "Sometimes it's better to follow in front. He'd never suspect us there."

Claerwen still did not understand, though she was amazed at all that had been accomplished in a short length of time and how so many people had been manipulated in a very simple but very coordinated ploy. For now, she decided to accept his odd logic, knowing it arose from his ten years of painfully learned experience. She held her hand to him, indicating she was ready to go on.

---

They reached the coast by sunrise, the sharp sea breeze stinging their eyes and noses. Familiar with the area from previous travels, Marcus trekked for a high promontory that overlooked a long expanse of the coastline. He found a place in the bracken to wait, watching a thick layer of mist hover just offshore. Within two hours, Pascentius and his men emerged from the coastbound road and turned south along the beach.

Rising from their hiding place, Marcus and Claerwen followed, moving along a high embankment that paralleled the beach. The shoreline curved broadly to the right, and at its apex, a tumble of boulders ran across the sand, all the way into the water. On the escarpment above, a tree-covered bump of land rose in the same place. As Pascentius and his men climbed over the rocks, they disappeared from view for several minutes.

Marcus, in the lead, plunged through the small wood, not willing to lose sight of his quarry for long. Reaching the last of the trees, he caught sight of the men again.

But looking beyond them, he abruptly halted, backed, and grabbed Claerwen around her waist. He flung himself down, pulling her with him, landing hard on thick roots gnarling out from an ancient oak.

Claerwen sprawled across his lap. Momentarily stunned, she pushed herself upright and looked to Marcus. He pressed a finger to her lips for silence, then pointed at the sea through a clump of tall, wind-whipped grass.

Like phantoms, more than a dozen ships rocked in the water, the mist promising to reveal more as it dissipated. A small landing party camped on the beach, and Pascentius marched towards it, his tired men straggling behind. As he neared the camp, he was recognized, and a signal was immediately conveyed to the nearest ship. A small landing curragh dropped from its side, filled with more men, and rowed for the shore.

Claerwen's eyes widened, and she sank down closer to Marcus. "All Saxons?" she whispered.

"Aye. That's what they were waiting for, besides me."

"Will they still ally themselves to Pascentius, without Octa?"

"They won't care who they follow as long as the price is right."

She watched Marcus' face grow grim and stony, then she asked, "The price being all the land they want in Britain?"

He nodded in confirmation and elaborated, "Land, plunder, all the terror they can wreak, all the women they can rape, all the Britons they can displace, enslave or outright kill. Pascentius won't care, as long as he gets the high kingship."

They stared at each other, chills crawling on their skin.

# Chapter 7

## The Kingdom of Ebrauc

"We've got to get horses," Marcus said. As his eyes came up and met Claerwen's, he clamped his hands onto her shoulders. "I can't sabotage this, not this time. There's too many of them. We must get to Caer Ebrauc and warn Ambrosius. He will have to fight them."

His face reflected his disappointment. Sanctioning a battle was the last of his intentions.

Marcus rose and caught Claerwen's hand, pulling her up with him. They ploughed inland through the embankment's heavy overgrowth and into a shallow hollow where they stopped, calculating the best path to take.

Glancing past Marcus, Claerwen's eyes stalled, then abruptly dropped, their expression evolving into a high rank of dread. She sidled slightly, keeping her face close to his shoulder, and whispered through clenched teeth, "There's a man behind you, just in the trees, watching us."

Marcus remained calm, his movements unchanging. He took the waterskin from her and fidgeted with its stopper, but his eyes locked onto hers, communicating that he understood. He whispered back, "He's likely a scout. Follow what I do."

He hung the waterskin over his left shoulder, letting it swing casually by its strap, and cocked his head in a motion barely discernible to his right, in the scout's direction. Slowly, he started walking that way, drawing Claerwen with him. He grinned, then started talking, joking, laughing, looking leisurely, as if simply out walking with his companion.

They crossed the hollow, approaching the trees. Marcus slowed, still talking inanities. Then he quieted, his expression slowly changing as his eyes locked onto a target to the south. A narrow breach ran between the woods to the right and the overgrown, rising escarpment to the left. Gazing intently down the breach, he halted, giving the impression that some incredible spectacle had caught his attention and refused to release it. From the edge of his eye, he saw the scout's interest perk.

"I don't believe it," Marcus muttered, tentatively lifting his hand as if to point, but he was too enthralled to carry through with the motion.

Claerwen stared along his line of sight, confused. Nothing was there, only turf, trees, rocks and the thicket-filled slope they had just descended. She frowned, wanting to protest, wondering what she was supposed to look at.

"I don't believe it," Marcus said again, the incredulous tone of his voice rising. This time he did point, his right hand straight and sure.

At the same time, his left hand down between them, lightly squeezed Claerwen's arm. Her eyes shifted to his face for an instant, and she saw the scout beyond him, edging closer for a better look. Marcus started backing, pulling her with him. He kept his eyes locked on his target, and they widened as his mouth dropped open.

"It's coming this way," he said, moving faster.

Claerwen kept her gaze in line with his and moved with him. Fear struck her when she glanced to his face again, not understanding what had placed such a look of alarm there. He was not given to showing even the slightest apprehension in the worst of situations, and his expression prompted her to grip his arm, forbidding any opportunity to be separated from him.

They had moved north through the hollow, past the scout, and halted again. Marcus watched the man out of his peripheral sight and reached for his sword hilt, but his hand stopped before he touched it. "It won't help, not against that," he said, his brows knotting, making his eyes look terrified. "Run! Run now!" he shouted and turned, his hand around Claerwen's arm. They dashed northward into the trees.

The scout stared after them. He took a few steps out into the hollow, stopped again. Pulling his own weapon, a huge knife, he cautiously scanned the area to the south, then in a circle all around.

Nothing was there. No war band, no beastly creature. Nothing stirred except the wind.

His confusion was visible. Swearing to himself, he turned back to the trees, staring at the path the strangers had taken. Curiosity compelled him to follow, but they had disappeared, leaving the woods as empty as the breach to the south. Stopping before he had gone more than a few yards, the man frowned at the abrupt, eerie quiet.

A pile of fallen leaves burst upward in front of the scout, and a pair of fists exploded out of them, plunging into his face. The man hurtled backward, dropping his knife, and plumped down into a motionless heap.

Claerwen emerged from behind a tree next to the fallen scout. Marcus walked forward, flexing his hands. Leaning over the Saxon, Marcus checked him for additional weapons, found none. He picked up the knife and flung it far into the bracken.

"He has a horse back there. I heard it whinny, just when I jumped up," he said.

They ran a short distance and found a solid roan gelding tethered to a rowan bush. Slowing, Marcus approached cautiously, clicking his tongue and speaking low, soothing words. The horse remained calm and accepted his hands on its neck and back. There was no saddle, only a thin blanket.

"Aye, this one'll do just fine...should be able to carry both of us," he said, picking up each hoof for inspection. "Claeri?" He looked up when no response came and saw her staring through the trees to the south again, confusion still in her face.

She heard him choke off something he tried to say to the horse, almost like a strangling sound, and she whipped around, afraid he had been attacked. But his left hand came up, covering his mouth, and he leaned his face into the gelding's blanket.

Claerwen paused, then rushed forward, thinking now that he was ill. His hair had fallen forward, hiding his face from her, and when she pushed it back, he turned his head, showing an uncontrollable grin in his eyes. In the same instant, she finally understood.

"You...you are such a lout!" she sputtered, playfully slapping at his arm as her fear and confusion drained away.

"I'm sorry, Claeri — " he began, then finally gave in to the laughter he had been holding back.

She pressed her fists onto her hips in mock indignation, and said, "Wait till I tell Padrig about *this* one," then she burst into giggles.

"You wouldn't dare," Marcus teased.

"Aye, I would now, wouldn't I?" she teased back.

"Ah, but it worked, didn't it? The scout didn't understand the words, but he knew from my tone of voice and expression that he should pay attention."

"And I fell for it as well. I'll forgive you this time...I think," she said, winking, and reached for the gelding's lead rein.

Serious again, Marcus signaled for her to wait. He pulled the smaller dagger he had in his boot and said, "Before we start for Caer Ebrauc, we should disguise ourselves." Turning to the horse, he trimmed a thick handful of hair from the underside of the animal's mane, then smoothed the top layer down over the short fringe he left. "No one will know the difference and neither will he," Marcus commented, patting the horse's neck.

"I thought Saxons didn't use horses," Claerwen remarked.

"Not usually. Perhaps this one is stolen," he suggested, then asked, "Can you find a small bit of tree sap for me, just a nip on the end of a twig?"

With dexterous fingers, he braided the horsehair into a knot at one end and tucked it through an adjustable thong loop sewn inside the crown of his cap. When Claerwen returned with the sap, he pushed the small dot of gluey material into the crown. He pressed the knot into it, tightened the loop, then mashed a small handful of withered grass over it to prevent the sap from straying.

Gathering his own hair up and pulling it back sharply, he maneuvered the cap on over it. The horsehair hung below the rear edge, falling to his shoulders.

"What do you think?" he asked, grinning at Claerwen.

She strolled around him, tucked up a piece of loose black hair in a few places, smoothed and patted the horsehair until it looked almost natural, then grinned back. "'Tis very good, but what about your moustache? And the black stubble? They don't match the reddish hair." She passed her fingertips over the rough growth beginning again on his chin.

He squatted, poking through the scattering of leaves, and showed her a bare patch of ground. "The soil is very reddish here. Rub a little on, and I will pass well enough."

"Remind me not to kiss you again until you've had a good bath," Claerwen grimaced as she watched him finish his preparations. "And for me?"

"You're ready as you are in that clothing, except for one or two things I want to change." Standing directly in front of her, he pulled off her cap. Her tawny-brown hair, plaited in one heavy braid, unwound and fell, the bound ends dropping nearly to her knees. Marcus moved the thin leather binding tie upward, loosening the last length of her hair, then wound the braid around her head again, put her cap over it, and left the free ends to hang down like a boy's long hair.

He studied her a few moments, then he looked at his fingers, still showing red soil on them. Lightly tracing his fingers over her face, running along her jawline and over her upper lip, he created a pale hint of masculinity. "Now we both need a good bath," he smiled. "Come, we are now a pair of peasants crossing to Caer Ebrauc."

Marcus looped the pouch and waterskin together by their straps and hung them over the horse's withers. He hid the long sword underneath the gear and the blanket; it would be out of place for poor peasants riding over the moors. Then he vaulted onto the horse, reached down to grip Claerwen's arm, and swung her up behind him. Seconds later, they rode away to the south.

———————————

Caer Ebrauc was a landmark not to be missed. Visible for miles, its massive stone structure was originally a legionary fortress built by the Romans four hundred years earlier. Rectangular in shape, it stared proudly across the surrounding moors at all those who approached. Ambrosius, in conjunction with the local king, had repaired and strengthened the buildings, its walled boundary, and the triple bank and ditch defenses. The king's garrison troops filled the entire area within the walls, camped in neat rows.

A small knot of men stood just within the open gates, in an area clear of soldiers and equipment. They were deep in the midst of a discussion when a horse suddenly appeared on the moors, streaking over a rise, dropping down between the hills, reappearing on the next rise. The setting sun flung an eerie golden light across the fields beneath a sky so clear and blue that it almost hurt the eyes, and in the stillness of it, even the soldiers were quiet, as if the golden-glow inspired them to hush. Now the racing horse disturbed the evening's solemnity, its hooves pounding the gilded grey turf. The men turned to watch.

"Halt! Announce yourselves!" challenged the guard at a post beyond the outermost defense ditch. A line of spearmen blocked the incoming road, their weapons crossed. They saw a mud-spattered man in rough deerskin clothing, a second rider holding on so tightly behind him, they could not see the face.

Marcus pulled up hard and the horse nearly reared, but he held control on the tired animal. "I have urgent news for the High King Ambrosius!" he shouted at the sentries. "I must speak with him immediately!" He felt Claerwen's arms hugging him tightly, her hands splayed over his chest, revealing she was as fatigued as the horse.

The ranking sentry stepped forward without giving an order to lift the crossed spears. "Who are you?"

"I am a messenger from Marcus ap Iorwerth of Dinas Beris."

He yanked the gauntlet off his right hand and thrust his fist out, showing his clan ring. Of heavy gold, it sparkled more brightly than usual in the strange light. "This ring gives me authority to speak for the Prince of Dinas Beris to King Ambrosius."

The guard stared at it a few moments, then again studied the horseman, whose straggly reddish hair fanned out wildly from his cap as if he was still galloping full tilt over the moors, following with a perusal of the youth who peered over Marcus' broad shoulders.

Marcus insisted, "We have extremely important news for the king."

The sentry hesitated, scowling. He had never heard of Marcus ap Iorwerth.

"Now, man!" Marcus roared, his deep voice filling the landscape.

Flinching, the guard spoke to a young servant, who set off running towards the knot of men. Marcus squinted through the brassy light at them, and thought they looked as if they all wore the same gold-colored costume, tinged so by the setting sun. Oddly, he was reminded of the rich robes Christian bishops wore. In the center, he recognized Ambrosius, taller than the others and wearing a helmet emblazoned with a simple, symbolic crown.

When the servant reached the group of men, Ambrosius turned his attention to the announcement. Abruptly, he looked up at the riders. He spoke a reply, sending the boy on a dash deeper inside the fortress. Walking out of the circle of men, he gestured at the sentries to allow the messengers into the compound.

The riders pulled up, and Claerwen swung down first.

"You come from Lord Marcus," the king began, saluting a welcome, then recognized Claerwen's unusual green-blue eyes as they lifted to meet his. Startled, he shifted his gaze to the dismounting man and realized Marcus ap Iorwerth himself now stood before him.

"Come," Ambrosius said softly. His face was serious, but his eyes belied amusement at the disguises. He waved away the others with whom he had been meeting, ordered a stable hand to care for the gelding, then led his new guests towards the largest stone building.

They passed several tents that were stationed to one side for the purpose of sheltering meetings when the weather turned foul. Quick briefings and messages were taken outside to keep the flow of information moving well. Longer, more serious meetings were held inside the large stone building when privacy was important. Ambrosius brought them there, passing through another set of gates and a spacious, flagged courtyard. The building's second floor was lined with private chambers, and the king stopped at a particular door, rapped twice, then pushed it in.

In that moment, the youth who had been sent running appeared from inside, just leaving Myrddin with the news of incoming messengers. The prince rose to his feet behind a rustic table. His brown eyes traveled from his father to the messengers, halting in a stare as he realized their true identities in the same way Ambrosius had. The door closed, the latch clicking shut.

"Don't say names and don't send for servants until we're done," Marcus cautioned in a low voice as he piled their gear on a table. He circuited the room, ignoring Ambrosius' and Myrddin's curious eyes following him as he checked that the door was truly shut, the small, lone window's shutters were locked, and there was no place for anyone to hide or listen from the walls, ceiling or floor. Satisfied, and with no further preface or greeting, he gave a succinct overview of what had transpired. From the pouch, he removed the two spearheads.

"These prove that Octa was supplying weapons. The patterns are the same, as you can see. However, he is not the true threat to you. Pascentius is." He then told of Macsen's ceremonial spearhead.

Ambrosius studied the common spearheads, turning them over in his hands, calculating the depth that Pascentius' threat posed, then exchanged a long, silent stare of understanding with Myrddin. He was amazed once more at the devotion Marcus and his wife had to his cause, and felt empathy rise within himself as he watched Claerwen sink onto a bench against the wall, too exhausted to stand longer.

His decision came quickly. He exited into the hallway, calling for his military second-in-command. The second arrived within minutes, and the king snapped out a string of commands as neat as the rows of his camped soldiers, including instructions for a series of scouts to report the Saxon war band's progress and that his army should go on full alert.

Turning back into the chamber, Ambrosius approached Marcus and momentarily touched the red horsehair. Smiling, he said, "Very clever. My son told me to expect the unusual, I see he was right yet again. You are welcome to stay and rest as long as you want, if you need anything, my son will see to whatever it is. And, if you wish, come watch the fun as we lure these fools in, even fight with us, if you are so inclined."

"Thank you, my Lord," Marcus answered, bowing slightly.

"Ah, thank you, my friends," the king countered and left the chamber.

Once the door closed again, Marcus went to the window and opened one shutter, letting the evening breeze refresh his face. He folded his arms on the casement and rested his brow there for a few moments, stretching his back to ease its tiredness.

Myrddin turned to speak to Claerwen, and saw her head droop forward. To Marcus he said, "She's asleep."

Marcus shut the window and crossed the room, knelt in front of Claerwen. "It's dark now. I'm going to take her down to the river to clean up. She'll feel better. When we come back, all we need is a hot meal and a bed. Nothing fancy, we are merely messengers here."

"It's cold in that river," Myrddin warned.

Marcus held his palm to Claerwen's cheek, softly calling her.

Her eyes opened. She had heard their talk and pushed up onto her feet, saying, "We are accustomed to the cold, Myrddin, 'tis not to be of concern."

"All we need is a safe conduct to get us through the gates," Marcus said.

Myrddin sucked in his breath. "Come with me," he said and led them a few doors away to another simply furnished chamber. He handed Marcus a small bronze badge with a dragon enameled on its face. "This will get you through the guards. Don't be long down there. I will have some clean clothes brought for you to change into, leave those you wear now outside your door overnight, and a servant will clean them for you. I'll have a meal waiting in this room by the time you return." He moved towards the door, called for a waiting servant and gave instructions for the clothing and meal.

In contrast to his father's brisk efficiency and though his commands were just as clear, Myrddin gave Marcus the impression that he only worked within his own ironclad deliberation. He was never to be rushed through anything, not even an emergency, yet he would still achieve the proper results in far less time than someone who was harried. Within minutes, a neat stack of clothing arrived at the doorway.

Marcus nodded his thanks as Myrddin left, then bundled the clothing into a blanket from the bed. He and Claerwen quietly exited the fortress from the south gates, heading straight for the river.

Once beyond the walls and ears of the fortress, Marcus commented, "Myrddin is still keeping something from us. He hides behind those cat eyes of his and watches, waits."

Claerwen concurred, "His reaction was completely different than his father's, that's true. But don't you think it's just because Ambrosius is thinking in the terms of a warrior, rather than a druid?"

"Perhaps. But it's the same sense I had at Dinas Beris, and it annoys me."

They reached the river and turned south. A few minutes later, they stopped, coming to a small natural pool carved into the bank and hidden by sweeping willow branches.

"You've been here before?" Claerwen asked as she followed him.

He pushed through the willows, dropped the bundle on the sandy shore's edge and pulled off the cap with the fake hair. Stripping, he answered, "Aye, and I hope no one sees us. It's fairly private and there's no moon, but even in this cold weather, there's bound to be someone about."

Claerwen watched him vigorously shake out his hair as he

waded into the hip-deep water. Smiling, she asked, "And when have you ever had a midge's worth of modesty?"

He looked over his shoulder, watching her pull off her dirty clothing. "I was thinking more that you don't exactly look like a boy," he countered admiringly.

She glided into the pool, sinking down until the water covered up to her neck. Her legs coiled under, she pushed off the rocky bottom to float along the surface.

Watching, Marcus suddenly forgot he was chilled and tired, fascinated by her gracefulness, and he contemplated how like an otter she was, turning around and around as fluidly as the water itself. Only starlight filtered through the willows, but its very faintness enhanced the dreamlike waterscape through which she swam, giving her skin a luminous sheen. He savored how her breasts rose from the black pool, taut and perfect, then withdrew as she turned again. Her braided hair flowed in a luxurious line from her shoulders down her back, streaming alongside, until she turned once more, as if part of some serene, ancient ritual. Only Claerwen could make an icy, unforgiving river warm, he thought, and marveled that in spite of her exhaustion, and though she was untrained in the secrets of their people's ancestral spirituality, she reveled in the sacredness of the water, creating a fulfilling celebration. He smiled at the peace she radiated, conveyed by the simple act of bathing.

Marcus drifted out of the trancelike state his mind had taken when he saw Claerwen leave the pool and reach for the blanket to dry herself. Finding he was now shivering, he quickly finished washing and plodded out of the water. As she passed the blanket to him, he almost expected to see the light of fire in the head in her eyes. Instead he saw exhaustion returning, intent on claiming her, evident in the fatigued way she dressed. Smiling encouragement that warmth, food and sleep would soon be theirs to enjoy, he quickly dried off, dressed, and led the way back into Caer Ebrauc.

---

Marcus woke long after sunrise. The only sound he heard

beyond the tiny chamber's shuttered window was the call of guards to each other on the ramparts. He knew Ambrosius had already marched with his army for the designated place they would await news of Pascentius' approach. Inside was silent except for Claerwen's deep, slow breath, drawing warm and comfortable on his skin as she slept curled beside him. His face almost pulled into a smile as he laid his fingers over her hand, resting in the middle of his chest, and he wished he could take her home, that the coming battle would put an end to the plotting. But even if Pascentius would die on the field, the scheming and treachery would always exist. It had been so, since time out of mind, and in spite of the efforts he and others had made to stop the butchery, this would only be one of many more fights. Disappointed, he watched Claerwen sleep; and he wished again, this time for more of the peace that she inspired in him. He gathered her into his arms and went back to sleep.

They were left undisturbed until late in the afternoon, when Marcus ventured briefly into the hallway and ordered a meal from a passing servant. A message was automatically relayed to Myrddin, who appeared at the chamber shortly after the meal arrived. Staying briefly, he reported the news brought by Ambrosius' stream of couriers. Pascentius was approaching slowly along a correctly anticipated path, no other Saxons had swollen his war band beyond the coastal group, and the two sides were expected to reach each other by early the next morning. Marcus listened with dour approval, then gave Myrddin his requests for gear — clothing, weapons, food — to replace all that had been lost in Brynaich. He cited the need to be ready for departure when the time made it necessary.

At first light on the second morning, Myrddin returned, knocking lightly at the chamber.

Marcus answered and pulled the door ajar, hiding himself behind it. He held a finger up for quiet, indicating Claerwen had not yet wakened that morning.

Myrddin said softly, "Another messenger just arrived. The war bands are within each other's sight."

"I'll get dressed."

Myrddin nodded, requesting Marcus meet him in his chamber as soon as possible.

Marcus closed the door. Padding softly through the dark room, he went to the table where his sword lay. The clothing had been cleaned and lay neatly folded next to the weapon. He fished his breeches from the pile and pulled them on, tied them.

"Where are you going with Myrddin?" Claerwen asked, startling him. She sat up, reaching for an oil lamp. As the flame lit the room, she saw he had picked up the sword. Throwing off the last of sleep, she launched out of the bed, dragging the blanket around herself, and crossed the tiny room. She took hold of his wrist. "You're not going to fight, are you? Marcus, please, please don't — "

He put down the sword and wrapped his arms around her. "I'm only going to observe, that's all. I should return by evening, sooner perhaps."

He felt her distress ease, then her arms slid up around his neck. She pressed her face into his thick hair, breathing in his scent, making him smile. He mumbled, "Two nights in a real bed and too bloody tired... Ah, but I must go. Myrddin's waiting."

"I have an idea," she whispered in his ear.

"And what would that be?" he asked, sensing mischief.

Her eyes flicked towards the bed. "Let him wait." She leaned against him, pushing. Catching her sense of fun, he complied, moving backward. His legs bumped into the bed, and he dropped down onto it, Claerwen falling with him, the blanket draping loosely over them.

"You are so tempting," Marcus murmured. He enjoyed her softness and warmth as she lay on him, his hands exploring her skin. In the discomfort of many long days of travel and sleeping out in the open every night, they had indulged very little in their normal affections, and he missed her.

Claerwen curled herself around him, luxuriating in his arms' embrace, missing him just as much. She caught his lips in hers with gloriously unending kisses.

Knocking came at the door again, dispelling the mood. "Are you coming?" Myrddin called.

Marcus groaned softly, his head falling back on the bed. "If he would know..." he whispered, making Claerwen giggle, then called aloud, "Aye, hold for a moment."

Claerwen rolled aside and said, "I will come with you."

"I think you should stay here and rest," he suggested, getting to his feet. He returned to the table and picked up the cap with the false hair. For a moment, he stared at it as if changing his mind.

Claerwen read his thoughts and spoke them as she began to dress, "But if there is trouble, I *should* come with you. We should take everything with us. Then you wouldn't need to come back here. And we will need the disguises again."

Exhaling roughly, Marcus nodded his agreement and began pulling on the rest of his clothes. For an instant he frowned, sensing a nuance in her tone, an underlying grain of certainty that she knew trouble was coming. He wondered if that trouble was the same as Myrddin kept secret. Puzzled, he decided there must be a purpose in it and that he must not upset the chain of events they had been entrusted to protect. And he trusted Claerwen.

Dressed, including their disguises, they opened the door to find Myrddin still waiting. With a hint of enlightenment regarding his interruption showing in his face, he led the way out of Caer Ebrauc.

---

The battle was filthy, like any other battle, but it was quickly over. The high king had chosen his ground well, fanning his men out along the top of a north-facing, high, rounded hill that swept down to boggy flatland. As Pascentius' war band moved south, Ambrosius placed a small group of advance warriors on the hill's crest and spread the remainder down the slopes behind and to the sides, beyond the curve of the skyline. They waited in silent patience.

The Saxons marched within sight and stalled, studying the Britons, astonished that so few had come out to meet them. Not waiting long, they charged, slinging contemptuous taunts as they raced over the moors.

The Britons waited, watching, still silent.

And then the Saxons reached the base of the hill.

The tan-grey turf belied sticky, sucking mud that dragged at their churning legs. Men fell, and the armor and long muscular arms and legs that had been their warriors' pride helped little as they flailed in the boggy earth. Other men struggled to them and found themselves in peril as well. Those that came behind halted and scattered around, looking for better footing, but found more of the same.

Then a great cry rose up from the Britons' hill. Saxons that could still look up saw the small group had expanded into an enormous army, well armed, well trained. The British pummeled those in the mire with arrows and spears; flanking forces descended the hill on solid ground, cutting off escape for those who had avoided the mud. Unable to flee, the Saxons were routed. Pascentius, with the first line that had attempted to cross the marsh, had disappeared, apparently having gone down with his men.

Marcus and Myrddin stood on the hill's crest after the king's army had charged. With their arms folded, they grimly watched the fighting. Claerwen sat on the ground several yards away, holding the gelding's tether while it grazed in peaceful contrast to the clashing noise below.

"Why don't you want to fight with them?" Myrddin suddenly asked, his curiosity overwhelming his aloofness.

Marcus' brows were jagged down, his face stony. "Some men like to fight, to kill. Some men even live just for the taking of a life."

"But not you?"

"You know I've killed my share. Out of necessity." He shook his head, his mouth pressing down into a flat line.

"You are a warrior, Lord Marcus, born of the warrior class. I have heard you called a swordmaster of the highest degree."

Marcus grunted. "I became a spy instead of a soldier for the purpose of stopping the fight before it could begin. Ideally, if I could sabotage the war before the war started, no one would have to die." He squinted across the view below him, hating the irony that he was watching a bloodbath he could not stop. He had little sympathy for the barbarian Saxons, but the smell of death wafting from the moor sickened him.

Myrddin's aloofness rose again. He scoffed, "Then you must be naïve to believe as such. You, of all people, would know better."

Taking his sword from its scabbard, Marcus held the hilt with both hands and lifted the tip skyward. The sparkling blade shone long and sensuously in the morning sun. He responded calmly to the criticism, "I was born to the warrior class — that was not my choice. I learned to fight because it was expected. Oddly, I enjoyed swordsmanship, and aye, I'm good at it. But I abhor killing. There is no honor in it. If that makes me a paradox, then so be it. I have my reasons."

He watched Myrddin, again disliking the prince's arrogance. Then, hoping to catch him off-guard, he asked, "When you first came to us, why did you say you should have sought out the Iron Hawk instead?"

From the edge of his eye, Marcus saw Claerwen react with astonishment, but she remained silent, listening with intense curiosity. Myrddin considered the question carefully. When he took too long to answer, Marcus prompted, "Do you know where to find the warrior? Or who he is?"

"No, do you?"

Marcus almost smiled. "There's not a soul in Britain who has not asked that. No one knows. His helmet always masks his face; he never speaks. He carries a massive sword that has a pommel made of iron in the shape of a hawk. I have never heard that he has been defeated. However, his activities have apparently been dormant for the last year or so. Nothing new has been heard of him. Perhaps he has fought one battle too many."

Myrddin's aloofness suddenly drained away. "My remark was only said in sarcasm. I would not trust the Iron Hawk. He is too elusive, too unpredictable, too dangerous. He has never shown loyalty to any side. Tell me, why do you ask of the Iron Hawk now? What do you know of him?"

"No more than what his legend speaks of and the fear created in men's minds at the mention of his name. He is a faction unto himself."

The men suddenly became aware that Claerwen had risen and was staring intently across the field. Marcus picked up her line of sight, finding a lone man catching a horse on an opposite hillside. Stiffening, the warrior in him sparked alive in spite of the words he had spoken. He struck the swordtip into the ground and paced a few steps forward to see more clearly.

Claerwen's eyes ran to the sword, following its sway as it stood alone, like a symbol of one against many. She moved across to Marcus and gripped his arms, asking, "You've seen him?"

"Aye," he confirmed, his eyes narrowing. He looked to Myrddin, then pointing, he said, "That man, there, the one taking the helmet off and walking the horse up the far hill. He is Pascentius. He's abandoning his Saxons."

Myrddin watched and saw a tall man whose closely cropped hair was out of place among hundreds of other men with shoulder-length or longer hair. Cursing, Myrddin started, "I will send a message to my father and — "

"No," Marcus interrupted. "We're going after him. He could lead us to more of his secrets. He's done this before, and I want to know why he's so intent on pulling me into this. Tell your father to be well vigilant in his security. We'll contact you again when we can." Marcus sheathed the sword and strode for the horse.

Seconds later, he was mounted, Claerwen behind him. They circled the blood-soaked battlefield full of Saxon dead and victorious Britons, and disappeared over the moors.

# Chapter 8

**Across the northern kingdoms into Alba**

Once beyond the borders of the kingdom of Ebrauc, Pascentius led a slow, winding and apparently undetermined path, generally towards the northwest. Marcus and Claerwen followed, tracking him easily. They kept within a range close enough to actually see him, especially when rain or snow threatened to obscure the trail. At night, to remain undetectable, they camped with no fire, bundled tightly against the sharpening cold winds. They watched their quarry in shifts. By day, they foraged for food on the run as needed, avoiding contact with those few people who were still about as winter settled onto the island.

"He must be looking for someone," Marcus commented, frustration showing through his quiet eyes as he settled down for another night of watching.

"Or someplace," Claerwen agreed.

"Aye. He's not familiar with this area."

"Do you think he's lost?"

"I think he knows we follow him." Marcus rummaged in a pack and pulled out a short thong. The foot of a small bird of prey was tied to one end.

Claerwen stared at it, frowning. "Where did you get that?" she asked, but her eyes were more clearly asking why he had it.

He grinned and dangled the talons alongside his face. "What do you think?"

"Utterly foul," she grimaced.

"Good, that's the reaction I want," he approved and began to braid the thong into his hair.

Claerwen's eyes widened, then she realized he was creating a new disguise. "Has Pascentius seen you before?"

"Many years ago, but not face to face. I was looking similar to this." He shook the cap with the horsehair.

Claerwen's eyes ran from the old disguise to the new one. "If he knows you're following him, and if you conveniently arrive in the same place, wherever he is going to, isn't he going to guess it's you, no matter how you look?"

"Probably, and that truly makes no difference. You know how I believe he has been drawing me into this scheme from the beginning? He knew I was in Caer Ebrauc, and although he could not predict if he would win or lose the battle, he knew I would follow him if he abandoned the fight. He needs me for a specific reason. Otherwise, he would have tried to kill us by now. I will have to offer myself as bait, give him some promise he can't refuse to turn down, then reverse the trap."

She poked at the talons, making them swing. "You've been planning this disguise, haven't you, since leaving Caer Ebrauc?"

He grinned again, "Aye, I want to create this now, because we don't know when or where he's going to stop. It could be on the morrow, it could be in a fortnight, so we should be prepared." He rumpled his hair, letting it fall over his eyes, then leaned forward, striking a crazed face at her.

Claerwen fell back, trying not to giggle out loud, then teased, "Try this." She hooked her fingers in his hair, splaying it out in all directions.

"It won't stay like that. It's too long."

"We can comb it back on itself, to make it look fuller. It's so thick, it would be easy. You'll be wilder than the Picts."

"If he keeps on the move a few days longer, then this should be well in and help," he added, scratching at the deepening beard on his face.

Claerwen smiled, knowing he disliked having to grow a full beard, but that he would tolerate it without complaint until he no longer needed it. Though she had never said so aloud, she was always glad when he did shave, thinking a beard never suited him well. She liked his appearance best when he wore his long hair in its usual layered unruliness, accompanied by the flowing moustache he favored. She asked, "What are you going to be this time?"

Marcus shrugged. "I won't know until we see where he's getting to. But for you, I think, you will be my slave woman. Meek, but fiercely loyal. You obey my every command, heed no other's."

"The perfect complement to any role you choose to play?"

He nodded, "It will also make it easy for you to follow my lead while you are learning what to do. But when it is time to begin, we must make it look real, even if it's true that Pascentius knows who we are. We will have to play it out exactly as if we are the people we intend to portray.

"How will I know when to begin?"

"You will know. It will be obvious. And there will be times when I cannot stop and explain what's happening or why I'm doing some act. You will need to follow my lead on trust."

He smiled again when she acknowledged her understanding, then he watched her lie down to seek sleep. His eyes held a hint of sadness. Her unwavering faith in him over the years had always awed him, that faith having led her to save his life more than once. He thought of himself as enormously fortunate to have earned such trust, and he cherished it, especially since a day three years before when she had suddenly said how safe she felt with him. Fear had long cast its torture inside her, and that day had been a significant point of change in her life. After years of fleeing the horrors of civil violence and living in borrowed homes, she had found herself moved into his house and no longer fearing what crept beyond the front door. Vowing to keep her and her trust safe, he moved his gaze across to Pascentius' camp, marked by a tiny fire, and glared discontent upon his prey.

More than a fortnight passed as they crossed the northern

kingdoms of Brynaich and Gododdin, entering the mountains of
Alba. Turning westward, they skirted long, deep lakes of frigid
water with ice forming at the edges, crossed ridge after valley and
stream after river, plodded around tarns, traversed mist-filled
vales. The snow turned into rain again, but the air remained icy
and damp. Though the pace remained consistently slow, fatigue
settled, caused by insufficient food, lack of warmth, and poor
sleep. They saw no one else, not even the hardy Picts showed
themselves, staying hidden and snug in their scattered shelters and
watching with wary eyes, certain that the earth goddess would
protect or destroy those who chose to test their endurance against
her wintry power.

A few days later, deep into the afternoon, Marcus and
Claerwen watched Pascentius crest another endless rocky ridge
and disappear over the top. Waiting until he was out of earshot,
they trudged after him. The slope was not particularly steep, but
it was covered in scree that slid out from under each step, forcing
the climb to take twice as long as normal. Marcus winced with
each movement, his left knee's pain worsening, and he used a
staff broken from a deadwood bough for support. He gently urged
the gelding upward and hoped the horse's weight would not be so
much as to cause the animal to unbalance and fall.

Claerwen climbed to Marcus' left, several yards behind, her
back and legs aching with the cold and strain. For a few minutes
she knelt, resting, and watched Marcus struggle to the top, pulling
the horse with him. As he gained the ridge, she resolved to
examine his knee that night to learn if she could ease the pain she
knew he had, though he had not complained of it, then dragged
herself upright to complete the ascent.

Reaching Marcus, Claerwen found him bent over, panting
hard, still holding the gelding's lead rein while he rubbed the
knee. He straightened, and as they looked down the next slope,
their attention was captured in astonishment.

Instead of another stark and rocky valley, thick woodland
swept away down the slope and ended at the sea. Small islands
were strewn across the water. In the midst of the heavy forest, lay
a tiny glen, looking like a basin of tan and white marble because

of its winter-dead grass and patches of snow. A small, fortified enclosure on a slight rise stood on the eastern side.

Pascentius moved downward, along an escarpment beyond the southern edge of the trees, heading straight for the sea. No boats lay there, but a trackway, barely discernible, led northward through the forest to the glen.

"Is that where he will stop?" Claerwen asked, taking the gelding's lead and tethering it.

"I hope it is," Marcus answered, leaning over again, the cold wind causing his knee to cramp.

Claerwen knelt next to him and looked up into his face. His eyes were shut, pain tightening them. "Sit down, and I will see if I can ease it a bit."

"Don't worry about my bloody knee, it'll get better again," Marcus said, straightening, then saw her hands were scraped. He limped to the horse, retrieved a waterskin and soaked his kerchief, but before he could take her hands to wash them, he found her kneeling again, tugging at the lashes on his leggings.

"You don't have to do that now," he said.

"I want to," she countered and asked him again to sit.

Giving in, he sank down.

"By the gods, you should have told me how bad this was getting," she exclaimed softly as she pulled the legging open and rolled up the leg of his breeches. The knee was badly swollen. "This needs a lot of rest."

"We need to keep moving, he's not going to wait for us." Marcus dipped his head in Pascentius' direction.

Claerwen's lips curled in consternation. "Then for now, the best we can do is wrap it well, for support." She went to their gear and extracted a soft, resilient piece of doeskin and neatly wrapped the joint with just the right tension.

"I hope I won't need to fight," he said and rolled the breech leg down again, stuffing it into his boot.

Claerwen stared into his black eyes, wishing he had not mentioned fighting, and her stomach twisted when he pulled his gaze away, his mouth in a grim line. He retied the legging's lashes.

The horse whinnied, sharply catching their thoughts, and they looked up. Beyond the gelding, a huge man loomed out of the trees.

Marcus ripped his sword out of its sheath. He leapt onto his feet, flexed and ready to spring, ignoring the pain in his knee. Claerwen nocked an arrow, drawing the bowstring halfway. She crouched low, waiting.

The man, tall and bulky, with very broad shoulders and huge arms, gave a brown-eyed stare from under scraggly grey brows, first at Marcus, then Claerwen, and back again. He was dressed in skins and a ragged cloak, and carried a rough bow. The cloak's hood barely covered his big head, curly unkempt grey-brown hair escaping it. He raised a hand in peace and backed a step.

Marcus saw that the man was as surprised as they were, probably not expecting to meet anyone. Straightening, he struck the swordtip into the ground between his feet and rested his hands on the pommel. His eyes grew coldly intense.

The man showed no malice as he waited for Marcus to speak. But Marcus remained silent, his lips pressed together and his eyes unchanging.

"I do not wish to intrude," the stranger offered in an odd dialect and again waited for a reaction. When he received no answer, he backed a few more paces, saying, "I am hunting, only hunting. I will leave you alone."

"Wait," Marcus broke his silence.

The man stopped.

"I am Bhruic," Marcus told him. Unable to guess how much of the conversation about his sore knee had been heard, he made his voice deep and gravelly in a way meant to negate any weakness that may have been indicated. The coldness in his eyes eased but did not leave.

The stranger shifted uneasily but decided to offer his name in return, "I am Girvyn."

Marcus' eyes swept to Claerwen and back in one smooth motion, and he said, "The woman and I have traveled far. I sought my brother's homestead but found he is dead and his family scattered." Marcus suspected Girvyn's dialect was a form of old

Celtic mixed with Pictish. He spoke slowly in his own language from Gwynedd, wondering how well the man understood. The languages were similar.

As the man chewed on the information, Claerwen realized Marcus had begun the ruse. Startled by how he roughened his voice to match his wild appearance, she was also amazed by the way his pattern of speech changed from the smoothness of education to the terse and bitter form of a man beaten down by misfortune. He had adopted a new personality with no rehearsal, no stumbling, and she became awkwardly aware of how his many years of experience compared starkly against her lack of it.

"Raiders?" the man asked Marcus.

"Aye," he replied. "Can't go back to where I lived before, raiders there as well."

"They are everywhere," the big man remarked, pointing into the distance behind. "Down there, in that clearing, is an old fort they took last spring. The local prince took them in on the promise of grand loot and glory in return for his hospitality. Instead they have forced all of us who live here into working for them. And I am just one of the fools that fell for their smarmy talk." Girvyn spat over his shoulder in contempt.

Marcus' eyebrows edged upward as he sheathed his sword. "It is nonsense?"

"Aye. I'm a blacksmith, and when they first came, they had me make piles of spearheads, arrowheads, even helmets, the like. They hauled it away and no more was said. There's only about a quarter war band there now, sitting on their fat arses all day, eating and drinking, gambling."

"The prince has no power to force them out?"

"Nay, he is under their sword as good as I. They bleed us dry of everything, food, shelter, they even took my tools except for one hammer. I can't work now, and anyone who objects is cut down. So we live in fear. And before winter is done, many of us will die because there will not be enough food. I had hoped they would leave soon because I had to make horseshoes with icenails for them for winter travel. Meanwhile, I hunt to try to ease the coming hunger, but it is futile because the soldiers will take everything with them when they go."

"What do they wait for?"

"I heard talk of a high commander, some displaced Briton who has been called a traitor. According to Banawr — he's the second-in-command and their swordmaster — this leader is to arrive soon, if you can believe Banawr, the arrogant rot." Girvyn spat over his shoulder again.

Marcus' brows lifted once more.

Girvyn continued without being asked, willingly glad to vent his stored anger. "Banawr thinks he's high king when his master's away. Stupid arrogant…a real killer, just for the sport of it, always picking fights. Don't get me wrong, I can defend myself, but I'm a blacksmith, not a soldier. I got no taste for killing unless there's a need to defend. Don't get within swordreach of him."

"Who is this leader?" Marcus fished, already knowing the answer.

"They only call him 'the commander.' I suspect when he arrives, they will all leave and he with them. Good riddance." Girvyn stomped a huge foot, spewing mud.

Marcus queried, "If they leave, where will they go?"

Girvyn shrugged. "*Iwerddon* possibly, because most of them are Irish. Unless they go somewhere along the coast to the afternoon country where there's a few of their villages left."

Marcus went silent. He had not heard the term "afternoon country" except from storytellers. It was an ancient name for the kingdoms his people had settled centuries before, from Ynys Môn to the peninsula where Mynyw lay. Related to the sun's direction in falling upon the land, it seemed perfectly appropriate to hear the name from this northern man.

Marcus thought of the southern "afternoon country" of Dyfed. Settlements of Irish were still scattered along its coast, perfect footholds for their countrymen to launch raids into Britain. Years before, many of the western kingdoms had purged their lands of Irish settlers, attempting to end such bloody attacks. Some of the British kings had been harshly criticized for the bloodshed, including Marcus' own king, Cunedda of Gwynedd, as well as his closest friend and ally, Ceredig of Strathclyde, but the relative peace that had resulted was never regretted.

Glancing at his wife, his stomach knotted up. One of those Irish raids had resulted in the killing of most of her family and clan when she was a girl of twelve summers. He remembered the pain in her eyes when she had told him; it was the first time she had ever spoken of it to anyone. Her face was unreadable now, but he knew she was thinking as he was, that Pascentius was not only allied with Saxons, but with Irish as well, and the fort in the glen below was his refuge.

Sadness filled Marcus' eyes briefly and he nodded slowly to Girvyn. Then his expression changed to one of curiosity as he dipped his head towards the bow. "What are you hunting?"

"I have a deer down. I came up here for some of these saplings, to build a frame so I can hang the carcass before predators get to it."

"The woman and I can use the horse to haul it into your camp," Marcus offered.

Girvyn's jaw dropped. He never expected help. His eyes ran to Claerwen, still crouching, and he asked, "Who is she?"

Marcus hoped that with her strange clothing and her readiness to attack, the big man would think she must be a wild woman of the woods, descended from ancient female warriors. Signaling that she should rise and put up her weapons, he answered, "Her name is Glân. She was taken as a slave when she was a young girl. A year ago, I saved her life. She is mine, ever since."

"And she cares for you well, I gather," Girvyn remarked with a near-smile, showing he knew the woman kept this stranger's bed nicely warmed.

Marcus' eyes leveled with Girvyn's and widened with an odd intensity. His head tilted slightly, and a similar near-smile curved his lips. In the next instant, the expression was gone.

Claerwen observed the big man try to disregard the image of Marcus' strange reaction, but it stuck, disturbing him. She was to be considered property and tampering would not be tolerated.

Gradually Girvyn recovered his composure and took Marcus' words about raiders for the sound of truth, tempered by the offer of help with the deer. His tongue rolled in his mouth as if he could taste freshly roasted venison, a tempting salve to the plague of his perpetually hungry belly. Finally he accepted the offer, glad to share part of his meat in return.

They cut three small saplings and tied them into a sledge to drag behind the gelding. The deer was neither large nor far away, and they easily lugged it onto the sledge and into Girvyn's camp. As dusk drew the daylight away, they hung, bled, skinned, and gutted the deer. Claerwen spitted a large hunk of the tenderest meat to roast and placed wild roots on the campfire's rocks to cook, sprinkling crushed fresh herbs on both the meat and the roots for seasoning.

Basking in the venison-flavored smoke from the campfire, Girvyn joyfully extracted a huge wineskin of mead from under his gear and presented it to Marcus. Surprised and pleased, Marcus took it and gulped an enormous swallow of the sweet wine. He passed it to Claerwen. She took a smaller share and returned the skin to Girvyn, who drank twice as much as Marcus. It passed many more times around by the time supper was cooked and eaten.

As the men settled into after-meal talk, Claerwen retreated to the shadows beyond the fire's ring of light. She watched Marcus as he half-sat, half-lay against a log, looking sleepy and content, waving his hands in the air as he spoke. But his eyes were sharp and intense, and she knew he was in control of the drink, either by not swallowing as much as he had shown, or by a will so tough that he overpowered the drink's effects.

"To bloody good food, the best I've had in weeks," Girvyn declared in a sloppy voice, then belched and drank another mouthful of mead.

"To more bloody good food, the best I've had in months." Marcus belched in answer. "Stinking, filthy raiders."

"Aye, may the lot of them drown before they reach our soil again!" Girvyn shouted to the night sky.

"May the lot of them be swallowed up by their own soil before they ever leave it!" Marcus howled.

They roared, laughing, each out-insulting the last, each borrowing from his own dialect's colorful coarseness.

Understanding the exact meaning of the words was not necessary; the tone of camaraderie was enough to easily carry the high mood. Finally, the mead ran out.

"Where will you go, Bhruic, after you bring the meat home for me?" Girvyn asked, his watery eyes seeing three of Marcus.

"Don't know. Don't know where my brother's family went, if they're even alive." He sneered and added, "Never cared much for the lot of them. Never cared much for my brother, at that. *Bedd a wna bawb yn gydradd!*"

"Eh?"

"An old proverb from my homeland. It means 'The grave makes everyone equal'." He spat into the darkness behind the log. "Raiders were probably Viking. Stinking Northmen, as stupid as Saxons."

"Aye, all of them!" Girvyn thumbed over his shoulder, trying to indicate the direction of the fort and missing.

"Perhaps I will go farther north from here," Marcus sighed, shrugging, layering frustration into his words. "All I can do is start again. It will be the third time. At least I will have the woman to help now, but I'm bloody tired of it. Perhaps in the north, no one will want to raid so far away."

Girvyn shook his head and waved a hand as if to flip aside the thought. "There's little to live from up there. It's nothing but barren land, cold and wind, rain, snow, ice. It's impossible to survive in a place like that."

"It's been impossible everywhere else I've been."

Girvyn's mouth opened to speak, but, unsure of what he wanted to say, he clamped it shut.

Marcus noticed. "You have a suggestion?"

Girvyn hesitated then attempted to answer, but the words slurred into a wad of incomprehension. He drew a long breath and tried again more slowly, "My life can get no worse. Would you consider rebuilding with me? There will be a lot of work to prepare for the winter after the soldiers leave."

"What about your family? They won't help?"

"What family?" Girvyn half-sneered. "I am alone. And most of the clan is old or very young."

Marcus glanced at Claerwen. She gave no indication of preference, staying within her slave's attitude. He cautioned, "I'm accustomed to working alone, you may not want me around."

Girvyn almost giggled then countered, "No more than you may want to stay around me." He belched again, drifting. In a barely comprehensible voice, he began ranting about Banawr once more.

As Marcus listened, he hummed acknowledgments where appropriate. In between he yawned, loud and obvious.

Girvyn continued on, his voice mumbling. Stretching, his thick arms reached far to each side and his neck curved back over the log he leaned upon. He fell asleep in the middle of his stretch.

Marcus sat up and leaned forward, lightly kicking Girvyn's foot, testing if the big man was truly asleep. Girvyn snorted and sighed, completely unconscious.

Claerwen moved into the firelight, propelled by curiosity. "You yawned on purpose, didn't you, to make him fall asleep?"

Marcus grinned and whispered, "I got what I wanted, there was no need for more talk. And he got what he wanted, someone to help him control Banawr."

They prepared for the night, laying out a leather tarpaulin that served as bedding, and Marcus placed his sword just under its edge within a hand's reach. Claerwen took her place next to him on the side away from the campfire, casting their blanket over them. When he turned towards the fire, folding his arms to keep warm, she curled tightly in behind him and whispered in his ear, "What kind of a name is Glân?"

He sighed softly, almost like a chuckle, the effects of the mead now more apparent. "It means sacred, which is what you are to me." Rolling over, he pulled her into a kiss, then said, "And, aye, I'm drunk, to answer the other question you want to ask. Now get some rest, the morrow will be rough."

Laying his head down, he fell asleep.

# Chapter 9

### Alba

Girvyn's holdings were little more than a low, turf-roofed, earthen-floored stone shack with two chambers, one in front for living space and the other, in back, for storage. Both rooms had a rough plank door to the outside. Drapes made of skins, meant to keep draughts in check, were hung inside each door, as well as in an opening between the chambers. A deep timber porch, housing the forge, drooped across in front like a frowning eyebrow. Squat and primitive, sitting on the western edge of the glen, the smithy appeared to stare defiantly across at the fort.

At midday, rain poured again.

Girvyn and Marcus dragged the deer carcass in under the timber roof. Together with Claerwen, they jointed the meat then cut most of it into thin strips for drying, spread on crude racks made of lashed-together branches. The rest filled a smoking chamber built into the forge's base. Done by late evening, they idled over a simple meal, discussing the work to be done inside the fort and agreeing to begin on the morrow.

Before putting out the lanterns and seeking his pallet for the night, Girvyn stood once more in his work area, surveying its emptiness. Joining him, Marcus saw the heartache of a man who had lost his livelihood. He gripped Girvyn's huge shoulder and consoled, "We'll get your tools back."

"How?"

"They must be in the fort. Tomorrow, we steal them back, I'd say." With slyness in his eyes, Marcus gazed across the dark glen.

Girvyn studied him. "You've got a few tricks in you, don't you?"

Marcus grinned, his eyes squinting tighter, adding a malicious layer to them.

"You are a strange man, Bhruic," Girvyn mused. "I think perhaps those occasional looks of madness tell me you just might be capable of outwitting the likes of Banawr. Perhaps you and I may get along very well. Go on, your woman is waiting for you." Girvyn tilted his head towards the rear chamber, saluted, and turned into his doorway.

As Marcus disappeared around the smithy's corner, a hollow voice shouted from beyond the porch, its owner obscured by the heavy rain. Smothered in contempt, the voice demanded, "And where have you been, smith?"

A short, husky man appeared just under the edge of the roof. His face was ruddy, pudgy and pockmarked, with cold, pale blue eyes sunk into sagging folds of skin. Unkempt reddish-blond hair straggled down, dripping with rain. He was dressed in a soldier's full gear, including a leather helmet carried under one arm and a broadsword of mediocre quality hung from his belt. A pair of sullen mercenaries shuffled in under the roof to his left, shifting uncomfortably in their soaking clothes.

Girvyn turned but gave no reply, merely glaring at the man.

The soldier demanded again, "I asked where you have been. Answer!"

Girvyn slowly puffed up his bulk. He waved a hand at the racks of drying deer meat and asked, "Isn't it obvious…Banawr? As if it's any of your concern?" He said the name loudly and in equal contempt to warn Marcus.

"I'll expect this to be in the fort tomorrow morning. The commander has returned and he favors venison," Banawr stated.

"You never deserved what you've already taken, none of you! You'll have no more from me, you hear? Nothing more!" Girvyn spat on the ground in front of Banawr's feet.

Pascentius' second-in-command flushed and clenched his fingers around his sword's hilt. The steady patter of the rain seemed to grow loud, swelling proportionally with the two men's anger. Then the sound changed, stirring differently, softly rustling behind Banawr.

A swordtip pricked between his shoulder blades before he could react. Stiffening, he slowly released his weapon's hilt then turned. "Who are you?" he sniffed, hiding his surprise at the long-reaching sword leveled at his belly and the black-haired man holding it.

Girvyn could not suppress a grin as Marcus' dark eyes slowly traveled down, then up, unperturbed in their assessment. They came to rest, intense yet unreadable, on Banawr's face.

"Well, man, answer! Who are you?" the soldier growled again.

As if considering the quality of cattle for sale, Marcus said evenly, "I am not one of your soldiers to order." He scratched at his beard with his free hand.

Banawr's fingers tensed again, hovering over his hilt. "Then leave. Now."

Marcus' heavy brows lowered farther, his penetrating expression unchanged. "Not likely."

"You instigated this!" Banawr seethed. Giving in to his rage, he dropped the helmet and sprang backward, beyond reach of Marcus' sword, allowing himself time to pull his own. He pounced, swinging furiously.

Marcus deftly caught the blade with the edge of his own sword. With a harsh, ringing scrape, he drove down, hooked against the crossguard and heaved, forcing Banawr out from under the porch roof, into the rain.

Banawr backed out of range, regained his composure, then bragged to the pair of mercenaries, "Move away, you incompetent louts! Watch how I skewer this surly stranger." Gripping the hilt with both hands, he sidled, to the left, then back again, looking for the right moment of surprise.

Marcus waited, watching for the telltale flinch that would warn of the next lunge. Banawr had slow reflexes, making his movements easy to read, and Marcus calmly calculated this. Gradually Banawr stalked forward through the water cascading over the roof's edge. They tested each other's patience, waiting deliberately, flexed and ready, but as expected, Marcus knew Banawr had no patience. The flinch came, and his responding block stopped Banawr's wild swing before it was halfway around. He drove the blade into the soaking earth, then rammed a foot into the soldier's side.

Banawr fell, skidding backward across the slippery turf. The sword ejected from his grip, bouncing several feet past his reach. Cursing, he jolted upright, pulling a dagger from his belt.

Marcus dropped, wrenching away to one side. A slick, hollow resonance sung past him, followed by a solid thud. Rolling up onto his feet, he saw an arrow, not a knife, had pounded into the earth, narrowly missing Banawr's feet. It was still quivering. Then he realized Claerwen stood just under the edge of the porch roof, already nocking a second arrow.

Still holding the dagger, Banawr stared at the arrow in disbelief, not understanding from where it had come. He had seen no one with a bow. Then he saw another figure in the smithy. "A woman…" he blurted. Enthralled, he forgot his abandoned sword and never saw Marcus pick it up.

"Drop the knife," Claerwen's voice cut clearly above the rainfall.

Girvyn grinned broadly, warning, "You'd best do as she says, man. She will cut you no quarter."

Claerwen held the bow comfortably, familiarly, watching Banawr turn towards her, compelled by his curiosity. She raised the bow and drew halfway, aiming steadily at the center of his chest.

Marcus grunted, "Do as she says, Banawr. Drop the weapon."

"She will kill you," Girvyn advised happily.

Banawr continued to stare, fascinated by her strange, boyish clothing, and slowly rose, taking a step towards her.

Claerwen drew fully, her eyes narrowing. Banawr halted.

"She *will* kill you," Marcus repeated, holding both swordtips ready. "With good reason, but if you mind your manners, perhaps she will spare you. Drop the dagger and kick it here."

Banawr twisted around, looking for help from his two mercenaries, but they refused, smirking, unwilling to fight Marcus. Frustrated, Banawr yielded.

Claerwen eased the bow's draw and retreated, but remained within the smithy.

"Lo, she is beautiful..." he mumbled, "...and defiant, full of fire. I'd wager that one could set your bed aflame in the night..."

Marcus drawled maliciously, "If I ordered her, she would burn you to ashes, with pleasure *I'd* wager." Then handing Banawr's sword to Girvyn, he ordered, "Break it."

The blacksmith complied. Proudly using the only tool he had left, he laid the sword across the anvil and struck, cracking the blade off midway.

The metal shattered. Banawr recoiled. To break a warrior's sword was considered the gravest insult against him, the insult of submission to a superior authority.

His own sword in hand, Marcus held the tip to Banawr's broad beltline and pressed the man back against one of the roof's support beams. Ignoring the pelting rain, he spoke, "You will leave us alone. We will live and work together in peace and no more. You will not demand any share of anything from us because it is not yours to demand. Do you understand?"

Banawr did not answer.

"Do you understand?" Marcus demanded again. He flicked the tip sideways, nicking him.

Banawr winced. It was only a scratch but one difficult to heal because his belt would rub against it. "You bastard — " Banawr grumbled, grabbing at the thin red line of blood soaking the cut edges of his tunic.

"You've been warned," Marcus shot back, swinging the blade upward, prodding him under the chin.

Banawr fumed but he finally gave up, muttering unintelligible curses as he trudged to his horse and struggled to mount. He rode slowly into the darkness, followed by his amused mercenaries.

Girvyn shook his head as Marcus turned back to the house. "Do you know what you just did?" he asked.

"Aye, I humiliated him."

"On purpose? Damn, man, you just earned a slit throat in the night. He won't bear being embarrassed like that, especially in front of his men. And he won't wait long, Bhruic, I've seen him do it before."

Scattering cold rainwater, Marcus shook out his hair. It stood out, making his profile look like the grotesquely blasted branches of a lightning-struck tree. The talons came to rest on his shoulder as if they were gripping it. "'Tis Banawr who needs to beware."

The grin that followed made Girvyn's skin crawl. Eyeing Claerwen, still watching vigilantly into the darkness with her bow in hand, Girvyn warned, "You should have kept your woman hidden, Bhruic. Banawr will come back and try to take her from you, first, just because he will want to, and second, for revenge."

Marcus exhaled, "No matter. He would have found out soon enough. She will be safe with me."

Girvyn's curiosity broke and he whispered, "Who are you?"

Marcus squinted across the glen then said quietly, "No one to fear." He walked away towards his side of the building, Claerwen following, leaving Girvyn with his tongue clamped in his teeth and wondering if he was being used again.

---

The rain stopped in the night, but the sky remained filled with thick clouds. A wind bore down on the land, oddly warm and scattering away the last of autumn's leaves like flocks of tiny russet-colored birds. As dawn drew into daylight, Marcus slipped off the woven straw mat that served as a bed for him and Claerwen, and dressed in the dark. Carrying the sword, he went out the rear door and around to tour the smithy.

Even if the tools had been there, he observed, the basic arrangement was very primitive. His own smithy at Dinas Beris was spare and simple, but by comparison, luxurious. Thinking that if he would be there longer, he might try to convince Girvyn of a way to restructure it for more efficiency. He wondered how much skill the big man had, or if it was as wanting as the smithy itself. He was studying the forge when Girvyn appeared, yawning in his doorway.

"How is the meat?" Girvyn asked, squatting to peer into the smoking chamber.

"Needs more peat," Marcus answered, handing him a dried brick of fuel. Are you ready to go to the fort now?"

"Aye, we can eat on the way," Girvyn replied, handing Marcus a cold oat farl.

"I will tell the woman."

He strode through to the rear room and found Claerwen awake and kneeling, already wearing the long shirt she wore under her tunics. "Wait. Wear this," he said softly and reached for the pack of clothing she had been given in Caer Ebrauc. He fished through its contents and pulled out a tightly rolled up dress.

Shaking it out, Claerwen realized it was far more appropriate to wear. A slave in typical garb would cause fewer questions among the fort's soldiers than a woman in boyish traveling clothes. Made of thin woolen cloth, its undershift the same weight, the dress would not give her nearly the protection and warmth of the heavy deerskin tunics, breeches and leggings, but she accepted the idea without complaint and hoped they would be working inside out of the wind. Leaving the long shirt on for warmth, she started to dress.

Marcus waited, briefly watching through the partially opened door. She was beginning to knot the bodice's ties together when he turned back into the room, moving to pick up his sword.

Claerwen's eyes followed him, and the memory of his harsh confrontation with Banawr flooded her. She understood there was a purpose behind it, more than mere defense and that it could somehow gain them access to Pascentius. She laid her hand on his arm, letting her eyes question him.

He hushed her, his finger against her lips. His face told her that he would explain when the time was right, when they were somewhere safe to talk. For a moment he listened for sounds beyond the room, and she hoped he would chance a few words in spite of his warning. But instead of speaking, he let his eyes slide down to the open neck of the dress, stopping to rest and soften for just an instant. She shivered involuntarily, cold bumps on her skin.

"Are you coming, Bhruic?" Girvyn called from the front room.

Marcus glanced up into her eyes and his lips curled into a smile as he turned away. He picked up his sword and an empty rucksack. Claerwen rushed to finish dressing and followed him out.

As they rounded the front of the smithy, Marcus held up the pouch and instructed Girvyn, "If you have one of these, bring it with you."

Already several strides into the glen, Girvyn halted, confused.

"Would be easier to carry your tools in something, I'd say," Marcus pointed out.

"And you think we can merely walk over there and take them?"

"Aye. That's exactly what we're going to do. You're going to show us what needs to be done there, and we'll find the tools for that work. The rest you will take, because you'll need them to do the metalwork here, no?" He left no chance for quibbling and strode out, heading straight across the glen with Claerwen, leaving Girvyn to follow.

Marcus expected Banawr to have circulated news of Claerwen's existence throughout the fort, mostly as a distraction from how he had lost his sword. At the gates, the guard saluted the men with sheer indifference, offering no challenge. But as Claerwen entered, the gatesman's curious eyes followed her, trying to see her face. She kept her eyes downcast and stayed close behind Marcus and Girvyn.

As they crossed into the courtyard, Marcus began a careful observance, noting that the mercenaries, like the gatesman, were a rough, undisciplined group of men, none of whom apparently belonged to any particular stock of loyalty. Taking advantage of a free place to live because they had nowhere else to go, they would scatter at any better offer, if one would be made. He counted nearly fifty men.

The fort was ancient and in poor repair, almost to the point of being dysfunctional. Some restoration had been done, but not done well, and Marcus guessed that only the most critical necessities had been performed during Pascentius' occupation. Girvyn led them towards a small stone hut at the back wall. It stood near a pair of other structures; one had once housed slaves, the other had been barracks for soldiers. All looked as if they would crumble in the next wind. Inside the hut, one work table leaned against a wall, a broad selection of hand tools scattered over it. As light from the doorway spilled across the interior, it struck a small pile of weapons underneath the table.

Marcus turned and paused, his attention caught by the weapons. They were spearheads and had the same pattern as those from Octa's homestead and the Saxon camp. His eyes came up, sweeping to Claerwen, and he saw she had discovered them as well and had realized this camp was where the weapons had been manufactured. Their eyes drifted apart, not wanting to alert Girvyn.

Inside Marcus' mind, excitement boiled. Pascentius had ordered the weapons, forcing unfortunate men like Girvyn to make them. From there, the spearheads and other weapons had been funneled through Octa's farmstead to the Saxon camp, intended for use against Ambrosius in Caer Ebrauc. When his alliance with Octa broke and the undermanned battle failed, Pascentius ran, as always, intending to evaporate like a spent thunderhead. But this time, a trail of spearheads offered proof of his conspiracy against the king.

Marcus asked, "How is Banawr controlling the local prince?"

"I don't know," Girvyn answered. He leaned comfortably against a wall and launched into a speculation. "Lord Engres, that's the prince, came about this place in an odd way, some years back. One day, he appeared from only the gods know where, looking like he'd been through a dozen wars. No one knows how he got here, and he either won't tell or can't remember. The prince before him, at the time, took Engres in and had a woodswoman come to heal him. Engres eventually became like a brother to the prince. And when the prince died, leaving no children or other kin, the people here liked Engres enough to ask him to take the prince's place. He had nothing of his own, like the rest of us, but he's always been fair in settling disputes and has fit in well with us. We were surprised and disappointed when he let these barbarians into our lands, but I'm sure he was given little choice."

Marcus studied the hut's interior and asked, "How much is he looking to have done on these buildings?"

"Enough to keep out the snow and wind for now, he told me. He needs a stone layer and a carpenter more than a smith. Most of the local people will be too busy trying to survive the winter without having to work here as well. With no family to feed, I thought I could afford some time to work, once the soldiers are gone."

They walked to the barracks, Girvyn chattering on about the fort and the surrounding area. From there, they toured the other buildings, except for the personal houses, and at each location, Marcus stalled, studied, evaluated, watched. He guided the conversation using carefully worded questions, and by midday he had gained a good working knowledge of the fort's guard system, layout and routines, as well as who belonged to each building. And in each location, more of Girvyn's tools were found. Marcus made certain all of them were swept into the rucksacks.

"How do you think they'll react when we walk out of here with these?" Girvyn queried when they reached the last building.

Marcus explained, "The lack of reaction from Banawr's two mercenaries yesterday told me they are tired of his tirades and will do most anything to either goad him or ignore him. They did not even try to defend him. The guards here won't care what you take. Does that belong to anyone?" He pointed at an old, ragged cloak hanging on a peg.

Girvyn shrugged. "It's always been there. I don't know."

Marcus took it down and gave it to Claerwen. He half-winked with one eye as she dipped in a near-curtsey and thanked her lord. They walked out into the courtyard again, and turning back to Girvyn, he asked, "Where are we to start work?"

"Engres wants the barracks done first. If the winter is hard, he may bring the people inside the fort. That would be the likely place to house them." Girvyn paused, watching Marcus scan again across the compound. Guessing, he asked, "You're looking for Banawr, aren't you, because we haven't seen him all day?"

Marcus made no reply, thinking not only of the second, but that he also had not seen Pascentius.

Girvyn said, "Banawr's certain to be drunk somewhere, unless he's with the commander. Then they'll be busy scheming together. That is, of course, unless the commander's with the woman he has stashed in one of the abandoned homesteads, then count on Banawr being drunk."

Marcus grinned, "He has a woman Banawr hasn't taken from him?"

Girvyn snorted a laugh, "Aye, and you know why the man keeps her hidden. But I've seen him ride into the trees on a track leading straight east from behind the fort. There's an old house by a spring that's been empty for a generation, and it's got to be where he keeps her. I've never seen the woman, she's probably just a camp follower."

Nodding amusement at his own remarks, Girvyn left Marcus and Claerwen with a hammer and a pair of chisels, then headed for the gates. He passed the keeper and received no challenge as to what the rucksacks contained.

Marcus turned back towards the barracks, Claerwen following. He had expected her presence would draw some attention, but as he led her across to the farthest chamber, a steady gathering of prying-eyed mercenaries filled the courtyard. Annoyed, he had hoped to remain undisturbed. They went inside to begin work.

"Get back to your posts!" a loud, disciplined voice cracked out from behind the men.

Marcus returned to the doorway. The body of soldiers dispersed, grumbling quietly as they tromped off through the muddy yard.

One man remained behind, the owner of the orders. Tall and still proudly wearing outdated Roman-style clothing, his curled brown hair plastered down by the wind, Pascentius stared coldly at Marcus.

# Chapter 10

## Alba

Marcus returned Pascentius' stare. Then a grey-haired man appeared, coming from across the yard and interrupting the commander's attention. As the two men spoke together, Marcus retreated inside the barrack chamber and began to inspect the dry stone building's structural damage. Keeping watch on the men from the edge of his eye, he lightly tapped on the walls with a hammer, testing their soundness.

He commented to Claerwen, "The local people have taken many of the better stones for use in their own holdings, leaving the walls to crumble. It's easier for them to take these than to dig rock out of the turf a few paces in front of their houses. We can't even consider installing hinges or doors until we've shored up this stonework. This was not built well originally and was only a thick, single wall, not a double wall filled with insulating gravel."

"They're coming this way," Claerwen whispered, taking the hammer from him while he hand-rocked one stone into a more secure position.

"The other man must be Lord Engres, from his description. Stay behind me as much as you can," Marcus warned, taking the hammer again. "This one needs to come out and be refit," he said, tapping on another loose stone. A protruding bulge on the far side kept it from being pulled out. Taking a chisel, he prodded, trying to dislodge it as the men approached.

Pascentius strode directly into the barrack to watch Marcus work. He stood with his arms folded, his long cloak tossed back arrogantly over his shoulders. Fluid mud dripped from its hem onto the floor. Marcus continued to work, ignoring him.

"My man Banawr says Girvyn has taken in someone to work with him. Are you that man?"

"Aye," Marcus clipped through his teeth.

Pascentius moved closer, purposely getting in the way of the hammer's swing. He was more than half a head taller, but wiry in build compared to Marcus' muscular solidity. "I understand you disarmed my second."

Marcus paused but did not turn to face Pascentius. He studied the rock for a few more seconds, then swung sideways, the hammerhead neatly slipping through the open space aside the stone and striking with a powerful shock. The rock split, spilling out of the wall in dusty chunks at Pascentius' feet.

Pascentius did not move, but his eyes rolled upward. He frowned nervously at the vibrating wall.

"Aye, that I did," Marcus answered at last.

"And this is the woman he's been bragging about?"

"Aye." Marcus' voice echoed roughly in the empty room. He picked up two of the chunks. Turning the pieces, he found one that would fill a gap perfectly with a little shaping. He tossed the second piece aside.

"You broke his sword."

Marcus knelt and chipped at the rock. After only a few strokes, he stood again and tried the stone, found it was ready, tapped it into place. He said, "Banawr should have minded himself better." To punctuate his remark, he dropped the hammer headfirst to the packed earth floor, narrowly missing Pascentius' feet.

Engres, standing sullenly in the doorway, suddenly seemed to come alive, snorting at Marcus' comment. He mumbled, "...the only decent event in this place for months..."

Pascentius glared at Engres, and the older man's eyes dropped in submissiveness.

Marcus raised an eyebrow and gave Engres a swift perusal. The man appeared to be past forty winters and had a thin, grey quality about him, as if he had absorbed the dismal bleakness of a snow sky. His body was forlorn to the point of fragility; his hair, moustache and beard all greyed completely and tinged slightly yellowish. Even his eyes were grey. Except in the brief moment of amusement, his expression held the lost look of a man whose life was nearing its end and its course had been utterly unfulfilled.

Marcus moved along the wall and knelt, finding another small gap to fill. The piece of rock he had dropped lay below the space, and he picked it up. Too large, he set it down again and asked Claerwen for a smaller chisel. After examining the grain lines, he positioned the tool carefully for the right split. "Someone had to discipline him," he barbed, knowing Pascentius, so proud of his Roman-style command that would dictate strict discipline, would be embarrassed by his second's complete lack of it. Marcus reached for the hammer and lifted it to swing. Pascentius was too close again, but Marcus swung anyway, barely missing his legs. The hammer rang on the chisel, and the stone split neatly in half.

Pascentius finally backed several paces and scowled. "Nothing ruffles you, does it?"

"Should it?" Marcus countered. Standing again, he glared hatred that strained to break away like a raging stallion. He knew Vortigern's son was testing him, analyzing how he would be trapped, tamed and used. But for a few moments, before he would allow himself to be given as bait, Marcus bared the scars of his soul through his eyes. He wanted the man to feel the agony suffered, not only for himself and the beatings he'd endured, but for all those who had been starved, maimed, terrorized and murdered by Vortigern's Saxons. Marcus held his temper, knowing that if he let it go, he would kill Pascentius with his bare hands in spite of his abhorrence for taking a life. Any chance of succeeding in his quest would be ruined. There were too many others tied to Pascentius in the ambition to steal the high kingship; he had to find all the loose ends of the conspiracy. Pascentius broke from Marcus' stare.

"Who are you?" Engres asked, eyeing the sword Marcus had

brought, propped in a corner.

"I am called Bhruic. Like Girvyn, I am a blacksmith. Raiders took my land. The woman and I met Girvyn some way south of here, and he and I decided to trade work. She and I earn our keep, just as he does." He turned back to the wall.

"Banawr's men say you are an excellent fighter. Where did you learn this?" the man persisted.

"By surviving," Marcus answered. He moved farther along the wall, testing each stone for stability, then said, "Banawr is not much of a warrior."

Pascentius interjected, "He trains my mercenaries."

"In what? Arrogance?" Marcus shot back.

Engres grunted and went outside. Pascentius followed, and they spoke quietly together as they watched Marcus complete the circuit of the barrack room.

"You need a new roof on this," Marcus interrupted them, pointing upward from the doorway. "Girvyn didn't say anything about new thatching. Slate would be better if you have a source nearby."

Engres said, "It will have to be thatch. Can you do that as well?"

"Aye, well enough. So be it."

"Come, Engres, I tire of this labor," Pascentius said in dismissal, and he turned for the great hall.

Engres moved to follow. He hesitated, looking as if he had thought of further instructions. Then he saw Claerwen, on her knees and sweeping rock chips into a pail with her hands. She looked up at Marcus, listening as he spoke about the roof. A beam of sunlight shook loose from the cloudy sky, brushing her face and illuminating her green-blue eyes. Engres stared, his jaw dropping in surprise.

Marcus saw his reaction and countered it, easing into his line of sight until the sunlight dimmed, darkening the room again. Engres turned away, a stunned helplessness on his face.

Claerwen looked up again as Marcus swung around, suddenly ending the talk about the roof, alarm in his eyes. She had not seen Engres' response, but her stomach cramped as Marcus came at her, taking her by the elbow. He raised her, pulling her into the farthest corner of the barrack room.

"Do you know that man, the grey-haired one?" he demanded in a heavy whisper.

"No. Why?"

"He looked at you like he knows you."

She gripped the pail of chips as if afraid to let go. "Lord Engres? No, I never saw him before. I'm certain."

Marcus silently reasoned through a handful of possibilities of why Engres had been so startled by her presence. Finally, he shook his head and nearly smiled, the deepening lines around his eyes giving him a sly look, and he said softly, "I hope it's only that he thinks you're beautiful." He went to the doorway, examining the opening's sides for the best way to mount a door.

Claerwen's brow rumpled at the out of place compliment, but she sensed that underneath his stern words and face, he was actually enjoying the intrigue. She shrugged off the incident.

Using wood Girvyn had previously prepared, they fitted a simple frame around the doorway and pegged it in tightly, then hung a door into place as dusk fell. "'Tis warm tonight, with little breeze," Marcus commented absently as he checked how well the door fit.

Claerwen agreed. "Odd this time of year, more mud than snow. 'Twill be a full moon as well, the sky is clearing."

"I need a wedge to keep this door open until I can make a latch for it. If the wind comes up hard, it could rip this all apart again."

"I'll find something," she offered and turned towards the doorway.

Marcus caught her arm, pulling her back. Using silent hand signals, he indicated that she should look in the storage hut, and if it was safe, try to conceal one of the Saxon spearheads under her cloak. She nodded her understanding and waded across, hitching her skirts up out of the mud.

Marcus waited, leaning in the doorway. A pair of soldiers lit torches throughout the courtyard, then returned to their posts on the ramparts. Off-duty mercenaries gathered in the great hall for the evening meal, their voices and laughter drifting from inside.

The yard became deserted.

From where he stood, Marcus could just see between the storage hut and the old slave quarters in the fading light. A pile of debris leaned against the compound's rear wall, frost-dead weeds overgrowing it. At first he did not know why his attention had been drawn in that direction. Gradually, he became aware of a sporadically moving shadow, then he realized a postern gate was beneath the debris. The gate had opened, forcing aside the overgrowth, and the shadow detached itself. Puzzled, he backed inside the doorway and stood absolutely still, watching.

Avoiding the torchlight and furtively darting from corner to corner, a woman approached, heavily cloaked, her hair covered in kerchiefs. Making certain no one still worked in the barracks, she slipped into the last room at the opposite end from where Marcus waited. She stayed only a few seconds, then retreated the way she had come.

Marcus emerged and paced along the row. The last room was doorless like the others, and as he looked in, he saw a set of muddy footprints that ran to a back corner and out again.

Then steps squished in the yard. Marcus swiftly rounded the end of the building, disappearing from sight. Banawr strode towards the room the woman had entered. Marcus pulled back and waited, hoping Claerwen would not come yet.

Banawr went inside, his footfalls marking the same path as the woman's. He halted in the rear corner, reversed, paused as he came into the doorway, then crossed to the great hall. He stood under one of the torches and held up a tiny piece of cloth. Gazing at it briefly, he then lit it in the flames. As the cloth began to burn, he dropped it and entered the hall.

As soon as the door thumped shut, Marcus dashed across the yard. He had seen the cloth fall into a patch of slush. Finding it, he picked it up. The flames had barely singed one edge before they were doused. Taking only an instant to scan it, he raised it to his nose, sniffed, frowned heavily, then stuffed the cloth inside his tunic. He turned again for the barracks.

Claerwen emerged from the hut with a chunk of scrap wood. Passing into the repaired room, she was alarmed to find Marcus gone but went about securely blocking the door. As she straightened, he was suddenly there, startling her again. She touched her hand lightly to his arm to show she had retrieved a spearhead.

Marcus squinted in return, acknowledging her success, but his eyes were clogged with an icy hardness. She knew instantly that his annoyance was not part of Bhruic's characteristic gruffness and that something serious had happened. Keeping her hand on his arm, she questioned him with her eyes.

Unchanging, his expression gave no hint of why he was vexed. With a brief signal that they were done for the day, he turned away and gathered the tools. In silence, they walked back to the smithy.

# Chapter 11

## Alba

At midnight the moon was high over the glen and bright enough to give the impression of twilight.

Since returning to the smithy, Claerwen had tried to learn what had suddenly struck Marcus so irritable, but he refused to answer, continuously hushing her. His mood did not lighten even when she gave him the spearhead. When she tried to coax him into going for a walk in the forest's privacy, he again refused, saying he needed to help Girvyn. But he only worked for a short while then came to bed, quickly falling asleep.

She watched him. A thin, pale beam of moonlight spilled through a crack in the wall, its tedious movement across the floor emulating his slow and steady breathing. Feeling isolated, she turned away and forced herself to give in to sleep.

Uncomfortable on the mat, Claerwen woke again before long. Without opening her eyes, she rolled over and reached, seeking to tuck her hand around Marcus' arm. Instead, she found his half of the blanket rumpled up and cold. Her eyes came open then, and she realized he was standing in the doorway to the outside, fully dressed, his sword buckled on its baldric. Before she could react, he stepped out, softly closing the door after himself. She heard him pace away.

Alarmed, Claerwen lurched out of the bed. Bounding to the door, she pulled it slightly ajar and stared incredulously as his figure disappeared into the forest. "What is he doing?" she asked herself and debated whether she should follow or not. If not and he stumbled into a trap, she might never see him again. But if she did go, she could disrupt a precarious situation and endanger his life as well. Dragging in a long breath to dispel her confusion, she decided to trust his judgement and stay in the house to wait.

She sat down on the mat. The air, both inside and outside the house, felt heavy and stifling as it had all evening, full of a damp and dreary stillness that made everything droop with an unnatural tiredness. No night sounds rustled anywhere, not a leaf or branch or blade of grass moved. Claerwen rested her face on her drawn up knees, giving in to the oppressiveness, and wished a thunderstorm would suddenly billow up and scrub the air clean.

Her nose tickled and she sniffed absently, rubbing a finger underneath. It tickled again, and she became aware of a pervading sweet odor in the room. Sniffing further, she traced its source to the mat she sat on and found Marcus' side smelled heavily of it. Hoping to shake it out, she lifted the mat's edge, and a crumpled piece of cloth fell from the underside, reeking of the smell. Holding it away from herself, she went to the door with the intention of throwing the cloth as far as she could. Why Marcus would ever have such a thing, he who objected to anything stronger than the mild scent of lavender she usually rinsed her hair with at home, Claerwen could not understand. But as she opened the door enough to pose a good swing, she saw the cloth had figures drawn on it. On the left side was a letter "B"; in the center, a symbol for the moon; and on the right, another symbol, for a farm.

Raising her eyes, she gazed at the spot where she had last seen Marcus. Her stomach sank as she realized he was going to meet a woman, one he knew, and the perfume-soaked cloth appeared connected to his brooding. Sighing heavily, she hoped he would explain when he returned, and that the meeting would alleviate the foulness of his mood. She had learned in the past that to judge his erratic and inexplicable actions before they were complete could lead to disastrous misunderstandings. Taking another long breath, she forced herself to count patience instead of time.

Then movement caught her attention. A figure walked from the glen, and though only visible as a dim shadow, Claerwen recognized Banawr by the way he moved. He entered the forest a short distance from the place Marcus had, heading in the same direction. Claerwen whirled and grabbed up her cloak, and was glad that she had worn her clothes to sleep in against the dampness in spite of the unseasonable warmth. Seconds later, she was running towards the trees.

The glaring moonlight showed Marcus' tracks clearly. He had made no effort to hide them. In the near distance, she heard Banawr's footsteps. Reverting to hunting skills, she stalked the men silently.

The tracks circled around to the east, going beyond the glen. Nearly a mile from the fort, Claerwen came upon a tiny clearing with a small farmstead to one side, a spring-fed pond to the other. The trees thinned as she closed in on the clearing and she slowed, approaching cautiously. Lanterns glowed both at the house and along the pond. Amid their dim flickering, someone prepared to bathe.

At the water's edge, a woman stepped out of her dress and undershift, then stretched, unfurling herself in a catlike reach, her long arms rolling out above her head, her hands extending into finger-clawed splays. Tall, well shaped, almost voluptuous, with thick dark red hair that flowed down her back, the woman obviously enjoyed the warm night on her skin. Humming softly, she waded into the pond.

Claerwen waited. The dead night air dragged at her patience, and she found herself sweating, breathing harder than normal, as if the air was too thick and wet to use. She exhaled softly, hoping to ease her tension. Leaves riffled slightly, but too far away to have been disturbed by her breath. She turned her head and saw Marcus only a short distance to her right, staring at the red-haired woman. His expression was dispassionately empty.

Soft footfalls in the humus approached from beyond him, and Claerwen knew Banawr would be upon them within seconds. But

Marcus' attention remained locked on the woman. Claerwen whistled a sharp, low warning. She saw his head jerk towards her as he recognized the signal. His eyes searched the trees, missing her. He heard the footsteps then and turned in their direction, his right hand reaching for the sword hilt behind his shoulder.

Claerwen slipped forward, running, and whistled again, almost in his ear. He turned back slightly and suddenly she was there, pouncing on him, her face gripped in urgency, her hands grabbing his tunic. Before he could react, she yanked hard and fell backward, dragging him down over her.

Claerwen grimaced, gritting her teeth as she crumpled under his weight, but she kept her eyes locked with his, conveying the necessity to keep still. She saw his astonishment change to questions, and she turned her head slightly, glaring at the empty space where he had just been standing.

Following her line of sight, he saw Banawr had stopped behind them within a few paces and had taken on a grin full of arrogance at his discovery of the bathing woman. Marcus turned his face back to Claerwen, and he blinked once in deliberate slowness to tell her he realized why she had come. He felt her shiver, then saw she was lying in soaking, rotting leaves, tense and uncomfortable underneath him, but he dared not move with Banawr so close.

They heard the woman splashing in the water, still humming. Banawr held his position, watching, oblivious to anything else. Several times, a guttural chuckling softly rolled in his throat. The woman's humming turned into singing, at last prompting Banawr to move. Slowly, he tramped out of the trees, going straight to the pond.

Marcus pushed up slightly, carefully peering through the bracken. He felt Claerwen take a rough breath, and he realized he'd been crushing her. He tried to pull back, but her hands were cramped and locked onto his tunic. Slowly, he eased upright and gently massaged her fingers free, then brought her to her feet.

Taking in a last glimpse of the clearing, they saw Banawr had stripped and was in the pond with the woman. Marcus' lips curled into a near smile as he shook his head, then he backed away, pulling Claerwen with him. Without a word, he began following his own tracks towards the smithy.

Halfway there, Claerwen balked. "We must talk," she whispered sharply, gripping his hand and pulling him to a stop.

He frowned heavily and shook his head. When he tried to walk away, she clamped her hands around his arm and held on. She insisted, "How can I help you when you're in trouble, if you don't tell me what you're doing, if I don't even know where you are?"

"We can't talk here," he responded.

"You could have told me you were going to meet her," she blurted, pulling the marked cloth from inside her cloak.

He squinted in consternation.

"Please," she pleaded. "You are angry, because I interrupted you, but it was a trap."

He took the cloth, then realized her thoughts. He explained, "The 'B' was meant for Banawr, not Bhruic. That is the woman Girvyn told about, that Pascentius has hidden, but now I see she is lovers with Banawr as well. He didn't know I found this, so it was not meant to be a trap, though it nearly turned into one. I'm not angry. In truth, you saved me another fight. You were right to come for me."

He went silent again, his heavy beard and wild hair giving his face a dark, looming quality in spite of the bright moonlight. When he did not smile along with his approval, Claerwen sensed his tacit regard of the red-haired woman indicated a well-burrowed secret. She studied his face, searching for the person he truly was behind the dusky appearance and found he had closed himself to her, expecting her to trust his judgement.

"Who is she?" Claerwen asked bluntly.

"I can't say," Marcus answered with equal bluntness.

He had worded his answer the way he always did to avoid lying. Her brow pinched together, showing her frustration, then she turned for the glen, exhaling roughly, "We should go, before Girvyn notices we're gone."

He laid a hand on her shoulder, stopping her. "I am too accustomed to working alone. I'm not trying to hurt you."

Hiding the pang of loneliness she felt, she faced him and said, "I know."

Disappointed, she turned and started once more for the smithy, this time letting him follow.

———————

A new storm, charging in from the sea in the early morning hours, abruptly curtained the clear night and covered the mud and slush with a fresh layer of snow. Marcus watched large flakes swirl in the lantern light just beyond the edge of the smithy's porch roof while he hammered a bolt latch into shape. After only a few hours of sleep, he had risen again to help Girvyn make them, enough for all the barrack doors.

By midday, the snow was nearly ankle deep and still falling. Few people were about, and when Marcus and Claerwen reached the fort, they were left undisturbed. Working with cold-numbed fingers, they installed a latch on the door they had hung the day before, then completed the next chamber's repairs.

At dusk, they fitted the second room's door into its frame. As they finished and packed away their tools, Pascentius emerged from behind the great hall, alone and stepping high through now mid-calf deep snow. His long Roman cloak dragged behind him, and he paused at the hall's steps to watch one of his men light torches.

As the guard withdrew, Banawr threw open one of the hall doors. It slammed back and bounced forward again, quivering awkwardly on leather hinges pegged to a rotting timber frame. Pascentius glared in obvious dislike of his second-in-command, who glowered in return, shaking a sheathed sword in his left hand.

"This is the best you have for me?" Banawr demanded.

Pascentius sighed harshly. "If you hadn't annoyed the blacksmith with your foul temper, perhaps you'd still have your own sword." He muttered the name "fool" as he turned around, no longer desiring to go into the hall.

"It's his fault!"

Pascentius paused, drawing a long breath to temper his own annoyance. Behind him, Banawr stalked down the steps, his eyes locked on the barracks.

"Get back here," Pascentius warned. He lunged, grabbing

Banawr's arm, and whispered tightly in his ear, "If you weren't so deeply involved in this, I'd gladly let him tear you up, and believe me, he can do it. Stop acting like a barbarian."

"You need me more than you need him," Banawr hissed and wrenched his arm free. He stripped the sword of its sheath and plodded across the courtyard, each foot sinking into the snow.

"Don't be so sure of yourself," Pascentius countered. Then, being ignored, he shouted, "Banawr! He did not disobey you because you have no authority over that man! Now get back here or you'll be put under house arrest!"

Not taking his eyes off the encounter, Marcus reached out towards Claerwen, asking for his sword. He heard her whisper to be careful as he freed the weapon from its scabbard, and he stepped out into the yard. Moving casually as if merely going out to talk with an acquaintance, he stopped midway with his left eyebrow perked upward.

Banawr seethed, annoyed that Marcus never broke into anger. "Fight me, you arrogant bastard. I know you want to."

Mild amusement showed in Marcus' eyes, and he splayed his left hand out questioningly. "I don't need to fight you."

"Bah!" Banawr ejected, then taunted, "I'm going to take your woman."

"Ah, I wouldn't try it," Marcus said benignly. "Should you manage to kill me, she'll fill you full of her arrows, and I can guess where she'll select her first target, if you understand me…" He heard Claerwen come from behind him, halting to his left, her bow creaking as she drew. Following his suggestion, she aimed a steel arrowhead at the second's groin.

Banawr's taunt earned him a completely different answer than expected, and his face flushed deep red. He could find nothing to say that would break through this hardheaded man's calm. Finally, he choked down the fear that threatened to undermine his rage and he yanked his sword back, hoping his jealousy and anger would bring him strength, cunning and victory.

Marcus sensed the change in Banawr instantly. In one lean motion, he swerved to his right, drawing the attack away from Claerwen. Banawr's blade arced around, narrowly missing.

Marcus turned, his weapon sweeping with momentum, and caught Banawr's sword edge at the end of its swing. He rammed the blades down, the tips crossing as they sliced through the snow and into the earth. Tightening his grip, Marcus used his sword for balance, vaulting up, and with one heel, he struck a hard kick high into Banawr's chest. The man flew backward, carving a deep furrow through the snow.

Banawr lay groaning, curled up on his side, his hands locked onto his shoulder. Pascentius strode to him and knelt, trying to assess the injury, but Banawr whined in pain, refusing to let him pull his hands down. Grunting in disgust, Pascentius shouted imperiously for a pair of guards and instructed them to hold the second in his quarters until further notice. They carried him away on a litter.

Pascentius turned back to Marcus and declared, "You injured my man."

Marcus took his scabbard and a rag from Claerwen, calmly wiped his sword clean and sheathed it, then held Banawr's weapon by its blade, offering the hilt to Pascentius. He said, "I broke his clavis bone."

Scornful of the proffered sword, Pascentius queried, "This was deliberate?"

"Aye," Marcus responded with blandness.

Oddly, Pascentius' reaction was quite passive. He directed, "When your work is done for today, we will speak, blacksmith. The first house, to the left, directly behind the hall, there." He pointed at a square building showing just past the great hall.

Marcus nodded and said, 'I am finished now."

The Romanized soldier turned and strode back across the courtyard. Marcus squinted at Claerwen, silently telling her to put up the bow and follow.

Pascentius marched up the steps of his house, stomping snow off his boots at the top. He pushed through the door, pausing for Marcus to come in, then saw Claerwen trailing up the steps after him. He snapped, "She stays outside. What I have to say is private. Close the door."

Marcus scowled, but Claerwen complied, backing away.

Pascentius passed through an anteroom and entered a central common room. Chambers opened from it, giving Marcus the impression the house was a compacted version of a Roman villa in the south. It was sparsely furnished in typical soldier's simplicity, and other than the great hall, was the only building within the fort on a raised foundation. Marcus halted just inside the inner doorway, letting his eyes grimly follow the Roman across the room.

Pascentius perched on the edge of a table, resting one foot on a chair seat. "If this works out, we both get what we want," he said and leveled a glare.

Marcus leaned in the doorway and drawled, "What is it you think I want?"

"Something better than smithing the rest of your life. Something better than drudging for someone else. We both know you could do more."

Smirking, Marcus replied, "Smithing is all I know. Why should I want more than that?"

"Oh, come now, we both know you're a warrior. No one disarms another like you've done. Sure, Banawr is a fool, I've known that since he first came to my camp. But I have my uses for him. I want to see how good you really are, Bhruic. You're built like a warrior and you think like a warrior. You command a presence Banawr couldn't ever dream of doing."

"You flatter too much and I have work to do. What do you want?"

"All business, aren't you, blacksmith?" Pascentius grumbled. "So be it. I have something different for you to do. But I need to learn something further."

Impatience filled Marcus' face, and he said, "In truth, you want to know whose side I'm on. If you can trust me. And what my price is."

Pascentius shifted uncomfortably under the assessment.

Marcus continued, "You want to use me, as you had planned to use Banawr, but you're hoping I won't give you the trouble he does — "

"I need a swordmaster," Pascentius interrupted. "I need one

now that the fool is injured, though it's probably just as well that he is."

"The contingent of men you have here now is only a token force. Your true warriors are disbursed for the winter and you won't need someone to train them until they come back in the spring...if they come back." Marcus moved from the doorway to a place behind a low, Roman-style chair, gripping its back with both hands and leaning on it. "Why would I be so useful to you now?"

Pascentius chewed on his lower lip, locking eyes with Marcus. "You know who I am, don't you?"

Marcus gave no flinch, no indication of surprise at the question. "You are called 'the commander,' and you know who I am as well," he answered without hesitation, then dipped his head towards the door, adding, "I gather that all this nonsense about smithing and swordsmanship is for their benefit?"

Pascentius smiled wryly in acknowledgment and said, "They are as stupid as dirt, everyone of them. But ignorance can be very useful, no?"

Marcus returned the smile, deliberately full of slyness, contempt and cynicism, satisfied that Pascentius was the only one who knew his identity and that Banawr and the other mercenaries were dupes, promised a grand future just as Engres and his people had been. He responded gruffly, "Get to the point."

"Octa will become an enormous problem to you."

"Because I sabotaged his camp instead of falling into his trap? You're warning me that he will seek revenge? I already know that."

"Aye, but he will also be my problem. He has ties to the Picts and will raise a war band with them against me."

"How ironic. Your father and his father created an alliance to fight together against the Picts. Now Octa is allied with them. What do you want from me?"

Pascentius glared, annoyed by Marcus' directness. He answered, "A trade for your services."

"My price is too high for you."

"Not for this. I know that Octa is planning to strike on the southern coast. I know where and when. I will give you Octa's head. In exchange, you will bring me the high king's."

That was a blatant bluff, Marcus mused, seriously doubting the commander truly knew anything of Octa's military activities. He had expected to be forced into the position of Ambrosius' assassin, with Claerwen and Dinas Beris as a guarantee against his unwillingness. It was why he had deliberately injured Banawr, to take the suspected assassin's place and twist the trap back onto Pascentius. And Pascentius had to know he would never agree to such a proposal, unless the commander was as stupid as his mercenaries. Waiting for the extortion, he kept a straight face and dug, "The powerless son of a dead Saxon leader, for a high king? No."

One eyebrow rose on Pascentius' face. "Octa will hound you eventually, and you will need to give attention to that, sooner or later, regardless of me. This trade would certainly be to your advantage."

Marcus released his grip on the chair, then pulled it next to the hearth and sat. Scratching at his beard, he gave the appearance that he was thinking seriously on the proposition. He watched as Pascentius walked to a tall, narrow table along the wall and poured two cups of wine from a pewter pitcher, offering one to Marcus. "We have not agreed on anything yet," Marcus reminded him, but took the cup.

Anger rose in Pascentius' face, reddening it, giving Marcus a fair gauge as to how desperate he was becoming. The commander rasped, "You are rather presumptuous, aren't you? If you think this is a bluff and you cross me, I will personally feed you to Octa. He will be well pleased to take you off my hands. And perhaps that pretty one you've been calling a slave as well?"

Marcus' eyes went cold as he banged the cup down on the hearthstones, slopping wine over the rim. "If you want my services, it will cost you more than Octa's head!"

"Cost?" Pascentius shot back. "It will cost you your wife and your lands if you don't — "

Marcus suddenly started laughing, "You Romans are so bloody predictable. Have you even thought of asking whether I have a good reason to want Ambrosius off the throne myself?"

"You jest," Pascentius accused sarcastically, returning to the table he liked to sit on.

Marcus' eyes narrowed, reverting to his cold stare. Letting rage rise to the surface of his face, his mouth twisted bitterly. He stalled, giving Pascentius time to realize the full effect of his expression, then said in a low, dangerous voice, "He has crossed me."

The Roman clearly did not believe him, ejecting a raw expletive.

Marcus leaned forward in the chair and hissed, "What do you know of *Y Gwalch Haearn*, the Iron Hawk?"

The arrogance on Pascentius' face froze, and he rose from the table as if a dog had bit him from behind. "What of him?" he ejected.

"Say it."

Pascentius found himself breathing with difficulty as he recalled an event from the past. He drank deeply from his wine and actually paled as he thought, fear claiming his face. Then, as if forgetting he faced one of his most mistrusted and dangerous enemies, he confided, "When my father was still alive, I was traveling with a small party of soldiers, marching to join his camp the next day. We were well hidden for the night. While we slept, the warrior came. No guard cried out an alarm. I never saw him, or heard him. But when I awoke at daybreak, the heads of all my men were struck onto the ends of tree branches, in a circle around me, each staring with those...dead eyes. A small banner with a black hawk on it was left behind. When I reached my father's camp, I showed it to him, told him what had happened. He identified the Iron Hawk's symbol. My father was very superstitious and greatly feared the Iron Hawk. He believed it was a portent and withdrew his plans to invade the kingdom of Cornwall. But I still don't understand why I alone was left alive."

"It was a warning. To your father. You were the messenger," Marcus said, his face hard and tight. "Such has happened in Caernarfon and other places over the years."

"I have heard rumors of worse atrocities."

"They are probably true."

Wariness filled Pascentius' face. "What are you suggesting? What does this have to do with Ambrosius?"

"Ambrosius is allied with the Iron Hawk."

Pascentius nearly sat down again, his mouth dropping open, clamping shut, then opening again. "This is nonsense!" he blurted. "The Iron Hawk is more elusive than vapors. He is allied with no one."

Marcus slowly shook his head, the hatred showing in his eyes again. He lied, "Ambrosius paid the warrior to destroy Dinas Beris, to take it from your father's people who occupied it at the time. He nearly succeeded. He also nearly killed my wife in the destruction he wreaked."

"That's not what I heard. It was said the Iron Hawk rescued your lands, for you. Why would Ambrosius want Dinas Beris?"

"Because it lies adjacent to his stronghold of Dinas Brenin, or Dinas Emrys, as he calls it now. He wants to join them into one *cantref*, what we call a type of political region of one hundred homesteads. The strategic value is obvious. What you heard was a lie fabricated by the king."

Marcus paused, picking up his cup, and fiercely scowled into it. He rose and refilled it. Returning to the chair, he studied the red liquid as he swirled it around. He liked the taste of the drink. It was grape wine, not mead, and probably had been imported from Gaul to satisfy the Roman's need to stay Roman. He looked up at Pascentius and said, "Aye...I will do as you propose, and you will bring me Octa in return, not later than the holiday of *Imbolc*. But be warned, should *Y Gwalch Haearn* learn of this, either you, or I, or both of us could be delivered to the Otherworld more assuredly than piss in the latrine pit." He quaffed the cup down.

The Roman paced imperiously around the room, considering the warning, trying to hide his growing uneasiness as Marcus' brooding eyes followed him. Thoughts ticked away behind the commander's stony face, reckoning the possibilities.

Marcus silently reviewed the offer. He needed Pascentius to believe this was not a bluff. By itself, the proposed trade of Octa for Ambrosius was ludicrous. But Pascentius was weak willed and growing desperate as his alliances had dissolved, one by one, each time he abandoned a battle. By implying the threat of the Iron Hawk's interference, Marcus gained important leverage in convincing the commander his agreement was legitimate, strengthened further by the possibility that he wanted revenge on Ambrosius, his most important ally.

"How soon are you looking to have this done?" Marcus interrupted Pascentius' thoughts.

"Not until after Midwinter."

"So long?" Marcus observed, putting his feet up on the fire pit's hearthstones. He absently fingered the talons hanging from his hair, purposely annoying the commander with their ugliness. "I could use a more private place to live while I have to wait."

Pascentius moved across to fill his cup again, then Marcus'. "There is a small house in the back of the fort that is empty. You can have that. We will call you the new swordmaster, just for the benefit of the mercenaries' ignorance." He paused, irritated by the request and that he had granted it so easily, then asked, "Do I gather we have an agreement?"

"Why do you think I let you draw me into this childish scheme of yours? I didn't need to follow your trail. I knew it was a sham from the beginning. But I knew you could be useful as well."

"And how do I know you won't take the crown for yourself?"

"Kingship is for those who like the fame of it. It's not for me."

"That's hard to believe."

"No more than the idea of you as high king." Marcus drank down the entire contents of his cup in one gulp, smacked it down again, and grinned arrogantly. "Aye, we have an agreement. And *you* know better than to cross me."

Pascentius paused in the middle of lifting his cup again and met the cold black eyes of his new partner. He knew Marcus ap Iorwerth was by far not the most powerful man in Britain, but his range of influence could be devastating when it came to sabotage. Grunting, the commander lifted the cup the rest of the way and drank it empty, then poured more for both.

Their talk continued, mostly about swordplay. Pascentius appeared genuinely interested to learn more details of Marcus' skills, including how he had disarmed Banawr so easily. Tempered by a continuous flow of wine, and using jokes and nonsense comments meant to foment trust and goodwill, Marcus further persuaded Pascentius that their agreement was ideal.

After nearly an hour of steady drinking, Pascentius passed out, his cup falling to the floor. Marcus abruptly stopped his chatter. Leaning forward, he toed the commander's leg, making certain the man was unconscious. Slowly, he placed his cup on the hearthstones and pushed himself out of his chair, shaking his head to clear it.

Taking a deep breath, he began moving from room to room, searching each one. Most were empty or used for storage. Two were bedchambers, one for Pascentius and another probably meant for guests. Only one door was locked, and Marcus picked it open with a small dagger. There he discovered a tiny, windowless room with a table placed in the center. Piled on another, smaller table at the back wall, were several rolls of parchment, each tied with twine. One roll, set a little aside from the others, was loose, and he spread it open. On a map of Britain lay the detailed plans for the failed invasion at Caer Ebrauc, including the locations of Octa's camp in Brynaich and the landing on the eastern coast.

Marcus squinted an indignant grimace through the doorway at Pascentius. Then he folded the map into a tiny square and tucked it under his tunic. He opened the other rolls, searching each for clues of future escapades. There were many more maps and contingency ideas, all of which, according to the scratchings marked across them, looked as if they had been scrapped. Apparently the plans he and Claerwen had foiled in Brynaich and Caer Ebrauc had been the only ones to come close to reality thus far. He nodded to himself, pleased with his discovery, but he was disappointed as well, knowing the plot for which he had just laid himself as bait was not among these. And, he wondered, where had Macsen's spearhead been hidden?

Marcus stacked the parchments on the small table as he had found them and locked the door. Leaning on the wall for several moments, he rubbed his eyes and shook his head again, the effects of the wine chewing at his self-control.

Exhaling roughly, he started across the common room. For a moment he paused, watching Pascentius snore in his drunken stupor. Marcus saluted formally, in the Roman style, then strode for the door.

# Chapter 12

### Alba

Claerwen brushed snow from the top step of Pascentius' house, making herself a place to huddle in the doorway's corner. After working with cold, wet metal, wood and stone, she stuffed her red and aching hands inside her sleeves for warmth. She leaned against the door, listening for the two men's voices, but only heard an unintelligible droning. Disappointed, she intended to study the fort's occupants instead, but few were out in the cold, driving wind, and they soon disappeared into the great hall. She leaned against the door and waited.

"You have beautiful eyes, Lady."

The voice and the comment startled Claerwen. She had seen no one approach then realized someone stood next to the steps, his head barely reaching to the top one. The face startled her even more. A boy of about seven summers looked up at her with very dark eyes full of earnest sincerity. An endless swath of ragged kerchiefs covered his head, neck and shoulders.

Claerwen had to smile. "Why, thank you very much indeed, young man. And what is your name?"

"I am Sinnoch," he answered. "Are you cold, Lady?"

"No, I'm accustomed to it."

"Why are you here?" the boy asked, climbing up beside her. He was poorly dressed in worn leathers that had been made over from larger garments.

"I'm waiting for my master," she answered.

"Is he in trouble?" A flash of fear crossed the boy's face.

"Trouble? No, why?"

"No one goes inside the commander's house unless they're in trouble. He's mean. I don't like him."

Claerwen laughed and said, "He does seem rather nasty, doesn't he?"

"Aye," the boy replied, then grinned a wide, toothy smile as he studied Claerwen's face.

"Why are you out here all by yourself in this cold wind, Sinnoch? You should be at your hearth, with your mother and father." She watched his smile dim and turn into an unexpected grimness that should have belonged to an old man. Alarmed, Claerwen touched his arm. "Sinnoch? I'm sorry — "

He smiled again and cut her off, "No matter, Lady. I should go now." But he remained seated and thoughtfully picked at the frayed hem of a cloth tunic showing between the layers of leather.

Claerwen sensed a troublesome loneliness that ached in the boy as much as any wound to the flesh. Sitting with her seemed to bring him comfort, and she found herself studying what she could see of his face, downturned, snowflakes catching and melting on his lowered lashes, his wide cheeks red with the cold.

Finally he looked up again and asked, "You said you wait for your master, Lady. Are you a slave?"

"Aye, that I am. My master is a blacksmith. He's been helping Master Girvyn, you know Master Girvyn, don't you?"

The boy nodded and said, "He lets me watch him work sometimes."

"I think the commander may give my master more work to do."

"Then perhaps I shall see you again." Sinnoch's eyes brightened.

"That would be very pleasant indeed."

"Then you are my new friend, Lady. What is your name?"

"I am called Glân."

"Lady Glân," Sinnoch repeated the name, memorizing it.

Claerwen smiled at the inappropriate title he gave her and she teased, "That's the first time anyone's called me a lady. But, it's rather nice."

The boy gazed up at her with guileless eyes. "You should be a lady. You look like a princess to me," he said and laid a small hand in hers.

Claerwen was astonished. Even at home she never thought of herself as a princess, though she had carried the title since she had married. Like Marcus, she mostly ignored her rank because it held no power, and her life, like his, had been filled with hardships and hard work and the acceptance of both. Unsure what to say, she smiled and squeezed Sinnoch's hand, but he still waited patiently for a reply.

Behind her, the door suddenly wrenched open and the boy's eyes jerked upward. For a few moments of startled apprehension, Sinnoch stared. Then he leapt, arcing over the side of the steps. He dashed away towards the rear of the fort.

Marcus leaned in the doorway, his face deeply flushed, and his eyes vaguely followed the boy. He gulped in cold, fresh air. Claerwen stood, stunned by his forced expression, and he gripped her shoulder for support. He muttered, "Don't say anything, just get me away from here."

Her eyes searched his face, at first thinking he was hiding a serious wound, then she smelled the sharp odor of alcohol on his breath. She backed down the steps, towing him along. Once on level ground, he straightened up and walked almost normally as they crossed the courtyard and passed through the gates.

Halfway across the glen, he said, "If Girvyn asks, just tell him I'm drunk...which I am. I can't fight it off much longer."

"If you're this bad, I'd hate to see the commander," she muttered in his ear.

Marcus laughed impulsively, then doggedly regained control of himself. He slowed, then spoke quietly with a sudden soberness, "We will move into the fort on the morrow. Now that Banawr is injured, I've been made swordmaster, among 'other' duties, which you can guess."

"And then you drank him onto the floor?"

"Absolutely," he said almost proudly, swaying, tightening his hand on her shoulder to steady himself. He asked, "Who was the boy?"

Claerwen smiled, remembering the conversation, and replied, "I don't know. He wouldn't talk about his family or home. He was suddenly there and gone just as quickly. In truth, he's quite a charmer…"

Marcus halted. His hand dropped from her shoulder and gripped her wrist. He dragged in a long breath, willing his nerve against the wine, then looked seriously into her eyes. "Be careful, children can tell you a lot, but they can be very dangerous as well if they accidentally repeat the wrong thing to the wrong person."

Claerwen's eyes fell and she nodded, understanding what he meant. When she did not look up again, he knew she was thinking of the child she had miscarried and the resulting barrenness. He touched her wrist again and asked, "He's already gotten to you, hasn't he?"

"Oh, I'm just being dull-witted." She waved a hand as if to clear the air of her own thoughts, then swiped at her cheeks as she turned and started again for the smithy.

"Wait," Marcus called, and he pulled her around. Nearly losing his balance, he planted his feet wide and clamped a hand on her shoulder again. When his eyes came back into focus, he found no sign of tears in her eyes, but his face softened, reflecting his empathy. As a distraction, he took the folded parchment from under his tunic and passed it into her palm, curled her fingers around it. He said, "I want you to hide this on you. It's a map. Never lose it, never show it to anyone unless I tell you when and to whom. The only exceptions are Myrddin or Ambrosius. If something happens to me, go to them. Do you understand?"

She held her breath, still fighting off the tears, and nodded.

"Good. I can see Girvyn from here, still at the forge. We'll go around the back."

They flanked the smithy, turning towards the rear door. In the dark, the snow-covered turf looked flat and smooth, and Marcus, slowly drifting into a deeper disorientation, misjudged the possibility of ice underneath the surface. He turned his head, intending to say something, and felt his right foot give, sliding away.

Claerwen grabbed for him, but her footing found the same patch of hidden ice and she lost her balance, knocking into him. With flailing arms and muffled grunts, they fell.

Marcus landed on his back. Slowly, he lifted his head and shook it roughly in the attempt to clear his hazy mind. Snow thickly covered his hair and beard, and it scattered as he moved. Then he realized Claerwen was pushing herself up, sitting on him, trying to dump snow out of her sleeves.

"Sorry," he mumbled, then heard a giggle escape her. "Are you all right?" he asked.

She whispered, teasing, "You should see yourself, my Lord Bhruic."

He laughed, "I know, I'm a lout and there is no remedy for such as me — "

Giving in to a sudden impulse, Claerwen hushed him with a kiss. The sound of his laughter and voice were almost normal for that moment, and she only wanted to prolong it before he gained control again, even if he was drunk, even if it risked an admonition. In reward, his arms went around her, and he pulled her down, clutching her tightly and rolling over, his mouth groping for hers and finding it. He kissed her, passionately warm and comfortable, familiar. She would have lain there all night, oblivious to the snow soaking through her clothing, just to have those few moments of his affection.

But gradually, as she expected, the gruff voice returned and the frowning crudeness crept once more into his face like a dark cloud of discontent, and he drew back. Kneeling over her, he looked as if standing would take too much effort.

Claerwen pushed up onto her elbows and asked, "How much did you drink?"

Blinking a few times, he tried to focus on her, still determined to hold control. He started to answer, but the words slurred, and he grunted, tried again. "You don't want to know," he muttered, "You truly...don't want to know. Damn, I have to piss." He lurched onto his feet then, and tromped across the few yards into the trees.

Claerwen exhaled tiredly and pulled herself onto her feet. She entered her side of the smithy, lit the lantern in her chamber. Moments later, Marcus followed. He staggered to the mat, dropping onto it.

She knew he would pass out soon. Kneeling, she began to pull off his boots. From out in front, she heard Girvyn set down his hammer and tongs on the anvil then enter his side of the building. His steps paced through and he thrust aside the leather curtain between the rooms. With one sweep of his eyes, he took in Marcus swaying on the mat and Claerwen shivering in wet clothes.

"What did he do to you?" Girvyn asked in a quiet but urgent voice. "Is he drunk again?"

"Oh, don't worry about him, this is normal."

"He does this a lot?"

She smiled innocently at Girvyn then glanced down at her wet clothing. "I just slipped on some ice."

Girvyn grunted and began to withdraw, but Marcus suddenly called out. With his voice fading, he said, "In the morning, the woman and I will move into the fort. The commander has ordered it." Through hazy eyes, he watched Girvyn's jaw drop and Claerwen start in astonishment.

Girvyn blurted, "And you accepted? You hate those people as much as I do! What did he do, buy you?" He swore a long string of oaths then concluded with, "I thought you were one of those rare ones who can't be ordered around or bought by traitors like them."

Marcus shot a hand out and grabbed Girvyn's arm to gain his attention. "Listen to me." He tightened his grip when the big man refused to calm. Drawing upon his iron will, he spoke with authority, "Listen to me! I tell you this once, only once, and you will understand. You will never repeat this to anyone." He paused again until he was sure Girvyn was listening and, gathering the last of his self-control, he whispered, "Sabotage."

Girvyn clamped his jaw shut. He glared into Marcus' face then slowly began to grin. "I thought there was more to you than horseshoes and hinges. I don't know who you are, but I will say nothing. You have my word…and my sympathy." He disappeared into his chamber.

Marcus closed his eyes and mumbled, "Good, now I can let go." He fell back, flat on the mat.

Claerwen sighed with relief and shook her head. She said softly, smiling, "Aye, and there is no remedy for such as you."

———————

Sometime before dawn, Marcus woke again, jolting upright. First he felt dizzy, then the headache started. Looking around, he realized he was on the wall side of the bed, still in his clothes, and that Claerwen must have pushed or rolled him there. She slept in his place, his sword ready by her hand, and he smiled wryly at both the incongruity of her delicate looks next to the deadly weapon, and the irony that although she was strong and had nearly the endurance of a man, she was no swordsman. Groaning softly, he climbed over her and out of the bed.

Claerwen woke as he shook the mat, and she watched as he leaned over a pail, pouring cold water on his head from a waterskin. His eyes slid towards her and he muttered, "*Pen mawr.*"

"I will make the willow bark drink," she said, smiling, and pulled on a shift.

"Thank you," he breathed, wiping his hair back from his face, still hanging over the pail.

Shortly she returned with a small iron pot of hot water. Measuring bark into her palm, she crushed it between her fingers and dropped it into the pot. Within minutes it was ready. He drank it quickly then rinsed his mouth with fresh water.

A short time later they had packed only the most essential items of their gear, leaving the rest neatly piled on the mat. Before Girvyn woke, they left for the fort, crossing the glen.

A small house of dubious quality was assigned to them, but of all the empty houses, it was the best. Situated near the rear wall, it was close to the postern gate and had a window that opened to view both the gate and a long section of the adjacent wall. Marcus was pleased. The house was in poor repair and filthy, but until Pascentius was ready to execute his plans, they would give the impression of waiting patiently and make the house livable enough.

A fortnight passed uneventfully as winter came into fullness. Repairs to the house were completed, and work continued on the barracks. Marcus knew the two-sided bluff was only meant to keep him in the camp. There was another purpose awaiting him, one Pascentius hid with the greatest of care, and the more Marcus pried, the more carefully he was watched.

Of Banawr, Marcus neither saw nor heard anything more. He suspected the second had been sent home or at least moved somewhere out of the fort, preventing him from causing more trouble. The whereabouts of Macsen's spearhead remained unknown. Frustrated, Marcus was forced to wait.

In the evening, two days before Midwinter, Marcus brooded before the house's fire pit, his feet resting on the hearthstones. Irritated that another day had been unproductive, he rose and padded across to the window. Seeking fresh air, he opened the shutters and gazed for several moments along the wall towards the postern gate.

Shutting the window again, he asked Claerwen, "Is there any of the cider left that Girvyn brought us?"

She was stacking bricks of dried peat neatly in a corner and answered, "There's only a little there. Help yourself to it."

"This is nearly full," he countered, picking up a large ceramic jug from the casement. "Do that later and come here." He sat on the table's corner and poured two cupfuls, setting one down for her.

Claerwen came towards the table, then stopped, staring at the waiting cup. The word "full" stuck in her mind. Why full? She was certain the jug had been nearly empty.

A sharp pain suddenly filled her head and she closed her eyes. The cloudy veil that flowed within her mind, closing off the visions, dissipated. Streaks of red flashed across her sight, twisting and curling, flashing, searing with pain. The streaks buckled, forming into a figure she could not quite recognize. Smoke plumed across and behind, swirling, churning, choking. For an instant, she thought the figure was a dragon, a red dragon, lying on a bed of stone. It disappeared in the smoke.

The vision vanished as suddenly as it had struck; the curtain of mist closed again. When her normal sight returned, her eyes focused on Marcus, his cup at his lips.

"NO!" she shrieked, jolting him. Diving, her fist squarely punched the cup out of his grip. It cracked against the wall next to him, shattering, the fluid splashing down, running to soak into the earthen floor.

Claerwen fell onto her hands and knees and watched the wet patch of whitewash slowly turn black. "Marcus..." she said his real name without thinking, "...it was meant for me."

He watched the blackened whitewash begin to smolder. Wispy smoke floated outward then faded away, leaving behind a cracked surface on the wall. When he realized she had just seen a warning that had saved both their lives, he slipped off the table and sank onto the floor. Pulling her into his arms, he spoke soft, comforting words.

Then gripping his arm, Claerwen whispered, "It's that perfume again."

Marcus muttered an expletive. Getting to his feet, he said, "I must go out. Stay here, be sure the door and the shutters are locked. Don't answer to anyone except me."

She rose, following as he moved to retrieve his sword. "What are you going to do? Where will you — "

He pressed his fingers to her lips, hushing her. "Not a sound, no light, just bolt the door after me. I won't be long." He tentatively took his fingers away, communicating with his eyes that he must go and she must wait for him. He snatched up his sword and swept out the door.

# Chapter 13

### Alba

Marcus moved swiftly along the rear wall. Heading for the postern gate, he intended to search the red-haired woman's farmstead. The night was especially dark, overcast with a heavy mist, and once outside the compound's dim light, negotiating the forest would be difficult. Undaunted, he was certain of finding the way.

Coming within yards of the gate, he heard the surrounding debris rustle. He halted, cramming himself between a pair of beams, and watched it open. A figure slipped inside, striding along the wall away from him, moving towards the barracks.

Marcus recognized the red-haired woman's flowing mane and was pleased with his luck. He scanned across the ramparts, noting the guards' usual lack of attention. Most of them gambled in a small knot by the front gates. Grinning at the results of Banawr's training, he followed the woman.

Approaching the barracks cautiously, Marcus saw her enter the first chamber. Pascentius arrived moments later and entered as well, closing the door. Marcus pressed against the chamber's wall and listened through the chinks between the stones.

"How much longer must we wait? I can't bear this hovel another day," whined the woman's voice from inside.

Pascentius sighed tiredly. "You can't bear a lot of things, Daracha. Hold that bitter tongue of yours and be patient. Now that we've got him in the position we want, the rest will come easily in a few days. Have you seen to his woman?"

"Aye, if she's taken that cider."

"Cider? Why cider? What if he drinks it by mistake?"

"You want him out of your way, don't you?"

"Not before I'm done with him. I still can't guess why he'd drag a woman with him, especially his wife."

Daracha huffed, "That man is the coldest man I've ever known. She must be no different — she proved that when she killed my kinsman Drakar. They both deserve a fitting punishment."

"I understand why you want vengeance on her, but the only thing he ever did to you was seduce your half-sister, instead of you, and that was a long time ago. Can't you leave it be?"

"He was Drakar's mortal enemy and hounded him for years, remember? No, I cannot leave it be. You want him strangled in this plot of yours, and I want my revenge. We both get what we want."

Pascentius warned, "If you do anything, anything whatsoever, so that he does not fulfill the purpose intended, I'll personally see that you rot in some dismal, cold place with none but the company of rats that will feed on you."

Pascentius stalked out of the barracks, passing within a few feet of Marcus, invisible in the shadows. Several minutes later, the woman stood in the open doorway, holding a dimly glowing lantern. She adjusted her cloak, preparing to return to the postern gate.

"Looking for me?" Marcus called flatly, suddenly before her. He pushed forward, forcing her back inside, and kicked the door shut.

"You!" she reacted.

"Aye, me. It's been a long time, Daracha." He kept his voice low and even, letting it take on a natural rhythm that was at once soothing and threatening. Hoping she would match his tone, he meant to inspire her into keeping her voice low as well, guessing she would be adamantly against Pascentius learning of a confrontation.

Standing close, she was as tall as he was and glared on an even level with him with wide grey eyes that tilted up at their outer corners.

"And you still use that bloody awful perfume," he remarked as the scent radiated on the heat of her skin. He winced as if his eyes were about to water.

Her eyes turned hard at the implied insult, and with one swift motion, she swung the lantern at his face.

Marcus dodged, knocking it from her hand. It clattered to the floor, oddly still upright and burning. He caught her wrist, twisting her arm down. Barely audible, he asked, "Now why would you want to do that when you need me so badly?"

"The only thing I want from you is your severed head," she fumed.

"You heard the 'commander.' You won't get what you want without me."

"Let go," she moaned, trying to pull her arm out of his iron grip.

"Not until you give me what *I* want. Be calm, then perhaps I'll release you."

Daracha's arm ached, her hand tingling for lack of circulation, but she continued to struggle. "What could you possibly want from me?" she snarled.

"Does Pascentius have Macsen's spearhead?" he asked pointedly.

Daracha abruptly stalled. "Macsen's spearhead? What are you talking about? What makes you think he has part of Macsen's Treasure?"

He watched her face, trying to determine if her ignorance was real or a practiced bluff. Ignoring her question, he asked, "Does he?"

"I don't have to tell you anything. Ah, you're hurting me."

He released her arm and let her move out of his reach. "You haven't answered me," he prodded, taking a step in her direction.

She rubbed her bruised wrist. "I don't have an answer for you. I don't know. Leave me alone." She reached for the door, but he blocked it.

"Does Pascentius know what you do with Banawr?" he asked, arrogance coming into his voice as he worked the loose link he knew would unravel her mental armor. As her eyes narrowed, he continued, "If he would know, he just might boot you out of his camp, his life, his whole scheme which — I'd be quite certain — you are rather desperate to be a part of. Am I right?"

She gave no answer, but rage pounded in her temples.

He added, "What would he think of his woman bedding down a wretch like Banawr? A possible future high queen of Britain?" He smirked and went on, "I think not. He is certainly no man of virtue himself, but his queen would have to be without fault to be accepted by the people. But you should know how he thinks by now, no?"

Daracha clenched her fists and shot back, "Banawr's a diversion. Pascentius is always too busy."

Marcus grinned sardonically and leaned casually on the door. "Diversions are the things that make nations crumble. Such as we see happening to Rome."

His relaxed stance eroded Daracha's anger a notch, giving rise to her curiosity. Unable to resist a game of wordplay, she said, "They can also be the foundation of a new nation. Like those that have been abandoned by Rome's tyranny. You, master of spies, should know about diversions."

"I, madam?"

Daracha laughed scornfully. She approached him, her steps slightly swaggering. "Don't tell me you've forgotten after all these years."

"Forgotten what? That you are a camp follower?"

Daracha's mouth snapped shut at the insult. Her anger gave her heat, and she loosened her cloak in spite of the cold night air. Then she took the challenge, holding herself up before him proudly. Locking eyes, she spat out, "I am a lady of noble birth, not a camp follower."

Marcus saw that Daracha's gown was loose far down from the neck and she wore no undershift. He surmised she had been expecting to spend the night with Pascentius and therefore had not bothered to dress properly. "You could have fooled me," he jabbed back.

"Nothing fools you," she hissed. "Nothing ever has. For that, I could even admire you."

Marcus laughed, short and harsh. "Must be my inherent honesty."

"You mock me."

"Ah, so be it, Daracha, and what will it be? You tell me what you know about Macsen's spearhead? Or do I tell Pascentius about Banawr, then disappear and let you feel his wrath for having spoiled his plans?"

He watched her features manipulate into a convincing display of earnestness, well aware that she knew what he was capable of, that extortion was one of his specialties along with his maddening disguises. He was certain she would choose a bluff to keep him there even if she truly had no information, because she dared not risk losing her alliance with Pascentius.

She said, "I don't know anything about the spearhead. He has not spoken to me about it, and I have not heard him say anything to anyone else."

Marcus paced around her, absently smoothing his beard, considering her answer, watching her eyes follow him. He sensed a new ploy coming. Before she could speak, he disarmed her by asking, "Will Pascentius marry you?"

She stared at him, not expecting such a question.

"You said you are of noble birth," he prompted.

"What do you care?"

"What if he decides not to marry you? Or if he does, and he does not succeed in taking the kingship, what will you do?"

She stalled, unable to decide if he was merely fishing or was going to make an offer. She knew he would never give up digging with his questions, considering how tenacious he could be. Leveling her eyes, she took the risk, suddenly smiling, "You have a suggestion for me?" She moved forward, letting the cloak slide farther back on her shoulders. "You are a dangerous man, Lord Marcus."

"And due to that, you think I'm fascinating?" Marcus played

on her flattery, but folded his arms like a block to her presence.

Daracha leaned towards him, resting her left hand on his arm. She lowered her lashes and peered coyly through them. She purred, "There is a certain appeal to danger..." Her right hand circled around behind him, seeking the dagger he had hidden in the back of his belt. Its hilt faced the opposite way, away from her hand, and she could not reach it.

"Ah, so you like danger," Marcus countered and caught her searching hand, pinning it down. With his other hand, he took hold of her belt and pulled up, actually lifting her. The cloak fell, dragging one shoulder of her gown down with it, and he moved her back against the stone wall. She jumped when her skin touched the cold, rough surface.

Marcus' voice lowered, taking on a gravelly, menacing tone, "What's wrong? I thought you liked it rough. You must if you take lovers such as Banawr."

Her face showed alarm at his unexpected aggression. Recovering her nerve, she masked her fear in a sudden smile, a smile not laced with the return sarcasm she had planned. "What happened to the casual charm you always used in the past? But, I suppose, this suits you better."

Then her left arm swooped up, clamping around behind his head. Her hand passed down along his face, and he saw in it the glint of a small blade. It stopped against the side of his neck. With her face almost touching his, she sneered, "You see, I can be just as dangerous. You should know. Now let me go and move back."

He released her. Shifting the knife to her other hand, she held it across under his chin, forcing him to the wall, his head tilted back against it. He was unable to see farther down than her face, but he felt her prying under the hem of his tunic, loosening the ties on one side of his breeches.

"Ah, wouldn't you say it's time at last?" she crooned, and her hand found its way inside, seeking his manhood.

He was not surprised by either her curious fingers or her attempt at force, thinking she must have had the dagger hidden in her dress or belt, in an awkward place she could not reach until the cloak was gone. Disgusted, he said, "Not in a thousand lifetimes, you ugly cow."

Before she could respond, his hand whipped up and gripped her wrist, violently twisting the dagger out of her fingers. It flew, thudding somewhere across the room. His other hand found his own dagger. She tried to pull out of his grip, but his big hand tightened around her wrist, enough that she thought he was going to break it.

"You're hurting me!" she shrilled.

He dragged her around, jamming her against the wall again, pinning her there with his hand to her throat. He rasped, "You wanted it like this, Daracha. So you shall have it." With his knife, he sliced through her belt, then slipped the tip into her gown's open neckline. Ripping down, he tore the dress from her until it fell around her ankles.

Pulling his sword, Marcus backed, aiming the blade at Daracha's belly. He kicked the dress away as he moved, then the discarded cloak, his eyes never leaving her face. "Perhaps you should have learned long ago that I am not an easy mark, such as Banawr, and that it will cost those who cross me rather dearly." Hacking down with the sword, he shattered the lantern. Oil sprayed out onto the clothing, setting it on fire. "It will cost even more, if you cross my woman."

Daracha gasped, horrified. "You bastard," she hissed. Propelled by outrage, she lunged forward. The swordtip flipped upward again and she stopped short.

"You're getting too old for nonsense such as this, Daracha," he said, his disgust blatantly showing. He held her at bay until the clothing burned beyond any possible use, then opened the door. He swept the sword in a smooth line, indicating she should start walking home.

Pulsating rage, she clutched her arms around herself and gradually edged away from him, then dashed past, racing for the postern gate.

Alone again, Marcus exhaled long and roughly. He waited for the flames to die, then sheathed his sword and dagger, picked up Daracha's knife. Pulling up his tunic, he retied the lashes of his breeches.

Rustling disturbed the quiet. He turned to the doorway. A face peered around the edge, and though Marcus could not see her features, he recognized Claerwen's silhouette.

"Glân!" he ejected. "What are you doing here?" As he emerged, he saw her eyes dart between him and the path the naked woman had taken. When her eyes stopped, landing on his face, they filled with a crushing disappointment. Barely holding on to a brittle thread of dignity, she turned away and ran to the house.

# Chapter 14

## Alba

The door slammed. Claerwen looked up.

Marcus paused just within the fire pit's light, his glittering eyes following around the house until he found her sitting cross-legged on the bed. Slowly, he pulled off his baldric and lay his sword on the table. He dragged a chair across to sit in front of her.

"Why didn't you stay here, as I told you?" he asked, his tone both stern and quiet.

"What have you done?" she whispered, not trusting her voice to keep from breaking if she spoke aloud.

"Not here. Not now. Please," he answered, sounding more tired than angry, though his eyes remained tense. He hated the disillusionment marring her beautiful eyes and that he had caused it. He sank his face into his hands, his fingers raking into his hair.

A thousand questions waited to be answered in Claerwen's mind, why she had seen the woman flee as she had, why she had seen Marcus dressing, why either act had anything to do with Pascentius' plottings against the high king. She struggled for control, not willing to let the rawness of emotion wrench free and lash out at him, no matter how well proven her suspicions appeared to be. If he had broken the marriage vow of faithfulness, the act was unforgivable, but she would not risk his life for the sake of pride, retribution, or the purity of anger. The answers were obvious, she believed, but she pushed them away, forcing them to wait for a later time. The truth would only serve to shatter her faith in him.

Claerwen leaned forward, critically observing how he rested his face in his hands, considering the way his fingers curved into his knotted, frazzled hair, the talons imitating the same configuration as they hung awkwardly between his thumb and forefinger. She began to sense that behind his hands, the flashing anger in his eyes upon entering had evolved into a profound melancholy. She also sensed he craved to voice the festering, unspoken truth as much as she needed to learn it.

Claerwen tried to see past Bhruic's ugliness, searching for the bond of love and trust that had allowed her and Marcus to endure separations, imprisonment, illness, war, sorrow, pain and longing. Recognizable from the instant they had met years before, that bond had always enabled them to communicate far more completely than with words. Compelled by sudden compassion, she touched his hair.

He looked up.

She leaned closer, tilting her head slightly, and let her eyes ask once more what had happened.

He shook his head.

Claerwen rested her hands on his shoulders. Her brows knotted up in frustration, and she tried again with pleading eyes.

Once more he shook his head.

Sighing with disappointment, she pulled away, letting her hands drop into her lap. In the dim light from the fire pit, she saw a smudge on her fingers and realized it was blood. Reaching again, she pushed his hair back and found a long, thin scratch on the side of his neck.

"That woman cut you," she breathed. "Why?"

"'Tis nothing," he answered.

Squinting consternation, Claerwen fetched a wineskin from the table. Sitting again on the bed, she carefully tested the skin's contents, soaked a kerchief, then cleaned and treated the wound.

"Don't bandage it. It's not worth the bother," he said when she finished.

She replaced the skin's wooden stopper. Gazing across at the blackened patch on the wall, she thought of the vision warning of the poisoned cider and wondered why a dragon had been shown. As with most of her visions, she remembered little but the pain that followed and guessed that because the red dragon was the symbol of their people, it had been fitting. Regardless, she was glad the warning had been given and she had reacted with swiftness. "It was her, wasn't it?" she asked mostly to herself, then, looking to Marcus, "Why won't you tell me who she is?"

His eyes clogged with stubborn silence. Again he answered, "Not here."

"Then where? When?"

He remained quiet and rose, turning away, and as he prepared to go to bed, tears filled Claerwen's eyes, threatening to spill. Her certainty that his silence was no part of the cynical and gruff Bhruic was confirmed. It was deeply personal, between him and the red-haired woman. Giving up for the evening, she returned the wineskin to the table and went to bed herself.

Neither she nor Marcus slept well that night.

---

By first light, Marcus had dressed and was ready to resume work on the barracks. Concerned about another attempt to poison or otherwise harm her, he asked for and received Claerwen's promise to remain in the house with the door and shutters bolted, and to answer only his call.

But after he left, Claerwen found the previous night's images still raging in her mind. She wondered if he was truly going to work or had another foray in mind regarding the red-haired woman. The house grew uncomfortable, as if it was closing in, choking off her breath. By dawn, she unbolted the door and slipped out. She heard Marcus speaking with Girvyn somewhere inside the barracks as she silently paced to the fort's rear wall. Hidden from their view, she left by the postern gate.

Looking forward to the solace of the lonely wilds, Claerwen sought to free her mind. Throughout the night she had tried to resurrect the sense of compassion that had struck her when Marcus' mood shifted from anger to gloom. She hoped with all her soul that the scene she had witnessed was merely misleading, but the memories of it countered that hope, and she realized she was only trying to rationalize her fears.

Claerwen climbed the first slope of the hills south of the fort as sunrise spread upward in the eastern sky. Most of the snow had melted except in the higher places and protected leas, and the pungent, familiar smells of forest, damp soil and decaying leaves released in a permeating and soothing aroma. She loved earthy, rich smells: leather, wood smoke, freshly dug roots, horses, pine pitch, heather in the sun. At the top of the hill, she halted for a moment, breathing in both the scents around her and those of her favorite memories.

"Horses and leather," she actually thought aloud, struck by a most-favored memory of long ago, one she had relived in her mind hundreds of times. Years before, on a cold night within Ceredig of Strathclyde's stronghold at Dun Breatann, she had met Marcus for the first time in a walled garden behind the great hall. He had smelled of horses and leather.

That meeting played out in her mind once more as she remembered how they had stumbled onto each other. With his intense eyes boring into hers and so clearly reflecting his purpose in life, she had understood within moments that he was a spy. Her instincts had driven her to trust him unquestioningly, though he had refused to tell her who he was, saying no more than his given name.

Claerwen looked down into the glen. Even from a distance, the fort looked raggedly forlorn and out of place, unlike the way Dinas Beris seemed to grow naturally out of the rock and trees of its hillspur. Homesickness filled her. Her thoughts returned uncontrollably to Marcus and the cruelties he had endured in his work. She thought aloud again, "He would not give of himself all these years, suffering, so often for my sake, to merely give it all away to a red-haired camp follower..."

Movement stirred below, shaking her out of her thoughts. A figure hiked up the hill, following in her direction. Fear struck her in the belly and she retreated, obscuring her tracks as she moved, and wedged herself behind a group of boulders.

The figure was slight, its movement slowing as it reached the steeper sections. Claerwen chided herself for not hiding her trail more carefully. She had seriously believed no one would venture out in the cold. Then the figure's face turned upward, searching for a path. Swathed in rags and ancient leathers as before, it was Sinnoch. She rose and waited.

Minutes later, he reached her. He stopped as she hailed him, astonishment rooting him to the earth.

Claerwen dropped to her knees before him. His dark eyes searched her face, giving the impression that he expected something to be terribly amiss. "What is wrong?" she questioned.

He finally spoke, "Are you well, Lady Glân?"

"Aye, fine enough. Why do you ask?"

"I heard them talking...the commander spoke...as if you would die soon. I don't understand. Why would they say this?"

"I can't say why, Sinnoch," Claerwen answered. She wondered why the boy was alone again, so far away from the people of his clan. But remembering his reaction when she had asked about his home before, she held her tongue, not risking to alienate him.

Instead, she proposed, "Come with me, then. I'm looking for late-season berries, and I'm hoping there could still be some clinging to briars scattered throughout the forest. Would you like to help?"

The boy nodded, showing eagerness for her companionship. He wrapped his arms around her neck and hugged, his face suddenly brimming with smiles.

As they looped across the hills, Claerwen taught Sinnoch about plants and their qualities for healing, as well as for food and flavor in cooking. Fascinated by her knowledge, he learned quickly. By the time they had nearly returned to the glen, late in the afternoon, they had acquired enough food for several meals and settled in a protected spot to rest.

"Lady?" The boy looked up at her with questions in his eyes.

Claerwen smiled, enjoying his refreshing wonder and eagerness to learn.

"Do you know about sorcery?"

Her brows arched upward. She had not expected such a question. "Why do you ask?"

He hesitated, then plunged in, his curiosity too strong to stop. "There is a woman who keeps a *hafod*, a summer house, with many strange things in it. She mixes potions that smoke and have foul smells, making them over and over until she gets them the way she wants them. She says words in a strange language I don't understand, and she is always waving her hands and arms around to make you watch her."

From his description, Claerwen was reminded of a story Myrddin had once told about a sorcerer who wove patterns in the air with his hands, distracting and mesmerizing those to whom he spoke. Myrddin, himself often regarded through ignorance as a sorcerer or enchanter, had explained the difference between the ways of a true holy man and a sorcerer, that a shaman with fire in the head never exploited his gift, while a sorcerer's power was false and only a display of trickery.

Sinnoch continued, "She caught me watching her once and tried to make me learn it. She said I would be her apprentice because I was so interested. But I couldn't do what she wanted, then she got angry and tried to hit me. I ran away and hid."

Claerwen was appalled. "Do you know why she does these things? What is their purpose?"

"I don't know. Yesterday, I saw her in the fort, carrying one of the crocks she uses, but I don't know what she did with it."

Claerwen shivered involuntarily. She asked, "Do you know how to find the *hafod*?"

"Please don't go there, Lady!" he protested. "I don't want her to hurt you."

"Oh, no, Sinnoch, I only want to avoid it," she assured him, then pressed on in another direction, hoping not to confuse or distress him further. "I want to ask you something."

He waited patiently, looking up at her with his solemn dark eyes. For a moment, she was struck by a vague familiarity in them. Believing he must resemble someone of his clan she had seen, she let it pass and asked, "Does this woman, when she is doing these odd things, get a strange look in her eyes? Like they glow a little?"

Sinnoch frowned, not understanding. He shook his head and asked, "What does it mean, Lady?"

"Have you ever heard of 'fire in the head?'"

Sinnoch's eyes widened. "You know what it is?"

Claerwen nearly laughed. "Does she think she has it?"

"That's what she says. But…"

"You don't believe her?"

"No."

Claerwen took his hands, leaning her face close to his, and carefully explained the difference between the fire and sorcery as she had learned from Myrddin. She concluded, "The fire is an ancient power that comes only from the gods. It is sacred, never to be flaunted. It should not be feared, but when the power is stirring, it cannot be denied. Sorcery is a practice, similar to a religion. It can be used for good or bad. It is magic a person creates, far less powerful than the fire."

Sinnoch thought on her words, then carefully asked, "Do you have fire in the head?"

Claerwen hesitated, not wishing to frighten him. But if she lied, she would lose his trust. She answered, "Aye, Sinnoch."

His eyes grew big, but not with fear. Instead, pride shone in them. He said, "This woman believes she can give her power to me."

Claerwen explained, "If she would truly have the power, she would know it is impossible to give it to another person. Those with the fire can recognize anyone else who has it. Equally, they know when someone does not."

"It is dangerous."

Claerwen laughed. "Aye, both can be dangerous, but I would fear sorcery more than the fire because people control it for their own use. The power of the fire cannot be used for selfish reasons."

Quiet for a while, Sinnoch considered what he had learned. His mood grew pensive; then, with a child's brutal forthrightness, he declared, "I wish my mother was like you."

Claerwen was stunned. He had never mentioned any kinfolk, and she hoped with all her soul that the red-haired woman was not his mother. Taking his hands again, she sensed he longed to tell her more and that he did not trust what he had been told in the past. "Where is your mother?" she asked.

"She stays in her house and weeps."

Claerwen closed her eyes momentarily in relief. The red-haired woman was not given to weeping in seclusion. "Why does she cry?"

The boy answered, "She never says, but I think it may be for my father." Sinnoch looked down, his mouth pouted out and shame in his eyes. "I don't know who my father is. They say he is dead. But I think it is a lie."

Claerwen's brows lifted. "Why?" she prodded.

"I heard the commander and the woman talking once as if my father was alive. But they never said his name or where he was. I am afraid to ask. I think the commander would beat me, like the woman tried before."

Claerwen winced and said, "They wouldn't tell you anything about him, even if it's true your father is alive."

Sinnoch nodded in agreement. Sorrow radiated from him, making Claerwen ache with empathy. She sighed raggedly, giving fleeting thought to the wish that she could just take the boy home and raise him as her own, but she pushed the idea aside, remembering Marcus' warning that she must not become attached to him.

"Why are you so sad, Lady?" Sinnoch asked.

She smiled and hugged him again. "I am sad for you, for the loneliness, and that I can't do anything to help you." She left out saying "yet."

Sinnoch reached out and pressed his hand to her cheek, a simple gesture that spoke his appreciation of her kindness.

Claerwen held her lips in a flat line and stood up, taking his hand. If she spoke, she would give in to tears. Silently, they made their farewells as the sun dropped below the western horizon, and in the place he parted from her, Claerwen stood a long time, watching the empty space he had occupied.

Darkness fell.

Claerwen slowly approached the edge of the woods, crouching down. From there, she saw the postern gate was closed. She hoped Marcus was still busy in the barracks and had not noticed she'd left the house. Though shamed that she had not kept her promise, she also hoped an opportunity to exchange news would at last arise and the important knowledge gained from Sinnoch would negate her broken word. She found herself stubbornly clinging to her faith in Marcus, looking forward to his companionship that night.

"Mistress?" A man's voice called from a few feet away.

Alarmed, Claerwen rose, searching the darkness. A dim face emerged, and she recognized Lord Engres.

"Your name is Glân, I believe?"

"Aye," she answered tentatively.

"I must speak with you." He stared at her in the way Marcus had described.

"I have work I must do for my master, Lord Engres. I must go now." She tried to back away.

"Lord Bhruic would not mind if you spoke a moment with me, I am sure. Don't be afraid, I only want to ask you —"

A hand landed on his shoulder from behind, and Claerwen watched Engres stiffen as the fingers compressed. Then Marcus' face suddenly appeared over the hand, his brows jagged down in Bhruic's perpetual frown. To Claerwen, Marcus ordered harshly, "Go inside. Now."

She exhaled, relieved to be free of Engres' questions, though now her hope to avoid Marcus' anger was eliminated. She started quickly down the slope. Passing the men, she heard Marcus speak a gruff warning to Engres that ended in a threat. Glancing back from the glen's perimeter, she saw Marcus catching up to her, leaving Engres behind to watch them in bewilderment.

Upon entering their house, Marcus handed his sword to Claerwen. He swore an oath, the anger in his eyes apparent, then closed the door behind himself. He muttered, "This place is bloody uncomfortable."

She hung the baldric on a peg, then stoked the fire. But before lighting any of the oil lamps, she went to him and laid a hand on his arm. Softly, she informed, "I have news I must tell you." His head turned sharply, and she saw grim hardness still in his black eyes.

"No, Glân —"

"This cannot wait," she insisted.

Knocking rattled the door, interrupting.

Marcus grunted through clenched teeth, "They are hornets that won't go away." He ordered her to light the lamps as he swung around and pulled open the door.

Pascentius strode inside without asking to be admitted. He greeted Marcus politely enough but nearly choked when he saw Claerwen at the fire pit, lighting a piece of straw to touch to the lamps' wicks. His mood fouled visibly. Then his eyes traveled to the ruined patch of whitewash on the wall.

"Care to drink, Commander?" Marcus asked in an even, almost congenial tone, but his face displayed the same unforgiveness as when he had warned of the consequences of crossing him. He and Claerwen steadily, silently watched Pascentius turn around.

The commander ignored both the question and their staring eyes. Without pause, he said, "Engres has informed me that his people will hold a yule feast beginning at sunset tomorrow, as it will be Midwinter. Unless you are of the new religion and only observe Christmas, which I doubt, you are expected to attend."

"So be it," Marcus said flatly.

"I suppose your woman is to come as well. Engres is feeling generous," Pascentius added, then strode out.

Marcus stood in the open doorway and watched the Romanized soldier disappear. The festival itself did not interest him, but the holiday's occurrence meant Pascentius' plans would at last be placed into action. Hopefully, the opportunity to complete the quest would follow closely behind. Then perhaps, Marcus wished, the damage done to his marriage could be mended. He closed the door.

Before he could cross the room, Claerwen caught his arm again and whispered tightly in his ear, "The woman practices sorcery."

"What...?"

"The boy told me, I came across him in the hills. No, don't be alarmed. He is frightened of her."

Marcus lifted his hand, moving to stop her from continuing, but she insisted, encouraged because he appeared genuinely surprised. Keeping her whisper very light, she went on, "She has a *hafod*, I don't know where it is, but it is her laboratory." Pausing, she swept a hand at the poisoned wall, letting this knowledge sink into his mind.

He frowned, thinking, "Sorcery...in a *hafod*? Aye, then perhaps it is good you have made friends with the boy. We can use him."

Taken aback, Claerwen said, "I don't like using him. 'Tis not fair."

"He won't mind being used if he saves our lives."

Stung, Claerwen released his arm. "You cannot fight sorcery with a sword. You must let me help you. Stop trying to protect me."

"And she is going try to kill you again, I suspect at the feast, in the midst of the noise and chaos."

"Who is she?"

"It doesn't matter who she is."

"Why won't you talk to me? Is it not more dangerous to force my ignorance?"

The house seemed to close in on her again as he clamped his mouth shut, smothering the minuscule progress she had made towards restoring their communication. She waited for the overwhelming silence to dissipate, but it remained. Dejected, she turned away and went back to working the embers in the fire pit, trying to overturn her thoughts as much as the ashes. It did not work, and though she could lay new peat and coax the flames, her attempt to stir new compassion into her thoughts failed. The night wore late, and she watched Marcus calmly slide between the bed covers and fall asleep. Giving up hope for another day, she went to bed as well, but when morning returned, she was still asking why.

# Chapter 15

## Alba

On Midwinter night, the people of Engres' clan and the mercenaries spilled out from the overfilled great hall, all across the courtyard. Nearly everyone was drunk. Using anything that could create music, they banged, blew and screeched mismatched melodies in a cacophony that was more irritating than joyful. A bonfire had been built just outside the front gates, but as the mead and ale thickened each mind, the flames died from neglect. In earlier times, before the Romans' influence, they would have started the evening before and celebrated with orderly and dignified rituals, but no druid was available to conduct either the preparations or the ceremonies. The disorganization descended into apathy and arguments.

Marcus entered the great hall through the rear doors, Claerwen trailing behind. Slipping unobtrusively along the back wall, they avoided the bulk of the crowd. Marcus had noticed a small lap harp in a corner inside the hall on previous days, and he hoped it would still be there, thinking that playing it would give him the chance to observe without having to mingle with the others. Pushing on along the wall, he found it, and sat on a nearby bench. He gestured to Claerwen to take a place on the floor behind him.

Leaning the harp against his shoulder, he lightly ran a thumb across the strings, listening to its tone, and began to tune the instrument. Gradually, he turned disconnected sounds into melodies, creating a soothing background to the hall's din. Few noticed, although several heads nodded in his direction and an occasional voice hummed or sang phrases from familiar tunes.

As Marcus settled into playing, he studied the large room. Seated, he could not see far, but a tall woman slowly threading her way through the hall caught his attention. She sauntered, wrapped in a ragged cloak, the hood drooping over her face. Several feet from his corner, she halted, drew back the hood, revealing tilted grey eyes. Once certain he was watching, she moved forward, stopping directly in front of him.

"So, you are a bard as well," Daracha taunted in a husky voice. "Just a blacksmith, you told the commander. But you are a swordmaster and a bard...what else are you, Master Bhruic? What else are you hiding?" Her eyes tilted even more as they roamed over him, slowly, as if in search of something she had missed in a previous examination.

"I could ask the same of you, Mistress," Marcus returned the insult of lower rank, not missing a note on the harp.

Tension rose, thick as mud. Then he saw her eyes go past him, locking onto Claerwen.

"Your slave woman is rude," Daracha objected.

He glanced to Claerwen and saw she was standing, coldly watching Daracha, ready to pounce in the same way she had when defending him against Banawr. Marcus smiled unexpectedly and quipped, "She has always shown much intelligence."

Pascentius abruptly appeared behind Daracha and caught her elbow before she could explode in retort. He wheeled her around, speaking too low to hear, but his face reflected anger, disgust and warning. Moments later, she departed the hall, Pascentius stalking behind her.

Marcus looked up at Claerwen and caught her eyes, finding them again filled with confusion and disappointment. His own were calm in the attempt to reassure her, but his face was blank for the sake of not alerting others that something was amiss. He dipped his head down once, indicating she should sit again, and he watched her sink onto her knees, her head bowed to hide her face. He continued playing.

Engres approached a short while later, carrying a full wineskin and a pair of drinking horns. Cautiously, he remarked, "You must show me how you create that startling glare of yours, Lord Bhruic. 'Tis rather powerful."

Marcus almost smiled again, curious that Engres had the nerve to approach so congenially after the warning he had been given the night before. "'Tis something I was born with, I believe. Can't help myself."

Engres laughed at the comment and tilted his head towards the harp. "You play well."

"This is yours?" Marcus asked, his fingers halting.

"Ah, 'tis mine, but you play better than I do. Please, continue if you wish. And I brought this to share, if you like." Engres offered the wineskin in conciliation, then opened it, poured both horns full.

Marcus' eyes narrowed as he took one, suspicious of the drink, but it had not burned through the wineskin or the horns. Engres saluted him and began to sip. Swirling the dark liquid a moment, Marcus sniffed at it and decided it was safe enough. He took a mouthful, found it was strong ale of good quality, then swallowed and handed the horn to Claerwen.

"Do you know this?" Marcus asked. He began to thump his foot steadily on the wooden plank floor and launched into a well-known tune, singing to his own accompaniment. People close by turned around, recognized it and began to sing along. The focus of the room shifted to the corner as more joined in. At the end of the song, a round of drinking and cheering filled the hall.

Marcus continued playing long into the night, at the same time watching the people descend into incredible drunkenness. Though he liked the ale himself, he only drank small amounts between songs, needing to retain a clear mind. He had seen neither Pascentius nor Daracha return, prickling his suspicion that trouble would come later in the night.

Engres spent the rest of the evening drinking and singing with the music, and sometime after midnight, he took the harp from

Marcus. "It's been a long time since I heard this one," he said, trying to coax a particular melody from the strings. "It's very pretty, though rather sad, and it needs a woman to sing it. Your slave has a pleasant speaking voice; I would wager she can sing as well. Do you know it, Mistress?" Engres gazed at Claerwen.

Claerwen stared back, instantly recognizing the tune. She nodded slowly, not sure if she wanted to sing. Normally she would love to, but not in an unfamiliar crowd. Looking up at Marcus, she waited for his permission and received it with his nod as he took the drinking horn from her.

She began softly, remembering the words with no difficulty, even though it had been many years since she had sung it. Her voice rose gradually, carving a beautiful sound in the smoky air of the hall, the words sad and haunting, her face reflecting the story of the song. Swept into it, she appeared to enter a trance of sorrow, swaying as she knelt next to Marcus.

He watched her, frowning. He had never heard the song before, but he recognized the lyrics' dialect came from an area along the Afon Dyfrdwy, once called the Cynnwyd, where Claerwen was born. At first he thought the fire had come into her, but there was no soft glow in her eyes this time, and she stared blankly past the people listening to her.

The harp music faded away, Claerwen's voice following it. For several moments she remained still, kneeling, not conscious of her surroundings, looking as if something deep within her mind had taken control.

"Glân?" Marcus called her quietly. She did not react. He realized her eyes had shifted, and she was now staring at Engres. "Glân?" he called louder then touched her arm.

Those around them suddenly went quiet, watching Marcus turn towards her, his face wrenched in horrified alarm. They saw he had realized she was not breathing, the color drained completely out of her face. Choking escaped her throat, like two quiet chuffs. Her eyes glazed, then closed, and she dropped, sprawling down under the bench as if she were spilled water.

"Glân!" Marcus ejected, launching himself off the bench, tossing the drinking horn aside. He pulled her up into his arms, but she drooped unresponsively.

Engres reached for one limp arm, trying to take her hand in his. Shocked, he repeatedly asked what had happened.

Marcus' black eyes swung up. "Leave her be," he raged hoarsely, lifting her. He started for the door, disregarding that Engres followed, still asking, all the way across the crowded yard. But when Engres tried to enter the house, Marcus abruptly turned, showing a raw cruelty in his eyes that halted the older man as if he had walked into a wall. Embracing Claerwen protectively, Marcus went inside and kicked the door shut.

"Claeri," he whispered, calling as he carried her across to the bed. She felt fragile in his arms, and he set her down gently among the rumpled bedding. Terrified that Daracha had found another way to poison her, he dredged through his mind to remember if he had seen Claerwen eat or drink anything different than he had, but he could recall nothing odd. Loosening the neck of her dress to make her more comfortable, he listened for her heart and was relieved when he heard it beating strongly, felt her breath, now even and deep.

Moaning, she opened her eyes. Confusion engulfed her, but as she began to focus, she realized she was comfortable and warm, lying with her head resting on Marcus' arm, looking up at him. His eyes were full of the kindness she had wished so much to return.

"You fainted," he told her, his voice soothing. "Do you remember what happened?"

She tried to organize her thoughts and took several deep breaths to speak, but could not find her voice or make sense of why she was in their house. Shaking her head, she took another deep breath. Then it came to her, like a storming billow of the sea. She sat up, struggling to speak. "That song..." The words stuck in her throat and she swallowed, tried again. "When the Irish came, when they killed my family...I was singing that song with my father."

Marcus' jaw dropped and his fear dissolved into compassion. "You never told me."

She continued in a shaking voice, "I have tried so hard to

forget…the screaming, running, hiding, seeing the dead across the valley, in the river. When I told you about it, I knew you had seen places like it. Once, you said you had seen too much death. I knew I didn't need to describe more. The song is beautiful, but I wish I'd never have to remember it again. I wish it would leave me alone." She let him pull her into his arms, accepting his comfort.

He began speculating, "There must be a reason Engres asked for that song. He must know you, or know something about that raid. Are you absolutely certain you've never seen him before?"

Claerwen pulled back and rubbed at her eyes. Shaking her head, she answered, "I don't know who he is. No, I've never seen him. But I tell you, for just a moment, I was so lost in those memories, it was as if I could see my father's eyes again. But I must have been just carried away. Engres' eyes are the same color my father's were, and for a moment, they reminded me of him. I'm sorry, I didn't know I would react so."

Marcus held a hand to her cheek, gently stroking her skin with his thumb. "I thought you had been poisoned," he whispered. "I'm so relieved that I was wrong."

Claerwen finally smiled, finding no sign of Bhruic's frowning rudeness and all of her husband's familiar warmth showing in his face. Catching his hand, she closed her eyes and kissed his palm.

When her eyes opened, he was watching her intently, longingly, his lips slightly parted. Slowly, he leaned forward, kissing her, at first gently, then with unabashed need. He pushed her down into the bedding. One hand slid down her leg and moved up under her skirts, the other underneath her shoulders, clasping her tightly to him.

Claerwen responded in kind, wrapping her arms around him, returning his kisses with uncontrollable indulgence. While they had not completely foregone each other's affections since leaving home, it had been markedly curtailed and very subdued from normal. Now, as his hand roamed its way up her legs, warm and seeking, she arched herself into him, expressing every craving.

Then he grunted softly, and his face, next to her ear, lifted slightly. Opening her eyes, she saw his expression had turned back into Bhruic's. His eyes stared down alongside her, and she turned her head to follow his line of sight. Among the bed covers was a thin and gauzy undergarment of the purest white linen. Elegant and luxurious, it belonged in a wealthy noblewoman's palace rather than the rustic house.

"What is this?" Claerwen asked, reaching for the fine piece of cloth.

"Don't touch it," Marcus ejected.

Claerwen's stomach wrenched, realizing the garment belonged to the red-haired woman and Marcus had recognized it. The sickeningly sweet perfume radiated from it. Her eyes flashed, returning to Marcus, and she demanded, "What else does that stinking thing hide?"

He was startled. Claerwen rarely expressed such sharpness. "No —" he blurted, but she pushed at him ferociously, shoving him aside. She bounded up, squirming past his hands as he tried to catch her.

Crossing the room, she stopped at the table, leaning on it. Needing time to think, she stalled, considering what she should say, if there was anything she could say. He rose and started across.

Before he was halfway there, the idea struck her. She clamped down her anger, forcing it into a reserve corner of her mind for a later time, and she said, "If you won't talk to me, then I will have to learn for myself, won't I?" Whirling around, she took up her cloak, wrenched open the door, and marched out.

The door slammed shut behind her.

---

Only two lanterns flickered at the red-haired woman's front door. One other glowed at the edge of the pond, the water rippling gently in its light. Claerwen watched from the wood as before. She waited, listening, hoping Marcus' footsteps would soon approach, that he was coming after her and she could force him to talk. But time passed, and she remained alone.

Then the red-haired woman appeared in the doorway. She picked up one lantern and closed the door after herself. Her hair was loose, sweeping down her back with the same motion as the thick, flowing robes she wore. Briskly, she strode around the pond and into the trees behind.

Claerwen turned towards the way she had come and stared into the trees, wishing Marcus would suddenly emerge from them, but no sound, no movement met her. Biting down on her lower lip, she gathered her skirts and turned again, moving forward silently along the edge of the clearing and then following an invisible path that descended into a low-lying area behind. Another clearing, larger than the farmstead's, expanded across it. To the far side stood the *hafod* Sinnoch had spoken of, a tiny stone hut that looked as ancient as Britain itself. The red-haired woman marched straight to it, entered and lit the interior with brightly glowing oil lamps.

From the trees' protection, Claerwen observed for the best part of an hour. Humming and singing drifted from the *hafod*, but instead of a cheerful sound, the tone was somber, almost morbid, and Claerwen was reminded of women keening at a funeral. She heard the clicking of crockery as it was moved, picked up, set down, pushed against. Gradually, the singing turned into a chant, unintelligible in a strange language, likely the tongue of which Sinnoch had spoken. Amidst it, the woman called Marcus' name.

The instinct to protect her husband jolted inside Claerwen like lightning. Hitching up her cloak to keep it from dragging, she walked across the turf directly towards the *hafod*, stopping just beyond the light that streamed from the open door. Remaining invisible in the darkness, she watched the woman work behind a small trestle table inside, pouring and mixing fluids, still chanting, waving her hands over them. Claerwen smiled at the performance's atrocious grandeur.

"You will not cast influence over Marcus with that," Claerwen said evenly as she strode into the light.

The woman's grey eyes jerked up, startled, then narrowed with hatred as she recognized Claerwen. Setting down a ceramic jug with a loud smack, the woman jeered, "What would you know of this, you addled-head little slave?"

"I know enough," Claerwen responded civilly. "I know you tried to kill me. I am certain you will try again."

"And you deserve to die, coward. For what you did to Drakar."

Claerwen stalled at the mention of Drakar, her brows slightly raised, but her face remained as inscrutable as Myrddin's could be.

The woman smiled maliciously. "You don't know, do you? He hasn't told you who I am. Then I shall enlighten you. I am Daracha, and my kinsman was Drakar."

Claerwen's stomach cramped as she realized what the revelation implied. Logic demanded that Marcus would have sought out all of Drakar's kin, hoping to locate his allies, anyone he could use to fulfill the quest of stopping the traitor's activities. Daracha's arrogant demeanor fit the ideal of a kinswoman loyal to a barbarian like Drakar, and that Claerwen had killed him gave focused meaning to revenge.

"I wonder what else he has not told you," Daracha taunted. "Has he said how he whores himself? How he uses women to get what he wants? Insipid women, like you, like my half-sister Elen, who have not the nerve to spit, let be defend themselves against a predator like Marcus ap Iorwerth. Ah, I can see from your face that he never told you any such things. I should feel pity for you then, eh?"

Claerwen knew Marcus had been well experienced with women before he had pledged himself to marry, and she believed Daracha's accusations were merely a ploy. Unmoved, Claerwen spoke again with calm, "Drakar died because of his greed. He helped to broker Saxon and Irish mercenaries for Vortigern. They were used in the annihilation of my clan, as well as that of countless innocent people. All for the sake of greed. Aye, he died by my hand, but not out of my revenge."

"That shows what a coward you are, doesn't it?"

"'Tis a coward who acts on revenge, because a coward has not the strength to make peace," Claerwen countered.

Not expecting Claerwen to maintain her composure, Daracha frowned with her mouth twisted bitterly. "It's true, you are no different from your husband, are you? Such a cold, miserable dog of a man is he, and you are the same." She moved into the doorway. "Beware," she warned. "There will be no escape."

Claerwen paced a step forward. For several moments, she held Daracha's stare and read the truth in the woman's eyes, that her revenge was for jealousy, not for Drakar's death. Claerwen nearly smiled and said, "So be it." With a gentle swirl of her cloak, she disappeared into the darkness.

———————

Torchlight showed through the mist-filled forest as Claerwen neared the fort. Tired enough to sleep on her feet, she walked swiftly in spite of her fatigue, eager to first find Marcus, then rest after the difficult night. Dawn would lighten the eastern sky soon.

But from below, rustling evolved into the sound of steps running up the slope. She stopped, dreading to meet anyone, and knelt down to wait in the thick, ferny overgrowth. Shortly, a man burst from between the trees, dodging low-sweeping branches, racing past her, his long dark hair whipping out, a sword across his back. Claerwen rose, whistling a low, sharp signal.

Marcus skidded, his boot heels scraping shallow trenches into the earth as he tried to turn and halt at the same time. Breathing hard, he swung around, seeking from where her whistle had come.

Claerwen walked out of the ferns. She watched his eyes find her. Intense, penetrating, they followed her as she moved towards him, questioning where she had been, what had happened. When she stopped before him, he rested his hand upon her shoulder, gently squeezing. His mouth flinched, then opened to speak.

"I know," she hushed him, slipping her hand to his arm.

He frowned, not understanding.

She tilted her head slightly and repeated, "I know. I know who she is. I know why she is doing this to us."

"How?" His brows knotted as he searched her face, then he realized what she had done. "You confronted her?"

Claerwen nodded.

His eyes widened, his jaw dropping. "She would never tell the truth."

"She didn't need to. The truth was in everything she *didn't* say."

Marcus was dumbfounded. Instead of a disaster, Claerwen had

taken control and sidestepped his overprotectiveness. She had learned the truth just as she had said she would. That perfectly explained why she was so calm, and why, when she had approached him, her steps had been so full of graceful serenity. He took her hands, pride filling his eyes, then finally found his voice, "You have a bloody lot of courage."

Claerwen shook her head. "No, 'twas not courage. I was angry. But now I understand. She is dangerous because she is jealous, because you never touched her. But she will try again to kill me, she is waiting for the right time."

"Pascentius has threatened her with abandonment if she does not follow his instructions, including when that attempt will be made. However, on the morrow, I believe, I will be able to begin unraveling his plans. He cornered me when I left the house — I tried to follow you — we are to leave for Winchester with him at sunset, tomorrow eve." Looking at the brightening sky, he added, "We had best get some sleep." He took a step towards the fort.

Claerwen held onto his sleeve, holding him back. She asked, "Who is Elen?"

Marcus froze, stunned by the question. Exhaling slowly, he asked, "Daracha told you of her half-sister?"

"She said that you used Elen, and other women like her, that you whored yourself."

Marcus winced.

"It is true?"

His eyes rolled to his right and down, like they were sliding off a cliff. He admitted it, nodding.

"And that is the true reason you refused to tell me about Daracha? You were afraid the truth about yourself would be told?"

Marcus sucked in his breath, stalling. Then he met her eyes. They were so beautiful, light and clear like the sea on a bright day, and he asked himself how he could lie to those eyes, even if by omission. He had heard no threat in her words, no malice, no anger, not even disappointment, only her compassionate, generous nature that he had always admired.

He began softly, keeping his eyes locked with hers. "Shortly after I met you in Dun Breatann, I went to Rhuddlan, along the Afon Clwyd, in the kingdom of Powys. Elen was there, and I knew she likely had information regarding Drakar's whereabouts. It is true, I used her. Twice. There were others after that...not often. I cannot tell you how many times or how many women. I'm certainly not the first man to do this, it was a convenient tool. And I'm not proud of it, even though it was useful for the results it brought me."

"Is that how you thought of me?"

"No. Never." His eyes did not waver. Continuing, he said, "Four years passed from the time I first met you, until I found you again in Caernarfon."

Claerwen responded, "I had no claim on you then. But you do not speak of those years between. Never. And I did not ask because the nature of your work demands secrecy."

"I believed then I would never see you again, so I did not pursue what I felt for you any further. I went back to the road, working, rarely home for another three years. It was in those three years that I did this. In the fourth year, I returned to Dinas Beris, exhausted from the constant traveling, the ruses, the fights, the frustration, all of it. By then my father Iorwerth was dying, and Drakar was threatening Dinas Beris so much that I needed to help defend our lands."

He paused, seeing that her expression had not changed and she still listened earnestly, without judgement. He finished, "I have been with no woman but you since I went home. I swear by all the gods my people swear by."

Claerwen studied his face through the frenzy of the disguise. The oath he swore bound him to the truth, and she knew him well enough that he would never forswear an oath he considered sacred. She said, "At first, I was not certain whether your brooding was just a facet of Bhruic. Then I realized it had only to do with Daracha. Every encounter pointed to one direction, but it was a false trail. I'll admit what she told me about your past is distressing, but done is done."

Marcus frowned, puzzled. "You accept what I did?"

Her eyes saddened. "It is an ugly thing, what you have done, but there is no point to keen over it now, just as sitting at home crying over my barrenness while you are gone would serve no purpose. I know who you are, inside here." A faint smile softened her eyes as she poked a finger to the middle of his chest.

Marcus folded his arms around her in an elegant embrace. For a few moments, he savored the feel of her leaning against him, her warmth under his hands. He pressed his face into her hair and lightly kissed it. Then pulling away, he saw a hint of mischief in her eyes and lifted an eyebrow in question.

She teased, "I'll never get used to that bird claw."

He fingered the dangling talons and laughed with a sudden light-heartedness. "Come, let us get some rest," he said, and led her back to the house.

# Chapter 16

## Alba

Somewhere there was tapping. Somewhere distant. A long, light tapping. Incessant. Annoying.

Claerwen turned her head aside, not wanting to wake, and pulled the pillow over her ears, wishing the tapping would go away. It must be a woodpecker, she thought.

Weight pressed down on her. Turning her head again, she forced herself to open her eyes. The talons, still braided into Marcus' hair, came into focus just next to her face. He was asleep, snoring lightly, sprawled halfway over her on his belly, his face leaning on her shoulder.

The tapping started again. Claerwen pushed herself out from under him and was surprised that she felt even more tired than when they had gone to bed. Her arms and legs had no strength, and her head ached almost as much as after a vision. Groggy, she listened for the noise and realized someone was at the door.

She shook Marcus' arm, but he only stirred slightly. Confused, she reached for a shift, sitting up to pull it on. The effort seemed immense. Then, crawling out of the bed, she tried to stand. Dizzy and weak, she nearly fell.

"What is happening?" she asked aloud, clinging to the edge of the bed. Shaking her head, the tapping came again. It stopped when she lurched onto her feet, and she struggled across.

"Who is there?" she called, finding her voice hoarse. Receiving no answer, she called twice more. Still no one answered.

Suspecting Daracha was there, Claerwen hesitated to open. She backed away, then saw a piece of cloth had been wedged underneath the door. Cautiously, she knelt and pulled. It was wrapped around a solid object and fit snugly in the gap under the door, but it passed through easily enough. The cloth unrolled as she picked it up, the object falling into her hand.

"By the gods," she ejected. In her palm lay a silver talisman, gleaming with traditional and elegant patterns of intertwining lines. Cylindrical in shape, a thong was attached to one end so that it could be worn around the neck. Claerwen turned the cloth over and found symbols on it. Smoothing it out, it had a rough sketch of three figures, apparently a mother and son, and another woman off to the side. A heart was drawn between the son and the second woman, with arrows pointing from the son to the heart and again from the heart to the second woman.

Claerwen frowned, not understanding. She examined the talisman and found a thin crack that ran all around lengthwise. Pressing a fingernail into it, she discovered it opened on tiny, hidden hinges and spread into two halves. Inside was a lock of dark hair, fine and soft like a baby's.

"By the gods," Claerwen said again, realizing what the symbols meant. Snapping the talisman shut, she rose and stumbled her way back to the bed.

"Wake up," she called to Marcus, now shaking his arms in earnest. "Wake up, please."

He stirred but not quickly, sputtering acknowledgment of her urgency.

"I must talk to you. It cannot wait."

Marcus slowly sat up, dropping his legs over the edge of the bed. He dug the heels of his hands into his eyes, rubbing them open, then shook his head to clear it, mumbling that he was ready to listen.

Claerwen explained what she had heard and found, then placed the object in his hand. "Look inside it, Mar — " She started to say his real name and caught herself, but his expression stopped her altogether.

The color drained out of his face as he held the silver talisman. His mouth opened then clamped shut again, and he grunted through gritted teeth. When his eyes came up, he said, "This is Elen's."

"Elen's?" Claerwen blurted, not expecting his reaction. "I don't understand, how did it get here?"

"Daracha," Marcus answered, giving the talisman back to Claerwen. He started to yank on his clothes and said, "This is trouble. Elen would never give that up willingly, it was the only thing in the world she had of value."

Studying the cloth, Claerwen said, "I don't think Daracha brought this here." She looked up at Marcus, waiting for his attention. He finished tying his belt, looping the end around and through itself next to the buckle, and he came to her as she held the cloth for him to see. "Daracha did not make these marks. They are drawn differently than those on the message to Banawr. And it is unlikely that she would have left it here with the talisman, it's not the kind of message she would give. I think Elen herself has been here."

She paused, waiting for his response.

"Go on," he said grimly. "Tell me what you are thinking."

Claerwen rubbed the silver pattern with her thumb. "I believe Sinnoch is her son, and the symbols on the cloth are meant to tell me to take care of the boy."

"Her son?" His brows lifted. "Are you sure?"

Claerwen nodded. "This talisman has a lock of a baby's hair inside. It is the kind the bearer wears to protect the child the lock belongs to. She must have seen that he likes me, and that I have been kind to him." Claerwen stopped, then asked, "Daracha is her half-sister?"

"Aye. They had the same father. Daracha was related to Drakar through her mother, only rather distantly. Elen has none of Drakar's blood kin in her family."

"Sinnoch said he was told his father is dead, but he heard

Pascentius and Daracha talk as if he is still living. And he spoke of his mother, that she weeps, he thinks for his father." She paused, thinking, then speculated, "Why would Pascentius and Daracha split a family of Engres' tiny, obscure clan? Unless, if Sinnoch's father is alive, could he be a hostage, and that is part of Pascentius' hold over Engres and his people, more than the false promise of wealth? If Sinnoch's mother *is* Elen, then it would make sense."

Marcus considered her theory, saying it was very possible, then added, "I don't think Elen is part of Engres' clan, and I would wager she and the boy have only been here as long as Daracha. Those two women have had a longstanding grudge that already existed when I knew Elen — I never knew its source. Jealousy, perhaps. It could even be over Sinnoch's father."

Claerwen suddenly grabbed his arm. "Do you think the grudge is violent? That Elen will try to hurt Daracha?"

Dread filled his face. "It's possible. I don't believe Elen is capable of violence, but Daracha is. And Elen is no match for Daracha."

"By the light, that could be why she left the talisman, to protect Sinnoch if she thought she could no longer care for him..."

They stared at each other, then abruptly rushed out of the house.

The fort was unusually quiet as they crossed towards the postern gate, and they reckoned that Engres' people were all home sleeping off the ale's effects. Broken crocks, food scraps, ashes and burnt sticks from the bonfires were scattered in drabs and heaps across the courtyard and between the houses.

Upon reaching the gate, Marcus paused, scanning the compound, and was struck by how empty it appeared. Puzzled, he listened, and became aware of Pascentius' voice speaking in a low, intent tone, somewhere out of sight. He moved a few steps towards the courtyard. Holding a hand out to Claerwen, indicating she should stay where she was, he caught a glimpse of a line of soldiers. Looking tired and cranky but not disobedient, they were dressed in full battle gear.

Marcus whipped around and took Claerwen by the elbow,

whisking her through the gate.

Once outside, he whispered, "Pascentius lied. They are leaving tonight, not tomorrow. They are in the courtyard, all of them, packed and ready."

She asked, "Why would he leave without you?"

"It's a trap," he answered.

"How?"

"I don't know yet."

Claerwen suddenly realized the sun was already well past its peak, bleak and forlorn in the cold winter sky, and that they had not only slept through the morning, but it was now late afternoon. She urged, "We must hurry."

They dashed through the woods in the direction of Daracha's farmstead, coming upon it minutes later. Marcus pounded on the door, rattling it with each hit of his fist. No one answered. He tried the latch, but the door was bolted from the inside. Without hesitation, he kicked at the bolt, breaking it off its pegs. The door crashed open, hit inside and sprang back, wobbling on its hinges until it nearly shut again. He cautiously pushed it with his foot.

"Stay here," he told Claerwen and took a step inside. He found an oil lamp on a table next to the door and lit it. Holding it high, he directed the light across the interior.

"*Cachi!*" Marcus burst out, following with a long string of additional curses. He set the lamp down hard and backed, turning, bracing an arm around Claerwen as he came out, pulling her with him.

"What is it? What's in there?" she implored, alarmed. When he took too long to answer, she wriggled out of his grip, bounding into the doorway.

The house was completely ruined inside, its contents torn up and scattered in broken pieces. The whitewashed walls were stained with soot, filth, and as Claerwen's eyes adjusted to the darkness, she realized blood was there as well. Then she saw Elen. Though she had neither seen the woman nor heard a description of her, she knew the body lying on the floor was hers, looking as if every bone was broken, her skin bruised and burned, a bloody dagger in one hand. Elen was as broken as the rest of the house.

Claerwen was too shocked to scream or even move. Marcus came up behind her and dragged her outside, folding his arms around her, needing to protect her.

Digging her fingernails into his tunic, Claerwen choked out, "Where is Sinnoch?" She forced herself out of his arms, calling again, louder, then tried to dash inside.

Marcus grabbed her once more, pulling her around. "I will look. Stay here," he ordered, holding her there until he was certain she would follow his command. Cautiously, he re-entered. Claerwen stood a half step outside the doorway, watching, afraid to lose sight of him. He thoroughly searched the house but found no trace of the boy.

Outside again, he asked, "Does he know Daracha is his aunt?"

"I don't think so," Claerwen shook her head.

"Can you find the *hafod* again?" he queried, taking her hand. "Perhaps he is there."

"Would she try to kill Sinnoch?" Claerwen stalled in horror.

"If he is being used, like we are, for some ultimate purpose, she and Pascentius will keep him well hidden until that purpose is done. His father may be the key. If he is alive, we need to locate him. But who is he? Elen did not belong in any court circles. Her status never gave her access to a man with a rank important enough that could be passed on to the boy."

Claerwen insisted, "We must find him, before they do."

Marcus laid his palm gently to her cheek, his compassion responding to her distress. "If they don't already have the boy, they will send some of those warriors to look for him. You are right, we must hurry."

Claerwen led him along the obscure track and quickly found the summer house. It was abandoned, torn up inside like the other house.

"No one will be coming back to this," Marcus concluded on seeing the state of the tiny shelter. He held still several moments, listening intently, then shook his head. "I hear no movement."

Claerwen felt as dismal as the disappointment sounded in Marcus' voice. No movement meant no soldiers were searching the woods, indicating they had already taken the boy. "I don't understand, Marcus. Why would they take Sinnoch and leave you behind, if you are both a necessary part of the plan? It makes no sense."

"No, it doesn't, not for the way it was organized. I expected Pascentius would cross me, as much as he expected me to cross him. He only wanted me to stay in the camp until a certain time, but he still needs me for some reason. There is more to it than this and somewhere, between here and Winchester, there will be a reckoning."

With his fists clenched in frustration, Marcus looked up at the darkening sky through the tree crowns. A storm approached, as imminent as nightfall. He needed to search the *hafod* for evidence of the conspiracy, but they needed to leave for Winchester just as urgently.

"Lady?" called a voice from behind them.

They whirled around. Sinnoch stood there, bundled as usual in his rags, his dark eyes reddened as he bravely held back tears. Claerwen dropped onto her knees and the boy rushed into her arms.

"I can't find my mother. No one has seen her," he said, clinging tightly to Claerwen. "There are soldiers in the woods on the other side of the glen, where all the houses are. They are searching each one."

Claerwen looked up at Marcus, her eyes asking what to say. She saw the same relief in his face as she felt, that apparently Sinnoch had not been inside Daracha's house.

He knelt, laying his hand on the boy's shoulder and asked, "Were any people of the clan there?"

Sinnoch nodded. "The people were told to leave their houses while the soldiers searched. If they refused, they were beaten. My mother wasn't there and no one knows where she is. I even went to Master Girvyn, but he has not seen her. Then I came here, because she had once spoken of the sorceress. Has she been here?"

"We don't know what happened to her," Marcus said, keeping a convincing face in spite of the half-truth. "I think it would be best if you stay with Master Girvyn until we know."

"Aye, Lord Bhruic." The boy agreed, calming.

Marcus rose, touching Claerwen's arm to draw her attention. "There is little time."

"I will take the boy," she offered, understanding his need to search the *hafod* before they left.

Marcus hesitated. It was against his judgement to send Claerwen and the boy without his protection. But he also knew she was as capable of stealth as he was, even more so in the wilds. Both tasks needed accomplishment and departure for Winchester grew steadily more urgent. Reluctantly, he gave his approval.

"Tell Girvyn to 'scatter.' He will understand what it means. If the gelding is still there, pack it and be ready. I will meet you shortly," Marcus instructed, then paused as his eyes swept the surrounding trees. "Please, take extraordinary care."

Claerwen nodded understanding. She took Sinnoch's hand and disappeared into the trees.

Marcus turned to the *hafod* and entered it. From the smells that rose from the broken contents, he was reminded of a druid camp he had searched years before. It had been a laboratory as well, preserving many of their secrets born of wisdom and persistent experimentation. Considered sacred, the druids protected those secrets with zeal, even violence, and if he had ever been found in possession of any of their arts, he would have been executed for desecration.

Methodically, he searched the *hafod*. Little was useful, but he found shards of tiny ceramic crocks, their spilled contents soaked into a fallen plank from the trestle table. Sniffing at the wet patches, he found they smelled similar to sulphur, yet not quite the same. A few drops remained pooled in one shard, and he carefully tipped it over, dropping the liquid onto a patch created from one of the other spills. A black stain spread, then a small puff of smoke rose.

Though perfect evidence of the destructive poison, there was none left to remove, and regardless, it would have been too dangerous to carry a long distance. Finished, he returned to the farmstead. He declined to go inside the house again, certain that any useful evidence had already been destroyed there as well. Instead, he carefully walked around the pond.

The banks were marshy, the result of seasonal rising and falling of the spring's water level. Autumn's debris still covered the ground, and Marcus scanned the leaf and pine needle layer, tilting his head to one side, then the other, studying the area section by section, squatting to see better, until he found what he was looking for.

Most of the humus was soaked, decaying, settled from the recent rains and layers of snow that had come and gone. Except in one tiny area. The leaves had been disturbed, no longer pressed together in quite the same, natural way as the rest. Sweeping them aside with his hand, he found the soil underneath was disturbed as well. With a knife, he dug into the soggy earth. The space he found was just big enough to have temporarily housed an oilskin-wrapped object the size of Macsen's ceremonial spearhead.

Disappointed but certainly not surprised, Marcus cleaned the knife and rose. There was no use in looking for any further evidence. It would be gone or destroyed. Marcus quickly retreated.

Running through the woods, he emerged several minutes later near Girvyn's smithy. The glen was windswept and lightning flashed in the west, but the smithy was silent. He approached warily, then saw the gelding neatly packed.

Smiling, he called, "Glân?" No answer came. He went through the house. It was empty. He called again and still received no answer.

Going outside, he found fresh tracks leading away, a large pair and a tiny pair, side by side. He followed them until they disappeared in a northerly direction inside the forest. No other tracks were fresh enough to have indicated a follower, and he felt secure that Girvyn had taken Sinnoch to a well-hidden cave the blacksmith had once spoken of.

"Claerwen?" he called this time, going back to the building and walking out through the rear door.

Marcus' eyes swept across to where the southbound track began through the wood. Under the nearest tree, lay a ragged old cloak. Sprinting to it, he picked it up, and saw two sets of tracks leading away. One set, clear and consisting of three men's and a woman's prints, headed to the way south. The other, more obscure, was only a single set of male prints, showing a path straight towards the fort.

His skin crept when his eyes rose and met the dilapidated timber enclosure. Heavy smoke rose from the roofs within the walls.

"No..." he moaned, and the first of the rain spit in his face.

# Chapter 17

**Alba**

The decision came instantly. Marcus knew either set of tracks could lead to Claerwen, but the way the heels of the single set of prints were pressed into the mud told him the man carried something more than battle gear. The smoke rising from the fort was too heavy to merely be from a fire pit, also indicating greater danger and the higher likelihood of her whereabouts. And should he be wrong, he would rather disclaim the worst of possibilities and catch up to her on the road to Winchester.

Still holding the crumpled cloak in his hand, Marcus crossed the glen on a dead run. The front gates were open, but as he neared them, he saw fire strung across the entrance. A line of dry straw had been scattered there, soaked with oil and set ablaze. The flames were spreading to the adjacent walls. Unable to cross through, he careened around the side of the enclosure, skidding on the turf, and ran for the postern gate. The fire was expanding in that direction as well, but the door was still accessible. Kicking it wide, he thrashed his way inside.

Through the thickening smoke, he saw every structure burned. Screaming Claerwen's name, Marcus fought his way to the house they had shared and smashed in the door. The roof had already collapsed, but he saw nothing of her there. Backing away, he turned and dashed for the great hall.

The front doors were barred from inside. Using the large dagger from his belt, Marcus slashed at the aging hinges, here made of leather, unlike the new ones of iron in the barracks. He wrenched one door free, sending it pounding to the ground, and the metal bar used to block the door fell with a ringing thud.

Smoke, thick and black, curled from under the top of the doorframe and billowed out, driving him backward. He had seen, many times before, the way smoke could gather under a ceiling then suddenly drop with deadly, all-encompassing purpose, smothering any living being below. He needed to stay down, close to the floor, not only to see his way through, but to avoid breathing the fouled air as much as possible. If Claerwen was inside and still alive, he knew he had only a few minutes, perhaps not even that long, to pull her to safety. He dropped to his knees and crawled in.

He saw her almost immediately. Calling out, he scrabbled across to where she lay, next to the rear door, one arm outstretched, her fingers moving slowly. Her eyes were open, blankly gazing, showing she was conscious but not coherent.

Hot debris showered down and the roof groaned. Marcus glanced up, and through gaps in the smoke he saw the beams were close to giving way. He threw the cloak over Claerwen then ran his arms underneath her, preparing to lift, but halted when he saw her hair, braided in one long, thick plait, was caught in the crack between the rear door and its frame. He tugged on the braid, just enough to confirm his suspicion that it could not be pulled out. Looking up, he saw the hinges were of iron, not leather, and though old and rusty, they were still too solid to hack through. Then he saw the door had been deliberately wedged shut with shims of wood all around, pounded in so tightly that it would take too long to dislodge them or try to destroy the door itself. Whoever had done this was determined that Claerwen should die in the fire.

The roof groaned again. Cinders landed on the cloak, singeing a pattern of holes. Marcus clamped his hands down, suppressing them, then took up his dagger and cut the braid, freeing Claerwen.

Glancing up once more, he saw the smoke begin its descent from the ceiling. Fighting his own desperation, he knew that to lift Claerwen and attempt to run out would be to risk too much, that he would never reach the front doors before he was overwhelmed. Instead, he wrapped himself around her and started rolling across the floor. He awkwardly crashed through the half-blocked front doorway, tumbling out and down the steps with her tangled in his arms. Seconds later, the thatch gave, great chunks pounding down inside the building, flames spraying out through the doorway.

Not pausing, Marcus launched himself onto his feet and pulled Claerwen up, lifting her this time, and ran for the postern door. But the fire had spread along that wall and engulfed the debris surrounding the gate, blocking his escape. He stopped and turned from one side to the other. The entire enclosure was ablaze. Panic rose, thicker than the smoke from which he had just fled, strong enough to feel it rack all through his body as he realized there was no other way out of the fort.

Heat boiled out from the timber walls, smelling of pitch and oil. Marcus cursed, now understanding the extent of the arson. One timber wall began to crackle, the pitch inside it hot enough to explode.

He turned back into the courtyard, running hard. The timber boomed behind him and he dropped, sprawling over Claerwen as deadly chunks of flying wood and splinters, big enough to kill like arrows, spewed over the yard in a rush of hot air.

The stinging shower of projectiles subsided, and Marcus cautiously raised his head. He realized he lay against the low stone rim of the compound's well. Its round, iron-ringed wooden cover was down. From drawing water there, he knew the surface was only a man's height below and a pail was suspended on a heavy rope from a thick beam that crossed the top of the narrow shaft. The pail hung several feet below the water's surface, and the interior wall was made of unevenly laid stones, some cracked, some even missing, inadvertently creating periodic footholds. He lifted the lid and reached for the rope.

"Marcus?" Claerwen suddenly called, struggling to sit up.

He turned to her, surprised that she had wakened and was fairly alert. "Stay down," he ejected, and before he could explain the pitch-sabotaged timbers, another one shattered. He pulled her down, covering her again. When the shower of debris slowed, he spoke softly, urgently, "We must get down inside this well. It's the only place we'll be safe. There is no way out of the fort until those walls run out of fuel and the fire burns itself out."

He yanked the pail up and removed it, hoping there would be enough length of rope to tie into a harness that would hold them just within the water. Listening for the telltale sound of another impending explosion, he worked quickly, knotting a double loop around his thighs. He sat on the edge of the well, his legs inside.

"Come," he said to Claerwen, and told her to lock her arms tightly around his shoulders and cling behind him. Then with great care, he began to climb down, wedging his feet in the pockets of space left by the missing stones, using the rope mostly for balance.

The water was frigid. Marcus felt Claerwen tense as their feet entered the water, but she did not cry out and he continued downward. When they were chest-deep, they reached the end of the rope's length. He cautiously gave it more of his weight and less to the footholds, using the loops like a seat.

"Come in front of me," he instructed once he was satisfied the rope would hold their weight. He helped her grope her way around until she sat on his belly, the rope behind her. Then he stretched, balancing, pressing his back against one side and wedging his feet into an open space on the other. His legs and lower body were immersed just below the surface of the water and Claerwen only from the hips down.

Another timber exploded above, sending splinters crashing across the top of the well. Again Marcus clutched Claerwen protectively, pulling her down to him. Several small pieces of charred wood fell inside, pelting them. One still burned, striking the shaft's stones, then the water, hissing when it hit, and sank. He silently prayed the fire would burn itself out soon, knowing the cold water could be just as lethal, only slower to kill. He could not depend on the approaching storm to douse the flames. Though it threatened to be well endowed with rain, it could also pass to either the north or south, missing the glen completely.

"Claeri?" Marcus called softly as she stirred against him. She moaned, fighting the urge to cough. From the difficult way she breathed, he guessed that she suffered from the smoke sickness.

"It's so cold..." She mumbled, starting to shiver, and leaned her face into his shoulder.

Marcus hated that she had to be miserable. "Do you remember what happened to you?" he asked.

She rubbed a sore place below her right ear. "They must have hit me from behind. I thought I was dreaming at first, of the fires when the Irish killed my family. Then I realized where I was and they'd left me to die."

"Mine was a stupid idea to let you wait alone in the smithy," Marcus reprimanded himself. He felt for the place where she held her hand and found a bump.

Claerwen slowly shook her head, "They would have found another way to separate us. Don't blame yourself. I will be fine enough soon."

Marcus explained how he had found her, then apologized, "I'm sorry, I had to cut your hair. I couldn't free you any other way."

She nearly smiled, pulling a long, thick lock up and seeing it now only reached to her waist. She responded, "'Tis no matter now. How long do you think we'll need to wait here?"

"I don't know, Claeri. I just cannot say." He felt the icy water seeping up, crawling into his hair, and he cleared his mind for the wait.

Time passed. Marcus could not guess how much. He watched the small circle of dark grey above, unsure if it was smoke or clouds. Occasionally, raindrops struck his face. He shook almost violently, and his feet were cramped, feeling like a hundred knife pricks tearing through them and up his legs. Though the water buoyed him partially, it was not enough to ease his discomfort, the rope loops cutting into his thighs, his back pressed against his sword scabbard and the uneven stones. No more explosions had come for some time, and he was growing increasingly restless, the pain unbearable. Finally, he decided the time had come; he had to move before he dropped Claerwen.

"Claeri, we must go up from here, now. I'm too cramped to hold on any longer, and I can't lift you. You'll have to go first, alone. Just the way we came down, using the footholds and the rope for balance. Can you move your legs?"

Though shivering as much as he, she had been resting quietly, curled down onto his chest. She lifted her head and in the dim light of the shaft, she saw his eyes were squinted, his teeth gritted. Slowly she straightened, reaching for the rope behind her. Her hands were so cold she was barely able to feel its roughness. Her feet were numb and she wriggled them for several minutes, but instead of regaining feeling, they churned with agony.

"I will try," she said, knowing her weight contributed to his pain. Cautiously, she reached her left foot to the wall, seeking a foothold. She missed, unable to feel the stones. She tried once more, missed again.

"You can't feel anything, can you?" he asked.

She paused, shaking her head, but she persisted, groping first with her hand under the water's surface until she found a large opening. Pressing her foot into it, she gritted her teeth and pulled on the rope, lifting herself from him. She held her breath at the needling pain and twisted herself around, slipping her free leg over Marcus. Clinging to the rope, she reached her right foot out, this time easily locating another foothold. Pausing to gain her bearings and gasp for air, she began the climb. After a few steps up, she heard Marcus groan.

"Go on, Claeri," he urged when she stopped and looked down. "It's not so far, you can do it. You must keep going."

Reluctantly, she went on, dragging herself up a little at a time. She found breathing difficult, but she fought off the urge to cough, stopping periodically to rest until the shortness of breath eased. Finally reaching the stone lip at the top, she crawled over it and rolled onto the yard's surface.

"I'm here! The fire is nearly out," she called but heard no response. She looked into the shaft and saw Marcus sitting upright, freely hanging on the rope. He tried to stretch his legs, but she could tell his muscles were severely cramped. "Marcus?" she called.

"I can't move," he finally answered, his face rumpled with pain.

"Press your feet against the wall again and push as hard as you can," she instructed.

He groaned, unable to do as she said.

"Marcus, do it now! Brace your back against the wall and push your feet on the other side. As hard as you can! You've got to do it or you'll never come out of there! Do it now!"

Gathering his iron will, he leaned back and struggled to lift his legs, pulling them up with his hands until he was in the right position. Grunting, he pushed, tensing the muscles until the pain rose unbearably, then he released. He repeated the act twice more, until the cramping eased.

Then he looked up and saw Claerwen's frightened face above. "I'm coming," he said and gripped the rope, calling on his remaining strength. Slowly, he pulled himself upward, hand over hand, foothold to foothold. Gaining the top at last, he sprawled over the edge into Claerwen's arms.

It began to rain steadily.

"Thank the gods for rain," Marcus muttered, wishing it had come earlier. After several minutes of catching his breath, he sat up and swept his dripping hair back from his face. He scanned the badly smoldering ruins of the fort. As the rain strengthened, the drifting smoke diminished.

"We'll go back to the smithy," he said, slowly getting to his feet. He pulled Claerwen up and stumbled with her to the front entrance. The gates had fallen and with them, the heavy crossbeam from above. The wreckage sprawled across the entrance, crumbled and smelling acridly of the fire, but a small space had been left unfettered to one side. Supporting each other, they picked their way through.

Before they were halfway across the glen, the rain turned into a heavy, stinging sleet, and upon reaching Girvyn's building, they found the gelding still patiently waiting with its head drooping, slushy ice clinging to its coat. Marcus pulled the animal in under the roof and threw a blanket over it.

"We've got to get warm," he said, trying to keep the shivering out of his voice while he examined the forge's fire pit. It still smoldered inside and he fed it chunks of dried peat until it burned steadily. Glancing up at Claerwen, he saw her lean on the building's wall. Though she appeared to be watching him, her eyes were not alert. She did not cough but still breathed with difficulty, and he was troubled by the sluggish way she moved and spoke. Afraid she might take fever from sitting in the cold water, he crossed the few steps to her and gently squeezed her hand.

When she felt his fingers, she tried to smile, saying, "You saved my life. Again."

Marcus smiled back, "Whenever the chance arises. Please, go in and change into dry clothing. I will make something for us to eat." He pulled the packs off the gelding and took them inside, dropping them onto the mat in the rear room.

"But...we need to start for Winchester," she protested, following him.

He smiled again briefly, then opened the rear door. "In that storm and with night falling, we would not get far. See the ice forming on those trees? If this continues for long, by morning it will be so thick it will break a great many of even the heaviest branches. And because we must pass through the forest, no matter which direction we take, it will be too dangerous. When ice like that falls, it will kill."

"We're trapped?"

"For now. And I hope Pascentius is caught in this as well." He grunted his frustration and returned to the forge.

A short while later, Claerwen rejoined him, now wearing her heavy traveling clothes. She brought him a blanket, citing that he should change into dry clothes as well. Instead of taking her suggestion, he handed her a wooden spit with some of Girvyn's smoked venison and pieces of dried apple on it. Realizing they had not eaten all day, she gratefully took the hot food and huddled close to the forge's heat with him. They ate slowly to make the meal last longer, wishing there would have been a wineskin of mead to fill it out, and hoping that Sinnoch and Girvyn were safe.

Finished with the meal, Marcus rose to check how the horse fared and found the blanket he had thrown on earlier was soaked through. Pulling it off, he rubbed the animal down until it was comfortable and apparently without complaint. He took the blanket Claerwen had given him from his own shoulders and covered the gelding once more. Done, he turned for the storage room and found Claerwen before him, holding dry clothes.

"You need to help yourself now, Marcus," she told him, insisting this time. "You're so tired and I know you're still in pain. Look at your hands, how they're shaking." She took one and held it to her face.

From the pallor of her skin, he knew she was exhausted and ill, and her head must be pounding like his hammer to the anvil, yet she still had compassion left to think of his comfort. He was glad to be done for the day; he felt his legs were close to giving out, his bad knee ached like a knife was stuck in it and he only wanted anymore to sleep. Giving in, he kissed her lightly and let her guide him to their mat in the storage room.

---

"Ah, my body feels like a sack of rocks," Marcus groaned at dawn, rolling onto his back and finding Claerwen coming awake as well. He pulled himself up and lit an oil lamp, then slowly got onto his feet. "By the gods..." he ejected as he opened the back door of the house. Ice hung down from the overhanging roof thatch in long, tapering fingers that reached the ground.

Claerwen rose, coming to see what he had discovered.

"Don't touch it, Claeri," he warned and pulled her away, handing her the lamp, then he leaned back and kicked out. A section broke, splintering, crashing outward, and he muttered a curse as he stared through the gap.

The entire landscape was coated in ice, grotesquely twisted from the capricious winds. It clung to absolutely everything, bending heavy branches, breaking off smaller trees at mid-trunk. The road was deeply layered, slick, impossible to walk on.

Marcus swung around, his face in utter amazement. "I've seen bad ice storms before, but this is far beyond the worst. We cannot hope to travel through that." He moved through the rooms, out into the smithy. The glen was coated as well, like thick cream, only hard, and the burned fort in the distance showed as a matter of iced-over lumps.

"'Tis beautiful...and eerie," Claerwen said quietly. "We must wait?"

"Aye." He squinted in consternation then conceded, "It will give us time to prepare."

"Prepare?"

"Aye. First, this bird claw that you like so well," he grinned, holding it up, "is going back to the Otherworld." Taking up a dagger, he sliced off the lock of hair the talons were woven into and threw the claw onto the ashes of the forge's fire. "The rest of this disguise is leaving as well." He ran a hand over his beard and saw her eyes lighten when she understood he was going to shave it.

"I will heat water for you," she offered and reached to tap down a chunk of ice from the roof.

"You don't need to." He went back inside, Claerwen following.

"How can you bear to do that without hot water?" she asked.

"You've seen me do this for years," he said, winking. He sat on their mat and started to scrape off the bulk of the beard, leaving a short bristle to shave with a smaller blade. "If you still have a comb, can you try to get it through my hair?"

Claerwen teased, "You'd best finish that before I start. It's going to take a bit of time and a lot of pulling."

She watched him trim around his moustache with short, smooth strokes, well accustomed to a lack of water and no mirror. Finished, he rubbed a hand over his lower face in search of any place he missed, then said, "We should sleep as much as possible, until it is safe to travel. How are you feeling by now?"

Claerwen sat down behind him and began to weed the knots out of his hair. "I can breathe almost normally, but my head is still in pain. In truth, I think I would be a burden to you without a day of rest. I would wager that you need it as well."

He hummed his agreement and waited patiently for her to work through his hair. Although each passing rainstorm had cleaned it, he had deliberately not combed it since beginning the ruse, letting it remain wild and fitful to enhance the disguise. As Claerwen untangled it with a comb carved of shell, it fell once again into its various layers, shining blue-black in the light of the lamp.

By mid-morning, the sky had cleared and the sun was strong enough to give warmth. The ice cracked and fell in chunks throughout the day, melting into racing rivulets by late afternoon. Mud puddled wherever no grass grew. The cold wind did not return and the air remained moderate, giving hope that the next morning would prove travelworthy. They slept through most of the day and that night.

At first light, Marcus and Claerwen began moving south, riding pillion. Weaving carefully, they sought the most unclogged paths and avoided dangerous places where ice still clung. Several times a clod fell near enough to splatter freezing mud on them.

Once beyond the confines of the forest, they gained speed. They had taken a supply of food from Girvyn's stores, eliminating a few days' need to hunt or forage. No more snow or rain fell, and on the evening of the second day, as the sun set, they came within sight of the Antonine Wall. They camped in an abandoned barn within a mile of it and Marcus briefly scouted before dark closed in, surveying the moorland to the south.

"It will be easier once we cross the wall," he commented later over his supper. "With the open land, we can move faster."

He looked up from his meal when Claerwen said nothing, disconcerted by her silence. Then he realized she had fallen asleep, sitting up, leaning on a beam, still holding a piece of smoked deer meat in her hand. Easing her down, he spread a blanket over her, finished his meal, and watched until he fell asleep himself.

Shortly before the next morning's first light, Claerwen began dreaming. Disconnected faces and images trailed fitfully across her mind. Even in sleep, she tried to string them together and make sense of them, but they seemed to be only so much nonsense. Nothing was clear except a dim glow that shuddered to one side, flaring up and radiating warmth. She turned away because it disturbed the images. Then she heard herself cry out, the sound of her own voice seeming to echo. A horse nickered somewhere. Then a hand touched her, and she realized she was awake.

When her eyes opened, she saw Marcus squatting next to her, a piece of wood in one hand from their campfire, held like a torch. His other hand was on her arm. The gelding whinnied softly in the corner behind her.

She breathed hard, feeling the hair on her neck had risen tautly. Slowly she sat up. For several moments, she remembered the sense of fear, but little more. Then she shook her head, as if to dismiss all of it.

"What did you see?" Marcus asked.

"It's gone," she answered, rubbing her eyes roughly. "I think I heard Myrddin's voice, but I don't know what he said. And I saw Dun Breatann, the walls, as if I was looking up at them. Nothing more. I don't think it was important, only a dream."

Marcus studied her face, his brows jagged down. "Are you sure?"

She saw he was worried, that he was searching for signs of the fire in her eyes, that he must have caught the sense of fear from her. To reassure him, she began to roll up their bedding, smiling softly, and said, "It was not meant for concern."

He grunted and rose, went to the barn door, opened it slightly, then closed it again. "It will be light soon," he commented. Turning around, he crossed to the horse, reaching for the saddle blanket.

The barn door slammed open.

In a rush of shouts and ringing metal, Pascentius burst in, a handful of guards following, all with drawn swords.

Claerwen whirled around, shielding Marcus as he reached for his own weapon's hilt. But Pascentius drove forward, the tip of his sword stopping just under her chin.

"Don't move or I will cut her!" he shouted.

Marcus froze, watching the soldiers circle them. Two grabbed his arms, a third unbuckled his baldric and took it with the sword.

"Search him!" Pascentius ordered.

Marcus kicked the soldier to his left, yanking his right arm free. In the same instant, Claerwen leaned to her right, avoiding Pascentius' blade. She dove for the horse, trying to leap astride, but the commander was too quick and tripped her, sending her sprawling into a pile of stale straw. He grabbed a handful of her hair and pulled back, arching her painfully. Lowering the sword, he held the blade against her neck and shouted, "I warn you, Marcus ap Iorwerth!"

Marcus smashed a fist into another soldier's face, marking the third man he had rendered unconscious. As he swung around at the shout, he saw Claerwen. "No!" he yelled, lunging, but two more men wrestled him down. They took the daggers from his belt and wristband.

Pascentius withdrew the sword and signaled for Claerwen to rise. Regaining her senses, she stood shakily. But on seeing Marcus pinned with his face jammed to the ground, she lurched forward. Pascentius caught her around the waist and dragged her back. She wriggled, kicking and smacking with her fists, trying to slide out of his grip, but the commander was tall and strong, lifting her under one arm as if she were a sack of squirming grain.

"I am taking your woman hostage, Marcus ap Iorwerth. By now, her worth has risen enough to warrant her keep," Pascentius taunted then ordered his men, "Tie him up."

"Marcus!" she screamed, reaching for him when she realized she was going to be taken away. He was on his feet again, straining forward. Wrenching one arm free, his fingertips brushed hers, but the men regained control, forcing him towards the back wall. He watched her fight, twisting and pounding with stinging ferocity, then she was gone. The soldiers lashed him tightly to a beam then left the barn, taking the gelding with them.

For a few moments, Marcus held still, listening to the hoofbeats canter swiftly away. He glared at the empty barn, from one side to the other, unable to move more than his head, horrified by his uselessness. Then he filled his lungs and screamed his rage.

# Chapter 18

## Dun Breatann, Kingdom of Strathclyde

The fortress of Dun Breatann perched upon a double-humped rock, rising straight up out of the River Clyde's northern shore. The rock's sides were so steep that bank and ditch defenses were unnecessary. On the landward side, a line of cut stone steps led to the front gates, easily defendable by only a few warriors. A boat landing filled a narrow breach on the riverside, and a second set of steps rose from there to the palace above. Marshes spread from the river to the northward lowland hills, a small settlement of farmsteads huddled close in to the rock's base, and a broad shore lined the river eastward from the stronghold.

The sun had almost set by the time Marcus reached Dun Breatann. He had found the beam to which he'd been lashed in the abandoned barn was rotted away both at the roof and ground. With much pushing and grunting, he had wrenched it backward, breaking out a section of the rickety wall and falling with it. He was stunned when he hit the ground, and the beam had nearly rolled with him lying precariously atop it, threatening to crush him. But it balanced, and he stretched himself long enough to extricate his tied ankles off the broken end. The soldiers had not found the knife in his boot, and by awkwardly twisting his legs up, he had just reached it with his fingertips, then cut the wrist bonds.

Finally free, his first desire had been to chase down Pascentius, but being nearly unarmed and on foot made it a ludicrous thought. Then he remembered Claerwen's dream. Following both instinct and logic, he had turned towards Dun Breatann, hoping to all the gods that his friend, mentor and ally Ceredig, King of Strathclyde was home, and that Myrddin was truly there as well.

Marcus carefully scouted the stronghold from the landward side then settled into a thick copse to wait for nightfall, watching up at the walled enclosure. Soldiers were abundant, mostly belonging to Ceredig's regular war band, but many others wore an unrecognizable badge and appeared to take authority over the king's men. The strange soldiers meant trouble, and even if carefully disguised, Marcus knew he would be searched and questioned at the gates. Then he felt chills creep up his neck as he remembered Claerwen's dream again. She had described the walls just as he saw them at that moment.

As night came into fullness, Marcus crept out of the copse. Slipping past the settlement, he emerged near the rivershore docks, busy with the day's returning fleet of fishing curraghs and coracles. Crouching in shadowed corners, he waited impatiently for a gap in the crowd to open. From there he watched a row of coracles beached on the shore, the last one conveniently close to the water's edge. It was no more than a tiny round frame covered with a heavily oiled hide.

Gradually, the fishermen drifted towards the houses. Marcus dashed across to the last coracle and slid it into the river. Curling down into the bowl-shaped bottom, he let the water's current pull the boat away.

Once free of the settlement's torchlight, Marcus came upright, sitting on his heels. He guided the boat, dipping its paddle silently to one side, then the other. Moving rapidly westward, he skirted the fortress and passed the boat landing, a shelf of low-lying shore hemmed in by a stone wall. More fishermen were gathered at a small gap in the wall's center, unloading their catch in trade with Ceredig's court. The shelf of land extended out from underneath the wall, and Marcus maneuvered his coracle to the western end where torchlight did not reach. He grounded the boat.

Pausing, he rubbed his left knee. Kneeling in a cold puddle brought shooting pain, but he forced himself to ignore it. Then he stood, balancing precariously in the unstable boat. Reaching high, he caught the top of the wall and dragged himself up it. He rolled over the top and fell down into a dark corner onto a lump of river-soaked turf. In a narrow shadow, he lay flat and still, listening intently, peering into the glaring torchlight of the unloading area.

Gradually, the fishermen finished their trading, wandered to their boats and cast off. Lackeys removed half the torches and retreated up the narrow passageway into the fortress, but more than the usual contingent of guards continued to patrol. Nearly all wore the unknown badges. Marcus waited until they were all turned away, then eased deeper into the corner where the wall became imbedded into the rock. The turf had crept up and hidden a small opening in the face. At a glance, it appeared to be merely a slight depression over which the grass had grown, but Marcus peeled the turf down, pulling its clinging roots away, and revealed a larger hole. Slowly, he eased his head and shoulders into the opening, his arms out in front for guidance, and pulled himself inside.

The opening sloped downward at first, and he had trouble to maneuver his wide shoulders through. A bigger man would never have been able to enter at all, and Marcus was pleased that his ancestors had passed to him their smaller solidity. Wriggling through, he came into a wider section and crawled on hands and knees. No light penetrated, but previous excursions gave him familiar bearings, and he continued a hundred feet straight into the rock base of the fortress.

The floor sloped farther downward, giving the tunnel enough height that he could stand. Dim light glowed, not far ahead, and Marcus knew he was approaching an intersection of three tunnels and that one guard would be posted there. He stopped for a moment, listening, and concluded the number of sentinels had not been increased.

Marcus sprinted, leaping into the small room. Locking an arm around the guard's throat, he pressed a thumb and forefinger into his neck, squeezing. The man struggled but quickly fell unconscious. Marcus posed him on a small stool, making him look as if he had merely fallen asleep.

The left tunnel rose sharply, a long series of roughly cut steps curving upward. Marcus followed them. At the top, he halted and listened again, hearing voices murmur on the other side of a tiny trap door in the ceiling. With the dagger from his boot, he poked into the crack on the door's long side, away from the hinges, running the blade until it stopped. A small piece of wood wedged into the crack acted as a bolt. He pressed the knife into the block and pushed up, popping it out. The tiny door opened into the rear of a small, dark storage room.

Marcus lifted himself through the opening and crawled to the door of the room beyond. Pressing his face to the floor, he peered underneath. Spaciously arranged around a large fire pit, it was the central room of Ceredig's palace chambers. Two pairs of feet warmed at the hearth.

The voices were silent for a while, as if to reconsider the path of their conversation, then one man suddenly spoke, anger and frustration marking his voice, "I still don't believe it! He would never do such as this. I have known him all his life, Lord Myrddin, and Marcus ap Iorwerth would not do this. He is no traitor."

"I don't want to believe it either, but apparently there is evidence."

The door to the storage room swung open, squeaking slightly, and the patterned wool drape over it was shoved aside.

"What wouldn't I do?"

Ceredig, Lord Strathclyde, husky, tall, red-haired symbol of the northern Celts, launched out of his chair. Behind him, Myrddin rose as well, his face pale in shock.

The Prince of Dinas Beris stood proudly before them, haggard, scuffed, dirty and partially wet, his hair in disarray, and a smoldering, controlled rage in his glittering black eyes. Even without his customary two-handed sword, he still looked wild and dangerous.

Ceredig's brown eyes smiled through his tired expression, and he clapped Marcus heartily on the shoulder. He declared, "I should have expected it. We were afraid you would come here. Nothing and no one can hold you, my old friend, not even Uther."

"Uther?" Marcus shot back.

Myrddin confirmed, "Aye, Uther. You must have seen his soldiers out there. You've been declared a fugitive."

Marcus' eyebrows jagged down, adding even more harshness to his already ragged face, and he demanded, "Why?"

Myrddin frowned coldly. "If you came from Winchester, why would you need to ask?"

"We were in the north, near the west islands. What do they think I've done?"

"The north?" Myrddin was honestly surprised, then after studying Marcus a few moments, asked, "You genuinely don't know what's happened, do you?"

Marcus warily shook his head, his stomach sinking.

Anger drained from Myrddin's face, revealing disappointment; then he turned away, unable to answer.

Ceredig said softly, "Ambrosius is dead. Uther is high king now."

Marcus stared at him. "When?"

"Eight days ago. A courier arrived with a statement and an edict from Uther. His soldiers came within hours after."

"Eight days?" Marcus repeated. The rage in his eyes grew intense. "That's impossible. Pascentius has been hiding with Irish mercenaries for weeks in a small fort two days' ride north of here. They left only five days ago and were still at the Antonine Wall at dawn, *this morning*. I saw him myself. It is impossible..."

When his voice drifted off, Ceredig said, "They say a low-ranking soldier disguised as a physician gave Ambrosius poison instead of medicine. The man disappeared from the palace within minutes. The king died very quickly after that."

Marcus spoke bitterly, "It must have been Banawr, Pascentius' second-in-command, or a man arranged by him. I believe he was originally to be the assassin. I injured him, breaking his clavis bone, then brokered a false bargain with Pascentius to take his place. It was meant to keep myself in the camp long enough to turn the trap back onto Pascentius. They must have sent Banawr south, just after I incapacitated him."

Myrddin queried, "But why would an assassin be sent ahead so early without a war band's support? Or Pascentius himself to make the claim?"

Marcus sighed heavily, "It's logical. They wanted Uther to take the crown — he will be the next target. Pascentius is on his way to Winchester now with about a quarter war band. I'd expect, as he nears the capital, plenty more warriors from the Saxon Shore will join him. I'm sure he still has Macsen's spearhead. And why am I a fugitive?"

Myrddin faced Marcus again. His eyes had the numb look of a grieving man. Moving a few paces forward, he answered, "The statement said there was a ring left where the poison was prepared. The symbol etched into it was identified as that of Dinas Beris, of Eryri, in the kingdom of Gwynedd. They believe the low-ranking soldier was you."

Marcus squinted with impotent fury. He slapped his hand against his tunic, feeling under the belt for the tiny patch into which he had sewn his clan ring for safekeeping. Finding a bump still there, he yanked off the tunic, turned it inside-out and cut open the patch. A rock fell out.

"I've been so stupid," he spit through clenched teeth. "They had planned to assassinate you on my lands, Myrddin, to cast the blame on me, but I spoiled it for them. They will try again. Now they've killed Ambrosius and succeeded in blaming me. Uther will be next. It is a plot of revenge against Claerwen and me." He spun around, thumping a fist into a beam. The impact shook the timber hard enough to loosen dust from the roof.

"Steady, man," Ceredig said, gripping Marcus' arm.

Then Marcus froze. Horror and dread mixed on his face, startling both other men. His brows knotted together and he said, "Claerwen has a map I stole from Pascentius. It proves he was in league with Octa and that they had planned the attack on Caer Ebrauc together. I gave it to her to keep, so she could bring it to you, Myrddin, in case of trouble, because it was more likely that I would be caught instead."

Myrddin's eyes widened as he realized what Marcus implied.

"She is a hostage?"

"Aye, they took her this morning…left me stranded. She had a dream connecting you with Dun Breatann. That's why I came here."

"But why? Why would he take her now when he's already had you accused?"

"Because he must force me to follow him to Winchester, to place me there by the time they try to murder Uther, and to validate the false evidence they already have."

"If you go, you'll fall directly into their plans. If you don't… What are you going to do?"

The seething desire to create violence raged in Marcus' eyes, sending alarm through both Ceredig and Myrddin. An uneasy silence smothered the room as he fought to stay calm. He watched Ceredig's face, drawing on their friendship and long alliance for reassurance that he was not going to make another mistake.

Then Ceredig's eyes nearly grinned. He said to Myrddin, "He is going to humiliate Pascentius in return for taking his wife. He will steal her out from under the man's bloody arse. Hah! I like it! Never make Marcus ap Iorwerth angry, Myrddin. He is proud and stubborn, and freedom means everything to him. He can be very creative in his revenge."

Ceredig's smile expanded, and he told Myrddin of the boy he had fostered for Iorwerth of Dinas Beris. He explained that as a raw youth, Marcus had been unpredictably wild to the point that his elders thought his mentality was more than a little questionable. But as he had matured into manhood, they had seen that contradictory nature evolve into a rare and passionate courage, tempered with the insight to understand the truth behind the truth of life, and not hide behind wishful hopes for what ought to have been.

Ceredig said to Marcus, "I was amazed when I learned that Claerwen had somehow tamed a wild loner like you. I have not seen her since the night you discredited that lout Drakar. Myrddin tells me she is no longer the shy little girl I remember, but a beautiful woman of strength and courage. You remember that she is distantly related to me? I am proud of that. Very proud. We will make the arrangements for you, my friend. What do you need?"

Marcus named the items he wanted. Ceredig led Myrddin out to quietly order the supplies from his own people, grinning to himself as he passed the watchful eyes of Uther's soldiers standing guard outside his doors.

Alone for a few minutes, Marcus poured himself a cup of mead, indulging his thirst. He thought of Claerwen, agonizing that he would be too late, that Pascentius would kill her out of impatience. He watched the mead spin as he held the cup's rim in his fingers, rotating it slowly. His mind wandered, remembering the night Ceredig had mentioned, the same night he had first met Claerwen in a tiny walled garden behind Dun Breatann's great hall, only a short stroll from where he stood now. In those few brief moments, all those years ago, he had found the only other driving force in his life that meant as much to him as freedom. And without Claerwen, he thought, he might as well give himself up to the Saxons.

Returning with Myrddin a short time later, Ceredig announced a horse would be packed and waiting at a designated place outside the fortress within the hour. He handed a thick bundle of clothing to Marcus, along with a sword.

"I honestly don't know how you got in without being caught," Myrddin commented.

"He's perfected it into an art," Ceredig quipped.

Myrddin fell quiet, watching with fascination as Marcus sat in a chair next to the fire pit and stared into a tiny bronze mirror propped up on the hearthstones. Rubbing pale grey ash from the edge of the pit into his hair, eyebrows and moustache, Marcus combed it in until it looked the color of iron. Brushing more lightly over his face and neck, he made his skin look pale and old, then etched kohl into the tiny lines around his eyes, adding even more age to his face. The hollows under his eyes were already dark with stress and fatigue, needing little attention. As he worked, he detailed the convoluted progress the quest had taken.

Ceredig said, "You know you have us as witnesses that you were here, proving it is impossible for you to have been in Winchester when Ambrosius was poisoned."

Marcus smiled wryly. "Thank you, my old friend, but you know Uther may not be willing to take your word. He will know that you and I have been close allies for many years." He looked up from the mirror and gazed into the shadows across the room. He said, mostly to himself, "I was certain, as soon as Pascentius moved out, that I could have unraveled his plans. Instead, it was only meant to keep me busy. 'Tis all for naught now."

Myrddin countered, "Not completely. If you can get that map back, it will serve us well to have the proof of Octa's original involvement. We will need it to help defend you as well."

Marcus grimaced, more concerned with how he was going to rescue Claerwen. He pulled off his boots, taking the dagger from one. Ceredig handed him two pieces of thick leather. Marcus placed them on the hearthstones, setting the boots on top. Using the dagger tip to trace around each boot, he cut the leather to fit inside. He then cut four more pieces, sized to fit only in the heel. Two small pieces went in each boot first, then the larger ones. When he tried them on, standing up, he was nearly an inch taller.

"It's not much of a difference, but it can be enough to confuse them," he said to Myrddin's curious face. Unrolling the final items from the bundle Ceredig had given him, he found a dark brown homespun hooded soutane, a silver Celtic cross and a dark grey full-length cloak. He arranged the sword, a hand-and-a-half size with a short crossbar, onto a baldric, placing the hilt low behind his shoulder and the blade's length tightly along his body. Then he pulled the soutane on over his clothes, letting only the sword's pommel free of the neck and hidden underneath his hair. The cross went around his neck, the cloak over his shoulders. He arranged his hair a little more, combing it flat in a pattern radiating from a central part at the crown, almost in a Roman style, except for its length.

Marcus walked into the room's shadows. Then he swept around, pulling up the cloak's broad hood, and came forward again slowly, stooping as he emerged into the light.

"He looks as if he's lived sixty winters," Myrddin remarked incredulously. "You would never know unless you'd seen him create it."

"I've seen him change like that many times, and I still can't believe it." Ceredig added.

"And this is only to get out of Dun Breatann," Marcus said. "Bless you, my sons."

Ceredig snorted, amused by Marcus' ironic face.

"Aye, me, a monk of the new religion. Claerwen would laugh at this," he grinned briefly, then went somber again. "I will leave immediately. You know I appreciate the help."

"I have owed you for years, more than I can count, for all the help you've given me."

Myrddin offered, "I will do all I can for you, but you know Uther and I don't get along. He has even placed some of the blame for his brother's death on me."

"But Ambrosius was your father," Marcus blurted.

"Uther has an overwhelming temper. In time, I hope, he will learn to examine the evidence more carefully, but for now he is angry and quick to blame. Unfortunately, you are the first choice due to the evidence, and I am the second because I asked you to help. When you rescue Claerwen, I have a place I can hide her while you are in Winchester."

Marcus pulled on his moustache, thinking, then grunted to himself and said, "She will come with me. There is no place to hide her safely."

"How in the gods' names will you protect her?"

"I can disguise her as well. It will allow us to move more freely."

"And if you're caught? Then she dies."

"And if we don't clear our names, we will die anyway. Even if I had left her at home, she still could have been taken. Or worse."

Myrddin clamped his jaw shut in concession then said, "I am returning to Winchester in a few days for my father's funeral. Perhaps there is a way I can get you into the palace."

"No," Marcus said. "We will do this on our own. But I appreciate your offer."

Ceredig suggested, "Don't you want to stay here until sunrise? You look exhausted."

"No, I will leave now. I don't want Claerwen to endure

Pascentius' treatment any longer than she must. She is waiting for me."

Saluting Ceredig and Myrddin, he strode for the tunnels.

# Chapter 19

**Winchester**

Claerwen shivered, watching the top of the tent shake in the wind, and she counted the end of the ninth day of her captivity.

Another storm approached.

She wished she could stand for a moment, pace the two steps to the end of the length of chain shackled to her ankle, then pace back to the bare pallet she had been given for a bed. The tent was not high enough to stand within. Sitting cross-legged on the pallet, she picked and tucked at a torn and filthy blanket until it covered her cold feet. Her boots had been confiscated to discourage her from attempting an escape.

Claerwen guessed they were nearing Winchester, judging from the terrain they had passed through; but no one was allowed to talk to her other than Pascentius himself, and he told her nothing of importance.

Each evening the commander appeared with her supper, taunting her with predictions that Marcus would never come for her. He tempted her with bathing and better food, but Claerwen responded with defiant, steadfast silence, no matter how her belly grumbled or how she itched with discomfort. Pascentius was only trying to trick her into revealing how Marcus might rescue her.

Soon supper would come again, a thin, foul tasting gruel

accompanied by a rock hard, rat-nibbled piece of bannock. She listened to the guards outside as they shifted uncomfortably in the windy darkness, one at each corner of the tent, stationed from the moment camp was set up until it was broken, just as two in front and two behind her were posted for each day's ride between camps. Then she heard Pascentius' approaching footsteps crunch in the snow. Claerwen sighed, wishing he would not belabor himself with his insults and cajoling.

"Well, Mistress Claerwen," he began as he pulled open the tent flap and squatted. He set her supper bowl on the ground. "We still haven't seen your husband. He must have become lost, I fear. What do you believe?"

Claerwen's eyes lifted and met the sarcastic face he always seemed to wear. "I think you waste your time," she returned, folded her arms and looked away.

"Not for long, Mistress. I assume you realize we lay near to Winchester now, and we are progressing well in the preparations for our entrance. And once that happens, if Marcus ap Iorwerth holds true to his standards, you will be witness to his forthcoming execution. And after that, we will be witness to yours."

When she did not react, he asked, "Do you remember having difficulty waking one day, not long ago? A day when you seemed incapable to rise, both of you?"

Claerwen remained silent, but Pascentius kept at his taunt, "You left your house. You weren't supposed to, you know. You were supposed to stay there, so we could take you, and kill you then, leaving Marcus ap Iorwerth to think we took you hostage. He would have followed us to Winchester. But you fouled our plan."

Claerwen nearly smiled. "And when you did find me, you put me in that burning building to die. But Marcus read the trail as false and found me. And now you take me hostage for true. You certainly go to a lot of bother, don't you?"

"Sometimes flexibility is appropriate."

"As when you flee from every battle you've instigated?"

Pascentius flushed red and tried to hide it, shoving the bowl of gruel towards Claerwen. It tilted slightly, spilling a little over the rim. "This is how Marcus ap Iorwerth feeds his women. Like dogs. Like the dog that he is. And mad dogs should be put out of their misery, don't you agree?"

Claerwen glared at him with unflinching calmness, shielded by her dignity.

Pascentius stood, remaining just outside the tent's opening. He went on, unmoved by her icy silence. "He did seduce Daracha's little sister Elen. Poor unsuspecting girl, took to his handsome face and kind words. Part of his trade, women are, more than his other talents, I should say. You fell for it as well, didn't you?"

For several moments, Claerwen watched Pascentius' smirk broaden, and she wondered how Marcus had ever been able to hold onto his temper while playing out the ruse in the northern camp. Her green-blue eyes held steady, coldly considering the commander. Behind them, her patience came to an end. She slapped at the bowl, flinging it upward into the Roman-style robe. It hit at mid-thigh, tipped up and slid down, leaving its contents smeared like splattered dung.

Pascentius jumped back, rage replacing the disparagement. "You miserable — "

"Don't waste your time," Claerwen cut him off, her voice thick and strong.

Pascentius avoided her eyes, frustrated by her unbreachable defense. He swept away from the tent, calling for his seneschal.

It was then that Claerwen realized Pascentius expected a rescue would come very soon. Worried since her capture that Marcus had been left dead in the barn, she now reasoned if that were true, Pascentius would not try so hard to learn how her deliverance might be staged. She believed the commander had not struck her or ordered her punishment out of fear of reprisals if she was found hurt. She smiled, knowing the havoc Marcus was capable of, hidden so well behind his calm face, and she wondered if Pascentius' confidence was once again waning.

Weak and lightheaded from a fortnight of inadequate food and disappointed that a precious meal had been wasted, even if it was the abominable gruel, Claerwen reached under the tent's hem to scoop a handful of snow. For a few moments she stared at it, vaguely amazed that it could still melt in her icy hands and the freezing air of the tent. She sucked its moisture slowly out of her palms while she tried to warm herself with thoughts of balmy summer days, then dried her hands on the ragged blanket.

---

Hours later, Claerwen lay listening for the midnight call. The camp itself was quiet, more so than usual. Only the rattling tent and the rustling of horses on the stake line were audible above the wind's howl. Restless, she turned over and finally concluded she had missed the call. She gave a long, unrepressed sigh as if to replace it.

Uncomfortable on the hard pallet, Claerwen drifted into a doze several times, unable to give in to true sleep. Her stomach continued to growl and ache from emptiness. For a while, she gazed at a guttering torch, visible through a small tear in the tent. The night temperature dropped further. Claerwen wound the blanket around herself tighter, drawing her feet up. The shackle felt as if it was frozen, preventing her leg from staying warm. She sighed again, trying to release her tension, and turned over once more to face the rear of the tent, her back to the tied-down flaps that were no shield to the wind. She forced her eyes to close.

Several minutes later she came alert again, blinking her eyes. A face appeared, floating in the top of the quivering tent. It was Marcus', and for an instant, she thought he was there, finally coming to rescue her, but she realized it was how he looked years before.

She blinked again, trying to make the vision clearer, but when she opened her eyes, Elen's face appeared instead. Though Claerwen had not seen the woman except in a horrible, fleeting glimpse of death, the image was as clear as if she stood there unharmed.

Claerwen closed her eyes once more, squeezing hard, now wanting to dispel the vision. It faded gradually, drifting behind a curtain of swirling clouds, and when her eyes reopened, Sinnoch emerged. But instead of just a face, she saw the boy in a summer meadow, dancing joyously to some unheard jig reeling in his mind. Fascinated by the image, she watched the boy cavort and smile, his hair whipping about his face.

Claerwen sat up abruptly. The image disappeared and she reached out, grasping as if she could recapture it and hold it in her hands. For a few more moments she searched, hoping more would come. Instead, foreboding swelled inside her, choking her with a frightening sense of loss. She felt as if it was a presence, like a source of heat in the tent somewhere behind her. Wary, she turned her head.

A cold hand slapped over her mouth, its force roughly shoving her down. Claerwen came fully awake, panic taking hold as she felt a steel-strong arm go underneath and around her waist, dragging her off the pallet. She wrenched sideways and glimpsed the dim silhouette of a man. Trying to roll out from his grip, she lashed out with her fists and her one unshackled leg, but he turned and sat, hauling her onto his lap. He braced her against his chest and forced her head back.

"It's me," came a sharp whisper, hot in her ear.

She froze.

"Claeri, it's me."

Her breath caught in her throat at Marcus' favorite endearing name for her. As his hand lifted from her mouth, she twisted in his lap and ran her hands over his face, searching for the familiar landmarks of his eyes, his moustache, the shape of his cheekbones. She could tell he was in one of his disguises by the strange feel of his hair and that he had let his beard grow again. Then she flung her arms around his neck, utterly relieved he had come at last and he was real, not another vision.

He hushed her when he heard her take breath to speak, pressing a finger to her lips. Leaning forward to whisper tightly in her ear, he said, "We must go quickly. There is little time."

She squeezed his hand in understanding as she slipped from his lap and pulled up the blanket to expose the shackle, guiding his hands to it.

He cursed under his breath, then slipped out a small dagger from his left sleeve. Picking at the lock, he found it difficult to negotiate in the dark, but he succeeded in opening it. As he slid the dagger back into its sheath, he leaned forward again, asking, "Boots?"

Claerwen answered, "Taken. No matter now. But, wait." She abruptly turned back to the pallet and thrust her hand underneath, digging out handfuls of dirt. Shortly, she pulled out two objects and placed them in his hands. Even without light, he could tell they were the folded map and the talisman, and he grunted his surprise and relief that she had been able to protect both. He stuffed the map inside his tunic, securely deep into a small pouch on a thong, then hung the talisman from Claerwen's neck, tucking it inside her clothing.

"Wait here," he whispered and left the tent. Within minutes, he returned with a pair of boots and helped her to pull them on.

"What did you do?" she asked, but he hushed her again and took her hands. She struggled to her feet, letting him guide her from the tent. Outside, she leaned on him, finding her legs weak from disuse and hunger.

"Can you walk?" he asked, holding her protectively.

Instead of answering, Claerwen stared at the camp. A few torches were still lit, showing that every warrior slept a deep, unnatural sleep, some snoring, some leaning against trees, others slumped over sideways. One near the tent was bootless. She frowned at Marcus.

He flashed a grin. "Come, before they waken."

Claerwen laid her hand on his sleeve, holding him back, her face still asking what he had done.

He leaned, whispering, "One of Myrddin's sleeping potions. I'll explain later."

She saw his eyes glint and she smiled, his familiar, oblique humor suddenly warming her, making her feel safe. Running her arms around him, she sought his comfort as he supported her, walking to a waiting horse. As they mounted, snow began to fall, and they disappeared into the swirling storm.

---

Marcus steadied Claerwen as she knelt, sinking onto a waiting bedroll. "Did they hurt you?" he asked, his intense eyes still showing the rage Ceredig and Myrddin had seen, though tempered now by the success of his rescue. He lit a small torch for light and was appalled when he saw the extent of her dismal condition, her clothing filthy, her thin-drawn face showing she had lost much weight.

"No, I will be fine enough…once I get warm. And have some real food." Her teeth chattered but she ventured a smile and reached to hold his face, her eyes telling him how much she appreciated his courage. She saw he had greyed his hair, moustache and beard with ash. "How long have you been here? And where is here?"

"Since morning," he answered, bringing her a thick woolen blanket. "These are the ruins of a Roman temple, honoring which of their gods, I don't know. It's not very elegant, but it's dry and hidden, and there's enough room to shelter a horse."

"You've been here before?"

"Aye, whenever I need to be close to Winchester." As he wrapped the blanket around her, he saw blood dried on her sleeve. "Are you sure they didn't hurt you? Don't try to save my feelings, Claeri."

"This is Pascentius' blood. You didn't see. When he took me away, I bit his arm. It didn't change his mind about taking me hostage, but at least he finally dropped me."

Mischief shone in her eyes in spite of how she drooped from her ordeal, and Marcus could not keep from smiling as her humor dispelled part of his anguish and guilt, even if only for a few moments. He rose to stoke the fire and began to prepare a simple meal for her.

Watching him, Claerwen waited for news. He stared long into the campfire, too long, gathering his thoughts. The more he hesitated to speak, the more thickly dread crowded into her mind. Finally, she prompted, "They told me nothing. All I did was ride all day, shackled to the saddle, then either sit or lie on the pallet, chained to the ground. I was always blindfolded except inside the tent. Marcus? What have you learned?"

"'Tis bad news," he finally said in a low voice. His eyes rose, leveling with hers, and he told her every detail he had learned from Ceredig and Myrddin.

The little color left in Claerwen's face drained away. "How many days ago?"

"Ten and seven."

Her eyes squeezed shut in anguish. As they opened again, she said, "It is so many days from when I was warned of the poisoned cider you nearly drank. In the vision I saw a red dragon lying on a stone bed. I didn't understand then. I thought it was to warn you and that the poison was meant for me. Now I realize it was a symbol for Ambrosius as well. That was his standard, wasn't it? And he will be entombed under a large flat stone at the Giant's Dance, on the Great Plain west of Winchester?"

Marcus nodded slowly, the hair on his neck rising. "Aye, it is exactly as Myrddin said it will be. A dragon will be carved into the stone. Uther carries the same standard; he now calls himself Uther Pendragon."

"Then, the dream was true as well? Myrddin was in Dun Breatann? And he gave you a sleeping potion for the soldiers?"

Marcus nodded and continued, "I heard Pascentius talking before I used it. The assassin Banawr hired was called Eopa."

"Eopa? Not Eosa, Octa's kinsman?"

"No. Eopa was the low-ranking soldier they accuse me of being. He was disguised as a doctor and sent with Ambrosius' other physicians when the king complained of illness. The poison was administered in place of medicines. Eopa left the palace minutes later, going straight to Banawr, who promptly murdered him. The body was thrown into a bog where it will never be found, and Banawr is back in Winchester now, hidden, waiting until it is time for the next assassination."

He stopped a moment, taking a long breath, then went on, "Most of the soldiers in the camp here are Saxons. The Irish who were in the north have been sent somewhere else, and I don't know where yet."

"Could that mean another invasion from another location? At the same time he expects to assassinate Uther?"

Marcus nodded grimly. For a time they were quiet, pondering. Marcus watched Claerwen slowly chew the meal he had made for her, knowing from having been nearly starved himself after his imprisonment that she would have difficulty to eat for some time, that she was nauseated, and her stomach was knotted up in pain. When she finished, he began to speak again, "Claeri, we will have to go into Winchester tomorrow. I have an idea how — "

"Marcus," she stopped him, gripping his arm. "I have something to tell you. It cannot wait."

His eyes held steady, patient, anxious.

"I just realized who Sinnoch's father is," she said.

One brow leapt upward and he queried, "You heard someone speak of him?"

She shook her head. "No...another vision. Just before you came for me. It just suddenly made sense now."

His eyes narrowed, squinting, and when she did not go on, he prompted, "Who?"

Her face tilted upward slightly. In her mind, memories of the image danced again. Barely breathing, she whispered, "You."

He merely stared, too stunned to react, his mouth gaping.

"Marcus, you are Sinnoch's father. He looks exactly like you."

His breath quickened and he searched his mind for words, but found none worth saying. Shaking his head slowly, side to side, he muttered, "It cannot be..."

"Count the years," Claerwen said. "You said you knew Elen just after you met me. He is the right age. And it makes sense. They are using him, as they have used me, as a way to get to you. Sooner or later they would have told you."

He brooded on her words, trying to understand the shock he felt. "That is why you saw a familiarity in him?"

She nodded. "I can't believe I missed it. He always wore those rags over his hair. But in the vision he didn't. He looks so much like you, just the way Padrig and Owein describe how you looked as a child. He even has some of the same mannerisms you have, like this." She laid her hand along his cheek, her thumb gently brushing his skin in the way he often showed affection.

His mouth opened and closed, but no sound emerged until another realization flooded his mind. He whispered, "My grandfather's name was Sinnoch. Elen must have named the boy for him. Why didn't she come to me for help?"

Claerwen slid her hand comfortingly along his arm and said, "I don't know, Marcus. There are a thousand answers we'll never know. But I pray he is safe with Girvyn."

Gradually he calmed, though a look of sadness remained in his face. Without speaking further, they left the plans for Winchester for the morrow and bedded down for the rest of the night. The temple was peaceful after the wind-whipped camp, and Claerwen let her taut and jangled nerves release, feeling safe alongside Marcus, hugging his arm. Just as she drifted towards sleep, she heard him softly say to himself, "A son...by the light..."

# Chapter 20

## Winchester

"I have an idea, but it entails much risk," Marcus said in a brooding voice. Kneeling before the campfire, he poked at the coals longer than needed. "How are you feeling this morning?"

Claerwen slowly pushed herself up onto her elbows. From her bedroll, she saw a high angle of light shining through a tiny window in the temple's eastern wall, indicating it was late morning. Smiling, she answered, "Fine enough."

Marcus knew she felt miserable, that every movement was an effort. Turning around, he sat next to her, wishing he did not need to voice his proposal. He asked, "May I see the talisman?"

Claerwen pulled it out from under her tunic, slipping the thong over her head, and she placed it in his hand. She watched him examine it, turning it over and over, the same way thoughts turned in his mind. "You are still thinking of Sinnoch."

Frowning at the talisman, he nodded. "Aye, but as you said, I hope he is safe with Girvyn." He squinted his anguish, wishing he had more time to consider his son, even just the idea that he had a son, but now he needed to remain focused on the quest. Going on, he said, "We need to create a trap once we are in Winchester. I thought that one of us should be the bait, but Uther's warriors are too many; we cannot risk being identified until we prove our innocence. Instead, we can use Uther himself, as he is the next target anyway."

"How do we know he hasn't already been killed by now?"

"We would know from the commotion. And it won't happen until Pascentius is prepared to move in behind the kill this time. He is not ready, but Saxons are gathering quickly in his camp. It won't be long."

Marcus paused, his eyes drilling intently into Claerwen's. "What I propose is that we shift the focus from me to you. You will pose as an exiled noblewoman from *Iwerddon*, and I will be your seneschal. You disguised yourself as a peasant to escape a Norse raid and were able to flee with only the clothes you were wearing. This talisman should be enough to convince them you are of a noble house. Then we will ask for asylum. In this way we can be close enough to Uther to watch him, and I will have the freedom to move around unchallenged, to lay the trap for Pascentius."

"From *Iwerddon*? Will I need to speak Gaelic?" she asked, sitting up fully.

"Uther won't want to speak it, if he even knows it. You can make a mild accent, and I can teach you enough phrases to use for effect. We will need to use the Gaelic names, like '*Eireann,*' instead of '*Iwerddon.*'"

Marcus saw doubt in her eyes as she considered the plan. He touched her cheek. "If you're not ready, I will think of something else." Then his lips twisted and he ventured, "Huh...perhaps the Iron Hawk should do this..." He saw Claerwen's eyes sharpen and he went on before she could stop him, "Because you would be acting as a woman whose strength is depleted, you won't be expected to do anything but rest. It will give you a chance to recover while I work, and we can still be together. But we need to move quickly. There's very little time."

"'Tis a good plan," she concurred. "What of Macsen's spearhead?"

"It will have to wait for now. Hopefully, we will recover it when Pascentius is captured."

"Aye, it would be good if we could bring it to Uther. When will we enter the fortress?"

"Tonight." He paused, realizing the significance of her question. "You are telling me you want to do this?"

Claerwen's lips curled inward a moment, then she nodded, answering, "For what they have done to us, for what they have done to Ambrosius. And most of all, for Sinnoch, I will do this."

Marcus grinned his approval. He rose and strode across the temple, retrieving a heavy pouch he had brought from Dun Breatann. Setting it down next to Claerwen, he began to unpack it.

"What is all this?" she asked, watching. "More disguises?"

"Aye, the makings of them." He spread out a selection of items as he spoke, explaining the purpose of each, then held up a small, round object. "I was very lucky to get this. It is called *sapo*. The Romans had been importing it from across the Narrow Sea and is virtually unknown here since the end of the occupation. Ceredig has a network of trading brokers he uses who can get him nearly anything he wants, and fortunately he had some on hand — I think he took it from one of his daughters' houses. It will dye your hair a reddish color, but will eventually fade. It can even make my hair look reddish, which is very hard to do."

Claerwen took the sphere and found it sticky. "What's in it?"

"He tells me it's made of ash from beechwood and goat's fat. It's actually like soap, and the Romans used it for that purpose."

"Then at least my hair will be clean," she speculated.

Marcus laughed and countered, "Actually, the more bedraggled you look, the more convincing you'll be. I have another dress for you, much like the one you had before. But you can't look too messy. Uther must like what he sees, and though he will be bound by the rules of hospitality, he must be willing to grant you asylum as well."

"And if he does not accept me?"

He grinned wryly, his brows flickering in amusement. "He will."

"What do you mean?"

"I hear he has an eye that tends to linger a bit on the women." Claerwen wrinkled her nose, but Marcus assured her, "He'll be well busy planning his brother's funeral instead of chasing after women. Come, I will help you with this."

Leading her to a low stone basin, he explained that it had been used as a font for the old temple. He swept leaves and dust from it, then assembled a crude bench out of stones for them to sit upon, just lower than the basin's rim. Facing the font, he sat, wedging one leg between its base and the bench, then guided Claerwen to sit closely, the opposite way. He leaned her backward until her shoulders rested on his leg, her neck on the basin's edge. Her hair filled the font, and he thoroughly soaked it with fresh water. Cutting a small piece from the *sapo*, he began to methodically massage the dye into her hair, moving evenly from hairline to ends.

As he worked, Claerwen closed her eyes. Her breath came slowly, evenly, almost as if she had fallen asleep, and she reposed comfortably against him. Marcus wondered at her thoughts as he rinsed her hair.

"You can sit up now, and stay by the fire," he said as he ran an arm under her shoulders and helped her upright. He squeezed the excess water out of her hair and wrapped a thick woolen cloth around her head.

Claerwen caught his hand and held it in both of her own. She remarked, studying his broad palm and thick fingers, "I am always fascinated by your hands. They have the strength to break a man's bones and pound a heavy hammer on the anvil for hours, yet you can play a harp as convincingly as any bard, or trace a pattern across my skin as gently as heather flowing in the breeze." She slowly, almost reverently, kissed his palm. "I have not yet thanked you for coming for me."

Marcus gazed wistfully into her green-blue eyes, oddly alive and passionate in her pale face, then he folded his arms around her protectively and murmured, "There is no need for it." She felt fragile and he tightened his embrace, needing to spare a few moments for the lost intimacy of the past weeks. He whispered, "Would that I could hold you so forever, Claeri, and have no need to place you in danger once again." They held each other a long while.

The afternoon progressed, and they continued with the preparations. As Claerwen's hair dried, Marcus showed her another dye produced by the women of Ceredig's clan, made from walnut skins. Using a tiny wooden stick soaked first in water then dipped into the dye, he carefully drew thin lines along the edges of her upper eyelids and part of her lower lids, angling the lines to give her eyes a slightly slanted appearance. Handing her a tiny mirror, he explained, "This is permanent, although it will wear off in time. Hopefully, we will not be there so long that we will need to refresh it."

"There's nothing we can do to hide the color of my eyes," Claerwen remarked, studying the way he had drawn the stain around them. She blinked several times, disliking the strange tautness it gave her skin. "If I wear drab colors, at least they won't be so noticeable. Blues and greens make them stand out like marsh lights. Yours are hard to disguise as well; few people have eyes so very black. Although you squint so much sometimes, they almost disappear."

Marcus snorted at her teasing and took the mirror from her. Following the natural contours of his face, he etched dye into the creases that radiated around his eyes, as well as the lines across his forehead, causing them to appear more pronounced. Next, with a small knife, he trimmed his beard into a short, neat, narrow fringe along his jawline from to ear to ear. His hair still had the grey ash coloring from Dun Breatann, and now he worked more into his hair, beard, moustache and eyebrows to further lighten them. Combing his hair straight back from his face until the excess ash was removed, he was left with a coarse mid-grey finish.

As he worked before the mirror, Claerwen watched, fascinated, and she leaned forward to see him better. Catching a glimpse of her own hair as it fell over her shoulders, she took up a handful and marveled, "By the light...it truly works."

Marcus grinned and handed her the knife and the mirror. He suggested, "Trim a few locks around your face. They will change how you look as much as the different color; and if you wear the rest down and loose, you could walk past someone you know and they won't realize it if they're not paying much attention."

Claerwen's brows arched upward, then she realized he had done similar changes to his own hair many times. She had seen it combed straight back as now, flattened down like a monk's, as well as wildly neglected and every length from as short as the base of his neck to long past his shoulders. She followed his advice.

Marcus sorted through the clothing he had brought from Dun Breatann. He found the dress he had mentioned and handed it to Claerwen. It was of heavy, coarse wool and had two undershifts for warmth. While she changed, he pulled on a chain link hauberk and coif, a thick, boss-studded leather tunic, and a helmet of heavy, formed leather surrounded by an ironwork frame.

Finishing their preparations simultaneously, Marcus stood in the shadows beyond the campfire's light and adjusted the sword across his back, then draped on a long cloak. He came forward into the light, his expression solemnly tired and careworn.

Claerwen was astonished. "You look the way I always imagined your father did," she remarked, moving towards him, then stopped, looking up. "Why are you so tall?"

He explained the extra chunks of leather in his boots.

She smiled proudly, shaking her head. "Lord Ceredig is risking much to help you, to give you all of this, isn't he?"

"Aye, he is," Marcus answered soberly. "By edict, he should have arrested me and handed me over to the high king's soldiers for transport to Winchester."

"Will he be punished?"

"Possibly, but Uther would be stupid to alienate Ceredig. He is an important ally, the most important of the northern kingdoms. Threat of a high king or no, Ceredig knows me well enough to realize the evidence is false. He alone among my allies would dare to defy Uther, because of our long friendship and because he thinks he owes me."

"And how is Myrddin taking his father's death? He must be furious with us."

"Surprisingly, he was very calm. Oh, he was angry, disappointed, frustrated, but he controls it well. By now, he will be on his way here for the funeral. He won't know how we will be entering Winchester, unless the fire tells him."

Marcus stopped himself and came forward, taking Claerwen's shoulders and examining her face in the light of the campfire. She was unusually pale and haggard, the hollows under her eyes very dark, the signs of her confinement and hunger showing starkly. Disconcerted, he went on, "As before, we will need to play this out exactly as if it were real. Everything we say and do will be scrutinized, although it may actually be possible that we have more privacy this time, depending upon the chambers we are given. This won't be easy, but if we keep our wits, it should work. Are you sure you are strong enough to do this?"

Claerwen gazed into his eyes, the one unfettered link to him through his disguise, and she smiled. "You look very distinguished, my lord," she commented, then tilted her face up. She kissed him, slowly, gently, full of longing. As she pulled away, she said, "That was for luck."

He smiled in return, admiring her determination. "So be it, then. We are ready."

---

Torchlight glimmered across Winchester at dusk. Bundled in a thick cloak and swaying with hunger and exhaustion, Claerwen was vaguely aware of the lights as she rode down from the empty, windswept plains, approaching the fortress and settlement. Marcus tramped in front, holding onto the horse's lead rein and encouraging the animal to keep moving.

Reaching the eastern gates, Marcus rang the bell and waited, one arm braced against a post, his brow leaning on his arm. When a guard slapped the small lookout window open and called for who was there, he raised his face.

"I am Faolan," Marcus announced in a faint Irish accent and a voice a few tones higher than usual. "I am seneschal to Lady Riona, who seeks to enter the fortress of Winchester." He waved an arm to indicate the woman upon the horse and watched the guard squint into the cold air past him.

"Lady Riona, from where?" the man asked, regarding

Claerwen with eyes that clearly showed he would rather be asleep on his pallet than staring at strangers.

"From Eireann, across the sea. Norsemen raided the palace of her noble family. She is the only one left and seeks an audience with your high king, to apply for asylum."

The guard's eyebrows lifted. He turned away from the lookout window when a second guard came up behind him. They consulted.

Marcus could not hear their discussion, and when the conversation droned on too long, he called out, "Please, sir, my lady is not accustomed to traveling so far, especially in this season. She is not well, and would seek the king's hospitality."

The guard returned to the window, his face clearly showing irritation. By invoking the request for hospitality, Marcus had forced the decision in his own favor. Such a request, by ancient tradition, could not be denied. Grumbling, the guard eased the gates open just enough for the horse to be led through, thumping them shut afterward.

Marcus approached the second guard, apparently one of a superior rank, seeking instructions. But before he could ask, Claerwen moaned softly and swayed. Her head leaned back inside the broad hood of her cloak, hiding her face, and she slid sideways, falling limply into the snow.

Marcus whipped around, surprise on his face, and dropped onto his knees next to her. Running an arm under her shoulders, he raised her into a sitting position. Her head lolled onto his shoulder. The guards watched, puzzled by her sudden fainting.

"Please! Do you have a place we could go?" Marcus shot at them as he lifted her from the ground. "The lady needs warmth. She has not eaten in days."

The ranking guard shrugged at last, and signaled at a lackey to stable the horse. He led Marcus into the great hall, marching directly to one end and into a private corner that was draped with thick woven curtains. Marcus kicked a low wooden bench against a wall and set Claerwen down.

"Lady Riona," he called softly, kneeling in front of her. He chafed her hands and asked the guard for water. "Lady?"

Claerwen moaned again, and her eyes gradually opened, focusing on Marcus' concerned face. "Faolan? What...what happened?" she asked, tingeing her words with an accent heavier than his.

"You fainted, Lady. We have reached Winchester."

She lifted a shaking hand to her mouth and her eyes moved, looking from his face to the others behind him and on through the gap left where the drape was pushed aside. People crowded just beyond, drawn by curiosity.

"You are not well, my Lady?" a deep, cold-roughened voice came thrusting through the drapes.

Her eyes sought the owner of the voice and located a tall, pleasant looking man with brown hair and blue eyes, a neatly trimmed beard. Pushing the gawkers aside, he strode into the alcove, gave Marcus a cursory glance, then met Claerwen's eyes.

His face evolved from curiosity and arrogance into a stunned fascination. "Get some help over here!" he roared to a nearby servant.

"My Lord?" the ranking guard from the gates spoke to the tall man, who turned with one raised eyebrow. "She was announced as Lady Riona, from Eireann. She has come to seek asylum from you."

Claerwen gasped roughly, realizing Uther stood before her, then recognized his vague resemblance to Ambrosius. She tried to sit higher, reaching to Marcus' shoulder for support, intending to force herself into a curtsey. The king stopped her, telling her to remain seated.

"Forgive me, my Lord. I had not realized," she said, bowing her head.

"No matter," Uther replied amiably enough. "He says you and your man have not eaten in days." His eyes softened and he knelt, taking her cold hands. He continued to study her eyes as if unable to turn away from them.

"'Tis true. Our food ran out and Faolan, my seneschal, tried to hunt, but in winter it is too hard to find game."

A woman-servant interrupted, bringing water; another came moments later with a blanket. Marcus took the water-filled goblet and helped Claerwen to drink.

Annoyed by the onlookers pressing closer to the alcove, Uther stood, ordering them to stand away and leave the lady some privacy.

"My Lord," Marcus broke in, "we do beseech your hospitality until my Lady is well enough again. 'Tis true, she seeks asylum from you."

"Why me? Why not some Irish king?" Uther glared imperiously down his long nose, then his eyes flicked to the bump behind Marcus' right shoulder, under his cloak. Recognizing the shape of a sword pommel, his suspicion flared into anger and he demanded, "Why hasn't this man been disarmed?"

Claerwen drew breath in sharply and picked at Uther's sleeve, distracting him before the guard could answer. She implored, "How can he defend me, if he has no sword?"

Confounded by Claerwen's reaction, Uther queried, "Why would you need to be defended?"

She hesitated, then answered, exhaustion slurring her words, "Forgive me, my Lord. We have come very far and through tremendous trouble. There was so much treachery within the court of my home that if Faolan had not been armed, I would not have survived. If he is unable to protect me, I would feel greatly distressed and uncomfortable, as if he had been dismissed and I were alone against my enemies."

"You believe you have enemies here, in my court?"

"I have no guaranty that I have not been followed all this way, though we have seen no one. But any court can be a place of danger, can it not? I must be able to protect myself, or I will need to find another sanctuary."

The king's anger slowly drained away as the startling beauty of her green-blue eyes struck him, so vividly full of earnest urgency in the midst of her disheveled appearance.

Marcus spoke low, to enhance rather than break the spell Uther seemed cast within, "Lady Riona has come to you because the Irish fight too much amongst themselves. She believes she will be more comfortable among the Britons. Losing her family has been too painful to remain in Eireann, bearing the reminders, too heavy. I have helped her as much as I can, but I am only one old man. She is a princess and deserves better than a simple guard."

Uther further softened, "Such loyalty is truly rare these days, and you have been very much so to her. Why?"

"I have served her all her life. She is a good and true woman, and she has not deserved the pain she suffers."

"So you pity her?" Uther tested.

Marcus held the king's gaze a moment. With pride he answered, "I believe in her kindness, her honesty."

Uther's lips curled almost into a smile. Looking again to Claerwen's tired face, he spoke over his shoulder to the woman-servant: "Prepare a guest chamber in the palace for the lady. See that she has a bath if she wishes, and bring her some decent clothing. When she is stronger, she may come to me. We will talk further of asylum." He turned, his eyes narrowing at Marcus, and added, "You may keep that sword for now, but if there is ever any trace of trouble, you know what to expect." Uther strode away.

"Thank you, my Lord," Marcus mumbled, though the king was already halfway across the great hall.

The servant helped Marcus pull Claerwen to her feet, then guided them outside. They skirted a broad, cobbled courtyard and approached another building set at right angles to the hall. This building, along with the hall and several others, were originally part of Winchester's most luxurious Roman-style villa, now converted into the king's palace. Each structure was two stories in height and surrounded by a wide, two-stepped terrace. Except for the great hall, a tiled roof overhung the steps on the first level.

The servant led Marcus and Claerwen up the terrace, through an arched doorway and into a long corridor. The hallway was lined with richly crafted wall hangings, numerous oil lamps hung in ironwork sconces, an intricately tessellated floor and a carved ceiling supported by heavy beams. Many rooms faced into the corridor, and the servant stated that this was the guest section of the palace and behind each door was a full suite of chambers. She walked halfway through the corridor and turned sharply into an alcoved doorway, opening a double set of doors.

Inside was a small anteroom, furnished with a table and stool.

Another chamber, in the left wall, was a seneschal's post, and the servant declared it would belong to Marcus. A spacious common room, meant for the suite's occupants to meet within, was straight ahead through a broad expanse of wool drapes. Several other chambers opened behind the common room, and all were furnished with simple but very fine appointments, placed in comfortable arrangements.

As she guided them through, the servant lit several oil lamps, warming the chambers with smoky, golden light, then led her new mistress into one particular bedchamber. She picked it for Claerwen not only because it was larger than the others, but because it also had a solid oak door for privacy instead of a simple drape.

"She looks like she's had quite a rough time of it," the servant chattered at Marcus while taking Claerwen's cloak and helping her to sit on the bed. "I'll see that food is brought straight away, and bath water for her. By the light, she has no shoes! She's come so far with no shoes? Well, we'll have her bathed and fed and dressed, right quick."

The servant flitted about the rooms, her wrenlike cheeriness out of place in the midst of winter and the gloomy mood of the palace. She introduced Marcus to all of the amenities, including a privy room adjacent to the large bedchamber, complete with a seated chamber pot, its associated pile of soft moss, and a small ceramic bathing vessel. She mentioned that the entire palace was in the process of being rebuilt, and that eventually the wooden plank floorboards in their chambers would be covered over with colored stone tiles as they had seen in the corridor. Finally, she assured him that she would retrieve the items necessary for their comfort and return shortly.

Marcus checked that the door to the corridor had latched shut, then began a thorough inspection of the entire chambers. He examined the walls, poking at their stucco surfaces with a dagger when he found a flaw, peering behind wall hangings, testing the floor planking, trying the shuttered glass window, even searching the furniture. Done, he returned to Claerwen, ready to speak, but a soft knock at the outer door interrupted. He stiffened, reverting into the aging seneschal, and met the servant in the anteroom. With her came a half dozen other women, carrying pails of warm water for the bath, platters of food, armloads of gowns, undershifts, shoes, and a pair of cloaks, as well as a variety of items for dressing hair. The servants marched past him and congregated in Claerwen's bedchamber.

Marcus retreated to his tiny chamber off the anteroom to wait. He shed his heavy outer tunic and the chain link armor. He could hear Claerwen speak to the women, but her voice was too low to understand. Minutes later, the servants filed past him again, arms and water pails empty. The wrenlike woman stopped at Marcus' room and spoke.

"She said she wished only for privacy and rest, my Lord, and to bring this to you." The woman held out one platter of food. As he took it, she added, "Strange that a princess would not want help to bathe or dress. But, that's none of my concern, now is it?" Eyeing him with curiosity, the woman smiled briefly, then left.

Marcus bolted the outer door, then set the platter on the common room's table as he paced back through to Claerwen's chamber. The door was still open and he could hear her moving about in the privy room beyond. Knocking lightly, he called, "Lady? Do you need anything?"

"I won't be long. Go on and eat," she answered.

He listened to her splashing in the bath and he sighed quietly, thinking of home. There, they almost always bathed together, partially for the sake of convenience, most often in a nearby spring or a pool temporarily created by the river when it flowed heavily after a good rain. In severe weather, they would fill their tiny oak vat with water heated over the fire pit. Barely big enough for one person to bathe in, they had often wedged themselves into the vat together; and he grinned almost involuntarily as he recalled the laughter and singing, the water spilled all over the floor, and the lovemaking that usually came after. He was still leaning in the open doorway when Claerwen suddenly appeared before him, wearing a fresh, loose undershift of soft, cream-colored wool, her hair shining like polished copper in the lamplight. As she gazed up at him, he marveled, almost believing she had just stepped out of his erotic daydream.

She said, "This feels so much better. But…is it warm tonight, or am I accustomed to being cold all the time?" She shook the neck of the shift, confirming her excessive warmth, and one side fell down her shoulder.

Smiling, he answered, "There's a hypocaust under the floor, it is like an open basement. A furnace is somewhere outside the building, and there is a tunnel that leads hot air from the furnace into the hypocaust. There are probably chimneys hidden in the walls that take heat up to the second floor as well. That's how most of these old, more luxurious Roman buildings are heated."

"I wondered why there are no fire pits. 'Tis almost too warm."

Marcus smelled the fresh scent of lavender radiating from her skin, and he took a step closer, his hand lifting towards her bare shoulder. Then he hesitated.

Claerwen watched as sadness claimed his black eyes. She leaned forward slightly and caressed his face, her eyes searching his.

He caught her hand against his face, holding it there, and said quietly, "You need to eat now, while the food is still warm." He moved to retrieve the platter, but she kept her hand on his cheek and shook her head slightly, keeping her eyes locked with his.

He felt her compassion reach into him then, pervading his soul, and he sighed softly, appreciating the way they could speak without words. With great gentleness, he leaned to her, catching her lips in an elegantly tender kiss.

Claerwen slid her arms around his neck, savoring his affection. When he tried to pull away, she spoke softly, "Would that my craving for you be not so implacable, and that a mere kiss be the only necessity for satisfaction." Then smiling, she added, "Of course, I shall never be satisfied of you, nor do I wish to be. Rather, I should spend forever seeking ways to treasure you."

He found himself swept into an easy enchantment by the beauty of her words, composed in the way of a court bard, conveying the same peace she had always inspired in him, given freely of her heart. For an instant, he let his eyes stray to the huge, comfortable bed across the chamber. Giving in to his own heart, he wound his arms around her.

Heat rose on Claerwen's skin as his lips opened and came down on hers in an endless, fervent kiss. She reveled in the feel of his arms around her and the taste of his mouth, and she curved herself to him, longing for his hands to be on every part of her naked skin.

They were halfway to the bed when a knock came at the outer door, quiet but insistent. Looking at each other in chagrin, they hoped the interruption could be ignored. Claerwen whispered, "They must have forgotten something."

The knocking came again, more urgently, too rough to belong to the servant.

Groaning, Marcus released her, communicating with his eyes that she should finish dressing. He whipped around, striding for the common room, and arranged the table as if the meal had already begun. He looked up, anxious for Claerwen to come, and saw her nervously trying to yank on a sleeveless beige tunic over the shift, miss the armholes, and try again. Succeeding at last, Claerwen rushed to the table and seated herself. Marcus gripped her shoulder, his eyes telling her to be calm, keep her wits and not forget her Irish accent.

The knock came once more, heavy handed, rattling the doors.

Dropping again into his stern expression, Marcus reached for the latch.

# Chapter 21

**Winchester**

The high king waited at the door.

Stunned, Marcus bowed stiffly and backed into the anteroom, his hand sweeping aside in welcome.

Uther waved his own hand absently as he entered, passing Marcus, and announced, "I came to see if Lady Riona is comfortable." Ignoring protocol, the king strode through the drapes and into the common room.

Claerwen, just lifting a goblet to her lips, abruptly set the wine down and made to rise, but Uther waved his hand again, gesturing for her to remain seated.

"Please, my Lord, will you join me?" she invited, indicating a place for him across the table. Her eyes sought Marcus' as he took up a place against the wall behind the king. He half-blinked, encouraging her, then folded his arms and solemnly gazed across from one dark corner to the next.

Uther remained standing and countered, "I will stay but a few minutes, as I have already eaten. I only wanted to be certain they brought everything you needed. I was surprised to learn you had dismissed the women so quickly." He slowly surveyed the room. When his eyes came to Marcus, they halted and frowned, then ultimately disregarded him.

Claerwen said, "We are not accustomed to such luxury where I come from, my Lord. The ladies were very helpful, but I wished for privacy and quiet. And, of course, if I need anything, I can send Faolan for it." She smiled warmly, then added, "I wish to thank you, my Lord, for your patience and your kindness. Once I am established again, I shall find a way to repay your graciousness."

Uther smiled in return, again clearly fascinated by her green-blue eyes, shining brightly in spite of the meager lamplight. He remarked, "You are flushed, Lady Riona. Are you feverish? Should I send for a physician?"

Claerwen shook her head, declining the offer. "'Tis that I am not accustomed to the heat after so long out in the icy mud and snow. 'Tis a little overwhelming, but wonderful for cold feet."

Uther raised an eyebrow, not understanding. When she kicked a foot from beneath the hem of her skirts, he saw she was barefoot. He frowned at first, smiled, laughed slightly, then asked, "Didn't they bring shoes?"

Claerwen pushed up from the table and poured wine for the king. She swept a hand towards the bedchamber, telling him there were six pairs from which to choose. Uther paced to the chamber's door, observed the piles of garments, then returned, taking the wine. Watching her figure as she moved about the room, he asked, "Is that the best gown they brought for you? It's so drab. I believe there may be another in there that would pay fine homage to those lovely eyes of yours. Ah, listen to me, sounding like a fishmonger's wife!"

Uther chuckled to himself. Then, eyeing Marcus, he turned sober again. He saw a tired, stern and steadfast man, probably fifteen years older than himself. "You protect her with your life, don't you?"

Marcus nodded.

"I wish such loyalty existed among my own people," Uther muttered pensively, his eyes dropping to the floor.

Claerwen approached the king, sensing he wanted to speak candidly but needed prompting. She drew a long breath, considering what would be the right question, then lost her nerve.

She moved forward one more step, drew another breath and said, "We heard what happened, my Lord. Is it known who took your brother's life?"

Glancing past the king, she saw the cords in Marcus' neck tense, but his face remained absolutely solemn and unreadable. Uther did not answer for a full minute, and as the silence closed in oppressively, Claerwen felt her skin creep with the fear that her question had been an enormous blunder.

Then Uther faced her, his eyes a combination of anger and loneliness. He replied bluntly, "A man called Marcus ap Iorwerth was the assassin. I'm told he is some kind of master of disguise, which means he could be anywhere, look like anyone. We have not found him yet. My nephew is the only one of us who has actually met the man, and once Myrddin arrives here, perhaps we will at last make progress if he can give us a true description. And with my brother's funeral to be held soon, many people will be arriving in Winchester, making the search even more difficult."

"You think this man is still here?" Claerwen showed deep alarm and edged closer to the king.

"Aye, for I will be the next target, Lady."

"By the gods, my Lord, is there no way to stop this assassin?" Then before he could answer, she blurted, "But I suppose if you don't know what he looks like, it would be quite difficult to catch him. However, by the same reasoning, how would you know he truly was the man who killed your brother?"

"A ring with his clan's symbol was left behind with the items he used to make the poison."

"A ring? That was careless."

"Aye, he must have removed it when he prepared the poison, to prevent its damage from the ingredients. Perhaps he had to run to escape discovery, leaving or forgetting it."

Claerwen puzzled over Uther's speculation, then confided, "A similar murder happened in my grandfather's time. A particular dagger was left behind. Years later, however, it was discovered that the man accused was not the murderer at all. His dagger had been stolen and deliberately struck into the dead man's body. Unfortunately, the assassin escaped and killed several others before he was finally caught. The innocent man was executed within days of the original murder. When the truth was discovered, war broke out between the innocent man's clan and those who'd executed him. Even now, they still feud."

"You sound as if you were close to one side or the other of that fight."

Claerwen gazed up at Uther, the lamplight flickering in her eyes. Tears hung on her lashes briefly. She whispered huskily, "'Tis why I fled my home, not only because of Norsemen." Abruptly she turned away, wiping the tears.

"Forgive me, Lady Riona." Uther turned her around, his hands lingering on her arms. "I did not mean to distress you."

Claerwen held his gaze and asked, "Why would this Marcus ap Iorwerth want to assassinate his king? Who is he?"

"It is said he is a minor prince from the mountains of Gwynedd. Other than that, I don't know. That is the most intriguing puzzle. My brother trusted him completely. So does his son Myrddin. I don't know Myrddin well enough to know the quality of his judgement, but I knew my brother's was unfailing. I was told in the first year of Ambrosius' reign, Marcus ap Iorwerth found a sacred torque, part of the lost sacred symbols of the high kingship, what we call Macsen's Treasure, and brought it to him along with his homage and loyalty. The man could have kept it for himself and attempted a claim on the throne, but he did not."

"Was the torque stolen when Ambrosius died?"

"No, I have it, safely hidden. But if I die, I have no heir except Myrddin. He is no warrior, and these lands can be held only with a strong sword. And he is the one who gave that damned spy access to my brother, on the pretext of helping him discover any plots against him. Instead, his spy *became* the assassin!" Uther's eyes blazed with sudden anger, and he pounded his fist on the table, causing the platters to jump.

Claerwen's face flashed with fear at the king's vehemence. She retreated slightly, instinctively moving towards Marcus. Then she halted, once more holding her head regally and showing serene eyes.

"The truth is often hidden very deeply and requires the calm of patience and the care of determination to bring its emergence. Would that those clans of my homeland had done so, to save an innocent man."

The king's blue eyes glared coldly. She held steady, her face calm and softly lit, aware of Marcus watching her from behind. Gradually, Uther's face showed tiredness and his eyes dropped.

"You are very forthright, Lady Riona. I can admire that. As much as I can admire your seneschal's loyalty." He paused, then concluded, "I would be very pleased if you would join me at supper tomorrow eve."

Claerwen smiled and curtsied, accepting his offer. Uther took her hand, raised it and brushed his lips over her fingers. Then he strode for the outer door, leaving it open as he left.

Marcus closed and bolted the door, momentarily leaning his head against it, pondering the irony of Uther's remark about loyalty, unknowingly said before the man he had accused of his brother's murder. When he turned back to the central room, he saw Claerwen suddenly sit down on an upholstered bench, her hand over her mouth. Her eyes were wide and seeking his, and when he knelt in front of her, she gripped his arm.

"Have I done wrong? 'Tis not what we had planned," she whispered.

His eyes moved back and forth over her face, full of incredulous wonder. Then he grinned broadly and pressed a hand over her fingers that were digging into his flesh.

"By the gods, you were perfection," he whispered back. "You played him better than Myrddin plays the harp. You planted the seeds of doubt in his mind as I never could have, because he wants very much to like you, because he is attracted to you, just as I thought he would be."

Grateful for Marcus' approval, Claerwen released her breath.

He rose and retrieved one of the platters of food. "This is getting cold," he said and sat with her on the bench, placing the platter across their knees and offering her a piece of roasted fowl. His grin broadened and he whispered, "Of course, if he knew the true reason you were flushed, he never would have told you as much." His teasing eyes flicked towards the bed, and she looked down at the food, trying not to laugh aloud.

Marcus smiled warmly, but he realized she was functioning solely on sheer nerve and was still having difficulty to eat. He said, "Finish as much as you can and go to bed. On the morrow, I want you to stay here and rest. I will scout the palace and the town, learn the guard patterns, study the servants and slaves. What you can do directly, I will do through the rear door, so to speak. If the second..." he lifted his brows to indicate Banawr without saying the name, "...is here, I will find him."

Claerwen's face suddenly filled with shock. She looked up at Marcus with wide eyes and asked, "If the commander is gathering a war band, will he attack the funeral, with all the nobles in attendance?"

"He may, and I have thought of that as well. But it would be foolish, for Uther will have his own war band there to guard. It would also serve no purpose towards future alliances by threatening the nobles' lives. The commander will need those alliances, he cannot stand alone among this island's factions."

They finished the meal in silence.

---

The next evening, dressed in an elegant dark blue gown, Claerwen entered the great hall. Her hair was loosely draped with a sheer linen kerchief worn with its ends gracefully crossed in front and cascading back over her shoulders. Upon arriving the previous night, she'd had little chance to notice the hall's enormity, and now, as she wove her way between rows of trestle tables and benches, she marveled at the high ceiling, the thick supporting pillars, the dais to one end with the vast table upon it. Uther was already seated there among his courtiers, overseeing scores of people crowding the hall, mostly men from his war band. Servants bustled in between, delivering the evening meal, filling and refilling drinking horns.

As Claerwen made her way across the hall, Marcus closely followed. Heads turned, watching, staring. Comments passed among them: "strange new woman — must be Uther's latest chase — who is the old man?" She scanned the unfamiliar faces, her own serenely steadfast, and as she reached the dais, Uther stood, bidding the man next to him to move aside. She took the vacated seat, and Marcus posted himself directly behind her at the base of the dais, proudly watching with unforced dignity. Guards moved in, intending to challenge him, but the king signaled them to leave him alone.

Serving women appeared with bread trenchers, knives, steaming cauldrons of stewed meat, platters of fruit and vegetables. As the meal began, Uther introduced Lady Riona to the courtiers, stating she would be sojourning at Winchester. Then he said privately to her, "You look as if the rest has done you well, my Lady." His eyes flicked towards Marcus and he added, "He does not need to guard you here. You are safe among us."

Claerwen leaned towards the king and confided, "He will not leave my side, for he has vowed to always protect me. You see, my Lord, I saved his life once, a long time ago. Now he has saved mine. I will not forswear his loyalty."

Uther stared seriously into her eyes several moments, then suddenly grinned, greatly approving of her answer. He squeezed her hand and continued to chat, holding to lighter subjects.

Midway through the meal, amidst the persistent commotion of people coming and going, another man entered the hall. As the king's seneschal greeted him, the man pushed back his travel-worn cloak's hood. Uther noticed and rose from the table, saying, "Good, my brother's son has arrived at last. Excuse me a moment, please."

Claerwen's eyes followed the king as he strode across to Myrddin. She watched both men bristle visibly as they acknowledged each other, but their tempers held. When they turned to approach the table, her eyes dropped, avoiding Myrddin's as he took a place directly across.

She was introduced, and he politely acknowledged her presence but was cool towards her, too well occupied with his private thoughts to give her attention. He fell into a strained conversation with Uther regarding the impending funeral. Their words were polite enough, but the two men's underlying animosity felt like a pair of volcanoes sitting across a narrow valley from each other, ready to spit rocks.

In the short time she had known the king, Claerwen had already learned he was given to using insult and mockery, traits she detested. Without looking up, she knew Myrddin was tensely glaring at Uther with his usual countenance of all-knowing wisdom. She nearly smiled. But as she tried to unobtrusively observe them, she felt Myrddin's aura of power stir, recognize hers, grip her like a stunning blow. She kept her eyes down, trying to cloud her own power by concentrating on the food before her, but it was too late, she felt Myrddin's eyes swing to her face and hold.

"…in two days, my Lady," she suddenly heard Uther speaking to her, "I would be honored if you will attend the funeral with us." He stared at Myrddin with defiance.

"'Twill be my honor, my Lord," she answered, picking at her meal with the knife's tip.

"You are very quiet. You are still not feeling well?"

Thickening her Irish accent, she answered, "Forgive me, my Lord. 'Twill be the fatigue yet from the long journey, I do believe."

"Then I shall return you safely to your chambers. Come." They rose, and with Marcus following, Uther guided Claerwen from the great hall, across the courtyard and into the guest building. Once inside the long corridor, Marcus went ahead, entering the chambers to light the lamps. Moving slowly after, Uther stopped short of the doors, drawing Claerwen to a halt as well. He said, "Join me again tomorrow eve, Lady. Perhaps you will be more rested by then."

"Aye, another day should see my strength returning. Then I will begin to decide what I shall do."

"Do not be in a rush," Uther smiled and lifted her hand to kiss goodnight. "I do not wish to be deprived soon of your company." His smile widened and he stepped back, hesitated, thinking, then said, "I have something you might like. Will you come? Just for a moment?" He held out his hand.

She stalled, looking to the open chamber doors for Marcus.

The king insisted, "It will only take a few minutes. Please?"

Claerwen smiled, hiding her apprehension, and called out, "Faolan? I will return shortly." Receiving no answer, she moved to step inside, but Uther tucked his hand around her arm, firmly guiding her away.

He led her out of the guest building and across the courtyard, into another wing on the opposite side. From the outside, the buildings looked identical. The lower floor's layout inside was similar as well, but upon beginning to climb a narrow set of stone steps, Claerwen saw that the rest of the interior was very different. At a landing midway up the stairs, a large, many-paned glass window looked out over a small garden and cobbled courtyard. Passing the window, she marveled, never having seen glass before. Another landing at the top led into a corridor that turned to the right and ended in an alcove. Thick oak doors opened into an enormous chamber. Many other rooms opened from it, apparently filling the entire second story.

She was awed by the luxury of the furnishings. Uther moved directly towards a large coffer and lifted the lid. Her curiosity piqued, she watched him remove a delicate gold *talaith*, a thin circlet worn upon the head that signified noble status.

"Because you have lost everything in your flight, I thought of this for you. It might make you feel more comfortable among the other royal dignitaries that will arrive for my brother's funeral. They won't need to know of your misfortunes." He placed the circlet on her head, gently positioning it across the center of her brow. It fit perfectly.

Stunned by his generosity, Claerwen took a small silver hand mirror from him and inspected the gift. Looking up into Uther's blue eyes, she said, "You are incredibly kind, but how may I accept this, when I have renounced my title? I do not wish to give false airs."

Uther laughed at her modesty and said, "In my eyes, Lady Riona, you will always be a princess. Your graciousness, your beauty, your lively company make you so, even if you had not been born of the rank. And please, call me 'Uther' instead of 'my Lord.'"

Claerwen smiled, holding his gaze. His eyes were softly happy, a little unsteady from too much wine at supper. Then a pang of fear struck as she realized the look in his eyes was too familiar, too full of his attraction for her. She blurted, "Faolan will be worried about me. I had best go now, my Lord."

Uther raised his brows, surprised by her sudden desire to leave, then shrugged, recalling her earlier complaint of fatigue. "Come then, we will return to your chambers. I have need to speak again with my nephew, his rooms are on the floor above yours."

He escorted Claerwen, returning her to her doors, where she thanked him once more for the *talaith* and reached for the latch. But Uther stopped her, taking her hand in his. Impulsively, he suddenly moved closer and cupped his hand behind her neck, brushing his lips to her mouth. Then, without another word, he turned and quickly retreated along the corridor, bounding up the stairs at the end.

*"Malwen ddŵr,"* Claerwen hissed under her breath as she watched the king disappear. *"Mochyn y coed!"* Feeling her face flush, she whirled and pushed the doors open.

The anteroom and the seneschal's post inside were dark. The heavy drapes to the interior were drawn, only allowing minimal light through a tiny gap between them. "Faolan?" Claerwen called for Marcus, feeling her way along the wall. No answer came. Alarmed, she called again. Moving closer to the drape, chills crept on her skin and she sensed someone behind her.

Whipping around, Claerwen expected to confront her follower, but an arm covered in chain link shoved her aside. The outer door slammed shut. Metal scraped and a flash of steel caught light from beyond the edge of the inner curtain. Shuffling and a pair of grunts followed, then Marcus sharply called, "Bring a lamp in here!"

Claerwen darted to the drapes and whipped them open, then grabbed up an oil lamp. Holding it high, she flooded the anteroom with light, revealing Marcus holding a huge dagger to a man's throat.

Claerwen sucked in her breath. "It's Myrddin," she said.

Marcus released him, but kept a hand clamped on his shoulder, guiding him into the common room. Claerwen bolted the outer door and followed them in.

"What are you doing, creeping like a lizard?" Marcus demanded in a low, harsh voice.

Myrddin shook himself out of Marcus' grip, anger in his dark eyes, and spit out, "What am *I* doing?" He swung around to Claerwen and questioned, "What in the bloody world are *you* doing? I saw what my uncle did. Are you mad?"

Claerwen had never known Myrddin to show anger so blatantly. In truth, she had never seen him openly angry at all, at best always giving a look of omnipotent disdain when someone had overstepped themselves in his presence, usually, except when it was aimed at Marcus, capable of withering even the most confident of souls.

"He didn't give me a chance to protest without offending him," she answered, then turned to Marcus. "I tried to tell you…he took me to his chambers, but — "

"You went to his chambers? Alone?" Marcus interrupted, then touched the *talaith*. "He gave you this?"

She nodded, her eyes acknowledging his unspoken understanding that the king had flirted with her.

He warned, "If you offend him by rejecting his advances, you could give yourself away."

"It would be only too welcome to reject him. His words flatter too much, then he hurls insults at the servants."

Myrddin moved forward until the three of them stood in a tight triangle. With bitterness in his voice, he added, "And if you don't reject him, he will pursue you tirelessly, until you either give in to what he wants or get yourself imprisoned, even executed, when he learns your true identities. I want you both out of here. Now."

Claerwen countered, pleading, "This is the only chance we have to save Uther's life and our own. And probably your life as well. Do not try to stop us. We must finish this, and you know why. You know *all* the reasons why. And he is looking for you right now. He was on his way to your chambers when he left here. He wants a description of Marcus."

Myrddin's already pale face blanched even more, his anger

subsiding, replaced with dismal aloofness. "We are all on the same side here," he whispered. "You speak the truth. And apparently now I have need to go lie to my uncle…yet again." He turned, striding swiftly for the door. It slammed shut after him.

Claerwen went to slide the bolt, momentarily resting her forehead against the door. She did not hear when Marcus approached from behind.

"What did Uther do?" he asked calmly, turning her around.

Claerwen winced and replied, "He kissed me." Her eyes closed briefly and she dreaded his reaction, but when she looked up again, he was smiling wryly. "You're not angry?"

The lines around his eyes deepened as his smile broadened and he shook his head. "What did you call him?"

She shrugged and answered, "A pond slug and a wood louse."

He pressed his lips together, suppressing a chuckle, then responded, "I thought so. No, I'm not angry at all. Because I know you well. And remember? Turn the disadvantage to the advantage? You know what his chambers look like now. We can use that…"

Claerwen moved away before he finished speaking and leaned her hands on a table. Marcus came aside her, watching her face. Her eyes moved as if reading. They were full of distress.

"What is it?" he asked quietly, thinking she had become ill.

Her breath came raggedly and she bowed her head as if in pain. She answered, "I have a terrible sense of foreboding. It's struck me now, several times, ever since Pascentius took me hostage, but I don't understand what it is. Or who it comes from."

"Who?" he echoed.

"Aye. It usually means someone is in trouble. I have felt this before, in the summer when you fought Drakar. I learned it was your distress I sensed."

"It is someone else this time?"

"I believe so."

"Can you guess who? And does it have to do with what you said to Myrddin, about all the reasons we must finish this quest?"

Her brows knotted together and the sense of dread worsened. "I don't know."

The midnight bell rang, echoing forlornly over the fortress. Marcus listened a moment, then strode to the outer door. He checked that it was bolted, then moved the anteroom's heavy table across in front of it. He set a pair of pewter cups on top, leaning them sideways onto their handles, then returned to Claerwen.

"If anyone tries to come through that door, the cups will fall and alert you. I'm going out. I need to stir up some trouble." He moved past her, going through to the bedchamber. Kneeling in front of the bed, he flipped away a small carpet spread over the floor. Using his smallest dagger, he pried out a short section of the planking, along with the one next to it, opening a square just big enough to pass through. He sat on the edge with his feet in the opening, then slipped down inside.

Claerwen felt heat drifting up from the hypocaust. She leaned over the edge and saw him gather up a long, narrow bundle from behind a support pillar. He lifted it through the opening, climbed out and unrolled it, revealing a thick, black leather tunic, a matching pair of breeches, tall boots, gauntlets and a helmet of formed leather with a full face visor. And inside, lay an enormous two-handed sword, adorned with an iron pommel in the shape of a hawk leaning to take flight.

Claerwen stared aghast at the contents. "How did you get this here? You said you would never use it again," she asked sharply, her face changing from dread to horror.

He hushed her with a finger to her lips. "I said I did not plan to use it again, but that I needed to leave the opportunity available. I'm sorry, I must do this."

"But why?"

He licked his dry lips. "Do you remember what I told you of the bargain I made with Pascentius? That I fed him the idea Ambrosius was allied to the Iron Hawk? I need to force the commander into an awkward position, to flush him out where I can openly prove he is guilty. It must happen now, because Myrddin won't be able to stall Uther very long. And even though he has been dormant for more than a year, *Y Gwalch Haearn* is the only one with enough power to accomplish this."

Claerwen stared at the black leather in disbelief as he changed clothes. "Is that what you meant? When you said we should have the Iron Hawk do this for us? You already had this hidden in the temple, didn't you?"

Marcus said, "Aye. You are correct. I have always kept a second set hidden in Dun Breatann, besides the one I keep at home. And no, Ceredig doesn't know about it. I took it with me when I left there and retrieved it yesterday from the temple. I found these loose floorboards and two other exits from the hypocaust as well."

"What are you going to do?"

"Banawr is hidden here, somewhere. He is Pascentius' eyes within the palace. If I go scare a few strategic people, he will run back to the commander with news of the Iron Hawk."

"To confuse Pascentius?"

"Aye, he won't know who the Iron Hawk is pursuing. Could be Uther, could be me. Could be Pascentius."

"Isn't that going to put you in worse trouble? Uther's men will certainly not tolerate the Iron Hawk's intrusion. They will be looking for you in two identities."

"That is true, but they can only catch me one at a time," he grinned and added, "And neither have they built a structure yet I couldn't free myself from."

She hooked her fingers into his belt and spoke urgently up into his face. "If they catch you, they will unmask your identity. Then they will kill you. It's not a game any longer."

"It never has been," he returned, suddenly serious. Drawing away from her, he unsheathed the big sword for a moment. It was even longer than his favored two-handed sword from home, and slightly broader. Hefting it, he watched the blade swing smoothly with admiring eyes, then he sheathed it again. Buckling it across his back, the iron pommel peered over his right shoulder.

For one more moment he paused, holding Claerwen's face in his hands and letting his eyes wander over her features. Then he kissed her roughly. "I won't be long," he said. Picking up the helmet and the gauntlets, he dropped down into the hypocaust.

# Chapter 22

## Winchester

The hypocaust was hot and only high enough to crawl through on hands and knees. The Iron Hawk heard Claerwen push the floorboards into place, their closure blocking all light, and he moved slowly in the direction of the main hall, groping from memory of his previous excursion. At the junction where the guest building and the hall met, the hypocaust narrowed into a square, ceramic flue pipe. He lay on his belly, adjusting the sword so it would not scrape, and wriggled through the narrow opening.

Under the main hall, another tunnel of flue pipes led from the back of the building. Flames showed in the distant end of the pipes, dim light reaching the warrior. The air was stifling, and he crawled quickly across. Another connecting flue turned to the left, joining the wing in which the high king's chambers were located. Crossing half the length of this side, the Iron Hawk groped for a marker he had left on the flooring above. He found it, a piece of cloth stuck in the crack of a small trap door. Pushing, he eased the door upward, then stood in the opening, breathing deeply from the cooler, refreshing air above, then vaulted up and out.

Now in a disused room, he crept to its outer door. Pulling it ajar, he peered into the corridor. At the end towards the right side, in the great hall's direction, a flight of steps led to the second floor, the same Claerwen had described after her visit with Uther. Two heavily armed guards were stationed at the foot. Two additional soldiers marched down from the second floor, their steps echoing, and turned into the corridor. The warrior closed the door, holding the latch to keep it from clicking. The men passed, exiting at the end to the left. He knew they would patrol through the other wings, returning within a quarter hour.

The Iron Hawk opened the door again. Oil lamps, guttering in a strong draught, were hung at intervals and dimly lit the corridor. Several had gone out. The warrior reached to another next to the door and pinched off the flame.

One guard turned his head. "Bloody lamps are going out," he muttered. "How many times is that now?"

"I'll light them again," offered the other soldier, boredom in his voice. He picked a small wooden stick from a wall container and lit it. Starting for the first dark lamp, he saw the door next to it was ajar. Suspicion struck him. He approached, gingerly pushing it in, and entered the disused room.

Out of the pitch-black interior, an arm thrust, hooking around his neck. A gauntleted hand clamped over his mouth, and he was wrestled to the floor. A fist thumped hard on the back of his head, and he slumped, unconscious.

The second soldier glanced down the corridor once, then again, not finding his partner. He called the man's name twice. Receiving no reply, he drew a dagger and began moving along the wall.

A latch clicked. The guard halted. Listening, he heard nothing more, then saw the open door. He reached for it, but he never touched the latch as the door pulled away from him, a black fist launching into his face. He fell in a heap against the opposite wall.

The Iron Hawk dragged him into the room, leaving him with the other unconscious guard. Returning to the corridor, he locked the door, listened, decided he had not been heard, then sprinted for the stairs, taking them two at a time. He whipped around the mid-flight landing, passing the tall, narrow window of small glass panes divided by wooden tracery. Moving more cautiously up the last few steps, he came to a halt on the upper landing, just before the brief passageway that led to Uther's chambers. He heard two guards speaking next to the closed doors.

Footsteps pattered from below, approaching. Scanning quickly, the Iron Hawk saw the roof's support beams were exposed, crossing under the open, peaked roof. He leapt, grappling one beam, swung his legs up, and heaved himself around until he lay on top, disappearing into the shadows.

A lone servant slowly climbed the steps, carrying a small platter covered with a cloth. He passed under the beams and stopped, the two guards approaching him. They did not seem surprised to see the servant, who announced he was delivering bakery goods that the king highly favored. He displayed the plate's contents, a stack of sweet cakes, and was led inside the chambers.

The Iron Hawk slid off the beam, dropping again onto the landing. Crouching along the wall, he crept forward to where the corridor turned towards the chambers' doors. There, he tapped lightly on the plastered wall.

One guard remained there. He heard the tap and called a terse alert to the other guard inside. Pressing himself along the wall, he moved to the corner, leaning to peer into the passageway, but saw nothing. Then he moved out, heading for the stairwell, stopped midway to listen, moved again. Aware of a trap, the guard sprinted to the landing, his sword slashing out, but he met only dark, empty air.

An instant later, a figure fell from above, hurtling down into him. The guard staggered backward, choking for breath. Holding his chest in agony, he tried to lift his sword, but he did not have the strength. Then he recognized the dark figure looming before him, the odd, visored helmet, the sword's pommel of iron in the shape of a hawk, *Y Gwalch Haearn.*

The guard struggled to draw enough air to scream, but he only gasped and fell on his knees, letting go of his sword. As the man helplessly watched the Iron Hawk advance, his face clearly told of his certainty that he would die in that moment. The last thing he remembered was the warrior leaning over him and pain squeezing his throat. Blacking out, he dropped.

The second guard dashed out through the doors, followed by two more and the servant, then Uther himself, disturbed by the scuffling. The guards halted, stunned at the warrior standing over their slumped man. One of them swore, then shouted an alarm, but as the man leapt in attack, the Iron Hawk sidestepped and grabbed his tunic, spun him around and heaved him into the others. All were propelled backward, falling against the king.

The Iron Hawk turned and ran, skidding down the steps to the midway landing, shouts and running footsteps following closely. But instead of whirling and dropping to the first floor, the warrior vaulted headfirst at the window, using his fists as a shield.

With a spectacular crash, he broke the glass and the tracery, his body rotating in a complete somersault until he landed, sitting upright on the veranda roof below. He cut a trench in the thin layer of snow on the tiles as he slid, his momentum carrying him with unstoppable force over the bumpy surface. He soared off the edge.

Shouts cried a general alarm, filling the night as he fell, and he braced for a painful landing. His legs narrowly missed a hedgerow planted several feet beyond the veranda's eave, but his body plowed into the thick shrubbery. Though his weight crushed the hard-tipped and twiggy hedge, there was enough resilience left in it that he bounced and flipped forward, landing facedown and skidding over slick, wet cobbles.

The Iron Hawk bounded up onto his feet and ran again, not allowing time to realize if he was hurt. He raced along the backside of the building and careened around the corner, past the hall, then along the guest wing. Nearing the end of the building, he slowed, but slid on a patch of well-trodden ice. He grabbed a support beam from the veranda and swung around it, aimed himself at another hedge and flew over. There, he rolled into the wall, grunting when he hit, then sat up and yanked furiously at a loose thin stone slab. Pulling it out, he exposed a hole in the foundation and wriggled through, coming once more into the hypocaust. He replaced the slab over the hole.

The warrior slid down a short incline and whipped off his helmet. He skittered across, counting the pillars he passed to reach the correct place and find the loose planks. Halting, he listened hard for sounds above and spared a few moments to catch his breath. Setting the helmet down, he knocked lightly on the floorboards.

Movement creaked above, not heavy enough to sound like footsteps, and he knew Claerwen had been waiting for him on the bed, stepping down lightly on bare feet. He pushed up and the boards gave easily, lifting into her hands.

As he hauled himself out of the hole, he instructed her in a quiet, intense voice, "Get me out of this gear as fast as you can, but be careful, there's a lot of broken glass. Throw everything down there, except the hauberk and coif." He pointed to the place where the helmet rested.

He wrenched the baldric off with the sword then started stripping frantically down to his loincloth, Claerwen untying laces and pulling the heavy leather and link armor from him. She piled the gear piece by piece as he dropped it, swinging it down into the hole. Bits of glass fell onto the floor and they sparkled in the lampglow, catching Marcus' attention. He swore and abruptly caught Claerwen's hand, telling her to stay back.

"I'll get a cloth to sweep it away," she whispered and circled to the privy room.

"Hurry," Marcus shot back and grabbed the sword, unbuckling it from the baldric, then thrust the weapon into the hypocaust.

Claerwen returned with two cloths, handing one to Marcus to dry the sweat from his body, then carefully whisked the glass through the hole. Finishing, she slipped the boards into place.

Shouts cried in the hall outside.

"They are coming to search the palace," he said sharply as he picked up the chain link armor, the baldric and the other clothing he had changed out of earlier. Running to the anteroom, he threw it all into the seneschal's post, then moved the table away from the door with Claerwen's help. He turned back to the bedchamber where he had left the other sword.

Pounding shook the outer door and the latch was tried.

Claerwen caught her breath as she watched Marcus stride away from her. He stopped at the sound she made, his eyes snapping around to her.

She went to him, whispering tightly in his ear, "Put a blanket around yourself. Your face and body don't match. I'll get the sword."

He looked down at himself and suddenly realized what she meant, that his black chest hair was not that of an older, grey-haired man. He snatched up a blanket from the pallet in the small front room. The door rattled again, harder, followed by an angry demand to open immediately. He reached for the bolt.

The door slapped open, banging so hard that plaster chipped off the wall where it hit. Marcus jumped back, tightly holding his blanket. A torch was thrust nearly into his face and four soldiers stared at him. He backed to the wool drape and stopped, refusing to go any farther. Behind him, he felt the drape move, and his unsheathed sword was placed into his right hand.

"Out of the way!" the foremost soldier growled.

"He is armed!" a second one shouted. All pulled their swords, ready to cut him down.

Instead of backing in fear as expected, Marcus stared at each one, his black eyes coldly assessing, his tenacious calm disconcerting them. "What do you want here?" he demanded, his voice booming harshly. "Why do you disturb Lady Riona?"

"The palace is to be searched. There has been an intruder."

"And who would that be?" Claerwen came from behind the drape, wrapped in a long fur coverlet from the bed, her hair down and flowing around her.

Her sudden presence startled the soldiers. "The warrior known as the Iron Hawk, my Lady," the leading soldier replied, his brashness diminishing in light of knowing how the king favored her.

Letting fear cloud her face, she thickened her accent and declared, "In Eireann, his legend is known, but we thought that was all he was, a legend."

"Ah, but he is very real, Lady, and dangerous. He was fighting the house guard, just outside the high king's chambers, only a few minutes ago."

"By the light!" Marcus swore.

Claerwen paled visibly. "Let them search, Faolan," she said, and pulled the drape aside. "As you can see, Faolan was in his room, and I in mine. We were both asleep."

The leader grunted and the men split up, checking the small chamber off the anteroom, and giving a cursory inspection of the inner rooms. Claerwen watched, sensing their embarrassment at disturbing her. The leader finally apologized for waking them, and led his men out.

Marcus bolted the door behind them. Going into Claerwen's chamber, he sat heavily on the bed's edge, his head down in relief. She knelt before him, her eyes asking what had happened. He detailed what he had done, his voice quiet and steady.

Utterly stunned by the description of his escape, Claerwen asked, "Are you hurt?" Not waiting for an answer, she climbed onto the bed behind him and pulled the blanket down. Several bruises were already forming.

"Nothing serious," he muttered.

"These are going to be dreadful," she said and probed to see if any ribs might be cracked. He winced when her gentle fingers touched a sore place.

"How is your back?" she asked, lightly pressing on the small bones down the center.

"Fine enough. I didn't twist when I landed." He pulled the blanket around himself again, protesting, "I'm all right, don't worry so much."

"Get some sleep. You've been awake all night," she said.

"They'll be back," he countered, jabbing a thumb towards the outer door. "The gear must be cleaned, I'll probably need it again."

"Sleep," she said once more, pushing him back onto the bed. "I will do it."

Smiling, he gave in to her offer. "Be careful, there's a lot of glass imbedded in it."

"I'm amazed you weren't cut anywhere."

"That's why I always use such heavy leather." Sitting up, he kissed her cheek, then walked slowly to the anteroom. He pulled the pallet across in front of the door and laid down on it, moaning when he rolled onto a bruise.

With her mouth open in surprise, Claerwen wondered why he would choose to sleep there instead of in the comfortable bed, then she realized he anticipated the soldiers' return would come very soon. She pried up the planks again and fished out the black leather. Most of the glass had already fallen out, and she picked the rest with her thumbnail. The helmet showed no damage, only dust from the hypocaust. Finished, she piled the gear neatly, ready to use. As she reached for the planks, she heard Marcus stir.

Seconds later, he appeared in the doorway, his eyes tired and solemn, and he watched heat from the hypocaust drift up and catch strands of her hair, making them float as if on a summer breeze. He smiled for the sake of its beauty, so incongruent in the dead of winter. Crossing the room, he helped her push the boards into place and spread the carpet over them.

"Someone is coming again," he said softly. "I can hear him going from door to door, knocking, talking." He returned to the front room and dressed quickly in his seneschal's clothes. The knock came as he pulled on his boots.

Myrddin's voice answered when Marcus called for identification. He let the prince in, formally bowing until the door closed.

"And I expected *you* to make trouble," Myrddin muttered. "Now the Iron Hawk is here as well. Is there a reason for this?"

Marcus sidestepped the question, asking, "What do they say?" He guided Myrddin to the common room and poured him a cup of wine.

Myrddin stared into the deep rose liquid, his face shadowed with unspoken dread and oddly free of his customary aloofness.

"Drink it, man," Marcus invited, then poured himself a cup. He drank it dry.

Myrddin eyed the empty cup and remarked, "Aye, you are a Celt to the heart, in spite of that Roman name your grandmother gave you."

Marcus poured a second cupful. Holding it up, he barbed, "You're as much a Celt as I, only from the south. *Iechyd da!*" He drank half of it in one gulp.

Myrddin snorted, took a sip, then bobbed his head towards the inner chambers. "Is she still awake?"

"Aye," Marcus answered and pushed the bedchamber's door aside, signaling to Claerwen.

Greeting her, Myrddin said, "I am actually here in an official capacity. Uther wants all visiting nobility to meet with him in his chambers, in one hour. And since you are nobility, true or imagined, he is requiring your presence."

"Because of the Iron Hawk?" Claerwen asked.

"I don't know exactly what he's going to announce, but I would expect so, as well as something to do with my father's funeral." He paused, looking from Claerwen to Marcus and back again, then sighed heavily, a sudden sadness coming over him. "I never had the chance to know my father well, until the last few years. I spent twenty years of my life secretly studying the druidic arts. That was my fosterage. I am the last of my kind. Before that, my mother kept me isolated, because she refused to name my father, to protect him, and me, and she followed the right path in doing so. I will not ask what you've been doing, but I'm going to trust that you are on that same path. I will see you within the hour."

---

When Marcus and Claerwen arrived in the great hall, it looked as if most of Uther's war band had been posted there. They were escorted across to the building where his chambers were, up the stairway, past the gaping broken window. Claerwen stopped there, asking their guard what had happened. When told it was where the Iron Hawk had made his escape, she approached the ragged opening. The rut in the roof's snow and the damaged shrubbery beyond showed how far he had fallen, the risk he had taken.

"Lady?" the escort interrupted her thoughts.

She silently turned back and continued up the stairs, placing her hand on Marcus' wrist as if in need of support. Her fingers curled around inside and squeezed.

Soldiers lined the second floor passageway, their faces suspiciously watching each noble who passed. Claerwen kept a serene countenance in spite of her knees that threatened to collapse. She marched past the sentinels, Marcus following, and entered through the chamber's doors.

Inside, their escort announced them, and they were admitted immediately, led through the large common room Claerwen had seen before, then into a sumptuous inner chamber. Myrddin had mentioned it as one Uther now used for meeting guests privately. It was also one Ambrosius had used the year before, only months after he had become king, when she and Marcus had brought him Macsen Wledig's magnificent torque. The room had been extremely spare then, reflecting Ambrosius' serious nature. Uther had taken the room for his own use just after that, and had turned it into part of his luxurious home.

A large number of nobles had already arrived, and across the chamber Uther and Myrddin tensely discussed the intrusion. Myrddin's controlled remoteness contrasted starkly to Uther's demeanor, a boiling resentment threatening to break into full-blown fury. The escort announced Lady Riona's entrance and the two men abruptly stopped talking.

Claerwen moved gracefully into the room, Marcus a pace behind her. Then the guard at the door clamped a hand on Marcus' shoulder, stopping him. Fear filled Claerwen's eyes as she turned, then she looked at Uther, her expression changing to questioning distress. Uther signaled at the guard to let Faolan enter.

"Lady Riona," Uther greeted her midway across the room. He attempted a smile, but his underlying anger remained in his tired face.

She curtsied deeply, keeping her eyes down.

Her formality puzzled the king, but he brushed it aside. He said, "I thought you should hear what we have to say, as this will affect your asylum. We are waiting for a few others to arrive, then we will begin. Please be my guest if you would like something to eat or drink." He swept his hand towards a table against a wall, set with platters and drinking horns, then returned to his discussion with Myrddin.

Claerwen seated herself in a chair, choosing to wait in a quiet corner away from the other people. Most of them were silent as well, eyeing each other warily; only the king's and his nephew's voices droned noticeably, punctuated by an occasional command or announced name from the guards.

The room was hot, making Claerwen sleepy, already tired from having been awake most of the night. She wondered how much pain Marcus felt. He stood directly behind her, and she glanced up. Maintaining a steady stare, he scanned slowly around the room, giving no indication of any injuries. She deeply admired his fortitude.

Two servants arrived with additional food and drink. The room grew silent, the occupants waiting for them to leave. Watching them set out more drinking horns and platters, Marcus noticed that one servant wore ill-fitting clothes. Uther's personal attendants all dressed in a standard tunic, belted at the waist. This man had a second tunic underneath that hung slightly below the hem of the outer garment, as well as a hood, worn up, not down as anyone would inside a warm building.

The servant carried a cloth-covered plate and a ceramic goblet. He placed them on a separate table next to Uther and removed the cloth, displaying sweet bakery goods, the same as had been delivered the previous evening. He drew the king's attention to the food.

Recognizing the baked goods, Marcus realized the hooded man was the same servant as he had seen in the night. He stepped sideways, attempting to see the man's face, but could not from where he stood. Making a pretense of picking something for Lady Riona to eat, he watched the man as he crossed the room.

Claerwen studied the tension in Marcus' movements, and she knew it did not come from his bruised body. She glanced at Myrddin, wondering at first if Marcus had sensed a betrayal coming, but Myrddin remained deep in his discussion with Uther.

Marcus returned to his post behind Claerwen. His hand gripped her shoulder and he leaned down to whisper in her ear. "That servant was here in the night. Now he brings a special plate and one goblet, only for Uther. I smell the same odor in the air as was in Daracha's house. I believe, when the food and the drink mix together, after they are taken, then it becomes poison. I am sure that man is the second, but I cannot see his face."

Claerwen stared at the servant, her eyes drilling across at his figure, and the power of the fire stirred within her unexpectedly. She fought it, afraid of the disruption it could cause, then sensed Myrddin's power come alive as well. He turned, meeting her eyes, his own glowing softly amber. As he took a step forward, the servant stood in his path. The man backed, avoiding a collision, then came around. Banawr's face showed dimly within the hood.

Uther began to call for the nobles' attention, but no one heard. Instead, Myrddin's pale face and changing eyes brought more notice from the crowd, spreading a terrible tension, and he moved slowly towards Claerwen. A moment later, the fire left him, and he realized she and Marcus had pinpointed the assassin.

Abruptly, Marcus started across the room again. He caught Myrddin's arm and whispered through clenched teeth, "This is the map." He thrust the folded parchment into Myrddin's palm and folded his fingers around it. "That man is the assassin. Try to keep the guards away from me."

Realizing he was discovered, Banawr dove across the room. Amidst rising gasps of confusion from the onlookers, he ran through a door, into another of the private chambers. Marcus whirled around, dashing after him.

"What's goes on here?" Uther demanded. "Why is Faolan chasing that servant?"

"That man! He is the assassin!" shrieked a woman's voice from the entrance.

"The servant is Marcus ap Iorwerth?"

"No! The other man! The one chasing the servant is the assassin!"

"That's not true!" Claerwen shouted, recognizing Daracha. "The servant is the assassin! And that woman is his accomplice! Don't let her deceive you."

The room seemed to stir of itself, murmurs rapidly spiraling into shouts. Uther stared from one woman to the other, unable to decide which told the truth. Claerwen launched out of the chair, striding across with clear rage in her eyes, shouting for Daracha's arrest.

"Guards!" Uther yelled. "Arrest those men! Both of them!"

Livid, he took up the goblet and put it to his lips.

"NO!" Claerwen shrieked. She lunged at Uther, running now. A guard grabbed for her, but she swerved, evading him. She slapped the goblet from Uther's fingers. It flew, banging into the small table with the sweet cakes, spilling, then skittered across the floor, leaving a trail of liquid.

The guard caught her, wrenching her arms behind her back. She struggled to free herself, but the guard was too strong. He forced her to stand in front of Uther, pulling her head up by her hair.

"Who are you?" Uther confronted her, outraged. "What have you to do with Marcus ap Iorwerth?"

"Let her go," Myrddin said.

"Let her go?" Uther turned on his nephew. "Are you mad? Marcus ap Iorwerth killed my brother — your father — a high king — and she is connected to him. You want to let her go?"

Myrddin gripped Uther's arm. He stared coldly into the king's face and growled, "This is Lady Claerwen of Dinas Beris. She is Marcus ap Iorwerth's wife. They have been trying to save your life, not kill you. In truth, I believe she just did save your life, if this is what I think it is. Look." He indicated the table with the sweet cakes. Several of them, soaked with the spilled drink, smoldered and turned black.

Uther stared bitterly at the cakes. Turning back to Claerwen, his eyes brooded on her. "And how do I know *you* did not make the poison, and you are merely using your failure to kill me to blame some poor servant?"

"That servant's name is Banawr; he is Pascentius' second-in-command," Claerwen countered, entreating him. "The woman who called Marcus the assassin is named Daracha. She produced the poison, both now and for when your brother was murdered. We found proof of it in her house, near a small fort two days north of Dun Breatann. Banawr hired a man called Eopa to give it to Ambrosius, and Banawr killed Eopa afterward. The body lies in a bog somewhere. Daracha stole Marcus' ring and deliberately left it here so the blame would be cast upon him. This is Pascentius' plan to regain the power his father Vortigern lost to Ambrosius."

"You deceived me, woman. I say Marcus ap Iorwerth is the usurper!"

Claerwen could not believe Uther's stupidity. Pleading desperately, she went on, "Why would he bring Ambrosius the torque of Macsen Wledig if he craved the power of the throne? He has spent his life trying to prevent those such as Pascentius from achieving the kingship. He has never been disloyal to Ambrosius, or to you, and he has suffered greatly for it."

Her rebuke stung Uther, and his wrath grew overwhelmingly. For a moment, he turned partially away, his jaw locked with tension. But an instant later, he whipped around again, the back of his hand striking her across the face with a sickening smack. Her head wrenched to the side, pausing as her eyes glazed over, and she fell from the guard's grip, sprawling onto the floor.

"Claerwen!" Myrddin knelt, cradling her head in his hands, horrified by Uther's violence. Every noble in the room held absolutely silent. When she did not respond, he stood again before his uncle. Hurling words, he condemned, "That was uncalled for, you stubborn fool! She told you the truth and you cannot see it for all your hot-headed blindness."

"She lied to me," Uther shot back. "And you, you, great 'Merlin the Enchanter' as you've been called — you are more likely the sorcerer who created the poison, used now, and used in that which coursed through my brother's veins. He was your father, by the gods! Did you hope to take the crown?"

Ignoring Uther's diatribe, Myrddin argued, "You allowed Marcus to carry his sword within the palace. He never tried to use it, did he? The opportunity was certainly available. But somehow he had to enter Winchester to find the assassin and prove his innocence. If you arrest him, then you lose the true killers and the chance to at last rid yourself of Pascentius!"

"And you believe this?"

"You know only too well how dangerous Pascentius is. Ambrosius trusted Marcus implicitly and wanted his help. Ceredig of Strathclyde has supported this. So do I."

Uther seemed to soften a moment, self-doubt creeping into his eyes as Myrddin's argument set into his mind. But glaring at

Claerwen's limp figure on the floor, his face grew cold again and he growled, "I don't."

Myrddin spit back, "Most of your anger exists because now you have learned she belongs to another man."

Uther opened his mouth, his blue eyes piercing out of a face gone crimson, then he turned away, effectively dismissing Myrddin. He gestured at two guards to take Claerwen prisoner.

"Uther, you can't do this," Myrddin protested.

"Not another word, nephew, or I will have you locked up as well."

"Then at least keep her only under house arrest. Don't put her in that hovel with the other prisoners. Even you have to have physical proof." Myrddin wanted to whip out the map, but it alone was not enough to be convincing, and the stubbornness in Uther's face told him the king was not yet willing to listen to reason of any sort. He held his tongue.

Uther's rage boiled. As he scowled in contempt at Claerwen, an idea struck him. He said to the guard, "So be it, house arrest it will be. Take her to one of the empty rooms, upstairs in the old building, across the courtyard. Marcus ap Iorwerth will come looking for her before long. She will be the bait in my trap."

# Chapter 23

## Winchester

Claerwen felt the pain in her jaw even before she woke.

Hoping it was a dream, a very bad dream, she vaguely remembered the big hand flying at her face, the thudding sound of how it had struck. The pain grew worse. Her eyes opened, slowly coming into focus on the ceiling above. Turning her head, she winced, her neck feeling as if it was pinched in a blacksmith's tongs, and she discovered she lay on a cold, unadorned floor in a room absolutely empty except for a tiny chamber pot. Running her tongue along the interior of her mouth, she found her left cheek swollen and the inside cut in a pattern that matched her teeth. Thirsty, she tasted blood.

Claerwen slowly eased up, and as she drew her legs inward, metal scraped. Her right ankle was shackled to a chain bolted into the center of the floor. She jolted upright, realizing with full intensity that she was a prisoner and this was no dream.

Pushing up onto her feet and dragging the chain, she made her way across to a single door cut into one wall. The chain was just long enough to reach. She knew the door would be bolted from the outside even before she tried the latch, but she tried it anyway, just for the satisfaction.

Turning around, she crossed to a tiny window in the opposite wall. Barred in iron, it had shutters to the outside. They were closed, but unlocked. She swung them out and saw she was on the second floor of a building opposite the great hall. Dusk approached.

Her head pounded with the cold air streaming in through the window, and she touched her cheek, wincing again. She probed it anyway and concluded that her cheekbone and jaw were not broken. None of her teeth were loose, but she figured she must have a bruise to rival some of Marcus'.

"Where are you...?" she exhaled. Dredging her mind, she realized she had no recollection of his fate.

The bolt on the door slid. Claerwen turned towards the noise. A female servant entered and set a small tray of food on the floor, just within the doorway. The woman retreated, deliberately avoiding Claerwen's eyes. The door shut, clicking, the bolt ramming home.

Claerwen stared at the cloth-covered tray. She hoped the food underneath was better fare than the pitiful gruel Pascentius had fed her. Then she wondered if it was poisoned. Sighing harshly, she approached the tray, intending to inspect it, then saw a tiny, folded piece of parchment peeking from underneath. Surprised, she greedily picked it up, hoping Marcus had found a way to send her a message.

It was a letter from Myrddin. It read:

*I pray to the gods that this will find you conscious and unhurt. I begged Uther to let me see you, to attend to the certain pain you will have from his hand, damn him, but he is refusing you any visitors. Therefore, I have bribed one of the serving maids to bring this to you.*

*I have attempted to rationalize his destructive outbursts, citing he is still in grief for Ambrosius, but I fear I cannot convince even myself. Of Marcus, I know nothing, except that he either escaped the town wall, or is well hidden within. Neither was Banawr found, nor the woman. Uther continues the search and has ordered your execution along with Marcus', to take place once Marcus is found.*

*My father's funeral goes on as scheduled. If you are able to watch, the palace will be quite empty on the morrow as most of us will be in Amesbury and the Giant's Dance.*

*I continue to plead your innocence to Uther, though he does not listen to me. My hope is that Marcus has enough good sense to stay away until I can secure proof and affect your release, or he will be doomed. He is smarter than most men, but I have seen his rage in Dun Breatann when you were hostage before, and I fear one day it will drive him to a mistake from which he cannot extricate himself.*

*I do now beg your patience, dear friend. I shall do everything within my power to help.*

*Your beloved servant, Myrddin*

Claerwen read the letter twice more, having difficulty to see through the tears, starting now. She whispered, "He is right, Marcus, you must stay away."

But she knew he would not, not as long as he lived. He would come for her, somehow, or die trying.

She sank to the floor and wept.

———————————

The bathhouses behind the palace had not been maintained or repaired since the Romans' departure more than sixty years earlier. Many of the stones had been stolen for use in other buildings. Because the mortar between them had been pried loose, the walls had become precariously unstable, sometimes even collapsing, and now few people braved getting near.

A priest strolled along the palace wall near the baths that night, heavily cloaked and hooded, his breath streaming in the cold air. Stopping, he studied the ruins, intently scanning, like a night bird seeking a mouse burrowed within the fallen stones. He remained motionless, listening as much as he watched, for the slightest movement, sound or sign of life. His eyes halted, staring at a particular gap in the rubble. In the night air, the disintegrated buildings looked like grey, rippling waves of stone. But one depression differed, its darkness just a bit more alive than the rest.

It moved upward slightly and took on the shape of a head, the face a puffy, pock-marked shadow that glared back.

The priest slowly moved again, edging towards a stone bench oddly still intact along a toppled wall. He sat and let the hood of his cloak partially fall back, revealing intense eyes, long dark hair, and a neatly trimmed dark beard.

The face in the ruins dropped down into the gap.

The palace and its surroundings were still, nearly deserted except for the token guards left behind while the court's residents and their guests had gone to Ambrosius' funeral. Time passed slowly for both Banawr and Marcus, each waiting for the other to move.

Another storm gradually approached, and after more than an hour, an icy wind sprang up, blowing out much of the torchlight. With the thickening clouds, the last of the starlight disappeared.

Emboldened by the nearly complete darkness, Banawr crawled out of the ruins. Still dressed in the servant's clothing, he now wore a small pouch strapped across his chest and a sword buckled around his hips as well. Cautiously watching in all directions, he started for the alley between the great hall and the guest wing, saw no one, then sprinted through, running for the palace courtyard. But halfway across the yard, he halted, his jaw dropping in astonishment as he stared at the far edge. Barely visible, another man stood there, not in a guardsman's livery, but in the highly recognizable, black, masked helmet of the Iron Hawk.

Urgent to complete his trap before the king's return, Banawr hesitated, glancing up at Uther's chambers. The Iron Hawk noted the look's direction and took advantage of the second's indecision. He circled, cutting off access to the building. Reluctantly, Banawr drew his sword.

Several house guards appeared around the yard's perimeter, at first with the intention of halting the inevitable fight, then curiosity overpowered them. Mumbling among themselves, they did not approach either man, preferring to leave the Iron Hawk's temper unchallenged. They watched as the warrior slowly drew his weapon and swung it in long, low strokes, side to side, as if to test its weight and balance.

Finally Banawr accepted the challenge, pushing back his tunic's hood, needing to see peripherally. With his face snarled up like a burl on an oak tree, he gripped his sword's hilt tightly and began circling, concentrating on the Iron Hawk's steps.

The warrior rushed at Banawr, swinging with precision and strength, his boots crunching on the packed snow. Banawr met the blow, blocking and turning it aside, but the warrior advanced again, slashing with tremendous force. Banawr backed with each hit, struggling for footing on the icy ground. He neared the terraced steps of the guest wing and lost his concentration when he stumbled on the lowest step, then backed into a support beam. Distracted, he watched in terror as the Iron Hawk's blade arced into a blinding descent.

Banawr wrenched himself aside and the warrior's sword struck the pillar. Shards of stone chipped, scattering. Banawr whipped around and kicked out, hitting the Iron Hawk in the side. The warrior grunted, staggering back. His boot found a patch of ice and slid. Banawr advanced, sure of the advantage, but the Iron Hawk twisted, boosting himself around in a full circle. He slashed across again, using the full force of his turn. Jarred roughly, Banawr went down, nearly losing his sword. With one hand, he yanked a dagger from his belt and hurled it. A collective gasp hissed from the guards as the knife spun straight for the Iron Hawk's chest.

But the dark warrior sidestepped with graceful agility, and the guards standing behind him scattered like seed hulls in the wind. The dagger clattered harmlessly across the cobbles, spinning away. Frustrated, Banawr rose again and charged, desperation marking his posture. He slashed and thrust, over and over, trying to wear down the other man.

The great hall's doors opened, and Uther's seneschal appeared. For a moment, he stared in disbelief at the fight, then dashed back inside. Myrddin appeared in the doorway, then descended the steps. Seconds later, the high king marched out, demanding, "What do you mean the Iron Hawk is here again?" He paused, staring, then blurted, "Why does he fight a servant?"

Myrddin gripped Uther's shoulder. "Do you not see? That man

is the one who tried to poison you. And he is no servant. That is Pascentius' second-in-command."

From the edge of his eye, Myrddin saw a motion streaming towards him. He jerked his head around as Banawr's pouch landed at his feet. The Iron Hawk had cut it away and thrown it. Picking it up, Myrddin found inside a small vial of liquid and more of the bakery goods. Carefully opening the vial, he spilled a few drops onto one of the tiny cakes. Within seconds, it smoldered.

Myrddin's eyes narrowed as he produced the map Marcus had given him. He spoke with calm but undeniable authority, "This is your proof, Uther. That man tried to kill you. Not Marcus ap Iorwerth, not anyone else. That man and his people provided the same poison that killed my father. And this map details the attack Pascentius and Octa plotted together, the attack Marcus ap Iorwerth sabotaged. He is innocent, as is his wife. The Iron Hawk has championed their cause because you allowed them no chance to clear their names. You will need to learn patience, Uther, and fairness along with it. Will you believe the truth now?"

The king frowned at the disintegrating cake, then at the fighting men.

Myrddin continued when Uther remained silent, "Do you know what you have cost Lady Claerwen and her husband? It is time to release her and make amends. Let her go. Lift the fugitive status."

Uther countered, "I want her here."

Incredulous, Myrddin demanded, "For what purpose?"

A flurry of clanging swords interrupted. Both fighters grunted, frantically hacking in a spectacular display of swordsmanship. Though each had achieved a steady rhythm of strength, stealth, and concentration, the Iron Hawk had more stamina and agility. He began a new tactic, whirling and flashing the long blade in a pattern, its movement too quick to focus upon.

Myrddin watched Banawr. Mesmerized by the dancing blade as it sparkled in the torchlight, the second reminded Myrddin of a child watching madly fluttering birch leaves in the summer wind. Confused, frightened, Banawr knew the blade would fall, and fall with fatal brutality, but how and when, he could not guess.

Then, with the full depth of his lungs, the Iron Hawk screamed an unintelligible war cry. The fatal blow came, crossing at Banawr's neck, cleanly severing the head. The body fell, the head dropping almost in the place it should have been if it had remained attached. Blood soaked into the trampled snow.

The surrounding men went absolutely silent, stunned by the Iron Hawk's cruelty. Only the warrior's heavy breathing and his boots crunching as he washed his blade with snow and slid it back into its sheath disturbed the courtyard's stillness. For a moment he stood, unmoving, his posture almost like a grieving man, then he slowly strode to Banawr's body and picked up the head by its hair. He faced the high king, his lips pressed in a solid line of disgust below the lower edge of the mask, and held out the ghastly head.

The king's face recoiled in horror and fear.

Then the Iron Hawk threw the head, rolling it to within an inch of Uther's feet. He turned and walked calmly out of the courtyard.

Uther stared at the head, utterly appalled. It stared back at him, the eyes frozen in their moment of final terror. "Why?" Uther whispered, barely finding his voice. "Why?" he repeated, and his throat constricted, preventing him from speaking further.

Myrddin's attention was caught elsewhere.

Wiping tears from her face, Claerwen stared down from her room of imprisonment, her eyes locked onto the path the Iron Hawk had taken from the courtyard. Even at that distance, Myrddin saw both terror and relief in her face.

He turned once more to Uther. "I'm going to speak plainly. You will have to face the fact that you were wrong. If you do not release Lady Claerwen now and lift the fugitive status from her husband, the future disgrace you will put yourself in will be by far harder to reconcile than the embarrassment of rectifying a false accusation now."

Uther's face appeared like stone, his blue eyes colder than the ice he stood upon.

Myrddin continued, "Marcus ap Iorwerth is a selfless, incorruptible man who has only two passions in life. One is his wife. The other is freedom. Did you know that when you and my father were planning the return to Britain to reclaim the kingship, Vortigern imprisoned Marcus? The traitor's Saxon mercenaries beat him, tortured him, attempting to make him betray your plans. Then he was left to die. But he never broke his honor; he did not reveal what he knew. Lady Claerwen says he never even gave Vortigern the satisfaction of crying out with the pain. And I would wager on my life that he would endure it all again to ensure Britain's freedom from the Saxons' tyranny. Do not forswear that man's loyalty, for he will not take his wife's imprisonment lightly."

Myrddin spun around, striding for the hall, leaving Uther alone in the courtyard with his conscience.

# Chapter 24

**Winchester**

Claerwen waited, sitting in the dark, listening to the tap of sleet at the window. Cold draughts stole around the ill-fitting shutters, and as the sleet melted on the casement, droplets of water ran down inside the wall and onto the floor.

Shivering, she waited half the night, past the midnight bells, anticipating that Banawr's death would bring her freedom, but no one came, not even a guard to ask, or an official to tell her she would remain a prisoner. She was enormously relieved to know Marcus had evaded Uther's intense searches, survived the fight with Banawr and found the evidence to prove their innocence. But nothing had changed, and he had disappeared again. Frustrated, she wondered what had befallen him since. Finally, she lay down again, curled into a tight ball against the cold air, and fell asleep.

Morning dawned dim and icy. Voices echoed in the courtyard, waking Claerwen. She rose, stiff and deeply chilled, and crossed to the window. Ice that had accumulated on the shutters cracked and shattered, falling out as she pushed them open. She leaned her face against the cold iron bars to see the yard below. More courtiers had returned and were listening intently to a pair of guards describe the swordfight from the previous evening.

The bolt suddenly clicked and slapped. Claerwen turned as the door came open, revealing the serving maid with another tray of food.

"Have they said anything, when they will let me go?" Claerwen asked, rushing forward, hungrier for news than food.

The maid kept her eyes down, more concerned with setting the small platter on the floor without spilling it and picking up the previous day's leftovers.

"Please," Claerwen pleaded, "Tell me if you've heard anything."

But the maid turned and moved swiftly for the door. Claerwen followed. "What have they said? Please!"

A tall guard blocked the door with a heavy spear. He gripped Claerwen's shoulder and pushed her back, then slammed the door shut. The bolt rammed.

"Please," she called again, but she already knew there would be no answer. Turning back, she seized the platter, searching underneath for another message from Myrddin. Nothing was there. Pulling off the cloth cover, she only found cold food.

Her hope deflated, she sat down hard on the floor, wondering now if Uther had again begrudged the truth and dismissed the evidence. "What happened to you..." she begged of Marcus, wishing he could hear her, wherever he was. She hoped to all the gods he had not been caught and imprisoned, or worse...

---

The sun emerged by midday and melted most of the snow. Disheartened and bored, Claerwen spent most of the time watching out of her window, hoping to see Myrddin cross the courtyard. She had intended to try to catch his attention, but she never saw him. In the intervening time, she studied the naked room, trying to guess how Marcus would attempt an escape from it. Although strong for a woman, she did not have his strength for overpowering a guard or breaking structures. Giving up, she sat on the floor again, waiting for the escape of sleep.

Dusk had nearly settled into night when voices rose again in the courtyard. The palace had been quiet all day, the returning courtiers still sunk deeply in the solemn mood of the funeral.

Claerwen heard sharp words exchanged, and she returned to the window.

A monk waited at the gates, speaking rapidly with the guard. At that distance, the words were unclear. But she guessed his message carried importance — when the guard sent a page running to the great hall, Myrddin appeared immediately after, pacing quickly across the yard.

Myrddin greeted the monk, then paused, staring into the man's hood. They took a few steps into the yard and stopped again, debating together, striving to keep their voices hushed. The monk's hands moved in pointed gestures, indicating anger.

Then Uther descended the hall's steps, walking towards the guest building. The monk caught sight of him and turned, moving away from Myrddin. He shouted at the king, his voice echoing harshly between the buildings. Uther halted, his face registering annoyance, then surprise.

"By the gods my people swear by," Claerwen whispered, her eyes returning to the monk. He dropped his cloak and pushed back the hood of his soutane. Joy swelled inside her as she gazed at Marcus below, alive and apparently unhurt.

He dropped the soutane, revealing full battle gear. The beard and grey coloring were gone; his long black hair whipped in the wind. "Why hasn't my wife been released?" he shouted at Uther. Curious courtiers watched and guards paused, waiting for orders from the king.

Uther stared at him, then at Myrddin, several paces behind.

Marcus shouted again, "Why is Claerwen of Dinas Beris still held prisoner? You have all the proof of her innocence you need." With his right fist raised and ramming the air to punctuate his rage, he abruptly started across the courtyard on long, determined strides.

The king frowned, then suddenly made the connection between Claerwen and the approaching man, seeing Marcus for the first time without a disguise. He signaled to the guards to hold their position, then folded his arms in contempt, studying the bold confrontation. "Your wife is a hostage, not a prisoner." Uther picked his words carefully, pronouncing them with deliberate calm, his eyes not quite holding Marcus' glare.

"There is no difference. You have no reason to hold her against her will," Marcus countered. "Or are we still fugitives?"

"She will remain my hostage until Pascentius is brought down."

Appalled, Myrddin joined Marcus, demanding in a low, hoarse voice, "When have you decided this? What possible use could she be as a hostage?"

Uther shot back, "Pascentius is as great a threat as ever. He can hire other assassins. But as long as Lady Claerwen is my hostage, I have the assurance that Marcus ap Iorwerth will continue to sabotage his plots to gain the crown."

"You still don't trust Marcus?" Myrddin questioned.

"He has not offered to swear fealty. Instead he confronts me."

Marcus' eyes narrowed and he said low, facing Uther but speaking to Myrddin, "He asks for fealty? He has not earned it."

Horrified that Marcus would publicly insult Uther, Myrddin sucked in his breath. But the king held still, watching Marcus' face, his own nearly blank except for the hint of a smirk. Then he returned the insult, "And he has not earned his wife's release."

"This is not the time for children's games, uncle," Myrddin ejected. "You cannot afford to offend Marcus ap Iorwerth. You need his support, and while he may not have the power to break you, he can certainly, over time, undermine you, if he would choose to do so. You would do better to take a war band out and face Pascentius yourself instead of sending a lone man — "

"No," Marcus interrupted. "A war band is not appropriate. And you do not need a hostage to guarantee my conduct."

"And how do I know this?" Uther queried.

"In place of a hostage, I will pledge my life."

A chorus of stunned gasps rose from the courtyard. In the window above, Claerwen gripped the iron bars as her stomach sank.

Uther smiled greedily as he assessed the possibilities. "Dinas Beris is in a fine strategic location, and is adjacent to Dinas Emrys, which lies in Pendragon crown lands. As to your life, well, I cannot trust you to turn yourself in, but I can hold your lands and

Myrddin smiled wryly. "Don't ever tell him I said this, but you would have made a better king. I have seen you with enough anger to slay all the Germanic tribes, but you held your temper and still saw things fairly. Instead of spending so much on all the trappings of luxury, Uther should spend time learning kingship."

Marcus looked up at him tiredly with one eyebrow lifted. He said, "Uther is a man who has not yet learned to see the truth for what it is and that's why I spoke to him the way I did. He thinks he has control of me, and I'm letting that stand, but he does not. I procured Claerwen's release so that I would have the freedom to chase down Pascentius without being tied to Winchester. She would be an easy target here, too easy; I would not be able to protect her. Uther just won't admit that we all have the same goal."

"Did he take me as a hostage because I hurt his pride?" Claerwen asked.

Myrddin answered, "Partially, I believe that is true. However, Uther has a short memory when it comes to women. He will recover soon enough. But he will not overlook any mistakes or shortcomings regarding Pascentius. You will have to succeed."

"I will need to succeed, regardless," Marcus said, then cited that Pascentius would look for revenge sooner or later.

Claerwen asked, "Why did you say a war band is inappropriate?"

Marcus winced as he massaged a particularly sore place on the side of his knee, then answered, "Pascentius has at least one other hostage."

"Who?" Claerwen and Myrddin asked at the same time.

"I don't know. I scouted his camp all day. That's why I was so long getting here. Daracha is with them, and I saw a young girl, bound like you were, Claeri. I don't know who she is. There may be others, and I suspect so, because of the way the camp is organized. We will have to confirm this before I can decide what we will do. And there are still Saxons coming, a few at a time, all from the south coast."

Myrddin rose from his chair, picked up a lamp, and walked to a closed door in the rear of his chambers. He said, "I'm going to change clothes then go for a walk, and try to think of something profoundly wise to convince Uther into proceeding cautiously."

He smiled wryly again and handed the lamp to Claerwen. As he opened the door and led them through, he added, "Inside here is a complete set of rooms. They are yours for as long as you want them. I had your things from the guest chambers brought here for safekeeping. The servants would have stolen everything. It's all in here for you. I will see you in the morning." He disappeared into his own rooms.

Marcus softly shut the door. He leaned his back on it, resting with his eyes closed, listening to the quiet. He never heard Claerwen approach, but he felt her arms slip around him, comfortable and familiar, and as her empathy engulfed him, filling his spirit, he found a supreme calm within himself, a self-contained peace to be savored. He wished he could cork that peace inside a jug for later use when the need would arise. That need would truly come, and soon.

His eyes opened, and he found that she had placed the lamp inside a bedchamber within the private rooms beyond. Now she watched up into his face, her eyes tracing every detail. He wrapped his arms around her and pulled her up, his lips opening to meet hers in a kiss filled with passion held back for so long. He whispered, "I swear, no one has the gift of compassion such as you have, Claeri."

She offered, "Just for one night, before the next storm of trouble, let you and I enjoy a few hours of this privacy."

"It may be all we have for a long while again," he agreed, and searching her eyes, he knew she understood what he had truly meant, that it was all they may have together, ever again.

Marcus' black eyes glittered in the lamplight, and he lightly traced the bruise that still showed on her cheek. But before he could speak his concern, Claerwen raised up and hushed him, caressing his face and pressing his lips with kisses.

She pulled back, taking his hands, drawing him with her. Reaching the doorway of the bedchamber, he began to drop his gear, piece by piece. Clothing followed, scattered shoes, boots, belts, tunics, her gown, one undershift, then another, his breeches, a loincloth, all across the floor.

Marcus savored the feel of her warm nakedness as his big hands slid around her and he drew her down onto the bed. The soft swish of her palms rushing over his skin brought heat to his soul, and he abandoned all thoughts of the ordeals they had endured. Their muffled murmurs of pleasure filled the room as they molded to each other like hot, malleable iron, unabashedly exploring the delight of being together. Filled with earthy passion and boundless, ethereal joy, at last, and with completeness, they gave in to their craving for each other.

---

Midnight bells rang.

The oil lamp still burned, and as Claerwen lay curled into Marcus' arms, she watched him rest, comfortably serene, his eyes closed. Not wishing to disturb him, she held very still, yet she could not help but to run a finger along one side of his long, flowing moustache. He stirred, opening his eyes, and smiled.

"I thought you had gone to sleep," she whispered.

"I was enjoying this moment of contentment."

"And I spoiled it for you," she lamented.

He smiled and kissed her, "Never. I'd best put out the lamp now." He eased himself from the bed and paced across, but a tall ewer caught his eye. Checking it, he found it filled with wine. "Want some?" he asked, then picked up his loincloth from the floor.

Claerwen answered that she did and rose, pulling on a loose shift against the night chill. "How long will it take for this dye to wash out?" she asked, studying a handful of her hair.

"You don't like it?" he returned as he poured the wine into a pair of cups on the table.

She grimaced mischievously and shook her head, answering, "I'm always surprised when I see it."

He grinned and teased, "I'll always know it's you, even if you were as bald as Padrig at home…"

With mock indignation, Claerwen turned, fists planted on her hips. She declared, "You wouldn't like it much if I looked like

Padrig, though, would you now?" She whirled around, deliberately showering him with her loose hair.

He winked, "Perhaps, when we go home, he can comment on both your hair and mine this time, eh?" Scratching plaintively at his head, he wryly mimicked their seneschal's favorite greeting each time Marcus returned from one of his journeys. Padrig would always lament his own sparse hair in a thinly disguised but good natured expression of jealousy over Marcus' thick, full head of hair that promised to remain so into old age as his father's and grandfather's had. Laughing heartily, they picked up their wine and drank to Padrig, his long duty at Dinas Beris, his crusty humor, his grandfatherly wisdom, and the hope that they would be home soon.

Content, Marcus took the empty cups and set them down. Drawing close to Claerwen again, he grinned when he felt her fingers begin to explore under his loincloth. He pulled the ties apart on her shift and slipped his hands inside. The shift fell off her shoulders, catching in the bend of her elbows, and he admired her breasts' fullness as he curved his hands around them, lifting, caressing, gently squeezing. He leaned as she tilted her face upward, and his lips opened, reaching for hers.

A loud thump smacked behind them, followed by heavy footsteps, grunts and a shout.

Claerwen's head jerked around as Marcus' arms swung up around her protectively. Expecting to see soldiers or even Myrddin, they were stunned to find Engres standing in the doorway, the oak door wide open, a guard catching up to him.

"What in the gods' names..." Marcus started, shoving Claerwen behind him as she yanked her shift up and tied it together. He sprinted forward and caught Engres by the throat, jamming him hard to the wall, nearly lifting him from the floor. The man hung limply, not attempting to fight back.

The guard, rubbing a bump on his chin from a sound hit, apologized, "Forgive me, my lord, he tricked us and got through the door. He said he has a message for you, but he wouldn't wait to be announced."

"Leave him to me. Go back to your post," Marcus commanded.

He waited for the guard to retreat, then demanded from Engres, "What do you want here?"

Engres whined slightly, roughly turning his head in Marcus' grip, enough to watch Claerwen search among the scattered clothing, pull out a dagger and press it into Marcus' free hand. His eyes lifted, noting the difference in Marcus' appearance since shedding the Bhruic disguise, then traveled to the rumpled bedding, back to Marcus, on to Claerwen. Engres' nostrils flared, smelling the strong, musky scent of their lovemaking. Disappointment filled his face.

Claerwen glared at Engres, outraged at the inference of his expression. "Why are you here, intruding on our privacy?" She turned and whipped up a bed robe, dragging it on, then placed another around Marcus' shoulders.

Receiving no answer, Marcus flicked the dagger blade, indicating the older man should sit on the floor. Pulling the robe tighter around himself, he straddled a bench in front of him and leaned down to glare with icy eyes, prodding, "Answer the lady. Why are you here?"

Engres looked again from one to the other, confusion on his face. Clearing his throat, he spoke, "I was sent here with a message from Pascentius. Until tonight, I was his hostage."

Marcus raised an eyebrow, wary of a trap, but held quiet, waiting for more.

Engres continued, encouraged. "I was told to take a message to Marcus ap Iorwerth. I was told that you are he. The message is that Pascentius holds two other hostages."

"I knew of one, a young girl," Marcus confirmed.

Engres' face crumpled in anxiety, nearly giving in to tears. "Aye, she is my youngest daughter."

Marcus' eyes softened, recognizing the pain was not false. "Who is the other?"

Engres sniffled and answered, "The young boy, the nephew of that miserable woman, Daracha."

"No..." Claerwen exhaled, sinking to her knees. "That must be the foreboding I have sensed. It's Sinnoch's distress. By the gods...when was he taken hostage?"

"He and I were both taken on the day Pascentius left the northern fort."

"They must have taken him from Girvyn," Claerwen muttered. She looked up at Marcus and saw his face reflect her exact thoughts, that when he had rescued her, Sinnoch had been in the camp as well.

"They probably killed Girvyn," Marcus regretted. "It never crossed my mind to look for other hostages when I came for you."

Stunned, Engres asked Claerwen, "You were in the camp?"

"Aye. Pascentius kept me chained inside a small tent. I was not allowed to see or speak to anyone but him. On the first night they camped outside Winchester, Marcus came for me."

Marcus said, "Pascentius is very careful to keep his hostages separated. I drugged the camp's water and wine, but I had so little time and I was so intent to free Claerwen, I didn't look for anyone else." He raked his fingers through his hair, then touched her cheek, "I'm sorry."

She leaned against his leg, her hand resting on his wrist, and said, "We didn't know."

Engres' eyes followed the tender gestures of affection between them. He frowned then asked, "Why is the boy of so much concern to you?"

Marcus exhaled his frustration, answering, "He is my son."

Engres digested this information and said quietly, "That would make sense then."

Marcus stood and paced, hefting the dagger. "And why does Pascentius hold your daughter?"

Instead of answering, Engres spoke directly to Claerwen, "There is something more you must know. I tried to tell you before, but you wouldn't listen, and he wouldn't let me near you." Engres jerked his head towards Marcus, bitterness in his eyes.

Marcus swung around and spoke harshly, "Know that I will always protect her first, from anything and anyone, whatever is necessary."

Engres recoiled at Marcus' sudden vehemence, then slowly calmed again. When he saw they waited for him to tell what he knew, he asked, "You still don't recognize me, do you, Claerwen, after all these years? I thought, perhaps, you nearly had. Or rather, you have chosen to deny it?"

"Recognize you? I've never seen you before we arrived at the fort."

Engres shook his head. "I've thought of a thousand ways to tell you, but they all sound wrong to me. So I'll just say it. My true name is not Engres. It is Rhodri ap Gwallter, of the lands of the Cynnwyd, in Gwynedd, along the banks of the Afon Dyfrdwy. My daughter, whom Pascentius holds, is my youngest child, called Drysi..."

Claerwen's chin shook as her mouth dropped open, and the color drained from her face as she realized he had just told her he was her dead father. Barely audible, she murmured, "It cannot be...it's impossible. No one survived the massacre of the Cynnwyd in Gwynedd, except me. No one was left alive when my mother and my cousin came home from visiting down the river and they found me. Everyone else was dead, every one."

"No, Claerwen. I survived the Irish raid. So did Drysi. Only much later did I learn that you had as well and had fled to Strathclyde."

Her eyes stared wide and unblinkingly at Engres, and she rose to move closer to Marcus, her hand reaching to curve around his arm for reassurance. Engres watched, frowning again at how she touched him.

"I saw them all die," Claerwen countered, her voice going hollow. "Drysi was only two summers old. But I *saw* her dead; I saw all of them dead. You couldn't possibly be my father. His body was burned in the fires." Her fingers tightened on Marcus' arm.

Engres sighed, his grey eyes dropping to the floor. Shaking his head slowly, he said, "I was badly injured, with swordcuts, stabbed several times with a dagger. But I crawled away and hid until the soldiers left. I intended to go back, but I couldn't do it, I was too badly hurt. Those soldiers raided the neighboring valley as well, and survivors from there found me, helped me. I learned later that someone from the south, from the kingdom of Dyfed, found a baby girl and took her into their home for a while. When

I recovered enough, I began to search for her. I learned she was Drysi, and I had hoped to find her soon, but she had been sent from Christian orphanage to Christian orphanage. One clue led me into the northern kingdoms."

Engres' eyes rose to meet Claerwen's, tears hanging in them. Drawing a breath to steady himself, he finished, "On my way north, I learned from a stranger, purely by accident, that you had gone to Strathclyde with your mother and cousin. By the time I arrived there, you were gone again and your mother had died. I went on, and the clan around the old fort took me in. I changed my name to protect myself, and them, in case trouble would follow me. It is true, Claerwen, I am your father. I am Rhodri ap Gwallter of Cynnwyd."

Unable to find her voice, Claerwen only stared at him, looking for clues to his honesty. She shook so hard that Marcus helped her sit on the bench. He approached Engres, his eyes still cold, and asked, "Is that why you had her sing that song, to remind her, hoping she would guess?"

Engres nodded, his eyes dropping again.

Marcus looked at Claerwen, remembering her remarks about Engres' eyes, how they had given her a startling reminder of her father. He took another step towards the man, asking, "We were told how you became the clan's leader. How did you become involved with Pascentius?"

"Last spring, before his men set up camp, a man came to me. He knew who I was, he knew of the massacre in Cynnwyd. He also told me Drysi had been kidnapped, that the story about a family taking her in was false. She had been moved around by Pascentius' people and kept in orphanages and convents, all these years. He had proof. That man was Banawr. Pascentius needed a place to use until he was ready to attack Winchester, and by using Drysi, he forced me to support him."

"Where did they hold her?"

"I don't know. It wasn't in the fort, and they kept me on a very short tether. She may not even know why she is being held." Engres, unnerved as if an unforgiving dragon stalked him, finally met Marcus' gaze. "When I saw Claerwen, I couldn't believe it at first, but I knew those beautiful eyes were hers. No one I have ever seen has eyes such as those. They were beautiful from the day she was born."

Marcus softened then, moved by the anguish in Engres' words. He sat on the bench again with Claerwen and asked, "If this is true, why doesn't she recognize you? She was old enough to remember."

"I have changed much in the dozen years since she saw me last. I have greyed, my face fallen with injury, age, a hard life. She remembers me not as the broken man I am now."

Claerwen leaned closer to Engres, studying his eyes. "I am not certain I believe it yet. It has been a dozen years, and as you say, you are very different than I remember — "

"Claerwen," Marcus interrupted. "You know there is one thing that will prove who he is. One thing only your father could know."

She looked up, saw his eyes move from her to Engres. Squinting, he said, "Tell us how the torque of Macsen Wledig was hidden."

Engres' eyes widened with shock. "How do you know of the torque?" he demanded. He rose from the floor almost involuntarily, lurching towards Marcus. "It must not fall into the wrong hands! It must not! It must be given to the rightful high king!"

Claerwen grabbed his arm before he could stumble and be accidentally caught on the dagger Marcus still held. "Listen to me!" She shook his arm, drawing his attention as Marcus stood and backed away. "Listen to us. The torque is safe. Uther has it. Just tell us how it was hidden."

She watched Engres' eyes as he sank onto the floor again. Slowly he calmed. He spoke low, "Just before the last of the Romans were to leave Britain with the emperor Constantine, the five sacred symbols of the high kingship known as Macsen's Treasure were divided. For safekeeping, each piece was entrusted to a fostermate of his eldest son Constans, of which I was one. The crown was sent with Ambrosius and Uther when they were exiled to Armorica. The torque was entrusted to my care. I encased it in a plain ceramic coating, making it look like an ugly armband. I had given it to your mother, and she kept it with her clothing. She never knew what it was. I went back after I was well enough to travel and searched where the house had been, but nothing was left, only ashes, dust. I prayed that your mother had taken it with her, but I presumed she never would have found much to take at all when she fled. Nor was she sentimental enough to keep such an ugly looking thing...Claerwen? What's wrong?"

She stepped back from him, her eyes still holding his gaze. Her lips moved as if to speak, but she remained silent for several moments. Then she whispered to Marcus, "It is true."

He said, "He speaks correctly of the torque."

Tears filled Claerwen's eyes. "Aye, but Marcus, it is more than that. I *can* see it in his eyes. He truly is my father." She knelt in front of Engres. Taking his hands, she lifted them and pressed them to her face.

Engres' chin shook as he tried to control his own joy, surging in the midst of so much trouble. He squeezed Claerwen's hands, then pulled them slowly to his lips. He kissed each finger, one by one. Tears filled his eyes as well, and he tenderly took her into his arms. "Ah, my daughter, my daughter," he whispered, gently rocking her. "When I learned you were alive, I had so hoped you would be luckier than the rest of us. But when I saw fate had made you a slave, I was greatly saddened. I wish so much I could have protected you. They told me he was a prince, but even as a slave, you should not have to submit to such...things." His eyes returned to the rumpled bedding.

Claerwen frowned, confused, and pulled away. "Submit?"

Marcus' mouth perked nearly into a smile. "He doesn't know, Claerwen. They didn't tell him."

"Know what?" Engres scowled up at him.

Claerwen looked to Marcus and realized what he meant. Ejecting a short laugh, she explained, "If you know that he is a spy and that acting as a displaced blacksmith and swordmaster were ruses, then you should realize that the slave I played was just as false." She paused and her eyes filled with pride. "Marcus ap Iorwerth is my husband. We have been married for over three years."

Engres nearly choked on his surprise. "Your husband..." He clamped his mouth shut and reviewed his memories of Bhruic, the rough and crude man capable of out-drinking Pascentius, out-fighting Banawr and out-maneuvering Daracha's machinations. He looked at the bruise on Claerwen's cheek and reached tentatively, brushing it with his fingertips, then glared once more at Marcus.

Claerwen broke into his thoughts, "My Marcus would never do such a thing. He is not that kind of man. What you saw in the north was an image he created. What you see now is my husband protecting me. He has always been kind and generous; I could ask for no better man."

She rose then and went to Marcus, slipping her hands around his arm. With mutual adoration clearly on their faces, Engres saw no ruse for them to hide behind now. Drained, he sighed, then with great effort to remain calm, he said, "There is something else you must know, Lord Marcus, of Macsen's Treasure. I do not know the whereabouts of the sword or the grail. But Pascentius has the spearhead."

Marcus' eyes grew pensive again. "I know, I have seen. Any one of those symbols in the hands of Pascentius and his people can, and will, become the catalyst to rupture Uther's fragile support. The many factions of these lands are too easily swayed by promises of glory backed by symbols, instead of the hard work that is freedom. The symbols are important and belong to the house of Pendragon, but I would rather see the commitment to retain independence become Uther's highest goal."

Engres peered into Marcus' face, glanced to Claerwen, then back. "By the light," the older man whispered, "Now I understand what you've been attempting to do." Then he suddenly smiled, "And it seems...that you are my son-in-law!"

# Chapter 25

## Winchester

When Claerwen woke the next morning, her eyes opened to see Marcus seated in a chair across the room, his legs sprawled out in front of him, his chin leaning on his hand. A single lamp, straining to dispel the surrounding shadows, starkly lit the left side of his face. His black eyes brooded into the darkness, then she realized he was already dressed.

She rose from the bed, pulled a thick coverlet around herself, and paced silently across. As she came into the light, his eyes lifted, and by the depth of the lines around them, she knew he was very tired. She sat on the floor by his feet, and when he leaned forward to stroke her hair, he asked how she had slept.

Instead of answering, she queried, "It's so early. What are you going to do? Or should I ask what have you done?"

Marcus smiled slightly and touched her cheek. "I need to scout Pascentius' camp again, they were moving westward yesterday. By the time I needed to return here, they hadn't settled. And I need to confirm how many hostages he has. Until I learn more, I cannot decide how to approach them."

"I will go with you."

In her eyes, he saw her sense of commitment had not diminished. His mouth nearly flickered into another smile. He said, "I would understand if you want to stay here with your father instead."

"No, I want to go with you. He will be fine enough here with Myrddin, and he needs time to recover from his captivity as well, just as I did. We spoke quite a long time last night, and I explained just enough of what we've been doing, what we need to do yet, and a bit about Sinnoch. I do want to know him better again, but it will have to wait. I can do more by coming with you. I want to free Sinnoch. And Drysi. And ourselves."

He grinned then, the creases around his eyes deepening even more. "So be it, then, get dressed. Wear something warm and simple, not catching to the eye. That dark green dress would do well, I think, and a dark cloak."

"You've been out somewhere, haven't you? You weren't there when I went to bed, after I finished speaking with my father and he went to sleep. And now I find you here this morning."

He responded, winking, "Aye, and you'll know why soon. I don't want to speak here." His eyes shifted towards Engres' room, then to Myrddin's chambers. He held up a small pouch of leather in which they normally carried food. He said, "Come, we are going to raid the great hall then leave Winchester for a bit."

Once dressed for cold weather, Claerwen accompanied Marcus to the great hall. There, they nibbled on cheese and fruit, filling the pouch with more food, but they tarried only briefly as Uther appeared early, obviously in a foul mood. Claerwen saw Marcus' eyes glint with mischief in the midst of his solemn expression, watching the king order his household staff with extra rudeness. She suspected a connection. "What have you done now?" she whispered.

The mischief spread over his face. "Come," he said and took her by the elbow, guiding her to the front doors. Serious again, he paused, catching Uther's eye with one last sweeping scan of the crowded space. They stared at one another a full minute, neither willing to be the first to break away. Claerwen sensed the tension rise, and she feared an explosive outburst from the king, but his seneschal interrupted, barging into his concentration. Marcus led her through the doors and out into the courtyard.

"Are you the cause of his mood?" she prodded, her curiosity becoming insatiable. But he only answered with another wink.

They crossed near the spot where Banawr had been killed. Marcus asked, "You saw it, didn't you?" In the narrow cracks between the cobbles, blood still showed, congealed by the cold.

She nodded, pointing up to the window from where she had watched. His face showed sadness, and she touched his arm, her eyes grimly acknowledging what he had done.

He nodded, accepting her understanding, and they moved out of the gates and into the town, circuiting the streets near the palace walls, observing, watching, speaking casually. As they circled around, returning towards the palace's entrance, Marcus finally broke his banter and indicated with his eyes a tall blond man wearing king's livery. He whispered, "That man has been following us."

"He is from Uther?"

"No. Pascentius. He is Saxon. Two more were inside the palace, but only this one came out. They are spies. I recognize them from the camp. Come, we will lose this hound."

He backed between two buildings, pulling her with him, and they started running, light and quick, threading from alley to alley. They emerged near a stable that stood at the town's northern gates.

"Wait here," Marcus instructed, showing Claerwen a place to hide behind a stone wall. He pulled up his cloak's hood, hiding his sword hilt, and walked across the street into the stables.

Several minutes later, she watched him ride out of the building on a big chestnut stallion, the hoofbeats clopping slowly down the street and out of earshot as he disappeared around a corner. She waited, wondering how long he would be and hoping no one would discover her in the meantime. Crouched down, she had a limited view of her surroundings, but from what she had seen of the town, she would be glad to leave it. It reminded her of Caernarfon, where she had spent four years, with its old, dilapidated Roman buildings and newer native buildings that had been no more than rough huts crammed together and made of cast-off materials from the older structures. She had disliked

Caernarfon as well, including all of its stenches, filth, crowding, and loneliness.

Shortly, a low, soughing whistle came from behind, and she turned. Marcus, still astride the horse, waited in the street at the stone wall's end. Gathering her skirts, she darted to him. He caught her arm, swinging her up behind him. They rode to the gates, casually saluted the keepers as if merely going out for a brief ride, passed through, and disappeared over the plains.

Marcus urged the stallion to the top of a wooded knoll and stopped within the trees' edge. "We will wait here," he said. From there, they could see Winchester's northern side. He tucked Claerwen's hands around in front of him, inside his cloak, to keep them warm.

"Are you going to tell me what you've been doing?" she teased, "Or do I need to guess?"

He laughed and said, "Sometime today, one of Pascentius' spies will return to his camp. All that walking around and nonsense was meant to draw them out for identification. There may be more than those three, but all I need now is one to show us where the camp was moved."

"How are you going isolate Pascentius — "

Marcus held up a hand for silence, distracted by movement at the gates. "Look, there's one leaving already, the one who followed us. I will tell you more later."

The man emerged from the town, and once he was well away, he turned off the road and proceeded west across the plains. Marcus and Claerwen followed, paralleling his path, just keeping him in sight.

By sunset, they had traveled more than twenty-five miles. Within another mile, a tree-covered hill rose sharply from the rolling land. Marcus reined in and pulled back, dropping behind a low ridge. He spoke at last, "Within those trees is an old hillfort. Most of its defenses are still intact, although it hasn't been truly in use for about three hundred and fifty years. It's an excellent place to hide a small war band so close to Winchester. We'll go around and approach from the north side."

By dark, they found a shallow ravine filled with trees and thick shrubbery, and made a simple camp alongside a spring. They shared a cold meal from the pouch of food.

"I'm sorry we can't make a fire, Claeri," Marcus apologized for the cold. He dug inside his tunic and pulled out a kerchief-wrapped object. In the thin starlight that sifted through the trees, he showed her a small flask of mead. He offered it to her.

"You've been naughty," she remarked, recognizing it came from the palace. She pulled out the stopper, took a sip and handed the flask back to him. He responded with a grunt, lying down. Claerwen smiled and said, "You're limping again." She began to gently massage his bad knee.

"Aye, since that last fight, it's been bothersome." He stretched out, enjoying the feel of her fingers loosening the joint as he drank a long swallow of the wine. "I'm going to bluff Pascentius into a trade he can't resist."

"A trade for Sinnoch and Drysi?"

"Aye. And who does he want to eliminate more than anyone?"

"Probably you."

"Hah! That is probably true, but Uther's head is his ultimate goal."

"And how can you possibly trade Uther?"

Marcus grinned broadly. "I spoke with Myrddin last night, when he returned from his walk. He said Uther is leaving Winchester in two days on a campaign to strengthen his alliances in the western kingdoms. Pascentius will know that from the spies he has in the court. At first light, I will leave here to return for Winchester and identify the spies to Myrddin. He will have them arrested. By the time Pascentius realizes they've been taken, Uther will have left and Pascentius will have no viable source of knowledge about the king's exact whereabouts. At the same time I will spread the rumor that the Iron Hawk is causing trouble again, and that he has kidnapped you."

"Me?"

"Aye, then I will return here, and the Iron Hawk will present his offer. The one part of this I don't like at all is that I want you to stay here and watch the camp. I could be gone nearly two days. I don't want to leave you alone, but I do trust your ability to remain hidden. If you are not comfortable with this, tell me now."

"'Tis fine enough. You know I am more at ease in the wild than in a town like Winchester."

"Aye, but this is very, very dangerous, and you nearly died in a fire because I left you alone for only a short time."

"Marcus, I am capable," she reassured him. "I will be fine enough. At least you won't need to rescue me from the Iron Hawk."

He frowned, then realized her jest. "Ah, that would be interesting, to rescue you from myself, eh?" Serious again, he chewed on his lower lip a moment, then went on, "If they move out, don't follow them. Pascentius will think I'll be coming with a force. There is too much risk in a confrontation such as that, so we send *Y Gwalch Haearn* instead. You will speak for him, giving instructions for Pascentius to come out to negotiate, alone or with one man if he prefers. The warrior will offer him Uther and demand the hostages as his price of exchange."

"Why would the Iron Hawk want Sinnoch and Drysi?"

"I made it very clear to Pascentius that the Iron Hawk is my enemy as well. It is logical for him to believe the warrior would want to extort anything he can from me for control, and even though Pascentius has good reason to be bitter against the Iron Hawk, making such a trade will be too convenient for him to ignore. The commander will not want to hold his hostages much longer, they are only in his way. So if the Iron Hawk willingly takes them in trade for the one captive Pascentius wants most, he should give them up easily, especially when the warrior can prove he already has Uther in his hands."

"In his hands? That's impossible."

Marcus sat up, his face moving into the starlight. His eyes glittered like a pair of polished black stones, full of excitement. "I have Uther's sword."

Claerwen stared at him, speechless at first, then whispered, "Are you mad? How...oh, I shouldn't ask. How in the gods' names did you get it?"

He grinned again, "When I chased Banawr out of Uther's chambers, he went down a hidden stairway. It's the only reason I got out of there alive. I went back last night and stole the sword. And a few other things..." He reached inside his tunic and showed her a small pouch. Opening it, he spilled out a handful of silver coins. "This is how I bought that horse so fast."

"You *are* mad. After proving your innocence, you steal his sword? And silver?"

"They won't know it was me. They'll think it was the Iron Hawk. When we go after Pascentius, I'll have both you and the sword to show the Iron Hawk is fully capable of taking Uther. That's something no one has ever offered him, and he won't have his spies to tell him any different. And for a further reward, he gets revenge on me by giving my family to the Iron Hawk, or so he will think."

Claerwen wiped her hand over her mouth, shaking her head at him. Then something struck her funny, unknowingly as to why, but she started laughing. She told him, "You are the most audacious man that ever lived. It would take a bold plan to out-smart both Uther and Pascentius. This might just work. But when you can't actually deliver Uther, what happens? He won't hand over Sinnoch and Drysi without more assurance than a sword."

He touched her cheek on seeing the sudden sadness in her face, then said, "Pascentius is terrified of the Iron Hawk. If he does not hand over the children on the faith of a sword, he knows very well what the Iron Hawk is capable of doing. We will succeed, Claeri."

---

Marcus returned by mid-afternoon two days later, bringing full traveling gear and a fortnight's worth of food. He found Claerwen still watching the camp, and he reported that he had successfully planted the news of her capture by the Iron Hawk as well as identifying Pascentius' spies, causing their immediate arrest. Pleased when she stated she was still willing to go forward with the plan, he changed into the Iron Hawk identity.

Before donning the ominous helmet, he took Claerwen's hands in his, searching her eyes. "When we are out there, I will need to be rough towards you, to treat you like a prisoner. I won't hurt you, but expect me to be very nasty. I need you to show a lot of fear. We must make it look real, or they will not believe us."

"I understand," she acknowledged.

He squeezed her fingers, then studied her for a moment. Making a wry face, he said, "Sorry for this." He unwound her braided hair from around her head, loosening it to fall free, and mussed it. Then he took away her cloak and reached to the neck of her gown, ripping it in three places, enough to make the bodice sag slightly. He did the same to her skirts, in one place tearing it from mid-thigh to the hem. Her eyes came up, full of questions.

"I'm not trying to make a show of you," he assured her, brushing his fingers across her cheek. "Most people only know of the Iron Hawk as a violent, implacable, contradictory avenger. You are the first hostage he's ever had, so we must give Pascentius something to consider."

"And to promote the legend?"

His eyes met hers and held several moments. Then he replied, "Aye, you know me well. The Iron Hawk is mostly rumor and legend I've shaped very carefully over the years. And I'd rather fight by rumor than reality as well. If you don't want to do this, tell me now, and I'll think of something else." He touched her cheek again and smiled, "It's only an impression I want to create."

Claerwen returned the smile, "It's fine enough, I was only a bit surprised. But then, I shouldn't be by now, no?"

To complete the preparations, Marcus tied Claerwen's wrists together with a thin leather rope, leaving a long, loose end. He hauled himself onto the horse, then reached down to grip a hand around her wrists, pulling her up behind him. He tucked the rope's end into his belt. Pulling on the black leather helmet, he asked, "Are you ready?" She answered that she was, and he pressed his heels into the horse's flanks, urging it forward.

Mist blew in eerie clumps over the lowlands surrounding the hillfort as the afternoon faded into dusk. Two concentric ramparts protected the fort, an earthwork counterscarp bank between them. A deep ditch preceded each rampart. The remnants of a timber gatehouse interrupted the lower east-facing side. Saxons patrolled at close intervals across the façade.

The Iron Hawk rode up the grassed-over path to the entrance.

As he emerged from the mist, the guards halted, stared, and began shouting alarms to each other. Within seconds, both ramparts filled with bowmen. Their leader, identifiable by his heavier armor, shouted at the approaching intruder.

The Iron Hawk continued forward, deliberately ignoring the commands. The words were in Saxon, but even if they had been in his native tongue, he still would have disregarded them. The leader finally changed languages when he realized his demands for the warrior to dismount and identify himself were useless. Though the Iron Hawk finally halted, just beyond the range of bowshot, he remained straight, unmoving and silent upon the horse.

Then Pascentius appeared on the gatehouse. The commander froze, his face showing fear even from a distance. Indecision seemed to grip him, as if assessing which was worse, to face the Iron Hawk or his men's ridicule for choosing to flee. Peering between the sporadic drifts of mist beyond the warrior, he saw no advancing force, only the mounted man in black. Warily, he shouted into the gusting wind, "What do you want, warrior?"

The Iron Hawk swung his right leg over the horse's withers and vaulted off, revealing Claerwen's presence. He moved aside several paces, the loose end of the tether wound around his left hand. For a few moments, he gazed up at Pascentius, then suddenly yanked on the rope, wrenching Claerwen's arms sideways. She came off, falling hard, sprawled awkwardly on the ground.

As Claerwen's head came up and her eyes focused on Pascentius, she saw the commander's mouth agape in astonishment. His eyes studied her, taking in her handbound wrists, her torn and dirty gown, her struggle for the breath that had been forced from her. His face clearly showed wonder at what else the warrior had done. Though she knew Pascentius had little sympathy for hostages other than how they could be useful, she could see he was shaken by the Iron Hawk's brutality. She guessed at his thoughts, that he was weighing his hatred of both Marcus and the Iron Hawk, trying to decide which was most worthy of it, and how he might play them against each other.

Coming up behind Claerwen, the Iron Hawk dropped the tether and caught a handful of her hair. Pulling the huge sword with his free hand, he brought the flat of the blade down to rest on her shoulder, silently communicating that she should begin to speak.

"Lord Pascentius," she summoned, weakly at first. The blade pressed harder, pushing her shoulder downward, and she called louder, fear marking her words. "The Iron Hawk has a proposal for you. You may come here, accompanied by one man, to negotiate."

"Why would he want to negotiate?" Pascentius snapped in return. "What could he possibly have to offer me?"

"He has another hostage you will consider to trade for those you now hold."

"And who is that?"

"Uther Pendragon."

A stifling silence fell. Pascentius fidgeted, showing commingled mistrust and curiosity. "You have proof?" he finally asked.

"You may examine it."

Pascentius snapped his fingers at one of the bowmen, and the man followed him. They disappeared, going down inside the gatehouse. Moments later, the gates opened and the men emerged, moving cautiously along the path through the bank and ditches. Nearing the Iron Hawk, they slowed, peering intently at the eye slits of the masked helmet, but only saw dark against dark. The blade lifted slightly then pressed down again.

"He wants you to stop there," Claerwen relayed.

From underneath his cloak, the warrior produced another sword, smaller and bejeweled, in an ornately decorated scabbard. He held it flat and crosswise in front of Claerwen, indicating that he was going to lay it across her palms. She spread her hands awkwardly, straining to turn her wrists against the bonds, and took the weapon. Then he pulled her up by the hair until she stood, leaning back against him, and he swept his sword around to cross at her belly. She froze as she felt it press in, the steel cold through her gown.

Claerwen started shaking, genuinely afraid of the Iron Hawk at that moment, such as she had not felt since before learning his true identity. If she moved, even a little, the blade would cut her. Her mouth dried and she spoke with difficulty to Pascentius, "Take it. It is Uther Pendragon's sword. The Iron Hawk holds him captive. He will trade you the high king for the hostages you hold."

"Why would the Iron Hawk want Marcus ap Iorwerth's wife, and those two children? That makes no sense."

"He — "

She was not given the chance to finish. The Iron Hawk disengaged his hand from her hair and hooked his arm around her throat, jerking her back with him as he began to retreat. The king's sword dropped onto the ground. Moving upward, the warrior's blade settled across the line of her shoulders.

Claerwen tried to cry out, but the warrior's arm tightened, choking off her voice. She grabbed at his arm with her bound hands, trying to ease his grip, but he was too strong. When they were beyond bowshot of the place Uther's sword lay, the Iron Hawk halted, then released her, pushing her onto her knees again. She gasped for air, falling forward, and the sword came down once more, this time against the side of her neck. She winced as the razor edge scratched.

Pascentius warily picked up Uther's sword and examined it, then watched Claerwen cower on the ground at the Iron Hawk's feet. A line of blood trickled along her neck and he nearly smiled, rubbing his arm where she had bitten him. He looked up at the masked warrior, then said, "I agree to your proposal. When and where do you want to make the exchange?"

The Iron Hawk nudged Claerwen with his boot, and she looked up through tears at Pascentius. He and the Saxon bowman appeared almost as silhouettes as torches were lit across the ramparts behind them, dispelling the gathering darkness. She tried to calm her breathing, drawing great gulps of air, but before she found her voice, the bowman erupted, shouting animatedly in his own tongue, gesturing frantically in an arc from left to right at the plain behind Claerwen.

Pascentius moved a pace forward, glaring hard. Rumbling

vibrated the ground, gradually growing louder.

"You've brought a war band!" Pascentius shouted in outrage at the Iron Hawk when he realized the sound belonged to dozens of running feet. "I should have known this was no more than a bluff!" He flung Uther's sword towards the hillfort as if it was diseased with the pox and yanked his own from its scabbard.

The Iron Hawk whipped around, scanning the plain. Cries echoed from the south, rising from a long line of advancing warriors, far larger than Pascentius' force. He swore, feeling blood pound in his temples, and he wrenched off his cloak, throwing it at Claerwen. There was no time to wonder whose war band had ruined his plan.

Instantly turning back, he blocked the first blow of Pascentius' sword. Claerwen rolled away from them, scrambling towards the horse.

As he fought, Pascentius shouted orders at his bowman to abandon the hillfort and scatter into the surrounding plains to the north, avoiding entrapment within the stronghold by the larger force. The Saxon relayed the orders, screaming up at the ramparts, then joined Pascentius in fighting the Iron Hawk. The war band closed in, covering the ground at an alarming rate.

Claerwen reached the horse, grabbing the reins before the animal could bolt, the shouting and painful ringing of weapons distressing it. She located a dagger Marcus had hidden beneath the saddle and cut her bonds, then mounted. Gaining control, she turned the horse towards the fighting men. By now, the Saxon bowman lay still on the ground, a profusely bleeding gash across his belly. The Iron Hawk furiously pounded at Pascentius, driving him back towards the hillfort's gates. Then she saw that if the fight could not be finished within only another minute, the advancing force would overrun them all.

A shrieking war cry rose from the band's leader and Claerwen's head jerked around. Scanning across the line of racing warriors, she recognized Octa the Saxon. Her stomach plunged as she realized that Pascentius had told Marcus the truth — Octa had planned to invade with an army of Picts. Watching the Saxon leader's face, lit intermittently by guttering torches, Claerwen desperately rammed her heels into the horse's sides. The animal lurched, almost rearing.

"*Gwalch Haearn!*" she screamed for the Iron Hawk, her voice rising above the noise of the soldiers. She turned the horse straight at Pascentius and kicked the animal's flanks again. It shot forward, snorting discontent. "*Gwalch Haearn!*" she screamed once more, forcing the horse to follow her direction, but in the last second, the commander wrenched himself aside, avoiding the intended collision. Abandoning the fight, he disappeared into the trees surrounding the fort.

An instant later, the Iron Hawk sheathed his sword and sprinted from the interrupted fight. He shouted to Claerwen to keep moving as he raced alongside her, grasping at the saddle for a good grip. Leaping, he hooked an arm around her hips and clung, hanging awkwardly for a few seconds, then heaved himself on behind her. They gained speed, plunging westward down to the plains. The sound of running feet passed behind them, and as the sun neared its setting, the mist thickened, casting an obscuring glare between the war band and all those who fled.

# Chapter 26

**On the plains east of Winchester**

"There's a building yonder, it looks abandoned," Claerwen said.

A structure loomed out of the dusk. She had ridden hard for more than two miles, the Iron Hawk holding on tightly behind her. Here the mist had thinned again, allowing the last of the sunset through, and she saw the building was a dilapidated Roman-style villa, much smaller than the one converted into a palace in Winchester. Only the bare structure remained, its plaster chipped, beams fallen, parts of the roof crumbled. She coaxed the horse towards a tiny, walled courtyard.

"Pull up into it," the Iron Hawk instructed.

Reining in, Claerwen realized his voice had sounded more tired than normal, more clipped and strained. She felt his hands release from around her, and he slipped leftward, dropping away. Twisting around, she saw him fall, sprawling on the ground. He groaned, trying to push himself up. Instantly she understood it had been pain more than fatigue in his voice.

Calling him, Claerwen flung herself off the horse, landing next to him. As she helped him to sit upright, her hand passed over his right leg, her fingers coming away wet. But it was not mud or snow smeared there, it was blood, and her eyes lifted, filled with questions and fear.

"It's only a graze," he countered.

"No, it isn't. Don't move."

Claerwen ran to the villa's front door. It was jammed, but she kicked until it gave. The door slammed open, pushing up a rush of dust, and she coughed, waving at the mustiness with her hands. Quickly examining the room, she found it empty but dry.

By the time she turned around, Marcus was on his feet and leaning in the doorway, the Iron Hawk's helmet off and in his hand. Pain crumpled his face. He dropped the helmet and stumbled halfway across, reaching her, locking his arms around her for support.

"I didn't see it happen," she said, unbuckling the baldric and taking it with his sword from him. She dropped them, then helped him to a place where light still shone through a shutterless window. He sank onto his knees, then sat back against the wall.

"Just try to stop the bleeding for now," he said through clenched teeth as she started to loosen the ties of his tunic and hauberk. He pulled off his gauntlets. "I need to catch my breath."

Leaning over him, Claerwen found a slit cut into the side of his tunic, just above the belt, and a fall of blood ran all the way down his leg. She peered through the opening in the leather and gingerly pried apart the chain underneath. "You are right, it is a graze, messy, not deep, thank the gods."

"Those are more annoying than deeper cuts," he muttered.

"The chain link kept it from being worse..." Claerwen began, then she suddenly straightened and stared into Marcus' eyes, listening intently. Silence smothered the villa, but she felt a presence. The expression on her face told Marcus what she sensed and he reached a hand towards his sword. Then she turned her head sharply to the front door. Marcus tensed, ready to defend her, but she pressed a hand to his shoulder to stay.

Though the door had been left ajar, the opening was deeply shadowed, the courtyard wall blocking the last of the light. At first, the doorway looked empty. Then a shape moved, slowly at first, molding into a figure cloaked in black.

"Myrddin Emrys..." Claerwen exhaled softly, relief in her

voice. "How long have you been there?"

He stepped forward one pace, his dark brown eyes moving from her to Marcus, showing a moment of confusion. Moving a little farther, he stopped again at the sight of new blood shining on Marcus' clothing.

Without waiting to be asked, he flung aside his cloak and set about helping Claerwen examine the wound. Together, they quickly removed the leather tunic and hauberk, and pushed aside the thick woolen shirt Marcus wore underneath the chain. Myrddin directed Claerwen to bring a handful of mud. Packing it against the cut, it immediately halted the bleeding. When he asked for bandages, Claerwen looked at her torn gown, gave it a wry grimace, took hold of one of the undershifts' skirts and ripped away a broad portion. Tearing it into strips, she laid several folded pieces over the wound and bound it well in place. Done, Myrddin instructed them to change the bandages in the morning and to clean the wound well, citing that the mud should prevent the flesh from taking fever. He produced a tiny crock of salve from his traveling gear along with a wineskin.

"Drink some," Myrddin ordered, handing the skin to Marcus, then showed Claerwen the salve. "This will help to heal him faster. Apply it after you clean the wound in the morning, and bind him tightly again. He should be fine enough in a few days."

Claerwen thanked him, taking the crock, then watched his eyes slowly drift beyond her.

"I thought I was following the Iron Hawk..." Myrddin began, then paused. Bewildered, he stared at Marcus. "You got her back from him...already...but...I saw *him* on the horse behind you, Claerwen. I was sure." His eyes moved to her, then again to Marcus. "You couldn't have fought him off that quickly. Unless you ambushed him...but, you've been wounded...you must have fought..."

Claerwen hesitated, and her mouth opened and shut without speaking. Then she looked to Marcus, her expression asking him what to say. She saw his eyes follow the path of Myrddin's, from Claerwen to the huge sword, to the black tunic, back to the sword, then the helmet. Turning to Myrddin, she watched as he knelt and stared at the iron pommel. His head turned abruptly as he suddenly realized it was the same gear he had seen the Iron Hawk wear on the night Banawr died.

Myrddin locked eyes with Marcus. After several moments of silence, Marcus said very quietly, "Aye, 'tis true."

"You?" Myrddin ejected. He turned to Claerwen, shock plain in his face. "Long ago you said you didn't know, that the gods had not revealed his identity to you as they had not to me. How could you not know?"

"It is true, she did not," Marcus answered for her and took a long swallow of mead from the wineskin. "At least not for many years. She is the only one who knows...until now."

Claerwen said, "There were hints, but he kept his secret so well, I never guessed. And I had hated and feared the warrior for so long, I never gave credence to the thought that he and my Marcus could be the same man. In truth, even now, we only speak of him as if he were a separate man. You were right, Myrddin, when you once told me that perhaps the Iron Hawk's reasons were not as they seemed."

Marcus' eyes grew cold and brooding. "You will keep our secret," he demanded more than asked.

Myrddin stared back, equally stern, his customary aloofness rising as the power of the fire stirred, giving his eyes an amberish look. "No one will ever know. I swear by all the gods my people swear by."

Claerwen exhaled in relief. From her reaction, Marcus understood Myrddin would keep his word.

"Then that was merely a ploy when you came to me," Myrddin said, speculating. "You wanted me to spread a rumor." His eyes widened a bit. "*You* stole Uther's sword. Has your plan succeeded?"

"We were so close to freeing the hostages, but that war band destroyed everything. Now our options are severely limited. If you tell me those men were Uther's — "

"No," Claerwen cut in. "They were from Octa the Saxon. I saw him. And I think he did have mostly Picts with him."

Marcus muttered a bitter curse. "The one time Pascentius

actually told the truth...this interference has cost me three days' time and most of my leverage."

"A strange time to begin a battle...just before sunset," Myrddin noted. "I circled around to the north side of the hillfort to avoid getting caught between them. Pascentius' Saxons scattered in that direction. Oddly, Octa never went after them. He retreated to the south."

Marcus asked, "What of the hostages?"

"They went with the woman, riding north. Pascentius and a handful of men were close behind. All the others were left to fend for themselves on foot."

"Or to join Octa. I suspect that among those Saxons whom Pascentius abandoned tonight, there were quite a few loyal to Octa. That would explain the odd timing of the attack."

Claerwen added, "With the mist rising, Pascentius will not be able to go far in the dark, especially with Daracha and two children. We should be able to pick up their trails in the morning."

Squinting in pain, Marcus leaned forward and shook his head, countering, "We have two choices. Either track them as you say, or go back to the hillfort and look for clues of their destination. The second is the wiser move."

"And if there are no clues?" Claerwen asked.

"Then we waste some time. But we could waste far more time by losing their trail if it snows again." He looked across to Myrddin and queried, "Were you following us?"

"Not originally. I am on my way to join Uther; he should be close in to Mynyw, in the kingdom of Dyfed by now. When I received word of Octa's landing, I sent messengers ahead to both the king and to his military commander, Lord Gorlois of Tintagel, in Cornwall. Then it occurred to me that you might also need to be warned, that Octa may be actively looking for you as much as Pascentius, that if he had somehow heard of your pledge, he would expect you to be in the same area. Certainly he would take advantage of that in looking to fulfill his revenge after you sabotaged his camp. Uther will likely send a force after Octa."

Marcus considered Myrddin's warning, his head leaning back on the wall, his fists clenching and unclenching, betraying his anger. He speculated, "If Octa and Uther keep each other busy long enough, I can reach the hostages in time, then resolve the problem of Pascentius. But if Octa kills Pascentius, the pledge will be forfeited. My life, Claerwen's and those of my clan's, as well our home's fate, will be left to Uther's whim. If he continues his grudge, I'm a dead man."

"He needs your alliance. That would be stupid of him."

"Aye, and his is the same kind of distorted reasoning the people of our tribes have used against each other for centuries. It's why we cannot unite and drive out the Saxons. It's why we decimate our clans to the point we can barely function as a society in the face of the outsiders. Uther is one of us; he has the same goals, but he has the same bloody pride we all have. That pride gives us great strength, but it is also our greatest flaw. I believe peace will be a long time in coming."

For a while, they were silent, each pondering Marcus' words. The night's darkness drew in like an omen of the daunting future. They each knew that in any aspect, they faced continued civil violence, possibly all-out war, both amongst their own people and from outsiders. They also knew that they must keep on the quest, that discouragement was a thing too easy to grasp, that to begin questioning the purpose would bring on that discouragement more quickly and lethally than a raging plague. Suddenly very tired and needing to dispel the gloom, Claerwen rose and lit a lantern from their gear. It glowed, spreading the room with a shimmering golden softness.

"Will you stay with us tonight, Myrddin?" she asked quietly.

He shook his head, almost absently, still brooding. "I will go on. Gorlois is to meet me midway between here and Mynyw."

Claerwen came forward as he stood. "Myrddin," she called softly, touching his sleeve. "I am sorry your father is dead. I wish there had been more we could have done to prevent it."

Myrddin stared at the floor, sighing, "It would have happened anyway. I suppose I defied the gods when I asked you to try to stop his death."

Stunning silence followed Myrddin's statement. Marcus glowered heavily, then his deep voice suddenly ejected, "You mean to say that Ambrosius was doomed? In spite of all we have done? In spite of the danger I put Claerwen into?" He got to his feet and lurched forward, the rage welling in him again. "Before we ever left Dinas Beris? You mean to say — "

Claerwen grabbed the fist he had formed with both her hands. He stopped, clamping his jaw shut. She gazed calmly into his face, drawing him away from Myrddin, until she was certain he concentrated on her. She explained, "There was a purpose for what we have done, even in losing Ambrosius."

Tilting his head slightly with his brows knotted together, he sensed that she had spoken out of the deeper truth the fire gave her, that her words belonged to the same realm as the prophecy of the stronger king yet to come. He whispered, "You speak of the one you once called Arthur?"

Claerwen hushed him, placing her fingers against his lips, then nodded slightly.

His eyes flashed exasperation, thinking that Arthur was only a name, not flesh and blood that could wield a sword and speak words to inspire confused, hungry, angry people into uniting. But as he watched her eyes, he recalled his own thoughts from only a few minutes before. He glanced across to Myrddin and sensed a calm identical to Claerwen's. That calm was a portent as well, he realized, the portent of unspoken words he had sensed but not grasped since the beginning of the quest. His anger partially retreated.

Myrddin spoke softly, "I had no right to ask of you what I have. And yet I knew that I must. I need not mention that the path our lives take is sometimes a very perilous journey. My father's death does not mean failure; it was but another leg along that journey. I cannot blame you as Uther has; he does not understand now, but he will, one day in the distant future."

Marcus nodded slowly in acknowledgement.

Myrddin gazed a moment longer at Claerwen, deep in secretive thought, then briefly smiled. He turned to Marcus and asked, "One question before I leave, about Banawr. Why the severed head?"

Marcus' brow lowered over his deep-set eyes, and he folded

his arms. "For Uther's poor judgement. A warning."

Marcus' implacability did not surprise Myrddin, and he understood that although the warning came through the Iron Hawk and could be construed as treasonous, it was meant to be a lesson. He nodded, mostly to himself, then said quietly, "I will leave you now. May the gods bring you luck; we will meet again, I am sure." He leaned to lightly kiss Claerwen's cheek with brotherly affection, then saluted Marcus. He turned, disappearing into the shadows as enigmatically as he had appeared.

Alone again, Marcus reached for Claerwen's hand, his mouth opening to speak, but he hesitated, frowning, and his hand slid to the side of her throat, pushing aside her hair. A dark smear showed. His eyes widened, and he lamented, "I hurt you, and you didn't say anything. Of course, you couldn't." His fingers lightly traced the scratch on her neck, then he took a leftover scrap of cloth, soaked it from the wineskin and cleaned the wound. His eyes dropped, searching to see if she was hurt elsewhere, then rose again, questioning.

"No, you didn't hurt me otherwise. Just scared me into a dull-witted fool."

"Forgive me, Claerwen."

"'Tis of no matter," she smiled, then asked, "You're in pain?"

"No," he replied too adamantly.

She knew he was hurting, from both the wound and his frustration. He began to pace, his brooding eyes concentrating already on the morrow, planning, deciding, willing himself to not feel the needling pain. More than anything else, she also knew he was thinking of his son, and her sister, and with as much determination as he had ever driven himself, he would find a way to free them.

Quietly, Claerwen went about cleaning the Iron Hawk's gear, packing it away and selecting other clothes for him to wear. Then she prepared a simple, cold supper. Marcus spoke little more that night, preferring to balance his anger and resoluteness in silence.

# Chapter 27

### Into the Afternoon Country

"Are we going to look in the latrine pit again, like at Octa's farmstead?" Claerwen asked.

Kneeling among the trees behind the hillfort, Marcus tossed her a crooked grimace. He answered, "If we need to, we will. Rather, we need to find their command post. Come."

Leading the horse, they moved slowly along the tree-lined track leading to the well-hidden rear entrance. At dawn, there was barely enough light to see. Though certain no one would be left inside, Marcus remained cautious, citing how too much certainty usually led to mistakes. Crossing through the crumbling wall, they paused to survey the interior.

Having been abandoned for many years, everything from weeds, shrubbery and saplings to full-grown trees profusely overgrew the entire enclosure. Several patches had been trampled or hacked down to make enough room for a small occupying force. The camp's filthy remains filled these spaces.

"How can you tell where the command post was?" Claerwen asked.

"They weren't here long enough to be formal. It could have been anywhere Pascentius sat down for a few moments or where he slept for the night. It's a mess, but I expected that. Anything we might have considered useful may have been destroyed last night."

They tethered the horse and circuited the trampled areas, studying the debris. Nothing worthwhile captured their attention. Disappointed, Marcus walked across to the break in the upper rampart above the old gatehouse. He leaned on the pile of stone that had once supported one side of the upper gates.

"We will have to attempt to track them, won't we?" Claerwen asked as she dragged her skirts off a broken and dried out thistle.

"Aye, and it won't be easy now. They have too much of a head start."

"At least Myrddin saw they were going north," Claerwen noted, leaning on the opposite side of the entrance. She pulled up the hem of her gown and picked cockleburs from it.

"I made a lot of trouble for you, didn't I?" Marcus asked, watching her try to control her ripped skirts under her cloak.

"'Tis a bit inconvenient. And rather daring at times," she teased, kicking a leg through the longest tear.

He smiled briefly, glad her humor was intact, but his grim expression quickly returned. Resuming his previous thoughts, he began, "Even though Myrddin saw them heading north, they could be going..."

When he didn't finish his thought, Claerwen looked up and saw his brows jagged down. Coming at her, he took her by the arms and moved her slightly aside. He crouched, studying the stone wall she had been leaning upon.

"Look at this," he said, poking a finger at the rock. Its surface showed a network of scratches. He traced one long convoluted outline, then several straight lines on each side, all of which converged together at one point on the outline.

"It's a map?"

"Aye, I think so."

"Of where? It looks like the western coast, in a way. It could be anywhere."

Marcus studied a few moments longer, then voiced his observations, "Assuming this is the western coast, this line could mean Uther's route. And this one could be Pascentius, following him."

"Who is this one, then?" Claerwen asked, tracing a third line, sweeping in from the seaside of the outline.

"Another landing by water?"

"Saxons?"

Marcus tilted his head and brushed at them with his fingertips. "No...this line moves in a southeasterly direction, coming from *Iwerddon*. If Pascentius is allied with an Irish leader, that would explain why he had Irish in the northern camp. If this is so, I would wager it is the last force willing to cooperate with him after all his other failures. Of course, even if he is able to join with them and defeat Uther, he will eventually need to face Octa and defeat the Saxons and Picts to hold the kingship."

"But where is the landing? Is this Cornwall? Or somewhere on Gwynedd's coast? It could even be the highland coast. It's so muddled."

"Aye, they were poor mapmakers here. It could also be Armorica, on the Gaulish coast, though I would doubt it." Marcus puzzled a bit longer, then finally stood, flexing his aching left knee. He paced slowly, thinking aloud, "Lord Gorlois is Uther's highest general. He rules Cornwall's military, tighter than its king, and has made it relatively safe from western invasions. Cunedda of Gwynedd has done even more for our lands. His sons rule the small kingdoms down the coast from Gwynedd and they are mostly solid leaders, closely allied with their father. Ceredig has been successful in Strathclyde as well. That leaves Dyfed. There has been a rapid succession of kings over the past few decades, making it very unstable. I've never been able to keep a good alliance there myself, because of it. And there are still a few Irish settlements there."

"You think this is the coast of Dyfed?"

"Aye. And knowing the lie of the ground, I'd give you odds that they will land at Mynyw."

"And Myrddin said Uther will soon be there."

"He is walking into a trap." He started across the compound, striding towards the horse.

"But, Marcus," Claerwen called after him, running to catch up.

"What of Sinnoch and Drysi?"

He halted and turned, took her hands, searched her eyes. "I had said we should go after them first, but this changes everything. Uther will know of Octa's landing from Myrddin's couriers, and he may turn back himself to fight the Saxons and Picts. But even if he doesn't, neither he nor Myrddin will know of this landing, unless Myrddin has a vision. We cannot depend on that. They'll be surrounded." He waited for her reaction, watched the thoughts turning behind her green-blue eyes.

She asked, "Will Daracha take the children to Mynyw as well?"

"In truth, it is very likely, because Daracha will seek an alliance with the survivor, even if it's Uther. She is as hungry for power as she is for vengeance."

Claerwen nodded agreement, adding, "It is an easy way to draw us into a trap as well."

Marcus concurred, saying, "Aye, and time is short."

They ran to the stallion. Marcus awkwardly hauled himself onto the animal, grabbing for the wound as he settled in the saddle, but again denied it gave him pain. He held his left foot stiffly at angle for Claerwen to use as a step, and she climbed up, wedging in behind him in front of their packed gear. Before she could arrange her skirts, he kicked the horse into motion.

---

Unencumbered by heavy gear, baggage, and an entourage such as the high king would possess, Marcus and Claerwen raced northwestward. They crossed the Afon Hafren with the ferryman and fled on into the west, cutting through mountainous country along river valleys, then straight over rolling hills as directly as the terrain allowed. Two days later, they caught up with Uther's war band, still one more day's hard ride to Mynyw.

On seeing the king's camp, Marcus cursed to himself. Only a portion of the war band was still with the king. He drove the horse on unsparingly and followed the land as it flowed down to the camp. The royal guardsmen were not far from the eastward edge, and Marcus hailed them as he approached. Alerted, they called for additional soldiers, some of them mounted, and formed a thick ring of protection along the perimeter. Marcus hailed again, still on a dead run towards them.

"Halt! Or be challenged!" one of the guards ordered in a loud, booming voice as they drew swords and crossed spears.

Marcus let his horse run close in, leaving just enough distance to pull up tightly before them. Hauling on the reins, his animal nearly skidded, then came around abruptly.

"Identify yourself!" a second man ordered.

Marcus gave his name and rank, then demanded to speak with the high king.

The guards eyed his road-weary and travel-stained clothing, the hand-and-a-half sword resting in its scabbard across his back. Moving around, they were surprised to find a woman clinging tightly on behind him.

"Prove who you say you are."

Marcus held the heaving horse in place with his knees and countered, "You're going to have to take my word for it, I am Marcus ap Iorwerth. We must speak with the king."

A mounted guard, apparently of a superior rank, moved forward, thrusting his horse between the men. "'Tis true, he is the Prince of Dinas Beris," he stated, his eyes leveling with Marcus'. "And that is his wife. I saw them in Winchester when he demanded her release from the king. What do you want here?"

"I need to speak with King Uther, immediately," Marcus answered, risking bluntness.

"What is your business with him?"

"Where is he?" Marcus insisted, ignoring the question. His eyes glared at each man coldly, one by one.

The guards shifted uncomfortably. Marcus' restive animal sparked nervousness in their mounts, and the ranking officer backed his horse a pair of steps, anticipating a fight to break out. He growled, "You will not be considered for an audience with the high king unless you state your business."

Marcus' eyes squinted into narrow slits, showing only heavily shadowed black. "There will be an invasion at Mynyw. Pascentius is there, waiting for Irish boats."

"Irish! And how do we know this is true?"

"There's no time for arguing, man! Where is Uther? There's an Irish landing about to take place at the end of that piece of land — if it hasn't already — and you don't have half of your force here because they're off fighting Octa somewhere in the south. Take me to the king now or risk his wrath — if you survive."

The men stared, stunned by his declaration. Moments later, a commotion stirred out of the tents behind the line of guards, and several men emerged. Uther extracted himself from them and pushed through, demanding to know what caused the shouting. He stopped mid-query when he recognized Marcus.

"What is he doing here?" the king roared at his guards.

Marcus swung his leg over the horse's withers and dropped to the ground. He pressed his way between the guards and repeated his warning.

The two men studied each other, both exhibiting a calm façade, a rippling urgency just beneath. Then Uther demanded, "You have proof of this?"

Before Marcus could answer, a shout cracked across the camp. Myrddin appeared, striding swiftly, weaving through the gathered men. A young scout followed him, jogging to keep up with the prince's long-legged steps. Myrddin halted at the king's side. He announced that the scout had just arrived from the coast and had seen the landing in progress.

Marcus exhaled, relieved.

Uther whirled around, shouting orders. Within seconds, the camp began to break, the warriors heading out ahead of the supporters. The king swung back around to Marcus. For a moment, his blue eyes drilled into Marcus', then Claerwen's. He said nothing, then called for his war horse and walked away.

Marcus stalked back to his animal and mounted. As Claerwen's arms went around him again, he heard her whisper in his ear, "Was that his way of saying 'thank you'?"

He twisted his head back and answered softly, "Most likely. And that was bloody luck Myrddin's scout came when he did. There's no chance I could have proven that landing by words alone. There's too much mist to see any boats from here, thirty miles inland, even from the highest hill."

Myrddin approached them. He asked, tilting his head towards the departing war band, "Are you going with them? Or going on alone?"

"Alone," Marcus answered tersely. Moments later, he and Claerwen raced away from the camp.

Marcus avoided the road, knowing the area well enough to keep out of Uther's way and circumvent Pascentius' scouts. He and Claerwen pressed on into the night, slowing only for safety and brief periods of rest. They arrived above the coastal settlement an hour before dawn.

On a hilltop overlooking the land's end, they came to a halt and crawled in under heavy brush that crowned the ridge. Below, one large hut stood in a hollow, a sparse settlement of smaller huts scattered around it. Beyond, off the coast, half-hidden in moonlit mist, a fleet of Irish boats floated, landing curraghs already beached on the shore. Camped in a field east of the village, the soldiers prepared for battle.

Marcus pointed at the large hut and stated it was currently used as a Christian church, built on the site of an ancient pagan grove burnt down many years earlier. All the huts appeared abandoned, their inhabitants scattered into the hills for safety.

"There's Pascentius, see him, conferring with another man?" He jabbed a finger at a central point in the war band, marked by a group of standards. Then he ejected, "By the gods. That standard from the Irish is Gilloman's."

"That is bad?"

"He is a king. Of course, there can be about six hundred kings of varying degrees in *Iwerddon* over a ten-year period, so kingship there is cheap. But Gilloman is a strong fighter and a bloody good military leader."

"Tell me the truth, Marcus. Will Uther be able to defeat them?"

He squinted into the distance, studying the Irish forces. "They are fairly matched in numbers. The test will be in tactics. What Pascentius lacks, Gilloman will make up. Uther is a good general. But Gorlois is not here; he must have been sent to fight Octa. Who could save this, oddly enough, is Myrddin. He may be no warrior, but he is wily, and I have heard he has given excellent advice on other occasions."

"So it is said," spoke a voice behind them.

Marcus whipped around, one hand shoving Claerwen aside, the other hand already pulling a dagger. Then he halted, cursing. For a moment he let his head roll back with relief, then he sheathed the knife.

Claerwen came up sputtering, "Myrddin Emrys! You must stop doing that!"

"It's his nature, Claeri," Marcus muttered, then asked Myrddin, "Are you here to watch us for Uther, or watch Uther for us?"

"Both, I suppose," Myrddin replied. "I will not interfere with what you need to do. But Uther is just beyond those hills, and at sunrise, the battle will begin."

Marcus' eyes narrowed, and he grunted acknowledgment. He said, "I'm going to search those huts. My gut says Daracha is there with those children."

"Then you'd best hurry. The moon is setting, and it will be first light soon," Myrddin responded.

Marcus felt the hair on his neck rise. He turned to Claerwen. "I want you to stay here with Myrddin. Whatever happens, stay with Myrddin."

"I want to go with you — "

"No, Claeri. Not this time. If they're in those buildings, it's got to be the church. It's difficult to approach unseen, which makes it the logical choice. And the most likely trap as well. I will have to do this by force, there is no time left for stealth." He pulled his sword.

"Marcus, please — "

"Stay here," he whispered one last time, his patience eroding as he listened to the din rise from the war bands' preparations. His brows knotted, hanging low over the ache in his eyes, and he moved forward to kiss her, hard and fast, leaving her lips to tingle for minutes after. Then he was up and running, moving down the hill fast, threading his way through the bracken and scrub oak, disappearing from sight at the bottom of the slope.

Claerwen gazed into the distance, her eyes locked on the spot she had last seen Marcus. She waited, hoping to see him emerge from the brush, but the minutes passed and nothing happened. In the adjacent field, both armies were forming lines, screaming insults at each other. Soon the battlefield would be strewn with carnage, the smell of it wafting up to them, and Marcus would have to confront Pascentius.

Claerwen lifted her hands, palms towards the sky. She leaned her head back and spoke softly in prayer, "By all the gods my people swear by, please be with him and keep him safe. By all the ancestors of our ancient clan, please fight with him and protect him. With all of the essence of my soul, let me walk with him in spirit to shield him and guide him back to me. Blessed be."

"Blessed be," Myrddin echoed, squeezing her shoulder. They waited.

---

Marcus quickly covered the distance to the abandoned village, sliding to a halt behind the outermost hut. He waited, watching, listening, then decided no one had discovered him. Slipping from one hut to the next, he came upon the one that housed the church, edging along the wall, ducking under its windows.

Dawn broke as Marcus made the last sprint to the church's door, crashing through it. Only a rough bunch of lashed-together tree branches, it broke lengthwise down the middle, one side's pieces scattering, the other side left hanging drunkenly by leather hinges. Inside, the building appeared larger than it did from outside, its floor slightly sunken into the earth to give it insulation and height. Its only furnishing was a rustic bench that had served as an altar.

The weak morning light only caught the general movement of two Irish soldiers coming at him, yelling in confusion. He met them, just inside, his sword already swinging. It made contact with the first man, deeply cutting his arm, then ripping across the flesh of his belly with a soft swish. The man watched his own guts spill out; then he dropped, falling onto them as he died. Before the blade was free, Marcus turned, his right foot kicking high and accurate, crushing the second man's face. That man was flung backward and slammed against a wall. When he fell forward, landing in an awkward heap, his skull showed a deep fissure.

Marcus stopped, listening. The church was silent, but his warrior's instinct prickled, feeling a presence.

Out of the darkness of the building's farthest shadows, a howl came rushing, and Marcus moved again, like an ethereal force, his dark clothing and hair keeping him difficult to see. A brief flash of steel sparkled as his sword's blade swung around and bit into a third Irishman's shoulder. The man yelped, dropping onto his knees.

Standing over the last soldier, Marcus panted softly with his head bowed, holding his bloody sword with its tip resting on the floor. The man groaned. Then in one lean motion, Marcus pulled the dagger from the back of his belt and threw it. The weapon thunked into the center of the Irishman's chest, killing him instantly.

Marcus let his breath go, not realizing he had been holding it. Listening again, he felt no more soldiers present within the church. He pulled the dagger free and cleaned it. The daylight grew stronger. Straightening, he scanned the destruction he had created and felt his belly gnawing, reflecting how much he had come to hate killing, even if those lives had belonged to the traitors' dreaded mercenaries.

A whimper slipped out of the shadows from behind the altar bench, interrupting his thoughts.

Startled, he whirled around, lifting the sword again. But as he moved forward and to one side, allowing the light to reach into the rear of the church, he saw a girl on the floor behind the bench, bound and gagged. And in the corner to her right lay Sinnoch, restrained in the same manner. Daracha was not with them.

He put up the sword. With the dagger, he cut Sinnoch's bonds, then the girl's, talking as he moved, "We must hurry, before more of them come."

The girl whimpered again, terror absolute in her face, her eyes flicking from Marcus, to the dead men, to Sinnoch, back to Marcus. He spoke softly, "I know that your name is Drysi. I am called Marcus. I am not going to hurt you, but we must leave this place now. Do you understand?"

Unable to answer, she remained frozen in wide-eyed fear. Sinnoch crawled to her and gripped her arm. "He is helping us. We must go with him."

Impatient when she did not react, Marcus reached, attempting to force Drysi onto her feet. She whined and scrabbled back towards the wall, trying to avoid him.

He swore under his breath, frustrated, and warned, "If you don't come with me now...this church will be swarming with Irish warriors. If you want to die, then so be it, but my wife is your sister and I would not forgive myself if I let that happen."

Drysi's eyes rolled upward to stare at him again, white showing all around opaque green irises, but she finally found the courage to stand.

Marcus led them to the gaping doorway, a hand on each child's shoulder. Cautiously peering outside, he saw a line of soldiers marching across the path he had come down, cutting it off as a way to escape. He directed the children to head for a fold in the opposite hill instead, hoping to circle around to Claerwen and Myrddin.

Reaching the top of their climb, they crawled into a copse of young willows as the lingering mist took on a brighter illumination. The sun fought its way over the eastern hills. Minutes later, the battle began. Marcus turned towards the roaring war bands, Sinnoch joining him. They watched as the two sides rushed in, the front lines coming together in a jarring crash.

Marcus exhaled wearily. He turned to watch Drysi for a few moments as she sank into the willows a short distance behind them. His eyes softened as he saw a vague resemblance to Claerwen, though the girl was plainer and the stark fear in her expression gave her an almost sour look. He wagered to himself that his wife's inspiring compassion would ease the girl's trauma. And how he wished that they could all just go home and live in peace. But the time had come to finish his pledge to Uther.

He muttered a mild curse at their situation, then turned as Sinnoch caught his attention.

The boy looked up and asked, "Is it true...what the woman Daracha says? That you are my father?"

Marcus was speechless, as much from the bold earnestness in Sinnoch's dark eyes as from the question itself. For a child of seven years, the boy had the seriousness of a grown man. Marcus had hoped to tell the boy of his parentage himself, with Claerwen, when they were home. But Daracha had stolen that from him as much as she had stolen his clan ring, and he wondered what else she had said, what other blame she had left for him to disprove.

Now as he studied his son's face, Marcus felt he looked at his own reflection, though more from the question-filled expression than the physical resemblance. He wanted desperately to take the time and speak all that needed to be said, for to put aside his son's questions until later would give Daracha's lies credibility and he might never recover from them in Sinnoch's eyes.

But if he waited too long and Pascentius was either killed in battle by another's hand or abandoned the field like all the others that had gone sour, Marcus could lose this last chance to free himself from the pledge and Uther's tyranny. Sinnoch would have no home to go to, perhaps not even a family if the clan of Dinas Beris was permanently scattered. And always, the possibility of dying in the battle loomed as much as any other option.

He moaned, burying his face in his hands. Then, looking up once more, he held his eyes steady. He answered, "It is true."

Sinnoch took the confirmation as if he had been physically nudged, but he held Marcus' eyes without flinching. He began speaking about Daracha, "She said you were hateful and evil. She said your name wasn't Bhruic, and that you lied about everything. Everything you ever did. She said your name is Marcus ap Iorwerth, and I hear others call you that, so it must be true. But I don't want to hate you as she says I must. And your lady has been kind to me...I don't understand."

Marcus raked his fingers through his hair, relieved that Sinnoch had a mind of his own and a sense of fair judgement. Not knowing where to start, he thought of how Claerwen might word the answer. A smile flickered in his eyes and he began, "When you first saw us, you were given to understand that the lady was my slave and I a blacksmith and a swordmaster."

The boy frowned slightly, catching Marcus' tone.

"We came to that fort in the north intending for everyone there to believe that."

"But you are a swordmaster. I have seen you. You fought Banawr."

"Aye, that is true. But the lady and I were there for another purpose. We were trying to stop the man you know as the commander from having the high king assassinated. We needed to get into the fort and learn his plans. The only way to do that safely was to use disguises and false names. The lady you know as Glân, is my wife. Her true name is Claerwen, Lady Claerwen."

Sinnoch digested all that Marcus said, then stated, "Daracha said King Ambrosius died. She had a hand in that, didn't she?"

Marcus confirmed it and briefly explained what had happened since, that he had been blamed for the killing, how he had been absolved of it, and the purpose of the pledge. Then he guessed, "You now know who Daracha is, don't you?"

After a long pause, Sinnoch nodded. With his dark eyes searching his father's, he spoke again, "She is my aunt. Why is she like that?"

Marcus felt his heart jump, not knowing how to answer. He bowed his head, shaking it, and said, "She is driven by hatred, revenge, greed."

The boy confided, "I don't want to ever see her again. She said my mother is dead and that she is my aunt, and that I will have to live with her now. Then she said you were my father. But my mother always said my father died before I was born. She would never tell me his name. I begged her, but she would only cry and walk away from me."

Marcus sighed, disheartened, then confirmed, "'Tis true that Daracha was your mother's sister, actually a half-sister, and that your mother died, though we don't know how." It was not quite a lie; he did not know exactly how Daracha had murdered Elen. All he knew was that Elen's death had sickened him, and he vowed to himself that Sinnoch would not suffer any more because of Daracha.

Marcus sensed the thoughts churning in his son's mind, that the boy was judging the lies he had heard all of his short lifetime and was wondering now if this was the truth. He squeezed Sinnoch's shoulder, and said, "I wish I had more time to give you now. Damn, I've lost seven years of your life because no one told me of you. And now I have to go down to that battlefield before the commander runs away again. If I don't bring him to the high king, I could be imprisoned." He omitted the likelihood that he would be executed.

"Imprisoned?" Sinnoch's eyes grew huge. "Why?"

"Because I pledged that I would bring him the traitor within a fortnight. That time is nearly gone now. The king does not forgive failure."

"But...if you go to fight...if you don't come back...I would have to go to my aunt?"

Marcus shook his head. "What I'm going to ask you to do, right now, is to go to Lady Claerwen. She is not far away, just across on that hill there." He pointed. "She is waiting for us with a friend of ours. Take Drysi with you. Regardless of what happens to me, you will always have a home with Lady Claerwen, she will see to that. I promise this, by all the gods my people swear by."

For just a moment, tears nearly came to Sinnoch's eyes.

Marcus found himself filling with pride, a father's pride, understanding now why Claerwen had become so attached to the boy, so quickly. He wondered how Sinnoch had survived Elen's poverty of spirit and Daracha's cruelty to become a strong child who promised to grow into a fine man.

The battle rang louder, distracting them. For a few moments, they watched together. Then Marcus said, "Son, go to Lady Claerwen, now. You will be safe with her. If you stay low and follow just along the ridge there, you will find her." He looked up to see Drysi already moving in that direction.

Sinnoch hesitated, wanting to talk longer. His hands rested on Marcus' arm, his brows knotting in the same pattern as his father's. He said, "I don't understand why my mother didn't come to you. I think you might have helped her."

Marcus shook his head and replied, "I don't understand either. I wish she had. Perhaps she thought she was protecting you and me from Daracha, but I doubt it. Perhaps she was too proud. Or she may have feared me, and had thought she would lose her child to a prince."

"A prince?"

Marcus explained, "Aye, I carry the title of Prince of Dinas Beris. It's a small holding in the mountains of Gwynedd, to the north of here. But the rank is so minor that I hardly pay attention to it. It carries no power."

"But you must be important to know the high king."

Marcus smiled wryly, countering, "I have learned to make myself useful, but not because of the title."

Awed, Sinnoch slowly reached out and touched his father's face, as if to test if he were real. He said, "I was afraid of you, the first time I saw you. But now you just look sad, instead of trying to be mean."

Marcus smiled with irony, the lines around his eyes crinkling, then fading. He said, "Tell the lady, I will be with her as soon as I can. Tell her…"

Sinnoch watched his father's eyes grow sadder as the words stopped. He did not know much more about Marcus than what he had just learned and from what he had sensed of Claerwen's unquestioning love for this man. Now he saw the uncertainty Marcus felt at the possibility of dying on the battlefield and his unknown fate that would be left to Uther's whim if he survived. Always having relied on instinct when trouble came, and it had come often in his brief life, Sinnoch's instinct now told him he could trust Marcus.

"I will tell her," the boy said, solemnly earnest, his small hands gripping Marcus' arm. Then the boy turned and started for the ridge, following Drysi's tracks.

Marcus squeezed his eyes shut for a moment, forcing himself to tear his thoughts away from the boy and to concentrate on the battle. Slowly, he pulled his sword again, gazing across to the spot where Claerwen waited with Myrddin, and he wished he could see her, just once more. But as long as she was hidden, she would most likely be safe. For that he was glad. Then, locking his mind onto the quest for Pascentius, he suddenly spun around and disappeared down the hillside.

# Chapter 28

## Mynyw

Marcus pulled on his helmet, the same one of iron and leather he had used in Winchester when posing as the seneschal Faolan. Securing it tightly, he entered the battle, deliberately detaching himself from his emotions and letting his dark side take over. There was no time to think, no time to feel, only react. Time disappeared for him, and he worked his sword methodically — block, kick, thrust to one side; block, turn, slice to the other. The pain in his side hindered his usual agility, but in spite of it, he moved with determination and power, pushing his way directly towards the Irish standards.

Hour after hour passed, and close to sunset, Marcus neared the center of the battlefield. By that time, the standards had been thrown down and trampled upon, masses of butchered bodies intermingled with their remains. The intensity of the fighting there had spread to the surrounding areas, leaving a lull where he stood; and for a few moments, he rested his aching, weary body, peeled his cramped fingers from around the sword hilt, and wiped sweat and layers of spattered blood from his face.

He watched as Uther and his mounted entourage of highly trained guards approached the same area. Finding the ruined standards, they dismounted. Several minutes later, one of the guards announced that he had found Gilloman, run through and so covered in mud and blood he was recognizable only by the gold pennanular brooch still pinned to the shoulder of his tunic. Uther strode across and took the brooch, wiping it off. Then he ordered the body to be removed from the field and prepared for transport back to *Iwerddon* with the notice of the man's treachery and a warning to be spread throughout the Irish nobility against any further such interference in Britain's politics. In the instant Uther finished his remarks, a shout rose, catching his attention.

Marcus looked across as well. Several of Uther's soldiers had surrounded a small group of Saxons, Pascentius in the center of them. The Saxons attempted to slash their way free, but the king's men picked them off, one after the next. Pascentius valiantly hacked with his sword, but the Britons were too many, too strong, and closed inward. Sensing doom, Pascentius suddenly bolted, narrowly slipping through a gap in the men. He half-ran, half-slid in desperation down a steep, narrow, bracken-filled channel that cut away from the field.

Without hesitation, Marcus picked up his sword and raced after Pascentius. He heard Uther shout behind him on the field, ordering a small patrol to follow, but to let the Prince of Dinas Beris take the lead.

Marcus circumvented the channel, taking an easier descent to the right side. There the slope turned and leveled out at the bottom. Flying down, he emerged within minutes into mostly open moorland, strewn with pale grey rocks. He landed behind a large boulder, skidding to a halt, and waited.

Pascentius was gasping in air hard by the time he reached the channel's bottom. His sword still in his hand, he glanced over his shoulder several times, certain Uther's men were following, but he saw no one. Slowing with fatigue, he began to walk, listening, hearing only the bracken rustle in the wind and muffled voices of the dying on the battlefield. Placing his weapon's tip into the scabbard that dragged alongside his left leg, he started to push it inward.

A screeching cry burst from behind a large rock, and a sword raised high filled his line of sight.

"You bastard!" Pascentius spat bitterly, recognizing Marcus. He fumbled in desperation for his weapon, finally pulling it out again to block the sweeping thrust. The swords rang harshly, shattering the dull sound of moans rolling over the moors.

The commander grunted. His sword was turned awkwardly, its tip in the dirt, Marcus' blade wedging it down tightly. To pull back and free it would place him in a precariously unsteady position with his footing and invite a wound, probably fatal. Neither did he have the strength to counter Marcus' heavy hold for long. He used his only other option and kicked out, striking Marcus in the right hip.

Anticipating the hit, Marcus shifted his weight to prevent much damage. The wound in his right side stung as he twisted, and he was unable to rebalance himself as quickly as he needed. Pascentius recovered his sword and lashed out. Marcus blocked it, and the swords rang again, recoiled, crashed, recoiled again, over and over.

Pascentius fought in the precise and unimaginative Roman style. Marcus recognized the moves, having studied them himself during his fosterage. Finding Roman swordplay stiff and easily out-witted, Marcus had eventually learned a more compelling style that suited his physical agility. That agility, and the audacity that marked his courage, compensated well for him now as the wound needled him increasingly, and his bad knee weakened.

Pascentius sensed Marcus was in pain, noting how he occasionally favored his left leg and carefully protected his right side. Taking advantage and encouragement, he gained his second wind and struggled forward. They moved across the moor, hacking and blocking.

Uther arrived as the fight progressed, content to merely watch.

Marcus lunged forward with another heaving thrust, but suddenly pulled back, confusing Pascentius. Instead of continuing the steady pattern of hack, block and parry, he spun the flashing blade once around between them. As the blade came back up and over, it caught Pascentius' edge, knocking the weapon downward. Marcus forced its tip into the ground, then he vaulted, using his own sword for balance while it held the other in place. He kicked out, his heel driving his weight and momentum hard into Pascentius' wrists.

Pascentius shrieked in agony as he heard bones crack. He fell back, releasing the hilt, and sprawled unceremoniously on the turf.

Marcus caught Pascentius' sword before it fell, flung it far. In one further motion, he was down, one knee bent across the commander's legs, and leaning forward with his sword braced over the man's neck as if to slice a ham.

They stared at each other a full minute, both breathing harsh and raspy, Pascentius in pain and showing the fear of a condemned man.

Uther moved forward and stood over them as if he was about to officiate at a ritual. "Well, finish it, man!" he called to Marcus.

Fury boiled in Marcus' eyes as he looked up at the king, but he forced himself to speak calmly, very clearly, his deep voice drawing words carefully. "Is this what you want? For me to be *your* assassin? For you to sink to the same degree of cruelty as he has?"

Marcus' sudden query unnerved Uther. "You know the agreement we made. If you forswear it, you will be no better off than he."

"Think of this: if he so dies, you and I can — and will — be called murderers. It matters not if it was in battle, a legitimate challenge, or with a knife in his back in the dead of night. The factions that still support this traitor will call it what they will in spite of the truth."

"Then what would you suggest?"

"Hold a tribunal. Let those who support him show their faces and deny the truth. We have enough evidence and witnesses to prove to the world whom the traitors in Britain are. It could rally many of the minor kings and princes to your side. And the timing is perfect with the coronation so soon. To be the strongest is not always what makes the most right."

Uther silently considered the idea a few moments, hidden in a mask of solemnity, then conceded with a nod. "So be it, then. I will agree to this tribunal." He signaled to his officers and ordered, "Shackle him. He will be transported to Winchester."

Two of Uther's men dragged Pascentius out from under Marcus. Slowly getting to his feet, Marcus straightened and glared at the king, demanding, "And what of the pledge?"

Uther answered tersely, "Two conditions. You testify at this tribunal, and you swear fealty at the coronation."

"Done," Marcus agreed.

Uther turned and strode away, his men following with their prisoner.

Marcus cleaned and sheathed his weapon. Untying the straps of his helmet, he pulled it off, dropped it on the ground. For a few moments he stretched his tired muscles, flexing his aching hands and arms, his head leaning back. He let his mind drift, needing to absent himself from the ugliness of battle and death. But Myrddin's voice suddenly overrode the moment of near quiet, calling his name.

Turning, Marcus saw he was riding swiftly towards him, Drysi holding on behind, and he realized from the look on the prince's face that something was terribly wrong. "Where is she? And the boy?" Marcus questioned before Myrddin could drop off the horse.

As he reached the ground, Myrddin launched into a hurried explanation. "The girl here said Sinnoch was following her, but he never arrived. Claerwen went back across the ridge, looking for him. There were signs of a struggle. Then we saw a group of five riders, four men and a woman, across the hills to the north, partially hidden by trees. A sixth rider rode towards them. He had Sinnoch over the horse's withers. These were Saxon warriors, not Irish, all in full battle gear. She went after them —"

"How long ago?" Marcus cut him off. He felt like a rock had been rammed into his belly.

"Just after the battle began."

"Did they go north?"

"Aye. Claerwen was near to panic. She was certain it was trap for you and her, with your son as bait. She believes they will go to Dinas Beris, her reasoning being that if Pascentius dies here, the woman Daracha will have nothing left except revenge against you. I tried to stop her, but she was determined, hoping to reach your cousin Owein for help. She forced her way past me and took your horse."

Marcus raked his fingers through his filthy hair, muttering a long line of curses to himself. He wanted to blame someone, anyone, but knew it was no one's fault, and everyone's, including his own. "Her reasoning is probably true, Myrddin," he said, the worry plain in his face, then briefly told him of the proposed tribunal. Then he ordered, "I want you to have Drysi escorted to Engres in Winchester. When it is safe at Dinas Beris, I will send for both of them. I'm going to take your horse. Perhaps I can reach her, before it is too late…"

He moved towards the horse, gesturing for Drysi to dismount. Her face ashen and terrified, the girl recoiled. He stopped, aware that his muddy, sweaty, blood-covered face and clothing were ominous to a sheltered girl of fourteen summers. Irritated, he turned aside, signaling to Myrddin to speak to her.

"Come, girl," Myrddin coaxed, laying warmth and kindness into his soothing voice. He reached for Drysi, and she let him pull her off the horse.

Myrddin spoke quickly and quietly to Marcus as he handed him the reins. "Uther will be furious if you go now, without his leave. He may not release you from the pledge if you don't testify at the tribunal, but I will try to stall him," Myrddin offered.

"Tell him I will return to make amends, when I am able. But for now, I must go home." He swung up onto the animal and raced away, lost from sight within minutes.

# Chapter 29

## Dinas Beris

After two days of relentless riding, Marcus halted at the foot of the pass below Dinas Beris. Rising up by his knees on the saddle, he squinted into the cold wind, his hair whipping about his face as he scanned in all directions. He gazed up at dramatic golden plumes of mist swirling among the crags as the sun began to set, and he suddenly realized how much he had missed home. Finding nothing out of the ordinary, he sank down onto his horse.

A horn sounded, faint and distant, carried on the gusting air. Long and mournful, it was the tone of a ram's horn that Owein used to call alarms and announce those approaching the fort. Marcus began up the rocky path into the pass. His clan would be waiting for him.

As he neared the summit, his cousin appeared, riding down. They hailed each other heartily, pulling up their horses close together and leaning across to clasp arms. Before Owein could speak, Marcus asked, "Has my wife been here? Or any strangers, within the last two days? Have you seen anything unusual at all?"

Owein, tall, taciturn, dark blond with a moustache identical to Marcus' in style, and a ragged look that was almost ugly, shook his head, puzzled by his cousin's bluntness. Then, realizing Marcus was alone, he asked, "Where is Claerwen?"

Marcus exhaled roughly, "She was on her way here, alone, following another woman and a few Saxon soldiers. There should also be a young boy with them. Scatter the clan, Owein. There's going to be trouble and I don't know to what degree." He described Daracha, warning of her danger and ordering her arrest if she was found.

"Aye, cousin," Owein acknowledged, then asked, "Who is the boy?"

Marcus' eyes came up, dark and brooding. He answered, "My son."

Owein's jaw dropped.

"You heard me right," Marcus countered the reaction, then indicated for the alert to be sounded.

Wheeling his horse around, Owein put the ram's horn to his lips again and filled the air with a series of sharp calls. Moments later, Dinas Beris' able-bodied men raced towards predetermined patrols and postings, and the rest of the clan set to flight, disappearing into the mountains on either side of the pass and taking only what could easily be carried. As he watched the people move out, Marcus briefly explained about Sinnoch and why Claerwen was alone. As he finished, rumbling vibrated the ground.

"Rider coming," Owein stated. "Alone. From the southeast."

They turned to face the downward sloping road, and several minutes later Myrddin approached at a gallop. Dust-covered and wind-blown, he pulled up before them.

"I have news," he announced.

Marcus edged his horse forward, surprised that Myrddin had followed him to Dinas Beris, and even more surprised they had reached that destination so close in time yet had not encountered each other in traveling north. Suspecting they had taken different routes, he dismissed the odd occurrence and asked, "You have seen Claerwen?"

"No, I wish it were so."

Disappointed, Marcus muttered to Owein, "Start looking for Daracha. I will join you shortly."

As Owein left them, Myrddin continued, "I felt I should warn you, just after you left Mynyw, Uther had Pascentius executed."

Marcus' mouth curled in exasperation. "He took back his word?"

"When he learned you had gone without his leave or further promise to fulfill your side of the pledge, he denounced the tribunal and gave the order. Of course, he would not listen to me."

"Then I am a fugitive again?"

"Probably. I left without his leave as well, therefore, I am likely so along with you."

Marcus nearly smiled at their odd pairing, then said, "So be it. I have a place you can wait until we have secured — "

"I'm coming with you," Myrddin interrupted. "Claerwen is my friend, and I owe her as much as I owe you."

Marcus started to protest, but another ram's horn called from below, different than Owein's. From the tone and the series of sounds, he knew it came from a particular area in the southeast corner of his lands and a hostile intruder had been captured. Pulling his horse around, he started down the road again, leaving Myrddin to follow.

The mountainside curved downward as if an enormous hand had shaped it with a long, smooth swipe, ending in a broad shelf of land edged by a river. Forest covered the lower slopes. A sparkling tarn lay to the river's north side, marking the border of Marcus' lands and the base of the pass. Not far away, the pass road split; one fork followed the river to the west, the other turned east. A small convent within a timber enclosure lay a half-mile from the tarn, shut and silent against the entire world.

Marcus hauled up roughly near the tarn and dismounted. Myrddin arrived moments later. A circle of eight clansmen surrounded a Saxon staked to the ground. Several weapons had been taken, and Owein stood in the center, his drawn swordtip at the man's throat.

Marching into the circle, Marcus asked his cousin, "Has he told you anything yet?"

"No, but apparently your wife has had quite an adventure," Owein replied, then grinned.

Marcus stared at him in confusion. His cousin's grin grew

broad and toothy, his head tipping slightly to indicate something should be seen beyond the circle of men.

Looking up, Marcus saw Claerwen walking towards them. She still wore the cloak over the torn gown she had been wearing since the attempted hostage trade, both now so filthy they barely showed their original color. "By the gods..." he mumbled and strode across the circle, pushing his way between his men, reaching for her.

She rushed into his arms and hugged him with all her strength, utterly relieved to know he was there and apparently unscathed from the battle of Mynyw. Then gripping his hands, she urged, "We must hurry. Daracha still holds Sinnoch. I tried to free him late yesterday, but they had all but one man guarding him. I couldn't get close enough, and then they saw me. This one," she indicated the Saxon, "was sent to capture me, and I eluded him as far as the borders here. He caught me, and knowing the patrols were so close, I struggled enough to get their attention. They took him, then Owein came as well. And I am certain Daracha is carrying Macsen's spearhead."

She watched his eyes roam over her, taking in how travel worn she appeared and the condition of her clothing, the concern in his face blatant. She answered his unspoken question, "I am fine enough, but we must hurry."

Marcus started in amazement, "And you say I'm the audacious one." For a moment, he cupped his hand to her cheek, letting his eyes speak of his pride in her and his relief that she was apparently as well as she said. Then he turned and pulled his sword, squinting his determination to rescue his son, and strode once more into the circle of his men.

Standing over the Saxon, his eyes roiled like thunderclouds, and he held his sword's tip to the man's throat, pressing until he could see fear rise in a palpable force.

"Where is the woman called Daracha?" he demanded. The Saxon held Marcus' cold stare but gave no answer. Marcus repeated the question, his resolve growing more iron willed, but again he received no reply.

Myrddin knelt next to the captive man and repeated the

demand, but in Saxon.

The soldier's eyes widened in surprise at the high prince's knowledge of the language. The Saxon spoke back, his tone sharp and guttural. Myrddin countered, speaking rapidly and with firm confidence. The Saxon replied again.

Myrddin straightened and spoke quietly to Marcus and Owein. "He says he was to meet the woman known as Daracha once he had captured Claerwen. He was to take her to the other side of the pass, on the northern border of your lands. He says that is where they hold the boy."

Marcus turned for his mount, but Myrddin caught his arm, speaking urgently, "The man is lying. Take out your dagger, the biggest one. I want you to grin at him in your slyest, most cruel way. Do it now."

Not understanding but trusting him, Marcus complied, pulling the knife from the back of his belt. He twisted it, admiring the wide, finely crafted blade, then chuckled mirthlessly. Gesturing broadly, Myrddin spoke again to the Saxon.

The soldier's eyes showed white all around as they widened again, and he began talking rapidly, running out of breath but plunging on anyway. Finished, he waited for a reaction.

Myrddin paused several moments, intentionally letting the man fret the outcome of his answer. Finally, he drew Marcus and Owein several yards away.

Impatient, Marcus queried, "What did you say? What did *he* say?"

With a full measure of aloof dignity, Myrddin answered, "I told him that you are well known to take the most prized part of a man's body for a trophy, and that you had done so to an entire war band in exchange for their lives. You have decorated the inside of your house with them, from ground to roof, to remind you of all your victories."

Marcus stared at Myrddin in disbelief.

Owein burst into laughter.

Mischief broke through Myrddin's otherwise dreary expression and he said, "He also told me that Daracha and four other warriors are on the river beyond the convent."

Suddenly realizing the ploy, Marcus blurted, "Hah! The Enchanter does have a sense of humor! How did you know he was lying?"

Myrddin only smiled in return.

Marcus lifted an eyebrow and decided that it was either a good guess or fire in the head. Not caring which, he clapped him on the shoulder and heartily declared in thanks, "*Diolch yn fawr, cyfaill!*" To his cousin, he gave orders for two men to bring the prisoner with them and to send another dozen men immediately, prepared to fight Saxons, but to hold back until signaled to join in.

Turning to Claerwen, he took her hands. Hope glittered in his eyes. He whispered, "I shall see that your wish comes true, that we will raise the boy together. He will be *our* son, and he will be safely home with us within the hour. With my whole heart and soul, this I promise you."

# Chapter 30

### Dinas Beris

"Use the silent signals as long as there is light," Marcus said quietly to Owein. "Only set the torches to burning when it becomes necessary. If it is true there are only four men and the woman, we already outnumber them."

They ran down through the thick wood, streaking over mushy leaves that kept their footfalls hushed, past eyes of unseen nuns watching from the convent, dodging low tree branches as the other men followed, bringing the captive Saxon with them. Claerwen and Myrddin came after.

Reaching the trees' perimeter, they halted, crouched, peered across the wide, scree-covered riverbank. Clumps of old snow and ice lay strewn along the shore. Daracha stood in the open, facing the river, holding a long staff. With its golden lines and jewels shining in the fading light, Macsen's priceless spearhead was attached to the shaft's end. The four Saxon warriors were stationed evenly around her; two crouched in wait, two standing on watch. Sinnoch was not visible.

Myrddin and Claerwen drew in behind Marcus as he whispered tersely to Owein, "You know what to do, but we must take them alive, because they hold my son and we need to find him first." His cousin nodded once and backed silently. To

Myrddin, Marcus said, "Stay here with Claerwen. Don't let yourselves be seen."

"You're not going to wait for the other men to arrive?"

"No," Marcus answered, then signaled for absolute silence. He pulled his sword and watched through the trees, patiently waiting for Owein to find his position directly across the field of range. Within minutes, his cousin appeared, pointing precisely to where each man was hidden. Then he raised a fist.

Marcus rose. Slowly, he moved forward to the edge of the trees. Claerwen and Myrddin took the place he had occupied. A moment later, he walked out into the open.

"Daracha!" he shouted, his voice booming harshly across the cold river basin.

Jarred by the sudden yell, the woman whipped around, lowering the staff defensively. Marcus moved steadily towards her, punching the air with his right fist, once, twice, then again. In his left hand, his sword leveled, the tip drawing in line with her throat.

Her face contorted into a combination of fear, hatred and rage, momentarily paralyzing her. She glanced to the right, then looked again when she saw the biggest of her Saxons go down, one man holding a knife to his throat, forcing his silence, while another handbound and hobbled him. Rustling pulled her attention to her left, and she saw another of her men taken down the same way. Turning in a circle, she saw the others captured just as easily. They were brought together and sat down in a row, including the first prisoner from the border. Owein stood over them, directing the confiscation of their weapons.

Hatred fought its way past her fear, and Daracha swept around.

"Where is the boy?" Marcus demanded before she could voice her rage.

"You cold, miserable — "

"Don't waste your time." Marcus cut her off, advancing. "Where is the boy?"

Lashing out with bitterness, she taunted, "Go on, cut me, I dare you. But you know only I can tell you where he is."

He continued forward, unhesitating, his face locked in an

unforgiving glare. Daracha reacted, brandishing the spearhead. Marcus flipped the sword upward and turned the blade edge vertically. With unerring accuracy, he hacked down, breaking the staff between her hands and knocking the pieces to the ground.

"Where is the boy? Next time it will be your fingers, then your hands."

"I shall bleed to death a thousand times before I will tell you!" she shrieked, but began slowly backing towards the edge of the water, until she came upon a barrier of boulders and could go no farther. Owein crept slowly inward, both his sword and a big dagger drawn, ready to block any attempts to escape.

With calm dignity, Marcus spoke, "You seek power and control, not revenge for the death of your kinsman Drakar. You never cared for him any more than for Elen. Your revenge is seated in the fact that you could never control me, because your sister gave me information I needed about Drakar's traitorous activities in return for a little affection. If it had not been for the child she bore, you would never have known. Am I correct?"

Fury filled Daracha as the truth spilled easily from his clean logic. She moved a pair of steps, stalking Marcus, and spit, "You always take what you want, then run. You never would have married Elen!"

"No, I would not. That is true. But she could have come to me for help, and I'd have given it freely. She didn't. Why? Because you threatened to kill her, or the boy, didn't you? Then you murdered her anyway and stole her child, so you could use him against me. By the gods, woman, they deserved better than the ugly way you treated them!"

Daracha held Marcus' unbreakable gaze, her tilted grey eyes seething with hatred, but she gave no reply.

Marcus continued, "Pascentius is dead. There is no longer a purpose to holding Sinnoch hostage. Where is he?"

Daracha slowly straightened then, and her mouth curved into a smile full of mockery. "Aye, that is true, there is no purpose...any more..." Her head swiveled slightly, swaying almost like a leaf in a breeze, her eyes squinting sarcasm. "Then you will have to find him yourself." Mirthless, hollow laughter rolled from her throat.

"I say you will bring him to me, now," Marcus countered, pressing the swordtip to the hollow of her throat.

The laughter ended, but Daracha held still, staring defiantly. Then her eyes moved, looking past him. Alarmed, fascinated, dumbfounded, she knelt in an empty gesture of reverence and mumbled in astonishment, "Merlin the Enchanter…"

Cautiously, Marcus turned his head. Myrddin emerged from the wood, walking slowly, each step deliberate, determined, and Marcus realized the prince was under the spell of fire in the head. On long, gangly legs, Myrddin waded into the stream, crossing the low-flowing water to the south side. There was no hesitation in his movements, no emotion in his face, no indication his feet stung with pain as the icy water soaked through his boots. Coming to a cluster of pale grey granite boulders on the opposite shore, he knelt, hidden for several minutes as those on the northern side watched for him to emerge again. Then he rose, lifting a bundle shrouded in a dark homespun, and he walked back through the water and onto the shore.

A small hand slipped from beneath the ragged cloth cover, bluishly pale, dirty, limp.

Dread pervaded Marcus to the depths of his soul as he watched the hand sway slightly with each of Myrddin's steps. He felt his scalp tighten and his jaw go achingly stiff as if someone had clamped his head between two rocks, and he held his breath as the realization of what lay beneath the filthy woolen came into fullness.

An instant later, a plaintive, eerie cry rose, chilling Marcus as he recognized Claerwen's voice. He turned towards the woods, taking several long strides in that direction, but he halted on seeing her walk out of the trees. With her eyes locked on the hand, any hope that had remained in her face gradually faded, wisping away like mist, leaving her expression so desolate, his gut cramped.

Marcus started across again, thinking she was going to faint, but suddenly, she burst forward, frantically running towards Myrddin.

"No, Claeri!" he shouted, chasing after her. She moved fast, sailing down the slope. Dropping his sword, he caught her midway, skidding with his heels dug into the scree to stop both himself and her. She fell into him, grasping at his tunic as she lost balance, and they went down on their knees together, crashing onto the rocky ground. She struggled to rise again, but Marcus tightly clutched her, gathering her flailing arms and pressing her face into his shoulder.

"There's nothing we can do, Claeri," he spoke in soft, desperate words, over and over, knowing from the way the body was limp that the stiffness of death had already passed and Sinnoch had been dead several hours. He knew that she realized this as well, and that there had never been any intention to negotiate the boy's release.

"He was just a little boy..." Claerwen tried to speak, but her voice choked as the tears began to spill. She sought Marcus' hands and twined her fingers through his. Her eyes came up, utterly heartbroken.

Marcus drew a long breath, trying to ease the wrenching pang of sorrow that gripped him as he beheld her grief. He exhaled, then drew another, several times, gathering his will. He lifted one hand and gently laid his palm along her cheek, his thumb brushing her skin. Quietly, firmly, he said, "I want you to stay here, Claeri. Can you do that for me? Stay here?"

The soothing sound of his rich voice and his intense gaze kept her attention focused, gradually calming her. She nodded.

Marcus squeezed her arms, her hands, leaned to kiss her cheek gently. Then he rose, retrieved his sword. Turning to Myrddin, he saw the prince's eyes lift, full of sorrow, all signs of the fire gone. The bundled body lay across his hands, held reverently, and he gently placed it on the ground. He wordlessly retreated.

Marcus moved forward, dreading every step, dragging in air to steel his nerves. He feared Sinnoch had been mutilated as his mother had been, and more than anything, he did not want Claerwen to see such cruelty again. Kneeling, he reached for the makeshift shroud. Pulling it slowly away, Sinnoch's face showed starkly in the waning light, pale as whitewash. A deep wound scored the boy's chest, straight into the heart, the same size and shape as Macsen's spearhead would make.

The sight was no worse than the average death he had seen in his life, and he had seen many, far too many, yet this time shock swarmed inside his head, like a hive of angry bees, buzzing, churning, distracting. For several minutes, he gazed at his son, trying to remember the details of the last moments he had seen the boy alive, the conversation that had bonded them as much as their blood. Those words between them, though few, strained and incomplete, had been precious.

Willing down his roiling stomach, Marcus replaced the homespun and rose once more. He stalked forward, each step heavy as if dragging along thick chains, and he turned back towards Daracha. She was still kneeling, Owein guarding her carefully, and a smirk played about her face. For several minutes, Marcus glared, clenching and unclenching his fists, over and over, considering the path his rage should be allowed to take. He was oblivious to all the faces watching him, waiting for his reaction; Owein, Myrddin, the prisoners, his own people slowly drawing in closer.

Then suddenly Claerwen stood beside him, straight and proud. Her eyes, though calmly steady, cast a gaze at Daracha that could have split the woman into halves. She moved another pace forward, then halted again.

No tears fell now. For several moments, she continued to stare. Then she spoke. "May the gods forever hound you…for the pain you have caused. So many have suffered because of you and your lies and your hatred…"

She paused and Marcus turned his head, thinking she was further gathering her thoughts. Instead, he felt his skin prickle as the light of fire in the head suddenly appeared in her eyes. Her voice took on a thicker, more authoritative flow, and she spoke again, "You will pass from this life and your soul shall be riven into a thousand-thousand pieces, scattered across the universe, such that it may never return in whole to pass your evil intent again. You are cursed by all the gods in unison, you are cursed by your ancestors, you are cursed by all of your kin and their descendants. You are not to be remembered by any soul, for a thousand-thousand lifetimes."

An instant later, the fire left Claerwen. She stepped backward, almost stumbling, and Marcus caught her before she could fall. Her breath exhaled hard as pain swelled in her head, the aftermath of the fire. Gradually, she steadied and assured Marcus that she was fine enough.

He released her, but watched for several moments until he was certain she would not faint. Then he turned again to Daracha. The smirk on the woman's face had gone, but no remorse showed. Finally, in a voice low and hoarse, each word bitten off and spit out, he said, "You did this for the sake of revenge. For the sake of watching us suffer, you murdered my son."

Those who watched stirred, their whispered astonishment at learning Sinnoch's identity rustling among them like wind-blown drapes. One of the prisoners, the biggest man and apparently the Saxons' unofficial leader, called out, "The boy...your son?"

Marcus turned towards him, scowling, but nodded acknowledgement, waiting for him to continue.

"Please," the Saxon went on, struggling to speak in Marcus' language. "We know nothing...of boy's death. Until now. We come here...she hide him from us. We told...we only should escort."

The leader then spoke with the other Saxons in their language, and their expressions collectively changed, showing surprise, disgust, empathy, sorrow. Marcus signaled for the leader to be untied and brought before him. Studying the soldier's face, he recognized true distress in his eyes, not a ploy.

The Saxon confided, "I have son...like him. Woman should pay blood price."

Marcus' heartbeat pounded in his temples, so loud he thought his head would burst. Roughly dragging in air, he fought to control his need to violently vent his anger. He paced, a few steps one way, a few in return. Raking his fingers through his hair, he halted again before the Saxon. For another full minute he glared intently into the man's eyes. Finally, he announced, "I will release you and your men if you see that the woman is punished. If not, I will transport all of you in chains to the high king of Britain for trial. That woman is certain to be executed for treason. Anyone with her will meet the same fate. If you do not understand, that man," he swept a hand towards Myrddin, "will translate my offer into your language. What say you?"

The Saxon looked beyond to Claerwen, kneeling alone, then to Myrddin standing several yards past. He scanned the entire area, giving each face of Marcus' people a brief perusal, all of them waiting for his answer. The soldier's eyes returned to Marcus, and he said, "I believe you...fair man, honorable man, because woman say you not. Because you offer blood price for freedom. You wife need you, go to her now."

He nodded once, confirming his statement, then waited until Marcus withdrew to Claerwen. As Daracha realized Marcus had given his consent, she began to protest, trying to scramble onto her feet and escape the rock bower in which she was cornered, but Owein blocked her, shoving her back while the Saxon retrieved his battle axe from the pile of confiscated weapons. As the soldier strode towards her, his face showed he had put aside his empathy regarding the boy. With a well-practiced swing, he struck. Daracha's skull shattered with a dull, sickening crunch.

Everyone along the river flinched.

Except Marcus. He pulled Claerwen to her feet, guiding her away from Sinnoch, away from Daracha, moving towards the river's edge where they stopped. Tears filled his eyes as he felt her hands come up around him, gripping his tunic. He clutched her closely and listened to his men cut the remaining Saxons' bonds. Gathering their weapons, the soldiers filed quietly past Sinnoch, one by one, saluting.

After the soldiers tramped away towards the valley to the south, the only sound left was the slow crinkling of the river on its way to the sea, flowing as Sinnoch's soul had passed on to *Annwn, y dan fyd,* the Other World, only hours before. The understanding that he would never know his son beyond the brief minutes they had shared sunk into Marcus' mind, spearing his conscience that he could not keep his promise to Claerwen.

Myrddin slowly approached. Halfway across, he picked up the broken shaft with the spearhead and studied it for several moments. He moved forward again, and looking up to meet Marcus' gaze, he received a simple nod acknowledging his right to take it.

"If you wish," Myrddin offered, "I will carry the boy to the fort for you."

Marcus again nodded. He hissed bitterly, "Sometimes I bloody hate being fair." Then to his cousin, he ordered, "Light the torches now. And send for the druid and the pipes. We have need of a funeral."

"And...that?" Owein queried, frowning at the dead woman.

Still clasping Claerwen tightly and keeping her face turned away, Marcus looked over her shoulder once more at Daracha's destroyed body. His nostrils flared at the smell of death. As he turned away, he answered, "Burn it."

# Chapter 31

## Dinas Beris

In Dinas Beris' great hall, on a trestle table next to the hearth, Sinnoch rested on a pallet woven of willow. A new shroud of linen wrapped his body; upon it, branches of sacred yew were arranged, the dark evergreen branches interlaced in a pattern that signified eternal life.

For a day and a night, Marcus had stood watch over him, only going out for brief rest periods, and now the end had nearly come to a second night. A steady stream of his clan's people had wandered in and out through the doors, attempting to follow the ancient tradition of feasting and celebrating the dead's rebirth in *Annwn*, but a pall had been cast upon the ritual by Marcus' tacit grief. He barely responded to the kind remarks said to him.

From across the hall, Claerwen held her own vigil, watching Marcus and hoping he would soon turn to her for comfort. Eventually he would, she knew, but the time had not yet come. As first light approached, Myrddin silently paced into the hall, joining her. "I'm leaving now," he said.

Turning to him, she saw he was already dressed in his traveling clothes. "So soon? Will you not stay for the funeral?"

"I must return to Winchester with this." He lifted the edge of his cloak and patted a thick leather pouch she knew contained

Macsen's spearhead.

"Don't you want an escort? That thing will make you a target."

Myrddin smiled. "I am always a target."

Claerwen grimaced at his self-deprecation. "In truth, I was thinking that on their return journey here, they could escort my father and sister."

"I should warn you that I don't believe your sister will want to come here to live. She was rather adamant about staying in Winchester. Apparently, there is a convent she had lived in for a while nearby, and she wishes to return there, and to perhaps become a nun."

Claerwen blurted, "My sister, a nun? By choice?"

Myrddin nodded. "Aye, that appears to be her wish. But I think the truth is that she is quite terrified of Marcus. She continually complained that he desecrated the church at Mynyw when he killed the men holding her and Sinnoch. I made no impression upon her when I pointed out that he had saved her life. The second time she saw him, he had just come from the battle and was looking rather ominous."

"I can imagine," Claerwen agreed. "I suppose she will need to decide for herself, but if she chooses to come here, she is welcome."

"Your father, however, I am certain, wants very much to come here, to be near you."

"Ah, I do look forward to that."

Myrddin smiled again. "Regarding the escort, I will be able to move more quickly if I am alone, and that suits me well enough. Uther will be planning his coronation, and he will have need of the spearhead for the ceremonies."

"And need of you as well."

"Perhaps," he said, then, observing Marcus across the hall, continued, "He is taking this with great difficulty."

"Aye," Claerwen responded. "He won't even talk to Owein, or Padrig. 'Tis not like him to brood, but I do understand."

"You said that you knew the boy better."

Claerwen's eyes went sad. "That is true, I spent more time with him. But Marcus was given that one brief moment when they spoke together as father and son. I believe that once he comes to terms with losing Sinnoch, he will cherish that memory. It is something I will never have, though I will cherish my memories of the boy just as much."

Myrddin nodded at the explanation, then asked, "Why did Marcus give the blood price to the Saxon?"

"He did not wish to show his dark side to us."

Myrddin's brows lifted in question.

She confided, "There are times when I lie next to him in the night, watching him sleep so peacefully, and I wonder at some of the things he has done. That side of him can be so cruel, yet I know he has never killed for the sake of cruelty itself. Now you fully know what he is capable of..." She paused, waving a hand over her face to mimic the Iron Hawk's mask.

"Why has he put himself in such jeopardy, all these years?" Myrddin asked. "What exactly inspired him to start?"

Claerwen sighed roughly, "I don't know, Myrddin. Sometimes I think he and I know each other better than any other two people in this world, but there are things about him I don't know, and perhaps I never will. There is always sadness about him, even when he seems to be at his most content. It is as if I can see every death he has ever seen, all there in his eyes. And he knows, no matter how much he hates to take a life, there will be times that he must again. There is no avoiding it. I believe some terrible event happened a long time ago, before I knew him, something he either experienced or witnessed that he never speaks of, and that is the thing which drives him so consummately."

"Aye, we all find it best to leave some things unsaid. In truth, most of us do not remember times of peace. Yet...you are so calm," Myrddin commented, his eyebrows lifting again.

Claerwen smiled, though still with sadness, and looked down at her hands, studying her marriage ring. "I wanted so much to raise Sinnoch as my own. It is not my fate to raise children in this lifetime, but to accompany Marcus on his journeys, his quests. For that I have no regrets."

She looked up and smiled again, this time with joy, "To me, the side he shows is one of profound kindness. Myrddin, I do so treasure that man, more than I ever thought could be possible."

Myrddin grinned a rare, broad smile, then he leaned to brush her cheek with a brotherly kiss. "I shall see you at the coronation, my dear friend. Tell Marcus, if Uther gives any bother regarding our leaving Mynyw without his permission, I will find a way to pacify him. And I trust you will say my farewells for me."

He began to move away, turning for the doors, then stopped, returning. Taking Claerwen's hand, he pressed a small object into her palm and closed her fingers around it. He glanced across towards Marcus. Nodding, he lightly kissed her cheek once more, a slight smile perking the corner of his mouth, and strode away through the doors.

Claerwen opened her hand. In it lay the carved wooden piece representing the high king from the game *gwyddbwyll*. She gazed at it, too tired to guess its significance, then tucked it into a small cloth pouch hung from her belt. Sinking onto a bench, she crossed her arms on a table, lay her head on them, and quickly gave in to much needed sleep.

---

"I am ready now, Claeri," Marcus spoke in his rich voice.

Claerwen felt his hand lying on her arm, gently pressing her skin, and she struggled to pull free from the spell of deep sleep. Opening her eyes, she found him sitting beside her, his face calm, though the air of loss remained profoundly evident.

"What time is it?" she asked.

"The sun is just rising," he said, "I have told the druid. We will go to the standing stone now, and let Sinnoch go on to celebrate his new life."

Claerwen leaned into him, embracing him tightly.

---

By late in the afternoon that day, the people of Dinas Beris had all gone home, relieved that Marcus had ended the waking and allowed the funeral to proceed. The ritual had been brief, consisting only of a lamentation spoken over Sinnoch's body at the standing stone, then the cremation. The ashes had been carried to the summit of the mountain called *Glyder Fawr* and placed in a *carnedd* built to keep them safe. A capstone was laid atop the *carnedd*, its surface carved with a simple *triskele* of birds, the triple-spiraled symbol that represented both the clan of Dinas Beris and the spirituality the local people had practiced since time out of mind.

Marcus and Claerwen lingered after everyone else had gone, wanting to say their last farewells together and in privacy. They planted a young, sturdy tree with the hope that part of Sinnoch's soul would grow into it and remain close to them. Several other trees were scattered along the summit ridge of the mountain, marking other graves of the clan.

When they were done, Marcus sat down on the scree surface next to the *carnedd*, his knees drawn up and his arms looped around them. For several minutes, he rested his face on his arms. When he looked up again, he watched Claerwen kneeling a few feet away, squinting against the cold, wind-blown mist that billowed in from the northwest. Tears hung in her eyes as she patiently studied the various graves, and he knew she would wait for him without complaint, no matter how cold she was or how long he took to finish his thoughts. He sighed quietly, then apologized, "I cannot keep my promise to you."

Claerwen turned to him, blinking back the tears. "'Tis I who should apologize. If I had been more careful…or less bold…"

"No, Claeri. It was not your fault. The boy was doomed whether you had gone after them or not. There never would have been a negotiation. I think you sensed that, before you left Mynyw."

Her face filled with questions, not following his logic.

Continuing his thought, he remarked, "Sinnoch was a sacrifice, wasn't he? In the way that Ambrosius was."

Claerwen's hand came up, covering her mouth, her eyes searching his tired face.

He finished, "It is the gods' way to keep me tied to this ongoing quest, isn't it? And I believe it is to keep you with me as well, instead of home, raising babies."

When her hand dropped into her lap and her mouth fell open,

his eyes almost smiled. He said, "I don't think I ever told you this, but when you learned you could not bear children, I was secretly relieved."

"But I thought you wanted children," she countered.

"Aye, I did, very much so. But remember, my mother died of the childbirth fever when I was but four winters old. Each time I bragged about having a child, I also dreaded it, because it could have meant losing you."

"Ah, Marcus," she sighed, moving across to him. Touching his face, she smiled at the irony, thinking how many times they had nearly lost each other in the last months.

"'Tis good to be home," Marcus said quietly. On a clear day, the fort could be seen in the pass below. Now it disappeared as the wind drove the cold mist down over them.

Claerwen hoped the familiar comfort of Dinas Beris would ease the anguish of finding, then losing Sinnoch; then she suddenly remembered the game piece Myrddin had given her. Telling Marcus of the odd exchange, she dug the wooden figure from her belt's pouch.

One eyebrow lifted, and he speculated, "He gave me that same piece before we began this quest. I thought he meant to say that you trust your life to me as much as to the gods. That thought came to me several times, like an echo, especially when we were in trouble, and it always seemed to be appropriate. But why he keeps referring to this piece, I don't understand."

She gently squeezed the wooden figure, as if to sense a spirit within it. "Perhaps it is meant to say that now he believes how much you do trust the fire, even though you have not experienced it within yourself. And that you trust the portent and accept the path the gods have lain out before us. And him as well, of course."

He frowned, confused, taking the game piece from her. "We have acted almost blindly in this. You don't know when, or where, or how this great king will come about any more than I do. And I'd wager Myrddin doesn't specifically know either."

"No, we don't. You are right."

"But it will happen. Someday. Soon, perhaps? Or just as likely, after we are all gone?"

Claerwen nodded, confirming. She took the game piece back from him. "I think this is symbolic. Myrddin doesn't know that you carved this piece. But it is more handsome than the originals of the game, more well made."

"But that piece is flawed."

Claerwen's eyes came up. "Flawed? Yet...better than what went on before..." She paused, her voice drifting away.

Marcus interjected, "This represents the king yet to come? And though he will be flawed..." His eyes held hers, watching for fire in the head, and instead found their beauty entrancing him as much as they did the first time he ever saw them.

She nodded, smiling, and finished, "Aye, though he will be flawed, as Uther is flawed, as we all are in some way, he will still represent peace, and freedom...this king whom Myrddin will one day name...Arthur."

Chills shivered on Marcus' skin, more from the eerie mention of the yet unborn king's name than the dampness that crept through his clothing. Getting to his feet, he reached for Claerwen's hand and pulled her up. "'Tis time to go home," he said, wrapping his cloak around both of them. They started down the mountainside, silently wondering what more would need to be sacrificed.

# Epílogue

**Winchester
Spring, AD 471**

On the day before the holiday of Alban Eilir, the spring equinox, Winchester bustled with final preparations for Uther's coronation. The city was filled with visitors, most hoping to glimpse the king as he passed by in the traditional procession through the streets. Inside the palace courtyard, a high platform had been built and was being richly decorated. The king would be crowned there in grand style on the holiday before hundreds of invited dignitaries.

Marcus and Claerwen arrived at mid-afternoon and met Myrddin in the palace. He lent them the use of the same rooms within his apartments where they had previously stayed. Fatigued from the travel, Claerwen indulged in a nap shortly after they settled in.

With Myrddin busy and Claerwen resting, Marcus went outside again, exploring the grounds behind the palace. There he recognized the small courtyard he had escaped through when, as the Iron Hawk, he had crashed through the second-story window and sprawled across ice-covered cobbles. Now in the plainness of brilliant spring daylight, he saw a garden edged the courtyard, filled with resplendent flowers and cropped grass, not a hint of winter.

"I would speak with you if I may," Uther's voice suddenly interrupted the peaceful afternoon quiet.

Marcus turned, surprised to see the king alone and even more surprised at his fine manners. He surmised Uther was seeking a brief moment of solitude from the hustle. "Certainly, my lord," Marcus answered, bowing slightly.

"Your wife is well, I hope?" the king asked, still polite though with some stiffness.

Marcus nodded. "We would like to thank you for your generosity in sending the escort with us." He knew the escort was in truth a forced watch, sent to make certain he would arrive in time for the coronation's homage ceremony. Though they had traveled in comfort this time, stopping each night at inns, and half of the guard was made up of clansmen from Dinas Beris, the other half from Uther was as heavily armed as a prison transport detachment.

The king grunted acknowledgment, then said, "They've left me little time to spend talking today, so I will move straight to the point, as you are so good at doing." He eyed Marcus, waiting for his reaction, and receiving none but a look of curiosity, he proceeded, "You are a fine warrior and tactician, Lord Marcus." A hint of sarcasm laced his tone.

Marcus folded his arms, his lips pressing together with impatience. Always wary of flattery, he did not take the compliment seriously. He responded blandly, "I only follow the same path as my ancestors have done."

Uther's eyes narrowed, but he continued in the same line of thought, "I have seen at Mynyw that you have fine battle experience. Such valuable skills should not be wasted away in those remote mountains of yours — "

"Are you making an offer?" Marcus stopped him.

"As my military leader, your life could be made far more comfortable than it has ever been. You and your family would want for nothing."

Marcus countered, a little more sternly than intended, "You have a capable commander in the Lord of Tintagel."

"Gorlois is getting old."

"Age would not stop him from commanding well, even if he is no longer on the battlefield himself. No, I will not displace a man who serves you well."

"But you would make an excellent commander, a symbol of force to follow."

"I will not be made a symbol. Such things can be important as a point for rallying the people. But that symbol should be you, only you, to unite the people, not create more leaders. Too many leaders will cause more splits among the factions. You call yourself the Pendragon, make that the symbol of force, and reconciliation."

Uther glared, annoyed at Marcus' obstinacy. He tried a new tactic, "Then if war is not to your liking, I could use your knowledge of Britain's underground politics. You are well-educated and would make an excellent addition to my council."

"No, my lord," Marcus told him again.

Uther scowled, his anger rising. "Perhaps I didn't make myself understood. I will pay you well in land, cattle, or — "

"No," Marcus cut him off once more.

"By the light, man!" Uther erupted. "Are you so daft? Any other man would lick his fingers at the opportunity to be my second-in-command and the promise of a lifetime of wealth. Can't you see I'm trying to reward you? What more could you want?"

As Uther's tone deepened in its arrogance, Marcus' patience strained. His eyes squinted as if to hold onto his temper, and they lifted, boring into the king's. He said, "I will work for you as I do for others within my alliance of Celtic kings and princes. It will be on my terms, which you will find more than reasonable. Because the nature of my work demands secrecy, it can be no other way, not where my identity would become well known. I will not jeopardize my work, your position, or the lives of my family and clan."

Uther demanded, "How can I be certain of your loyalty when you are not easily within reach?"

Marcus bristled, but he spoke steadily. "You have spoken of

symbols. They are passed around and celebrated for the glory they represent. But glory is false and fades more quickly than light at dusk. Rather, seek freedom, which is far more important and far more difficult to achieve. It is kept only by day to day, year to year, hard, backbreaking work. It is a matter of survival, not glory. All I have ever wanted is freedom, and for now, we still have it. Nor will I give in as long as I am in this lifetime. You revoked your word when you had Pascentius executed. You could have made a far deeper impression on your allies if you had not given in to impulsive arrogance."

The king sucked in his breath, but held his face in calm aloofness, taking several moments to decide how he should counter the rebuke.

Marcus turned towards the guest building, intending to walk away, but Uther gripped his sleeve, pulling him around. The king locked eyes with him, needing to see if he told the truth. Marcus took the stare with gracious dignity. Finding no lie, Uther suddenly had the eerie sense he was gazing into the proud eyes of several generations of Marcus ap Iorwerth's ancestors.

Unnerved, Uther said, "You let no one push you around. Not even a king. I could have required your arrest for executing the woman Daracha instead of having her transported here for judgement. But when my nephew told me of the circumstances, I understood why."

Marcus said, "What I did was not meant to undermine your authority over the woman and her deeds."

Struck again by Marcus' humility, the king said, "Myrddin — in his words — calls you utterly incorruptible, brutally honest and selflessly loyal in the depth of your heart of courage. I see that it must be so. You have fought your own way a long time."

"Aye, a long time," Marcus repeated dryly. "For more than ten years now. I have counted six and twenty winters, but I have seen more trouble than my father who passed at sixty."

Uther's eyes widened. "Six and twenty..." he echoed, his anger and arrogance abruptly subsiding. "I would have guessed you were at least forty, or more..."

Across the yard, a door opened at the guest wing's far end,

distracting them. A woman stepped out, followed by three serving ladies. Uther turned and gazed at her, his eyes full of admiration as they closely followed her movement. Marcus noted the woman was beautiful, dark-haired and graceful, but he did not recognize her. He suspected Uther was either already in pursuit of her attentions, or would be so very soon.

The king reached under his cloak and pulled out a small leather pouch. "After the ceremonies we will talk again and settle your price as you requested to Myrddin. For now, please accept this as an advance on your services." Uther pressed the pouch into Marcus' hand.

Marcus moved slightly, his attention caught by activity stirring at the guest wing's opposite end. Claerwen appeared, emerging from a small group of palace servants, and he smiled as he watched her stroll into the golden twilight, looking rested and elegant. Hefting the pouch in his hand, he did not open it for inspection before stuffing it inside his tunic. From how it clinked, he knew gold was inside.

The dark-haired woman walked towards them, and Uther's eyes followed her again. She turned, heading for the great hall, her ladies surrounding her. Uther mumbled, "By the light, she is beautiful."

"Aye, that she is," Marcus reiterated, watching Claerwen. She looked up, catching sight of him, and his smile broadened as she approached. He kissed her cheek as she joined him.

Uther continued to watch the dark-haired woman until she disappeared into the great hall, then he realized Claerwen had greeted him. The corner of his mouth flinched as he met her eyes. He said to Marcus, "I realize now, in thinking on what you have told me, that the achievements of my life compared to those of yours are rather cheap. At the age of five and thirty, the only thing I have done is become high king by default when my brother was killed. Though I was with him at every step, it was his incredible tenacity that regained control of Britain from Vortigern. You are correct to criticize my actions, and I do understand that a public apology regarding my poor treatment of you is not what you wish. I shall respect that. Although I must demand your presence at the ceremonies, both of you have demonstrated your loyalty beyond any doubt. I am releasing you now from your pledge. This belongs to you."

Uther held out his upturned fist. As the king's fingers unfolded, Marcus saw his clan ring lying in the palm. In that moment, he knew Uther had come to accept, possibly even admire, his occasionally unorthodox methods to achieve his passion for freedom. He took the ring and placed it on his finger.

"Thank you, my lord." Marcus said, bowing his head.

Uther saluted and said, "The gods be with you. I must return to the court." He moved away, following the woman's path.

Grinning broadly, Marcus said softly, "I don't know who she is, but I believe he's hot on her scent already."

"I heard them call her Lady Ygerna."

Marcus' grin abruptly changed to surprise; then he exhaled chagrin.

"You know the name?" Claerwen asked.

"She is Lord Gorlois' wife."

Claerwen's face reflected her recognition of future trouble, but when she waited for Marcus to elaborate, he only smiled, refusing to dwell on Uther's promiscuity. Instead, she asked, "Is that what court life is all about? Scandals and affairs and gossip?"

He smiled wryly, answering, "Aye, very much so. Now you see the reasons why I never cared to be a prince or not, and why I never want to be at court. And the higher the court, the worse it is. Even Ceredig's and Cunedda's are full of such nonsense. Can you imagine me, dressed in that kind of gear all the time?" His eyes flicked in the direction Uther had taken, indicating the king's expensive garments.

Claerwen giggled and whispered in his ear, "You would be a bit out of place, such as when you work in the smithy, wearing only a loincloth, especially when there's a good breeze…?"

Her playful grin coaxed him into laughter. "Ah, but you'd like that, wouldn't you?" he teased. Then suddenly inspired by the joy in her smile, he drew her closely, seeking a kiss.

A throat cleared behind them.

Startled, Claerwen turned around. "Myrddin Emrys! You must

stop doing that."

Myrddin smiled, bowing. "Forgive me, 'tis a habit acquired that I seem unable to break. The evening meal will begin soon. Are you ready?"

Marcus shrugged, "As much as ever, I suppose." He moved a pace towards the great hall, but when Myrddin held still, looking from him to Claerwen and back with curiosity, he halted, lifting an eyebrow in question.

Myrddin smiled again. "I have often wondered how an ethereal, compassionate woman such as Claerwen and an elusive loner like you could…well…you know what I mean. I see that my original perception has been rather lacking in detail."

They all laughed together, enjoying a few fleeting moments of unfettered camaraderie. Then slowly quieting, Myrddin mused, regarding the king, "I wonder how long it will last."

Marcus eyed him, wondering if the remark was aimed at Uther's latest infatuation or the relative peace they hoped to build under his reign. Wanting to tell Myrddin that he should be the one to know more than anyone else, Marcus held his comment and gave his opinion regarding peace: "Not for long. My work will continue. But for a little while, at least, we will gather with our cups held high and celebrate the illusion of an idyllic life, such that the court bards shall one day sing of it. We will believe we are invincible and make the pretenses that we are but one clan across all Britain. I wish it would be so."

He touched Claerwen's face, his eyes tracing her features with unabashed affection. "For as long as we are able, let us savor the peace."

# Acknowledgements

First, foremost and always, I wish to thank my husband Peter for the unique insights he has brought with him from all across the world. Without his inspiration, I would never have had the courage to undertake this enormous and wonderfully satisfying challenge.

To the scholars, historians, researchers, archaeologists, librarians and enthusiasts scattered across the earth who have shared their vast knowledge, I owe a debt too priceless to be counted. The quest to bring light and life to the Arthurian legend and Celtic history may be daunting, but it is a powerful self-induced mandate that we share and follow.

And to Harriet and the gang, I owe scads of gratitude for letting me share this adventure over the course of many weeks. Their critiques, knowledge, suggestions, and encouragement have contributed vastly to this work.

*Diolch yn fawr*, many thanks, to all of you!

# Bibliography

The following is a partial list of sources used for this book.

Ashe, Geoffrey. *The Discovery of King Arthur*. New York: Anchor Press/Doubleday, 1985.

——. *Kings and Queens of Early Britain*. Chicago: Academy Chicago Publishers, 1990.

——. *The Landscape of King Arthur*. New York: Henry Holt & Co., 1987.

——, ed. *The Quest for Arthur's Britain*. London: Granada Publishing Ltd., 1971.

Chadwick, Nora. *The Celts*. London: Penguin Books, 1971.

Clayton, Peter. *A Companion to Roman Britain*. Oxford: Phaidon Press Ltd., 1980.

Cowan, Tom. *Fire in the Head*. New York: HarperCollins, 1993.

Condry, William M. *The Natural History of Wales*. London: Bloomsbury Books, 1990.

Cunliffe, Barry. *The Celtic World*. New York: Greenwich House, 1986.

Davies, John. *A History of Wales*. London: Allen Lane/Penguin Press, 1993.

Evans, Gwynfor. *Wales, A History*. New York: Barnes & Noble Books, 1996.